Praise for The Chimera

"An ambitious and kinetic a
packed with neat ideas."

— Antony Johnston, NYT best-selling author

"Snappy prose, electric action, crackling intersection of magic and technology, nano noir, adventure—what more do you want? Fans of science/fantasy will get the ride they're looking for!"

— John Shirley, author of *Stormland*

"A full-throttle magical cyberpunk superhero thriller; Santos has really hit the ground running."

— Peter McLean

"Stylish, bad-ass, and above all immersive. Wayne Santos excels at the top goal of genre fiction: creating a novel you can open on any page, any paragraph, and deep-dive right into its world. Every line sings of holographs and sprawling megapolis, every sentence is an offering to cyberpunk gods. You emerge a part of the Chimera Team, as ready to die for Cloke, Marcus, and Zee as they are to die for you."

First published 2020 by Solaris
an imprint of Rebellion Publishing Ltd,
Riverside House, Osney Mead,
Oxford, OX2 0ES, UK

www.solarisbooks.com

ISBN: 978 1 78108 797 8

10 9 8 7 6 5 4 3 2 1

A CIP catalogue record for this book is available
from the British Library.

Designed & typeset by Rebellion Publishing

Cover art by Gemma Sheldrake

Printed in Denmark

THE CHIMERA CODE

WAYNE SANTOS

SOLARIS

For Charlene,
The horse didn't die;
it just took a while to hit the finish line.

THE CHIMERA CODE

Book One of the WitchWare Series

Prologue:
The Brass Ring

Hoboken, New Jersey, August 5th, 2119

CLOKE DIDN'T REALIZE it then, but her entire life had changed in the moment the tank decided to run her down.

Technically it wasn't actually a tank; it was a GCV Infantry Fighting Vehicle, a big, armored personnel carrier that was almost 100 years old and built for the kind of mechanized artillery-based wars that people back then had expected to fight. But it had tank DNA in it: the treads, the single cannon, the old American excess of being clunky enough to run roughshod over streets and cars with only some scratches to its paint. And Toriyama was driving it like he was drunk.

But he wasn't. He was just new to tanks, and mad. He had every reason to be mad. Cloke had just cooked his little brother. Probably to death.

"YOU FUCKING, FUCKING BITCH," Toriyama shouted over the tank's public address system. He plowed through the corner of a building as if to emphasize his point and Cloke just pumped her legs harder, trying to get to the corporate residential compound she knew was around here somewhere.

What had started as just another gang clash in the decaying slums of downtown Hoboken had gone south faster than anyone had expected. Cloke was the main "weapon" of the

9

Crosstowners; the black box that maintained their hold over their territory. Someone in the Darks had finally realized that guns and knives weren't going to cut it with a teenage girl who could throw fire and lightning out of her hands. The Crosstowners had been lured into a surplus military warehouse where the GCV had tried to do a number on all of them.

Toriyama, leader of the Darks, had run over Cloke's friends. Cloke had responded by flaming his brother.

And now here they were.

Cloke didn't see Toriyama anywhere behind her; she must have taken the corners too fast. She raised her hand, ran the keys through her mind and let fly with a flare soaring into the sky, just to make sure he kept up.

Then she saw it. The gate to the compound. Warm, cozy lights beyond it. Plenty of guns in front of it, keeping the riff raff out, like the street gangs.

The security at the gate entrance looked at her.

She was waving both arms at them now, never dropping the pace of her run.

"Help!" she shouted. "He's trying to fucking kill me!"

The security at the entrance put their hands to their holsters but didn't pull out their guns.

One of them, the bigger guy with more muscles, looked on; calm, but cautious. "What the hell are you talking about, kid? This is company property, authorized admittance only."

The GCV finally caught up with Cloke again, and rumbled in the distance, increasing its speed.

"You tell him that," she said. She moved closer to the guard. Toriyama, in the GCV, angled himself so that now he was in a straight line that was going to hit Cloke and whoever was standing too close to her.

"Hey," the other guard called out. "Hey, hey, hey!"

He pulled out his gun and waved his arms in warning. Toriyama didn't even hesitate or slow down.

The guard finally took a shot at the GCV. Cloke didn't think anyone was surprised when the round bounced off and did nothing. It was getting closer by the second. Both guards were firing now, but the bigger one with the muscles had finally gotten it into his head to call for back up. He murmured the situation to someone on a wireless while still keeping up the fire.

Neither of them noticed that Cloke had kept right on backing up until she was at the gate itself. It was only as she was hiking herself over that the muscled guard finally said, "Hey. HEY!"

She ignored him and dropped onto the other side. If he was going to shoot at her rather than at the tank that was coming down the pipe, he wasn't going to get a decent shot off before he got run over. If he was smart, he would be concentrating on the more immediate threat of trying to survive the next five seconds.

She sucked in her breath as she took in the scene around her.

Houses. Grass. No grit. No decay. This was a place she'd only seen in ads. The streetlights all worked, and there was a warm glow coming from many of the windows. She could see silhouettes of people sitting at tables, eating, the flickering of lights from a screen or maybe a sim unit. People could actually have a life here. A good one, without fear or uncertainty about whether they were still going to be able to sleep here in a month.

It was safe.

Cloke wondered what it would have been like. Growing up in a place like this, taking all this for granted.

Toriyama caught up to her. She could tell from the crash behind the walls, and the scream of at least one of the guards. She hoped someone had had the foresight to actually call this in.

She could see people moving to their windows to find out what was happening.

She cut through a lawn when Toriyama busted the GCV through the wall and lurched into the compound. The front of the tank and part of its treads were covered in dust and blood.

No going back. They were on company property now. It was only a question of just what flavor of Totally Fucked was coming down the pipe after this.

She didn't need to hold his attention anymore: now she just needed to stay alive long enough for whoever owned this compound to do something about him. She just needed to stay out of the way. The time for fireworks was over.

She kept a house between herself and the GCV she could hear trundling on the other side.

Once again, the speakers on the tank squawked to life. "You killed my brother, you fucking bitch," she heard Toriyama spit out. "You think you can hide from me?"

She was actually pretty goddamn sure she could, but she wasn't going to tell him that.

She heard a high-pitched whine come from the GCV. "Think I don't know shit about my new ride? Think I don't know about this little switch here? Terahertz imaging? Sees through fucking walls, bitch."

Cloke rabbited.

The GCV came through the house. She heard screaming. She didn't know how many people were in there, but they'd just been smeared by Toriyama. That *had* to get someone in one of the other houses making a call, there was no way they were going to let him just keep knocking houses down.

She staggered as a flying piece of broken house winged her back. It wasn't enough to knock her off her feet, but the pain slowed her down. She turned to see the GCV coming out of the new hole it had just made in some family's home. Where the fuck was the rest of the security in this place? Was this company that cheap?

She floundered, trying to keep her footing and headed for the next house. There was a fence in the way, but she was young and riding a charge of adrenaline the likes of which she'd never experienced. She almost bounced over the fence in her fear, and realized immediately that she finally had a real opportunity at hand.

She ran a quick circle around her potential salvation and waited for Toriyama to come through, hoping that his eyes were fixed on the Terahertz Imager and too untrained to read it properly.

She'd read the situation correctly.

Toriyama howled in triumph and came at a good speed through the fence. It was nothing to his tank, but he'd only cleared it by a few more feet when he tipped the entire thing forward into a swimming pool.

No hesitation from Cloke.

"You *fuck*," she hissed and put her hands out, fingers arched. Keys in her head, fast and big and full of pain.

Lightning.

The bolts lanced from her fingers and hit the pool with the GCV and Toriyama in it.

She heard him scream before the speakers on the tank shorted out. She laid on the electricity for a few more seconds, upping the power for good measure and then cut it off for the finish. He wouldn't be dead; he was probably at least tough enough to withstand a few seconds. Smoke was coming out of the seams in the tank's armor.

She waited. She heard the movement of the hatch.

Moving. Running around the pool, chest tight with anger now as her hand reached in to pull at the hilt of the knife. Pulling it out and twisting it in her hand so it was ready for a downward stab.

The hatch raised, Toriyama's arm visible.

Cloke jumped, landing on the tank, almost sliding off the wet armored surface. She regained her footing and scrambled to the top. Toriyama was out now, looking dazed. She raised the knife into the air.

Keys in her mind. Focused. Painful.

Lightning again, dancing around the blade.

She plunged it into Toriyama's shoulder, felt the tingle as the current briefly ran through her own body, throwing her clear and away from the pool, back onto the yard.

Toriyama screamed again, his body thrashing as the embedded knife delivered its charge. He flailed and slumped over the tank, completely finished.

Cloke watched from the edge of the pool, lying on her side, trying to catch her breath.

Up above her, shafts of light cut through the dark, first focusing on the totaled GCV, the body of its driver, finally settling on Cloke herself.

Another speaker kicked in, this time from above. "Throw down any and all weapons and remain on the ground."

She got to her knees and covered her eyes to stare up at the lights. She couldn't see what it was, but she could hear. A Gyro of some kind, one of those one-man, urban combat pacifiers, probably with an autocannon trained on her right now to turn her into a red paste if they so much as caught a glimpse of a gun.

Cloke turned and looked at the house that belonged to the pool. There was a family there: a father, a mother, one little girl. The father was looking at her with a mix of horror and venom. The mother was clearly not processing anything. Only the little girl looked at her with fearless curiosity. Another light was trained on her.

"ON THE GROUND. NOW," came the order from the second Gyro, with a pilot obviously much angrier.

Cloke sighed. She looked at the money around her. The comfort. Saw the smoke coming from Toriyama's body, from a failed, stupid ambush that had all come about because the Crosstowners had entered their territory one time too many. This had been the result. All this death because her mob couldn't afford to show weakness to the rival mob. This was her life. Fighting for scraps of pride while people like this family and the pilots above watched with morbid fascination as they killed themselves.

16 years old and she already had no future. One stupid fight had taken everything away from her.

It couldn't go any other way, could it? No matter what she did here, they were going to end her, one way or the other. That's what money did to people that didn't have any.

Money always crushed everything around it that wasn't money.

She looked up at the Gyros. They were the mobile kind, no cockpit to speak of, clear unobstructed view for the pilot, no shielding, largely patrol and recon, normally the first on the scene.

She raised her hands, apparently in surrender.

"That's right," she heard above her. "Just comply with the orders and—"

Keys. Simple. Straight. Fire.

Even as the fireball left her hand and hit the Gyro she was moving, diving for the pool and getting under the shelter of the GCV. The pilot in the Gyro was screaming, his 'copter spiraling away as he rocked back in forth in his seat and burned. She hit the pool with a splash and maneuvered herself under the tank, hearing the eruption of full auto rounds coming from the other Gyro, feeling them vibrate against the armor of the GCV.

A break in the fire and she leaned out, following the shaft of light to its source, unleashing her lightning. The second Gyro went screeching down towards some point in the middle of the compound and Cloke made her move.

Out, out, out. Out of the pool, running out of the yard, hearing the motors of more aerial vehicles whirring distantly and getting closer. She was wet, and cold, and angrier and sadder than she'd ever felt in her life. She was never going to see her sister again, and the stupid bitch probably wouldn't even notice.

More lights on her, throwing long shadows of her body across the ground.

She turned her hand back, let loose with another fireball, didn't even bother to aim it, and kept running.

She felt something hit her in the back, taking her off her feet. The ground rushed up to meet her.

As everything went black around her, Cloke found she only had one lingering thought left. She wished she'd turned around so she could at least get one final spit at the people who had killed her.

SHE WOKE TO find that she was not only alive, but clean.

The first thing she saw was black. Shiny black. She realized the ceiling had been polished to look like the keys of a giant synth keyboard. When she sat up, she saw the hospital gown she was wearing, the similarly black floor, and the pristine white walls around her. She was in a bed, and a machine was recording her vitals.

Dizziness hit her and she slowly sank back down. Even the act of sitting up had disoriented her.

The only thing she could do in relative comfort was blink and think. Extremely slowly.

Some time may have passed. Or none at all. She couldn't be sure. But the next time she could focus on anything, it was because a door she hadn't even known was there opened from no apparent joints, seams or other indicators in the wall, and a man walked through.

He was in a grey suit guaranteed to cost more money than Cloke had ever owned her entire life. Thin, fit looking, white old man. His hair was cut close and neat, and he hadn't bothered to dye the grey out of the sides. His brown eyes swept across her and seemed to evaluate her with the precision of a laser. She could almost feel him plugging her into some kind of equation to see what the end result would be.

She wanted that calm, confident look on his face to be set on fire. She tried pointing towards him, could barely raise her hand, let alone pull together the focus to run the keys properly through her head. Sitting up had almost wiped her out.

"Remarkable," he said. "Even after all that, you're still trying. You're so pumped full of drugs right now you've probably got to think just to breathe. Even if you weren't, the intensity of your attacks would have left you drained. You're in no condition to fight."

"Why am I not dead?"

"And here I thought you'd be grateful about that," the suit said. "Because orders came down to use the riot suppression gear instead, that's why. It's hard to question a pile of meat and blood on the pavement. You've got a bruise on your back in the shape of a big rubber 'x'. It'll fade in time, but it's the calling card of a non-lethal takedown. Now then, let's have a nice chat, shall we?"

The suit pulled at a stool, then at a nearby table for meals, and sat down. He reached into his inside pocket and Cloke almost choked when she saw him pull out a clear, clunky old OLED flex screen, unfolding it and setting it down on the table. He pushed at an icon to make it rigid and then another to make it opaque and accessed something on it.

"So. Your name is K—"

"I know what my name is," Cloke said, harsh but weak. "Who the fuck are you?"

The man's eyes fixed on the screen momentarily before shifting to her face. She could make out a smile at the edges of his mouth. "Irish father, Filipino mother. Sixteen years old, born May 10th, 2103, indeterminate time and location; insufficient funds for hospital supervised birth. No NEASA social or identification registration; insufficient funds for administration and processing. No formal schooling, one entry for a rejected application to the Thomas G. Conners elementary school; insufficient funds for admission. No prior police or corporate activity report, no credit record, no transaction history." The man set aside the display. He reached into his suit pocket once again and pulled out something small and white. "My name is Victor Chapman." He placed the small white thing at her bedside. "My card." He leaned back in the chair, seeming to appraise her. "I hope the accommodations are sufficient."

"Pretty nice digs for someone that just wrecked a neighborhood," Cloke said, turning away. "Unless jail is a lot better than I'd heard."

"You are not in jail because there are a number of questions that require answering," Victor said. "Like how does a sixteen-year-old girl singlehandedly take down a surplus tank and two trained urban recon Gyro pilots? How does that same girl with no education or formal training use N-rated thaumaturgical techniques?"

"Thauma-what?"

Victor shook his head and put his hands on his legs, smiling with something that looked like exasperation, maybe disbelief. Cloke couldn't be sure. "You don't even know what you're doing. You don't realize what you're capable of. Amazing. How did you get past the screening?"

Cloke picked up the card without looking at it. It was smooth in her hand. She let it drop to the floor. "Never got screened," she said. "Couldn't afford that either. Any other stupid questions?"

Victor leaned down, picking up the card Cloke had dropped to the floor. "Have you ever heard of General Information Systems?"

Cloke snorted. This guy may as well have been asking if she was familiar with gravity. "Sure. They hide everything."

Victor held the card up and put it in her hand. This time she read it. Below his name was the title, "Chief Diversity Officer," and the simple, familiar GIS logo, which appeared somewhere on nearly every data-related piece of software Cloke had ever used in her life.

"We don't actually do much hiding," Victor said. "But believe me when I say we know everyone who does. And we know where they put it."

"And that was your little commune that got trenched."

"That was one of our employee estates, yes. Significant staff loss, not inconsiderable property damage, and top of the line urban pacification hardware laid to waste like it was nothing. All because of one young woman who isn't even old enough to have a proper drink."

Cloke shut her eyes and turned away. "So, what do you want, a cheque?"

She heard Victor laugh. And it was in the dark, nestled in the warmth of the hospital bed, that she heard him say, "No, I was wondering if you'd be interested in a job."

Cloke crushed the card she was holding in her hand.

I
The Petition
October 19, 2138

Chapter 1:
Taking Stock

IT WAS WARM and humid in Singaraja. Cloke's clothes stuck to her skin with the sweat. She'd just have to deal with it. This wasn't the time to bitch about tropical heat, not with so many people crying.

It was exactly the kind of funeral that Darma would have hated.

She'd warned him, repeatedly, that he needed to be specific about this kind of thing in his will; it wasn't all just about who got the money, or ensuring that his request for an emulation was on paper. He hadn't listened, of course, and the end result was that he was getting the ceremony he'd been dreading: a traditional Balinese burial.

His body was undergoing Ngaben: the ornate process of cremation that was supposed to return his remains to the elements. It was an expensive ceremony, one that cost years' worth of salary for the average Balinese family. Cloke had paid for this one. She had little choice; no one was supposed to know how much money Darma had been worth when his location had been traced and the rail gun had turned his strategy and support post into a crater in Pescadero Creek. The only reason there was even any kind of body left to put in the elaborate temple-shaped coffin was because the gunnery crew had been in such a hurry to lock in his location, they were actually off by 30 feet.

Not that it mattered. Even at that range he was a goner unless he was willing to abandon his post. And he wasn't. He'd stayed at his station, keeping the doors open, constantly shifting code to keep the automated defenses offline, and making sure that Cloke and Marcus got out alive. He'd promised her he would look out for her no matter what it took. He'd kept that promise.

Beside her, Marcus stood by uncomfortably in a black suit of mourning that just barely managed to contain the suite of cybernetics weaved through his body. Including all the integrated enhancements, he was nearly 400 pounds of seven-foot, bald black Liverpudlian. The parts of him that were still factory original from the womb were beaded with sweat. His face was a flat, neutral mask, his eyes completely hidden behind the visor that he'd chosen to render opaque in the hot, tropical sun. Cloke knew he was probably taking this harder than she was.

Neither of them had read up properly for what you were supposed to do at a Balinese funeral, so they maintained their silence, moving, walking and politely mouthing to the air as everyone else went through the motions of the ceremony. None of this would have meant shit to Darma: he barely remembered Bali, let alone talked about it in the years since he'd run with her unit.

Cloke looked at the display running across her own not-surgically-implanted, not-ballistics-reinforced visor, noting the local time. It also showed that it was 3ish am back in New York and 4ish am in São Paulo. She wondered if Marcus had bothered to turn on his translator to read the funeral rites subtitled from Balinese. He probably had; it always bugged the shit out of him when he didn't know what was going on. Cloke preferred to let it all flow around and over her; she'd said her goodbyes. This wasn't for her, for Marcus, or even for Darma. This was for all the people who had known him once upon a time as a goofy kid with a flair for coding, and who had managed to get a career in network engineering consultancy.

Or at least, that's what he told his parents on visits and when he sent the checks back home.

Cloke still couldn't believe that part. That he actually sent money back to his parents. It's not like it would have been dangerous for him; he had been at the top of his game—in the circles they moved through he was recognized as one of the best code jockeys on the planet. Anything he did that was digital would never be traced.

It was just amazing to Cloke that after years of working out on the edge, running some of the most legendary corporate defections and burn jobs the biz had ever seen, this guy—who had brought multinational companies to their knees—had still taken the time to write and visit his parents, and make sure they got a nice nest egg from him every month.

And now they were burying him.

Cloke's chest throbbed as she watched the procession carry Darma's body, encased in what looked like a miniature Hindu and Chinese temple. Some of the poorer locals had already seen fit to attach the cremations of their own relatives to this funeral to take advantage of the day Cloke had paid for. She couldn't blame them; she would have done the same thing if money had been an issue.

Cloke waited patiently with Marcus, watching as Darma's family and hometown friends said their goodbyes. When it was over, Cloke, via her translator, accepted the thanks of Darma's family. Marcus promised them that they would take care of anything else required for the funeral and assured them that they would make all the arrangements for settling Darma's will.

She left the funeral feeling like she was under 30 feet of thick black water that squeezed against her lungs. But then that was the only way it could go when the guilt hit. She was alive, Darma was not. He'd made a choice. He had chosen his friends.

"I wonder if I'd have done the same," she said much later, in the car on the way to the tube terminal.

"Clueless here, C," Marcus said. The fingers on one of

his graphene hands were unconsciously tapping in perfect, rhythmic sequence, a testament to the precise Norwegian engineering that had crafted them.

"Just thinking out loud," Cloke said. "If it had been me in that tent, and it had been you and Darma on the line, and I knew a rail gun was trying to vector on me, would—"

"Yes," Marcus said, not even looking at her. "You've done it before, you'll do it again."

"There's a difference between maintaining useful assets and sacrificing yourself for the good of others," Cloke said. "I think a long time ago Darma decided to ignore the distinction." She turned to her own window, watched the emerald green of the Balinese jungle whip by as their car drove itself down the twisty roads of the mountain. "Don't know if I can."

"My wife and kid say otherwise," Marcus replied. "And while you constantly trip my bitchy alarm, the bitch detector remains silent. And you know how twitchy that can be. Hard doesn't mean heartless." He stopped tapping the armrest and the same hand capable of crushing reinforced polycarbon alloy gently put itself on her shoulder. "We square on this? We good?"

Cloke sighed and patted his hand. "I'm gonna miss him."

"Me too," Marcus said. "Fucker still owed me about 300 reals worth of daiquiris."

They both smiled. It wasn't going to be the same without him.

Marcus resumed his watch over the passing landscape. "When are you going to supervise emulation boot-up?"

"I haven't decided yet," Cloke said. "Guess I got off lucky that way. Darma said I had to do it, but the will didn't actually have a timeframe. I'm gonna assume I don't have all year, but as executor… yeah, I gotta figure that out."

"Do I have to be there?"

"No."

"Good," Marcus said. "No matter how many times I see that shit, it freaks me out. That quiet kind of freak out. I think that's worse."

"You going to be okay with this going forward?"

Marcus shook his head. "Dunno, C. Just dunno. I guess I'll just have to be, won't I? First time I've ever had to deal with an emulation on a regular basis."

They arrived at the ETT terminal. Cloke used the General Information Systems corporate ID that was attached to her official DNA records and was through in just a few seconds. She waited in the lounge for the 45 minutes it took Marcus to finish with the security checks on his cybernetics and the processing of his own DNA associated with a regular British passport.

"Remind me to get one of those things one of these days," he said, pointing to her wallet with its chip card, the corporate confirmation that signaled special processing. "Must be nice going through any airport or tube terminal with just a flash of the card like that."

"Be a ward and employee of the company for about 16 years and maybe you'll have the same luck," she said.

"Thanks, but no. Call me old fashioned, but I still like the idea of being a citizen of a place rather than a thing."

Cloke sat down in one of the chairs in the lounge. Marcus remained standing. "That's got its advantages too," she said. "A country can't fire you."

"You never wanted to keep your NEASA citizenship, then?"

"I barely had it. Didn't make enough of a dent in their database to qualify as anything except a point for the population statistics. Besides, if I wanted citizenship anywhere why stick with the North East? Central's not an option obviously, but I could have gone Texan or NoCal."

"Or Brazilian."

"I've flirted with the idea," Cloke admitted. "But I doubt I could hack learning to speak Portuguese."

"Maybe you shouldn't have moved to São Paulo then," he said.

"Like I had much choice. Everything that matters happens there. Besides, you didn't want to live there and neither did Darma, so that left me."

"I can't argue a truth," Marcus replied. His eyes flicked to a readout only he could see. "I'd better get going, the tube to London's going to be here in a few minutes. You looking for a free home-cooked meal?"

"Can't," Cloke said. "I have a meeting in New York."

"GIS?"

"Yup."

"They're going to take you to some ancient restaurant with piss poor food and try and get you drunk to work a deal. Don't. Sign. Anything."

"That's usually my line," Cloke said. She waved him off. "Go on, get outta here, you've got a kid that needs to be thrown 10 feet into the air with those baby crushing hands of yours."

He gave a casual salute. "You give me a holler if anything goes down, ya?"

"If I can still remember how to swipe an interface in the middle a drug-fueled orgy, sure," she said.

She watched Marcus wander over to the area of the terminal where all the Europe tubes were. Her own wait wasn't that long, as the New York Evacuated Tube Transport arrived. Even with her head start, he was still going to beat her; the tube to London was under two hours, but her New York tube was going to be about two and a half.

The Companhia Nacional de Logistica logo played out on the various displays in the lounge, announcing the tube's arrival. Cloke was always very particular about picking CNL tubes. It wasn't just that they had the most routes, they were Brazilian. That in itself guaranteed a certain amount of quality and safety. They'd been at it longer than anyone else in the business.

She boarded with only her small bag and sat down in the lounge seat. It was only a few minutes before the tube started up; she felt the brief motion of it as it accelerated up to cruising speed.

Once again, it was time to pick a sim. Riding the tube was one of those times that pretty much begged to use a simulation.

Cloke supposed it must have had to do with the constant, subliminal sense of motion and the lack of windows. There wasn't much point, since half the time they were traveling underground, and the other half through ocean, not a whole lot to see in what amounted to a cylinder maglev-ing its way through a frictionless, airless tube at 6400 kph. It was that sense of movement in an enclosed space without being able to see anything that made her uncomfortable about sitting there, just reading. She could feel the walls getting smaller around her. Not exactly a freak out situation, but not something she wanted to tolerate for a couple of hours either. Sims, of course, took care of all that.

She looked for the external neural inputs, the ones usually meant for children or people who couldn't afford the surgery for a direct wireless beam. They were nowhere to be found. She eventually had to ask another passenger for the cabling in his seat pouch and he handed it over after masking the pity on his face. She'd learned years ago to ignore the looks people gave her when she did this; they always assumed she had some kind of medical condition, possibly a neural disease. There was no point explaining the real reason. Magic and its vagaries were none of their fucking business.

She opened the packaging and put on the head and wrist bands with the electrodes weaved into the fabric, plugged the cables into the dirty, neglected jack in her armrest.

She closed her eyes, sank into her seat and watched the world bloom into whiteness as the sim clicked into her nervous system and artificially stimulated it.

The music began, soothing and banal as a female voice asked her in a variety of languages which one she preferred. She spoke the word "English," and watched the menu unfold before her as spheres of light with images inside them. She didn't feel like just watching more SimNet programs or rumormongering. Normally she would have chosen to link into the view of a bird or a drone equipped with the neurolink gear and just feel what it was like to fly through the air, but it didn't seem right considering she'd just come from a funeral.

She chose something lighter, more interactive; an adventure game in a high fantasy setting. Within the sphere she could see dragons and some kind of haggard warrior trading blows while a mage worked his mouth frantically, reciting powerful incantations no doubt.

She felt herself smile. Sure, incantations. Why the hell not?

She confirmed her selection, the sim reading her impulses, and watched as the globe approached her, preparing to surround her in whatever cheesy fantasy experience the developers had envisioned.

Her world once again went white.

And then she was on the ground, twitching, her mouth forced open in a scream of agony like nothing she'd experienced in years.

The pain stopped. Her flesh had wisps of smoke curling away from it, and her body instinctively curled into a fetal position.

Lightning.

She'd been hit with lightning.

She pushed herself up, looked around her.

Night. The buildings of Manhattan off in the distance. The smell of rain in the air, and the familiar industrial tang of Hoboken.

She looked down at herself. She was in the old cast-offs she'd worn years ago, before GIS, before everything, when she was still just running in the streets. She was curled up on the ground halfway between home plate and first base in an old baseball diamond. She sat up.

Suddenly it all crashed in on her in a horrible way.

The lightning. The baseball diamond. The clothes.

She looked in the direction she knew the lightning had come from, saw the crowd of onlookers from the different gangs, and there he was.

Drake.

Poised. Confident. Well fed. Educated.

She looked down at herself again at her hands, her shoes. She was 15. Her body, her clothes, they all said so. This was the baseball diamond where she'd fought her first duel. Against some fucking Thaumaturgy major out of MIT who'd thought it would be fun to slum it in Jersey.

She stood up. She didn't know what the hell was going on, but she knew, even back then, that Drake had just been learning. In this here and now that was inexplicably then and there, Cloke might have only had the body and nervous system of a teenager, but her mind still carried 19 years of experience as a combat mage. She got to her feet.

This would be even less fair than it had been the first time.

She raised her hands and ran the keys through her mind.

Drake raised his hands up in surrender.

"Apologies," he said. "I had little control over which assets the sim would pull as easiest to generate."

Cloke took a deep breath and let her brain crank into a higher gear while her combat reflexes dropped to a lower one. She felt for the energies that should have been there, in the air, and felt nothing.

"This isn't magic," she said.

"Oh, if only," he said. "No, I'm afraid this is just a little hijack of your simulation. A brief one, I assure you."

"That's impossible," she said.

Drake smiled, and Cloke knew in that instant she had to still be in the sim. The Drake she'd known, however briefly, couldn't have smiled like that. His eyes were too cold, and he had no wisdom in the lines of his mouth. "My dear, you of all people should know that very few things are impossible. It's just a question of whether it's worth the effort required."

"Simulation, end," Cloke said.

Nothing happened.

She held the same thought in her head, and still nothing happened. She gestured through the air, drawing an invisible rectangle and slashing it diagonally. Still nothing. She was locked in.

"There's no point," the simulated Drake said. "And we won't be here long. I have a very narrow window of access and it's already bleeding out. There's not much time to explain."

And that was even less like Drake than the smile had been. Someone else was behind that face. Cloke stared at the simulation, tried to listen to the cadence of the words; see if the speech pattern lined up with that of anyone she knew who might remotely be able to pull off a stunt like this.

"You're not saying anything," the simulation said. "I was expecting more questions."

"Just say your shit and get me out of here."

"I want to hire you," it said. "Money is not much of an issue if that's your concern: name your price, I'll meet it. But I can give you something far more important than that, something you'll actually care about." Again, that smile, the one that was too old for a face more suited to frat parties and date rapes.

"Okay, fine, you want a question, I'll give you two. What do you think I could want from you, and who the fuck are you?"

"You are a woman of magic," the Drake sim said. "A powerful one, I know. I've been watching you a long time. And you want what any creature of magic wants. More. I can teach you more. I know things you don't. And that's because of who I am."

That didn't seem likely. "You're with the College? I know everyone in the College, and I know I don't know you."

The Drake sim opened its mouth to speak and its image burst into the simulation equivalent of static; a loss of form and color that looked like a miniature aurora borealis exploding on the baseball diamond. It regained its signal integrity a second later.

"If you want more, find me," it said. "In Singapore—"

"Where?"

The Drake sim winced. "Apologies, I forget sometimes how much these things change; they stopped calling it that, didn't they? At the LUMO Orbital Elevator Terminal, there is a Majitsu lab in a science park near the university. In that lab is a computer, ninth floor, southwest corner of the building. It's wired, completely off the networks. If you can get in that room and access that terminal, we can talk more then."

"Wait, what abo—"

And then Cloke was flung, feeling the impact of the seat at her back and watching the baseball diamond, the rain, the lights of Manhattan and Drake recede away from her like trails of old stars flying off to die.

The tube snapped back into her perceptions with the brutality of a whip. The people seated around her were staring in alarm.

"Was that a seizure?" the man ahead of her asked with a heavy German accent. "I think that was a seizure," he said to the others around them.

"I'm all right," Cloke said. "Bad connection."

She ignored the flurry of concern around her and consulted her visor. It had felt like she'd been connected for at least a minute, but that was just time dilation; her visor clock showed only a few seconds had passed. It also showed that her vitals, including her brain wave patterns, had stopped during that interval. Someone, without even knowing which program she was going to use, had just brute forced their way into her simulation, and it had paused her life.

She spent the rest of the trip with her eyes closed, listening to music. She opened her eyes every few minutes to make sure she was still where she was supposed to be.

It was a long two hours.

SHE TRAVELED BACK into the past as she arrived in Manhattan. When she'd tubed out of Bali, it had been about four in the afternoon. Stepping into the main concourse of Grand Central, the local time was now just past 6:30am the same day. She never got used to it, no matter how often she did it, her circadian rhythms being one of the first and earliest of her physiological casualties when she stepped into her new company life. She looked at the people around her, obviously trudging off to an early start for the workday, and found herself envying them a little.

She caught a cab and directed it to the corporate headquarters for General Information Systems in the North Eastern Allied States of America, at what had once been known as One World Trade Center. It was an odd, baroque choice on the part of upper level management, but then they had a reputation for being a baroque bunch. They liked owning pieces of history. It made them feel like they had always been relevant in the grand scheme of things, instead of only recently so.

She didn't recognize the receptionist at the ground floor desk, but it didn't matter. Her card was all she needed to get through without even an arched eyebrow of curiosity.

She knew he was going to be up anyway. He was expecting her, and he was always an early riser.

Victor Chapman was sitting at the table tucked away at the side of the cavernous, sprawling office that was the due of a vice president. He already had breakfast laid out, and was sipping at a coffee and reading from the same old clunky OLED display he'd been using when Cloke had first met him over 19 years ago.

He hadn't really changed much in all that time. He was reasonably fit and attractive, and looked like someone that might have been in his mid-40s. That, of course, was because he also had access to the latest life extension therapies and, failing that, the GIS health plan had a contingency for the use of thaumaturgical Glamours in certain circumstances. Cloke wasn't sure just how extensive his regenerative treatments were, but it didn't stop him from actually using treadmills and elliptical machines a few days a week.

His eyes flicked up briefly from his display, and then back down again.

"Coffee is fresh if you're interested," he said.

She sat down and removed her visor, setting it down on the edge of the table. The rest of it was piled with dishes overrun with breakfastalia; Western standbys like home fries and pancakes rubbed elbows with Asian dishes like nasi lemak, and paratha with curry. GIS always gave their executives too much, but no one complained. "I'm not going to dignify that with a reply," she said, reaching for an empty cup. "What famous people are scandalized today?"

"Don't know, don't care." He pushed a dish piled with croissants in her direction. "Just reading a review about a little bar that's opened up called The Off-White Apocalypse." He stopped and looked at her, waiting for her reaction.

She didn't know what kind of reaction she was supposed to give, and so opted for grabbing a croissant and nibbling on it.

"The film?" he prompted.

She shook her head, reaching for the pot of coffee.

"Last year? The White Apocalypse? It's a play on the film's title, a bad one? Oscar for best picture?"

The croissant was so flakey in her mouth it practically melted. "I don't remember. I guess I've never heard of it," she said as she chewed, then sipped the coffee. Decent, but not quite as good as the standards she'd gotten used to back home in São Paulo.

Victor sighed. "You were at the after-party when it won. The lead actor was hitting on you."

"Who was that again?"

Victor frowned. "Now you're just being difficult. Vikram Shamdansi."

"Oh wait, yeah, I think I remember him. Cute. Also an asshole."

"That would be the one, yes," Victor said. He went back to his breakfast—eggs benedict with salmon—chewing on it in silence for a minute before speaking again. "Being rated for N-level elemental thaumaturgy isn't really an excuse for ignorance, Cloke." He drank more coffee and stopped his meal to look her directly in the eye. "How was the funeral?"

And there it was. She'd been waiting for it, but it still surprised her when she found it; that throb, somewhere in her chest that told her something she held dear was gone.

"It was good," she said quietly. "Well, as good as something like that can go. His family was there. His old friends. No one knew what to do about Marcus and me, but we were footing the bill, so they couldn't complain much."

Victor reached out a hand and put it on top of hers. She let it stay there, and was glad that he was still here, fretting over her monthly budgets, her diet, her exercising, her way of interacting with clients, and being the rock she could feel under her when it seemed like the rest of the world had dropped out around her.

"You know if it were practical for me to go, I would have. But it wouldn't do for a GIS executive to attend the funeral of a purported freelance programmer. Too many questions. Too much media. And Darma... Darma's family... they don't deserve that," he said. "I suspect Darma didn't like me very much, but I don't begrudge him that. If I were him, I wouldn't like me very much either. But I was always fond of him."

She let loose a heavy sigh and knew it would be far from the last. "Tell you a secret?"

"What?"

"It doesn't matter now, but... he did like you, Victor. A lot. He respected you a bunch. He'd just never tell you to your face."

Victor smiled and nodded. "That sounds like him. Even when he was filling my house video channels with pornography that I couldn't turn off for 48 hours—"

"It was affectionately done. He only inflicted porn floods on people he liked."

Victor laughed gently. Even Cloke found herself smiling, remembering.

"When do they initiate his emulation?"

"That's up to me, I think."

"If it will make you feel better, I can be there with you on the day."

She moved her hand to pat the top of his. "Thanks, Dad."

He smiled. "Is that a yes, or a no?"

She thought about how she'd feel on the day and couldn't even imagine. Marcus was right in not wanting to be there. "I'll take what I can get."

Victor nodded and went back to his breakfast. "You made

the right choice. It's a uniquely... unnerving... experience."

"How many have you been to?"

"Too many," Victor said, concentrating on his eggs benedict. "And it never gets any easier."

"Well that's reassuring," she said.

Victor shrugged and gestured his hand towards the conspicuous space she'd cleared amidst the cornucopia of breakfast food. He reached over and moved some chicken congee away from potential accident with her elbow. "Do you want anything? Eggs, pancakes, crepes, I can call for my assistant to—"

"I'm good with what I've got," she said. "It's all my stomach can handle right now."

"Jet lag?" he asked, chewing on his salmon with clear revelry.

"Not exactly," she said, taking another sip. "I flat-lined for a few seconds when someone hacked into my sim and told me he wanted to hire me."

Victor's chewing stopped. His eyes moved up to lock onto hers.

"Nope, not kidding," Cloke said. "You want the whole story?"

He nodded. She told him. It took the remainder of breakfast, and Cloke impressed herself with not getting angry at any point during the retelling. Usually something like this would have driven her batshit furious.

When she'd finished, Victor just sat there, rubbing at one temple with his finger. "Pursuing this further is an extremely bad idea with too many ways that it could go horribly, horribly wrong. I'm just going to assume that means there's no way to stop you."

"I'm glad we understand each other."

He laughed, but it was tired and devoid of genuine amusement. "There's an extremely small number of people that would have either the clearance or the know-how for that kind of access," he said. "And I don't think any of them are at Majitsu."

"What kind of relationship does GIS have with them right now?"

"Cordial. It's always been that way. I don't think anyone can really afford *not* to keep it as such. You don't get on the bad side of the biggest mass negation engineering firm in the industry."

"Do you know anyone over there?"

"Socially? No. I've had dealings with the management, of course, but only for the usual reasons, through the usual channels."

"So, if I were to do a little poking around…"

"The usual conditions apply," Victor said, sitting back and pouring more coffee for himself. "Technically you're no longer a registered, legally recognized employee here, so I can't lay down company law on you. Not that that's *ever* worked on you. But the retainer will make things very complicated if things go badly. The bigger issue is your… logistics deficiency."

She nodded. Darma.

Cloke herself was primarily combat and some infiltration. Marcus was almost nothing but combat. Darma had been their code jockey, and she was surprised at how quickly that lack was already being felt. Trying to run any kind of operation involving a hack on a high-security corporate network with no one on the deck was like trying to pull the family photos out of the home database with a baseball bat.

"I'm not going to ask for one of your kids," Cloke said. "Wouldn't be fair to them or you."

"Thank you for that," Victor said, and she heard the obvious relief in his voice.

"But I'm still going to have to find someone. Doesn't matter whether it's just temp or not, but it's got to be soon."

"Actually, I might be able to help with that," Victor said. "There's someone I've been keeping my eye on. They might be of some use, assuming they'll cooperate."

Cloke's suspicion meter rose a few degrees. "This is sounding more ambiguous than I'd like."

"Well, I don't know exactly who it is—all I have is a jockey handle, and a trail of destruction I've been following with great interest. 'Polychrome' has been at the heart of some very interesting runs that were being logged by security agencies and white hat cells. Data theft, data hostage encryption, some truly remarkable intrusions… This Polychrome is quite a talent, and was apparently getting very popular with the organized crime groups. Now all the activity coming in on the feeds seems to indicate the Triads are trying to hunt and kill them."

Cloke stared hard at Victor. She was sure that the disbelief she was radiating must have been detectable on the electromagnetic spectrum. "How is this in any way a good idea?"

Victor leaned forward and poured Cloke more coffee without asking. "I have learned from my experience with you that the kind of talent that proves the most useful, with the most potential, doesn't usually come from a prep school. It comes from being able to stay alive where it shouldn't. I've taken a look at the aftermath of this Polychrome's work. Whoever it is, they have flair." He went back to his own breakfast. "I can assign you one of our Data Processing Officers for a few days, if it'll help move things along, but no location work. That's non-negotiable: it all stays here."

Cloke took the coffee and sipped it. She didn't like where this was going. She didn't have a bad feeling about it; no instincts were kicking in about danger, and she knew Victor well enough after all these years to trust his intuition, but something in her bristled at this. It felt like someone was sitting her down at the table and making her eat her vegetables. "Who are you giving me?"

"Jenkins."

Cloke remembered her. 24 years old, bubbly, intelligent, cried and nearly fell apart when she'd realized a take-out sandwich she'd bought had the wrong price when it was scanned and she'd paid too little to the old lady that ran her favorite diner.

"I don't know if this is the kind of pressure she'd be able to take."

"She's not going to take any," Victor said. "The only thing she needs to do is keep you updated and narrow your hunt. She can do all that from a secure terminal here. The only thing she won't like about it is the operating hours."

"Oh Christ," Cloke said, and she wanted to laugh. There was almost no point in asking, but she knew she had to play this out. "You already know where this kid is, don't you?"

"Best guess is Sydney, Australia."

"Were you thinking recruitment?"

"I hadn't made up my mind," Victor admitted. "But I like to know where the most interesting potential assets are."

Cloke remembered the GPS trackers Victor used to leave for her to find when she was growing up and trying to sneak out. They'd been designed to deflect her from the real trackers she knew he'd hidden far better on her gear, her clothing, and even the make-up she used to wear before the paranoia of lipstick that told her guardian which club she was slumming it in had quit her of that interest.

She reached over to the pack of cigarettes he had left sitting on the table and pulled one out. "Shit. It would have to be Sydney, wouldn't it?"

"I thought you liked kangaroos, and surfing, and Pride festivals that party you to death."

"There's also Jimmy Tong. He wants me dead in a bad way. He's the 426 for Sydney's local Triad now, isn't he?"

Victor consulted his OLED. "He is. Though he may be out of town right now."

Cloke lit the cigarette. "What a mess." She felt the heat warm her throat as she inhaled.

Victor pushed the ashtray in her direction. "On the bright side, you can finally try that surf 'n' turf restaurant I told you about," he said. "Beautiful steak. Simply beautiful."

Cloke sighed. "It's going to have to be soon, isn't it?"

"I'd think so. Have you ever known the Triads to slack when they wanted someone dead?"

Another sigh. She took a long drag from the cigarette, stubbed it out and invaded Victor's side of the table. She took an empty plate, deprived him of a few slices of salmon from his plate, then went for the pile of pancakes he had left criminally ignored. "I'm going to eat this," she said with her mouth grimly set. "And then I'm going to go back to São Paulo and I'm going to sleep. I'm going to let Marcus see his family. And you are going to tell Jenkins that she's on and that she can start setting things up." She spotted some silog—a mix of fried egg and garlic fried rice from the Philippines— and heaped that on too. "24 hours. Just give me 24 more hours and we'll be on this. If this Polychrome guy can't keep himself alive for one more day, he's probably not as shit hot as you'd like to think."

She poured syrup on her pancakes, threw a cube of real butter on top of them, and then stuffed her face with food. Tomorrow was going to suck.

But at least Victor's people knew how to make a mean pancake.

Chapter II:
Resignation

THIS WASN'T THE way Zee had imagined death coming. Death wasn't supposed to be skulking around in the streets asking questions, showing pictures and video and slipping actual hard cash in people's hands if they gave answers. Zee wasn't supposed to be holed up in a 200-year-old bed and breakfast that had been converted over to a Sleep Pod franchise, with displays permanently stuck on SimNet tabloid shows talking about riots at Miriya's holographic concert. And there had never been anything in the cards about bringing down the local economy for simulated drugs.

That part hadn't hit the news feeds yet. By the time it did, if it did, the Blue Dragons would probably have already finished their job, and the Sydney cops would be fishing one more unidentifiable body out of Pyrmont Bay.

This wasn't a game that could be won; not easily anyway. Probably not without some kind of limb loss or permanent network sabotage that would make it almost impossible to operate online again. And if the net was no longer accessible, then what was the point?

Zee could feel the noose tightening. The last quick peek at local net traffic had tagged a couple of Blue Dragons on security cameras. Social and ambient surveillance feeds showed the same thing. It was like a ripple in the local media data, people suddenly mentioning rude Asians that asked questions in broken English and yelled at each other in Cantonese. Completely unsubtle, not giving a shit at all about who noted their presence. They were focused on being patient, methodical and relentless, sweeping every location, missing nothing. And soon they'd be here.

Things hadn't been this physical in a long time.

First order of business: get out of the sleep space and go somewhere with more escape options.

The roof.

Not the safest choice, but the most unlikely one, or so these Triad grunts would think. And now that it was down to playing the odds, the choices that would surprise the Triads the most were the ones with the best chance of survival.

Zee made for the stairs, slipping out of the fiber-reinforced biopolymer coffin that had been home for almost a week. The only thing worth taking was the visor, hardly an adequate substitute for a proper console, but still better than no net access at all, which was quickly becoming more a matter of survival than convenience.

Zee half walked, half ran past the other coffins—most of them shut, one improperly, from which the sounds of a man and woman moaning could be heard, punctuated by rhythmic thumping. There was a persistent, almost nauseating aroma of butterscotch in the air coming from the same pod.

At least someone's having a good time tonight, Zee thought.

And then it was through the doors, the clatter of shoes on metal, echoing in the cold space of the stairwell. Zee opened the door and breathed in the cool night air of Sydney.

It was really too bad things had to go catastrophic here. Zee had kind of been hoping that Sydney would be the town to finally settle down in. At least for a while.

The visor went back on and a quick consultation of the feeds showed that there was still a pursuit presence on the ground, moving in a clumsy, largely uncoordinated grid pattern. But it was still a net, and anyone that wasn't paying attention could get caught in it.

The Sleep Pod franchise was housed in a smaller building, only three floors, but then most of the buildings in this area were the same height. It made the roofs of the other buildings accessible to anyone who wasn't afraid to jump across the gaps. That had been a feature Zee had been hoping to not take advantage of, but it looked like the Blue Dragons could actually get their shit together when they were sufficiently pissed off.

Zee looked at the gap between the Sleep Pod and the neighboring building. One long, careful step was all it took to negotiate the space between them. The surrounding buildings had spaces between them that weren't much bigger. This was actually going to work.

Zee traversed a few more buildings, travelling deeper into the cluster of buildings that made up this block of the street. The visor showed the social feeds being absolutely ordinary now, which meant that the Triads had stopped interacting with the public. The taps in the surveillance also brought up nothing. Very, very bad.

Zee hopped more buildings and was on the opposite end of the block now, on what looked like a crumbling apartment building, the brick dated it as something from the 19th or 20th century; it was hard to tell. Noises filtered up from the street below, a cacophony of Australian accents mixed with Cantonese, Thai and German tourists. There was supposed to be a fire escape here.

There was. Zee had just enough time to register a silhouette rising up from about where the fire escape should have been, and then the gun went off.

Something pierced skin. Not a bullet tearing flesh and making a hole on one side and an even bigger hole on the other—this was a prick, a stab to the right leg followed immediately by white hot pain, and all the muscles in Zee's body pulsing with no control at all.

Zee could only watch as the gunner stood up and was joined by others. It was no surprise at all that Jimmy Tong was among them, smoking the clove cigarettes he thought were so classy. He wore a ridiculous red Hawaiian shirt that clashed with the shiny, spidery black of his prosthetic right arm.

Jimmy Tong looked down and clicked his tongue. He shook his head. "I'm really disappointed it had to come to this," he said finally. He got down on his knees to make eye contact, to make sure Zee could see he was smiling. "You could be dead right now, but you get a few minutes. We need to talk."

He pulled at whatever it was that had embedded itself into Zee's leg and held it up. "Shock round. Efficient, right? Neuromuscular incapacitation. Wears off after a while, but that just means I get to shoot you more, and if you get enough, you'll definitely be feeling that in the morning." He stopped, as if remembering something. "Oh, that's right, for you there won't be any more mornings."

Jimmy's foot went straight into the gut. Zee had been expecting it, but with no muscle control it was impossible to brace for, and the pain bloomed hot and sharp.

"Stupid, fucking *bitch*," Jimmy snarled. Another kick, this one even harder, Zee groaned, unable to even roll away. "Had a good thing going and you had to fuck it up. Had to fuck *everything* up. And for what?" This time he spat, and Zee could feel the saliva dripping down one cheek.

"Not… a bitch…" Zee gasped.

"I don't fucking care what you are anymore," Jimmy said. "Everyone's the same when they're dead. But you… you're gonna suffer a little first. No headshot for you. You know how long it took to get that gig going? Five years. Five of *my* years, and you just shit on that."

Another kick. More subordinates were gathering now either smiling down at Zee or keeping a straight face and nodding.

"I was going to make 438, I was gonna be a vanguard in year. Maybe less. And I was going to take you with me. We were going to be on easy fucking street, why'd you throw that away? Why?"

It was a rhetorical question. Zee couldn't even speak anymore, and Jimmy punctuated the question with yet another kick. There was probably going to be some kind of internal injury, not that it was really going to matter in a short while anyway.

Then Zee was hauled up by two myostatin enhanced thugs to stare Jimmy in the eye.

"Now I owe a fuck ton of money, a bunch of answers, and some serious apologies to the Dragon Head." He leaned in very close until the smell of something, possibly whiskey, was right in Zee's nose. "You're gonna be part of that apology. Old man Lun, I think he had a weird thing for you. I held him off, because you were making us money. Well you're not now. So he can have you. Which means you die, 'cause Lun, he likes to kill what he fucks. Drives his lieutenants nuts because of all the body disposal, but what can ya do? Lun keeps bringing in the money."

Jimmy took a few steps back and reached out his hand. The Triad that had taken the shot moved closer, passing the shock pistol over.

"You're only as useful as the money you make," Jimmy said. He casually pointed the shock pistol at Zee's stomach and pulled the trigger. More pain, doubling over, a scream that wouldn't stop.

Jimmy looked on sadly. "And the pisser is, I still don't even know why you fucking did it."

Zee could barely make out anything through the tears of pain. But even with blurred vision, it wasn't too hard to spot one of Jimmy's boys getting hit by a shaft of blue-white light coming in at a 45-degree angle, a sharp *crack* splitting the air, and then he fell backwards, twitching. The air was now thick with some smell that was vaguely familiar.

Jimmy's groove broke immediately. "What the fu—"

And then it happened again. The same ragged light, this time at a higher angle. Another of Jimmy's men went down, this one screaming.

Zee's eyes followed the afterimage of the light to a shape that was in the air, silhouetted by the lights from the office towers, closing the distance.

Jimmy reached for the holster at his shoulder and pulled out something a lot more serious than the shock pistol which he was now dropping to the ground. The new gun was the one Zee had seen him swagger around with whenever he was trying to make a point; some weird custom carbon revolver that he'd insisted was the sign of a true 22nd century cowboy.

Whatever the case, as he brought the pistol up and at the ready, there was another sharp, smaller crack from seemingly nowhere and his arm was yanked away. The pistol in his grip shattered and fell to the ground.

There was a loud crash somewhere behind Zee.

"Evening, Jimmy," a woman's voice said. "Fancy meeting you here."

Jimmy's only reply was an inarticulate cry of rage as he stared at his empty hand.

Zee rolled over, an act about as easy as rock climbing one handed with all the stomach pain rolling through like tidal waves.

It was like something from a movie poster.

There was something there, shaped like a man; a man at least two meters in height, hunched over and bulging with shiny black skin and muscles that threatened to engulf his body, his face completely covered by an opaque visor and mask. The roof had cratered where the man had landed and in his massive arms he was carrying a woman.

The woman had a holster slung to her equally black body armor, the gun still in it: but she, at least, had normal proportions—if you counted obscenely athletic as normal for the average human. She was not wearing a mask, only a visor, and Zee could make out the feathered, shoulder-length light brown hair; tanned, dark skin; and the brilliant blue eyes, all of which screamed Eurasian. "Been a while, huh?"

"You. Fucking. Witch," Jimmy said slowly.

The woman swung herself from the careful embrace of the cyborg—Zee assumed it *had* to be a cyborg if it could crater a roof just by dropping on it—and stepped lightly to the ground with a casual, almost careless grace. "How's the arm?" The accent was strong and clearly American. North Eastern Allied States for sure.

"That housing is pretty snazzy," the cyborg said through a harsh, obvious voice modulator. "German? Carbyne?"

Jimmy nodded.

"No, it's not," the cyborg said. "Probably an Indonesian knock off. Carbon fiber, you can tell from the way the light bounces off it. That's some second-tier clinic shit right there."

"It was all I could afford at the time," Jimmy said.

"I suggest a new career then," the cyborg said and now that Zee was really listening, the British accent was coming through. "Something with better pay and lower odds of getting you killed."

The men behind Jimmy, the ones still standing, readied their side-arms. The woman continued to stand by, seemingly unconcerned, although her mechanized bruiser visibly tensed, also ready to retaliate.

Jimmy held up his prosthetic hand to his lackeys. They lowered their guns, but didn't put them away.

"You didn't meet my friend the last time," the woman said. "I'm pretty sure you didn't anyway, or you would've needed way more than just a new arm."

"The fuck are you doing here, Cloke?"

"Not trying to make your life difficult," Cloke said. "But that might happen if we can't reach some kind of agreement."

One of Jimmy's men twitched his arms, raising his gun slightly.

The woman raised her hand, fingers open as if she were going to grab something. "Don't," she said in a tired voice. "You really don't want to start something now, not when I have a clear field of view."

Jimmy said something in Cantonese and the gunner backed down. Then he looked back to Cloke. "Just tell me what this is about so you can go die in a fire somewhere else."

Zee almost smiled. It was the first time Jimmy had ever sounded petulant.

Cloke diverted her attention to Zee, making firm eye contact. "You're Polychrome?"

Zee nodded.

Cloke's eyes turned back to Jimmy. "She's not your problem anymore. We'll be taking her off your hands."

Jimmy's face went carefully neutral and Zee knew that look. It was the same one he always had just before someone died. "Not gonna happen." Jimmy spat again, and Zee felt the saliva on exposed flesh. "Bitch owes me. Burned our whole operation to the ground, and it's coming out of her ass."

"Really?" Cloke sounded marginally more interested, like she was just asking about the soup of the day at a restaurant rather than being targeted by a Triad gang that wanted her dead. "And what did she do that was so heinous?"

"Doesn't matter," Jimmy said. "All that matters is that the payback is going to involve seeing her own intestines roped around her neck before she dies."

"We've got a problem then." She sighed and looked at Jimmy. Her eyes were everything: they said *don't fuck with me* in a way no words ever could.

Jimmy's face remained expressionless. He returned the stare.

"Here's what's going to happen, Jimmy. She comes with us, and maybe—and this all depends on how good a mood I'm in—maybe I compensate you for your trouble a little. I guarantee no one dies that way. Or we do it your way." She walked back to her cyborg partner and leaned against him. He was as immobile as a pillar. "Assuming you're one of the survivors, you'll be a 426 without soldiers. Congrats on the promotion by the way. You should be smart enough to know that means you now have more to lose." She opened a palm, and a tiny ball of flame burst into life and danced there in the air above her hand, like a butterfly made of fire. "So, what's it going to be? You want to walk away from here, or roll out in a meat wagon?"

For a few seconds the only sound on the roof was Zee's own haggard breathing. The rest of the Triads looked at Jimmy.

Jimmy raised his hands. "Take the bitch," he said, and Zee

tried to warn the woman, tried to tell her Jimmy never just rolled over for anything, but it came out a weak gurgle, and then the opportunity was gone. This was all going to go badly.

Cloke pushed herself away from the cyborg. "If you'll do the honors," she said to him, and walked a little closer to Jimmy, about level with Zee.

The cyborg walked over, and Zee felt the massive, reinforced limbs come around and lift. The cyborg turned around and as he did, his hand came up, making gentle contact with Zee's head and something vibrated through the fingers, conducting straight through the skull and right into the eardrum. *Shut your eyes.*

Zee would have to piece it together afterwards from fragments of memory and what they said later. But time slowed in the seconds it took for everything to go completely sideways.

First there was Jimmy raising a finger in the air, a patently obvious signal. Then he dove to his left, whipping his gun back up. There was the green dot of a laser sight strobing across the ground towards Cloke. The sensation of the cyborg's musculature flexing under whatever shell passed for his skin as he hunkered down. A sound like heavy machinery clicking and clacking into its open position as projections rose off his back. Cloke going into a roll as the opacity of her visor dropped to a solid, impenetrable black.

And finally, just as Zee's eyes shut, the cyborg's back projections flaring into a stark, blinding light that drowned everything in white.

Somewhere beyond the darkness of Zee's closed eyes, there was the sound of a lot of people crying out, probably because they'd just been blinded. Then the sound of something like an electric generator shorting out multiple times and another sound Zee couldn't identify at all, almost like a whip whistling through the air, but without the crack. There was that smell in the air again, and this time Zee placed it: ozone. Electricity. Cloke was throwing lightning.

By the time Zee's eyes opened again, it was halfway over.

Jimmy was on the ground, having fallen on his back when the flare whited out the vision of anyone with their eyes open. Somewhere off in the distance, on one of the taller buildings, a man was screaming as he fell to his death, his sniper rifle trailing not too far behind him.

The cyborg was on the move, hunched over to protect Zee, but his arm was extended backwards at an impossible angle and something—this was the something making the whip-whistling sound—was shooting out of his wrist at a speed too fast to see. The cyborg wasn't even looking behind himself, but Zee figured he probably had a targeting system wired either to his visor or directly into the optic nerve and it was feeding images from a targeting computer embedded in his arm.

Whatever it was he was shooting had already dropped two of the guys on the roof.

Cloke, meanwhile, was already hopping onto a neighboring roof, her arm extended. Lightning arced out of her hand while she was still in the air, hitting another Triad that Zee hadn't even seen hiding behind a solar panel array. Cloke landed, smoothly transitioning the impact into a roll and back onto her feet, both hands flung out in front of her as a sheet of flame crawled out from her fingers, melting whatever might still be behind the solar panels.

Zee finally understood that when Jimmy had been calling this woman a witch, it wasn't an insult.

Cloke bent and pivoted with almost mechanical grace, turning back to face the roof Zee and her cyborg partner were on. She was on one knee, drawing out a pistol which she carefully lined up on a blinded Triad that was just standing up. The Triad squealed as she fired and hit him somewhere in the back.

Jimmy was struggling just to get back on his knees as his men screamed and died all around him.

The cyborg turned back around, and Zee could feel him letting go. It was still a little unsteady to stand, but at least no one was spitting and hurling promises of execution anymore.

The cyborg adjusted something on his arm.

"What kind of bullets you got in that hand?" Zee asked with forced casualness. There was a pain building up somewhere below the ribcage now, but it was important to play this cool. People that could kill this fast needed to be humored.

The cyborg held up his right arm, showing a hole that looked like it might be a barrel for some kind of firearm protruding just below the palm of his hand. "Centrifugal gun in the forearm. Accelerates a ball in an electromagnetic spin chamber. No bang, no muzzle flash, no recoil."

Jimmy was staggering back and forth, grunting and rapidly blinking his eyes.

"You really should have listened to her," the cyborg said to Jimmy. "If you've had any kind of dealings with Cloke at all, you should know she doesn't joke about this shit. Hell, she doesn't joke about anything. The girl's got zero sense of humor."

"It goes with your zero sense of camaraderie," Cloke said, hopping back onto the roof. "Thanks for sticking up for me, as always." She walked up to Jimmy, who was still trying to regain his vision. She pushed him on the shoulder, and he fell on his ass with an angry shout.

Somewhere far below people were shouting. Which meant that a police response was probably just minutes away.

"So, where does this leave us now?" Cloke asked, standing in front of Jimmy. "You keep trying to fuck me over instead of just sticking to the deal, and end up getting totally fucked instead. Now how are you going to explain all this?" She kicked him gently in the side and he winced. She turned and walked back to Zee and the cyborg.

"You okay?" she asked.

Zee could only groan. "I think he broke something."

"Fair enough," Cloke said. She walked back over to Jimmy, who was now reaching for the gun with the shock rounds that was still lying close by. Cloke kicked it away and it harmlessly spun through the air, over the roof and down towards the ground below. She nodded down at Jimmy then met Zee's stare. "You wanna break something back? I'm big on parity."

Zee nodded and lurched over to Jimmy, leaning in close.

"Next time you're going to wreck a bunch of girls, don't get me to do it." Zee said, and kicked Jimmy in the jaw. There was a small sense of satisfaction in seeing his face cave under the impact.

The satisfaction only lasted a moment as Jimmy's disorientation disappeared, replaced by a focused glint in his eye. His prosthetic hand—a shock round firmly in its grip—found its home right in Zee's neck.

Zee screamed and crumpled.

Less than a second later, Jimmy also screamed when a bolt of lightning arced into his right arm. It exploded.

"Fuck," Cloke grunted.

The cyborg was already at Zee's side, checking the injury. "How bad is it?"

"I'm gonna need help," Zee gasped. "Lots of it."

Cloke had walked back over to Jimmy and stood over him. "Sorry about the arm," she said. "I'll pay for it."

"You fucking bitch," Jimmy hissed through teeth gritted with pain.

She stared at him for a second with a complete lack of expression. "Sorry about the eye. I'll pay for that too."

"What are y— WAIT, NO, N—"

Cloke pressed one hand down on the right side of Jimmy's face, on top of his eyelid. The bottom of her hand glowed warmly, and Zee could only speculate that flame was coming out of there, cooking Jimmy Tong's eyelid and the eye underneath it.

The cyborg looked down at Jimmy, noting his screams of pain the way some peopled noted the color of a car. "Maybe if she's footing the bill you can get something decent. Norwegian or Venezuelan instead of that Indonesian shit."

"Thank you, Marcus, I don't think he needs shopping tips right now." Cloke came back over to Zee, wiping her hand on her thigh. "You'll make it," she said. "We've got a Medivac and you're a tough girl."

"I'm not a girl," Zee said, vision dimming around the edges, getting dark. "I'm Zee," Zee said, and passed out.

Chapter III:
The New Deal

ZEE LAY UNCONSCIOUS—BUT stable—in the infirmary of the GIS Australasia Corporate HQ in Sydney. Cloke watched her from another room, looking over the shoulder of a doctor that had the security feed viewed as just one window amongst many on his display. The display he was using was called a slate; a smooth piece of alloy, about the size and shape of those old things Cloke had seen called bookmarks, but thicker for easier grip. It projected whatever image or interface was required along with a femtosecond laser constantly firing plasma so the user's fingers would feel like they actually touched something as they danced over the holographic interface in the air. It was something that Victor would have been using himself if he didn't have such a stubborn attachment to retro technology.

Marcus was leaning against the wall, being careful not to dent it. "So, Zee's a hermaphrodite," he said flatly.

"No," the doctor snapped testily. "A hermaphrodite is someone in which the sexual characteristics of both genders are potentially present. This... Zee, as you call them, lacks any kind of sexual organ or characteristic whatsoever."

"How is that possible?" Cloke asked.

"It's not," the doctor said. "Not naturally anyway. Certain telltale signs in the DNA suggest the patient's not natural at all. There are markers in the strands for the lymph development that are a key signature of Ribelix Labs in Brussels, for instance. Then the marrow system has Dr. Kamiya's fingerprints all over it from Kotsuzui Togo Shisutemu. And all the work was done in vitro, not gene therapy after the fact. The patient gestated with designer DNA from day one, it wasn't applied later."

"So, she's manufactured," Cloke said, not taking her eyes off Zee.

"That would be my guess," the doctor said. "But it's an amazing job. Very specific, very custom genetic engineering. The cost of this would be ludicrous."

"But not impossible."

"No, no, of course not, just... massive. The lab infrastructure alone would probably keep the Confederated Christian States operating for an entire year. I can't imagine why anyone would bother."

"I'm guessing your exposure to the obscenely wealthy is minimal," Cloke said, finally turning to look at the doctor. "Unique genetics aside, how is her actual state of health?"

"They'll live," the doctor said. "There's a fair amount of subdermal damage due to electrical burns. That's the shock pistol's work obviously. A little bit of internal bleeding, some cracked bones, including the left hand, but the fractures are easy to repair. Blunt trauma injury as well, but no surprises there. Minor internal damage to the spleen, nothing that isn't easily treatable with nanotherapy or we can get in our healing thaumaturge if you're really in a hurry."

"Nothing life threatening, then?"

"Not anymore, no. The trauma team knows what they're doing."

Cloke ran her hand through her hair. She badly wanted a cigarette now. She'd come here for a console jockey, and she'd gotten a mystery instead. "Was there a background check on this Zee? What came up?"

Marcus shrugged and the wall behind him groaned at his movement. "That Jenkins girl Victor assigned dug around. She said Zee has a footprint. It's thorough, but flimsy. There are legit transactions dating back about four years or so. Beyond that, the history is counterfeit, and she found the holes when she poked at it hard enough." He frowned at Cloke. "Some big question marks here, boss."

Cloke groaned, and it was only half theatrically. Wonderful. It had already been bad enough tangling with the Triads, now this extra layer had dropped into her lap like a grumpy cat that meant to use her knees as a litter box. "Is she up for questioning?"

The doctor snorted. "Would it make a difference if I said no?"

"Only insofar as I might keep it shorter."

"They need to rest, obviously, but one conversation isn't going to kill them."

Cloke shrugged. "So, she's not a girl, does that mean he's a..."

"Could be xie," Marcus said.

"This gets confusing," Cloke replied.

"Welcome to the 22nd century," the doctor said.

Cloke blew some hair out of her eyes. A genetically engineered console jockey was already becoming far more complicated than the contingencies anticipated. Victor was going to get an earful. "I'm going in to talk," she finally said. "At the very least maybe they can tell us what the hell we call them. You coming?"

"Sure," Marcus said. "Does this mean I'm the bad cop?"

"No, you're the 'in case of emergency break glass' fire axe."

Marcus grinned. "You always say the nicest things, love."

The room that Zee was recuperating in was typical GIS corporate interior decorating; a respectful adhering to local flavor that bordered on mania. This particular room had its walls painted to resemble a typical sunny day somewhere in the ridiculously posh suburb of Kirribili, across the bay and affording a view of the Sydney Opera House and the downtown skyline. It was tacky and entirely too eager to please, which was characteristic of most of the GIS executives she knew. The GIS logo itself was placed discreetly in unobvious places, an apologetic watermark of sorts to show they still ran the place.

Cloke took a chair and moved it closer to Zee, sitting down to get a closer look at them. She didn't care what the grouchy doctor said—until she got it straight from Zee's mouth, it was hard to see anything but a kid; a really messed up kid who obviously had a boat load of issues. But then being grown in tank was going to do that to anyone.

Somewhere behind her, she heard Marcus relaxing into a casual stance. By now he was all too aware that there likely wasn't a chair on this floor that could fit him without being deformed into a fascinating new shape suitable for public street art.

Cloke leaned in closer and took in Zee's sleeping face. Now that she knew Zee was manufactured, their looks made it an easy thing to believe.

Their face had been sculpted. Perhaps not literally, but there was a careful, mechanical precision to the way the DNA had created a slim, angular face with lines just hard enough to create sharp definition, but still soft and curved enough to avoid anything definitively masculine. The lips were a little smaller than what might be considered sexy on a woman, but still slightly too full to be comfortably male. And there was the dark hair, jet black, shiny. Zee hadn't done themself any favors whatsoever in the style department, choosing a short hairstyle that fell somewhere between a pixie and a pompadour. Their skin was wickedly pale, giving the impression that they were probably going to start feeling better once they'd ingested a few pints of blood.

Cloke touched their wrist lightly and watched Zee's eyes flutter. When they opened, their irises were grey, almost completely devoid of color.

"You are not what I would call a typical result," Cloke said, waiting until she was sure Zee was focused on her.

"Of what?" Zee asked.

"My ops," Cloke said. "I usually expect them to go sideways, not oblong."

Zee stared at Cloke. "I don't know what that means, or who you are."

Cloke noted the accent. American but western; maybe SoCal, NoCal or the Pacific Collective. "You can call me Cloke," she finally said. She leaned back in the chair and tilted her head to her left and behind her. "That's Marcus."

Marcus gave a single, slow nod. "Evening. You just let me know how I refer to you, and that's what I'll do."

Zee blinked a few times in unconcealed shock. Politeness, apparently, was not something they'd had much exposure to.

"Or we can table that for another day," Marcus said. "When you're ready."

"So, here's the deal," Cloke said, one part of her mind concentrating on looking as casual as possible, the other observing every reaction from this kid, right down to pupil dilation. "I'll tell you why you're not dead, but first, I want to know why Jimmy and his dance troupe wanted you that way."

"Where am I?" Zee asked.

"Still in Sydney for the moment."

"What does that mean exactly?" Zee asked, sounding calm, neutral. Now that Cloke was listening, she wasn't surprised at all to hear Zee's voice walk a fine line between that of a teenage boy, or a woman with a little timbre. If she was talking to them on an audio only channel, she'd probably never be completely sure of the gender of the speaker.

"Your future is variable," Cloke said. "And the determining factors are what kind of answers you give and whether I like them."

Zee looked down, fingering the gown. "I'm in a hospital? In Sydney?"

"Yeah. You've had some amazing work done. Or maybe I should say you're someone's amazing work. Raises a lot of questions."

"You mean who made me," Zee said, and there was a tenor in their voice that showed just how old this wound was. "But that's not why you kept me alive."

"No, it's not," Cloke said. "I still want to know why it turned into a job to keep you that way."

Zee smiled and it was devoid of amusement. "A job. You're

mercs, aren't you? Maybe PMC. Fine, I get it." They sighed. "It's standard practice for the Triad to want to kill someone when that someone fucks them over."

Cloke leaned back. "That sounds juicy."

"It's not really," Zee said. "Know much about the virtual drug industry?"

"That digital stuff?" Marcus asked. "Not really into that."

"It's more efficient," Cloke said. "You code up a program that neurologically simulates the effect of a speedball, LSD, whatever you like. It's perfect, all the effect with none of the actual physical side-effects, so no overdose, no loss of market. Customer buys the program, uses it on their sim unit, and after a set period of time, the program shuts down and locks out. If they want to use it again, they go back and buy a new digital key to unlock it. If they try to hack it, the program self-deletes, notifies the owners."

Zee nodded. "Jimmy had a nice little operation going here in Oz, thanks to me. I reverse-engineered some primeval code from the early Twenties. Completely re-cooked it with new input calibration data and it became a thing of beauty. Profit growth was weekly, it was good stuff."

Cloke looked at Zee appraisingly. This was no small thing. "And then you—"

"I modded the code in the product and disabled the lock and deletion mechanisms. Then I put it out online at a local public hub for a few hours. Yay, software piracy."

"Bloody fuck," Marcus said.

"A small group of people got free, unlimited access to virtual drugs. Someone probably duped them already and redistributed them on the Net. It'll get shut down, of course, but Jimmy and the Triads will have to find someone new to do it. They'll take a huge hit to their profits this year."

Cloke shook her head. "You were smart enough to do that, but not smart enough to figure out how stupid that was."

Zee shrugged. "I was mad."

"Mad enough to burn a reputation for being one of the region's up and coming jockeys," Cloke said. "You were on the cusp of getting noticed by the big fish in this part of the pond, and you threw it all away. That's pretty mad, all right. What did he do, shoot your parents in front of you while coming out of the theater?"

Zee made a face, a petulant one, and Cloke wondered just how old they actually were. They mumbled something while staring at their lap, but it was too soft for Cloke to hear.

"What? I didn't get that."

"He made me embed some rapeware into a custom version of the virtual drug."

Cloke's eyes narrowed.

"For parties," Zee said. The harsh tenor was back in their voice, the anger. "That's how he pitched it to me. It turned the user into a drugged-out, amped-up sex toy. He field-tested it with some girls he partied with, then decided it was commercial grade."

"What does that even mean?" Marcus asked.

"He wanted to start using it on his sex workers," Zee said. "Hooker 2.0, wetter and wilder than ever. He could start charging premium rates."

Cloke continued to stare. "And you just went along with it?"

Zee returned the stare. "You talked to Jimmy Tong like you knew him. Do you?"

"My acquaintance with him is strictly professional. Or as professional as anything gets in this business."

Zee snorted. "I tried to keep it that way too. Problem is, Jimmy can't stay away from his own product. And when he's on it, or just drunk, he makes sure he gets his way." Zee shrugged. "I figured it wasn't worth the trouble." There was a hitch in Zee's voice as they said this.

Cloke caught it. "That's not all of it."

Zee shrugged again and this time held up their left hand, the one that was now in a splint with nano-therapy units busily mending the broken finger bones there. "This is how Jimmy Tong persuades people. His favorite persuasive argument involves a wrench." Zee's eyes were fixed firmly on some point on the wall. "So yeah. I was mad."

Cloke looked to Marcus. His expression seemed to mirror her own feelings, namely that Zee had earned some karmic payback.

"He forgot about it, of course. Pretty much by the next day," Zee continued. "But I didn't."

"Okay," Cloke said, leaning back. "Okay. Thank you."

"For what?"

"Convincing me that this was not a complete waste of time."

"What's that supposed to mean?" Zee asked, finally meeting her gaze again. It was, Cloke decided, going to take some time to get used to the almost luminous elegance that had been built into Zee. Even a simple stare was arresting.

"Probation," Cloke said. "That's what you're on, if you want it."

"Probation for what?"

"I need a jockey. You might be it if we can make it work. If you want it to work." Cloke watched Zee's eyes carefully to see if any of this was sinking in. She knew she was offering a second chance, but would Zee?

From the absolute gravity that sank into their expression, apparently they did.

"It's not going to be that easy," Zee said with an air of forced calm, but Cloke could almost smell it on their breath now: hope. The same kind she'd had herself so many years ago. Cloke wondered now if Victor knew it was going to go down like this.

"No, it won't be," Cloke admitted. "There are going to be hoops to jump through. Big, flaming ones. But it might be worth it."

"How?"

"Keep me happy and you'll get administrative access to the GIS network infrastructure."

Cloke smiled, satisfied, as Zee was unable to suppress their reaction of shock. She'd just offered the Internet version of the keys to the kingdom. Only GIS had complete access to the global net since it had fractured into regional networks decades ago.

"That's impossible," Zee said.

"Not for me."

Zee's eyes locked with Cloke's. "Who are you?"

"My name is Cloke. That's all I'm giving you. The rest of it you can try and dig up yourself if you're half as good as you claim to be."

Zee arched one perfectly shaped eyebrow. "I got my start cleaning up personal online histories."

"Sounds juicy."

"Not as juicy as being a witch."

"I'm not that. Not even close," Cloke said. "The technical term is Thaumaturge. Elemental."

"The practical term is combat mage," Marcus said behind her.

"Throwing lightning and shit," Zee said.

"And fire. Ice. Gale force winds, bunch of other things," Cloke added.

"So, it's really real," Zee said, and for the first time there was neither defensiveness nor paranoia, just a genuine curiosity to glean more knowledge.

"You didn't think we were real?"

"Well, you hear about it," Zee said. "But that's about all. And anything without a lot of actual net coverage backing it up is probably just more online myths. Like Nigerian princes giving away money."

"Nigerian princes do give away money," Cloke said. "Well, maybe not for free, but if you run in the right circles, it's just something that no one likes to openly discuss."

Zee stared.

"I'm joking. Or am I?"

Cloke heard Marcus coughing down a laugh behind her.

"Combat magic is real," Cloke said. "Just not that common. It's part fluke, part discipline and not many people are cut out for it. At last count there were only nineteen Thaumaturges operationally rated for it from the College."

"That's it?"

Cloke shrugged. "There's always more training in the wings

but... yeah, we don't have a long shelf life. Getting killed by other people will do that to you. Occupational hazard."

"Well that sounds safe."

"That's half the fun of being in a Chimera unit," Marcus said.

"A what?"

"Industry slang," Cloke said. "What military and corporate higher-ups like to call combined arms combat groups. Any mix of conventional, digital and combat magic is a many-headed beast. And units that work well are top dollar in the market."

"Are you one of those units?" Zee asked.

"Depends on who you ask. Now you have a chance to find out."

Zee's eyes wandered to their lap, and it was clear they were thinking.

"It's a lot to take in. It always is." Cloke stood up. "We'll let you get more rest. Give it a think, but just remember this. Is it really any more dangerous than the situation we just pulled you out of?"

Cloke and Marcus headed towards the door. "If you decide to go ahead with it," Cloke said over her shoulder, "then we'll probably leave as soon as the docs give you the okay to travel."

"To where?"

Cloke stopped. "NoCal. You've got talent, but you've also got a temper. That's a dangerous mix. You need to get back in balance, so you'll need a teacher. He's in NoCal right now." She turned to look at Zee. "Treat him with respect."

Zee pulled their lip and it took years off their face, making them look like a teenager. "Why should I?"

"Because he's dead. There's nothing but bad karma in disrespecting the dead."

Cloke left the room, satisfied that she'd given Zee enough shocks to keep them occupied for the next few days.

Chapter IV:
Sensei No Konpyūtā e No Fusei Shin'nyū

THERE WAS A lot for Zee to take in over the next week.

For one thing, Cloke—at least so far—seemed to be that most rare of creatures, a woman of her word. The GIS med-center did their job and Zee was, if not completely recovered, at least not in considerable pain. There wasn't going to be any tennis in the future, but walking around and smoking cigarettes were possible again.

Cloke had also agreed to honoring a small list of requested items, including some clothes, a decent slate and a high-end consumer-level sim unit, but not a full-on console. "We'll save the big-ticket toys for once you're settled in," she'd said with what Zee was now realizing was her customary sense of mystery.

Marcus on the other hand, was much more approachable. Where Cloke tended to keep a lot of things to herself, Marcus was forthcoming. He was muscle; jacked-up muscle thanks to a string of synthetic adrenal enhancements and CNT fiber running through his cybernetic musculature, but still basically the primary hitter and shooter of things.

They were talking while Zee was en route to the fabled appointment, taking the tube to NoCal. Cloke had already gone on ahead a day earlier, and it was while they were talking that Marcus had shared—with no asking whatsoever—that he was married, a father, with a little girl.

"And your wife… she's okay with… all this?" Zee had asked, eyeing the barrel in his wrist that he'd earlier tagged as a centrifugal gun.

Marcus had shrugged. "It's work," he said. "It puts food on the table and money away for college. She wasn't always okay with it, always wondered if it was going to come back and bite us in the ass, but she's not so worried anymore."

"Why?"

"She trusts Cloke's judgment. Maybe more than mine," he said with a grin. "There are things Cloke won't do, and if I'm not doing them with her, Ginny's comfortable with that. The big money jobs, the *easy* big money jobs, are the ones we stay away from. No nuked shantytowns to make a statement to locals grumbling about revolution, no assassinating an up-and-coming unionizer. Hell, we actually ran protection once for a displaced Nigerian prince who was trying to get his throne back from a junta that was blowing up big civilian holes in the country after taking power."

Zee wasn't sure if having scruples was actually a strength or weakness in merc work, but it was definitely something worth filing away for future reference.

San Francisco felt different as Zee stepped out of the station and breathed in the Bay Area air. But then that was no surprise; San Francisco was always different. The city never stayed the same, which was probably one of the reasons why it had survived World War III with so little apparent damage.

Marcus, looking ludicrous in a massive shirt and pants that strained against his cybernetic frame, hailed a cab at the station and gave directions to the terminal. He waited by the open door for Zee. "This will take you where you gotta go," he said.

"You're not coming?"

Marcus shook his head. "Call me superstitious, but I don't truck with this. Don't want to be there when it happens. Not sure I want to deal with it at all afterwards."

Zee got in and Marcus took a few steps back. "You go and

have fun, or whatever it is you're supposed to have at such an occasion. I'll catch up with you two later. Got my own business to take care of while we're here."

The cab drove itself to the address Marcus had given, somewhere in the area still known, quaintly, as Silicon Valley—even though no chip manufacturing had occurred there for decades and the chips had switched over to carbon and graphene decades ago. It was a reminder of grander, less complicated times, when it had somehow not seemed pointless to have a single, unbroken nation spanning from the Pacific to the Atlantic. The area was a mix of new and old buildings, many over 200 years old, retrofitted with new additions and modern construction materials; ghosts of stone and brick being slowly covered over by a growth of polymer.

The cab arrived, automatically deducting the amount required from the small per diem account Cloke had assigned to Zee's DNA, finger and voice print. The building was an unmarked, unremarkable tan slab in the middle of many other slabs accented by cafes and restaurants with patio dining. The receptionist inside had been expecting someone, and it didn't take long for Zee to be shuffled into a large room, tastefully designed as an exercise in minimalism. It was adorned with a few rows of chairs facing a construct in the front of the room that was one third altar, one third podium and one third holographic display. A chapel for the digital faithful.

Cloke was waiting, looking grumpy, an older man with her. Zee didn't recognize him. Cloke nodded once in greeting, staring with the calm, icy blue eyes that were still unsettling; she always seemed to be sizing things up.

"How'd you find the trip?" Cloke asked.

"It was all right. Marcus talks a lot."

It was the man who spoke. "Marcus does that. You get used to it." He extended his hand. "Victor Chapman. Pleased to finally meet you."

Zee's mouth dropped as the name clicked. "Vice President of General Information Systems?"

"One of them," he said, with a small, sheepish smile. "It's

not as powerful as it sounds."

"Yeah, it is," Cloke said, rolling her eyes.

Zee saw Victor focus back down on the slate he was still holding in his hand. "You find out anything revealing about our Cloke yet?" he asked.

Zee frowned, and Cloke chuckled. "I'll take that as a no," she said.

It had been more difficult than Zee had anticipated to scrounge up even basic details about Cloke. She didn't even have a proper legal name in most records, going by the service designation of Cloke in what few high-level contracts were available to semi-public scrutiny or whatever back doors Zee could sneak in through. Some references to a Filipino and Irish descent were left here and there on a few medical records, which corroborated with the darker skin but weirdly chiseled features Cloke sported. Other than that, however, she had very little in the way of a digital footprint, something that was nearly impossible for the average attention-hungry human being in the 22nd century. A complete lack of any photo or video records was a sure sign that some kind of scrubber was at work, keeping her image off the various nets. That was only possible with high level GIS access, lending even more credence to Cloke's claim that she had connections.

Of course, the vice president of the most important company in the world standing right there and chiding her for not wearing enough make-up was proof enough at this point.

Cloke tamped down on Victor's make-up advice and looked at the elaborate holographic display. "You ever been to an emulation boot up before?"

"No," Zee replied. "But I've read about it."

"You ever interact with one of these things?"

"No."

"I have," Cloke said. She sighed, a gesture that seemed to reverberate through her entire body. "Maybe you get used to it with exposure, but it still creeps me out."

"It's just the question you don't like," Victor said. "That's the part you have a problem with, I suspect."

Cloke nodded. "I don't like that question, I'll admit."

"What question?" Zee asked.

"Is it really him?" Cloke said. "Or just some convincing code pretending it's him?"

"If the code believes it, does it matter?" Victor asked.

"Can code believe?"

"And thus the circular argument completes its circuit," Victor said.

An appropriately serious, older looking, formally dressed attendant entered the room and greeted Cloke. "You're the executor?"

She nodded and indicated Victor and Zee. "They're here for moral support."

"Of course, of course," the attendant said. "Our bandwidth here is pretty good, so we can broadcast a sim signal to you wirelessly, though we still have cabling for a direct jack if you prefer. Always cleaner and crisper, obviously."

"No," Cloke said, indicating the big altar with a nod of her head. "We'll use the display; I don't have any implants for receiving."

The attendant's face went into confused shock, mirroring Zee's own feelings.

"No receivers of any kind? At all?" Zee asked.

Cloke shook her head. "Virgin." She lifted her hair and turned her back to Zee to show the clean, unbroken flesh of the back of her neck.

"I assume your display is in working order," Victor said.

The attendant looked to the altar that dominated the room. "It's normally just used for saying a few words, accenting the presentation with some visuals, video reminiscing and the like... but yes, it'll work. Most people prefer the first meeting to occur in simulation. It's... a gentler transition."

"Holography will be fine," Cloke said. "I don't feel like applying saline paste to my head, and I don't know if you even have any analog interfaces lying around."

"How the hell do you run with GIS and not have any implants?" Zee asked, still in shock.

"It's complicated," Cloke said. "I'll tell you later. In the meantime, get ready to meet your new best friend."

The attendant produced a small carbon case no bigger than his palm, obviously some kind of cartridge, and slotted it into the terminal attached to the display. Zee watched as Victor moved away, taking a seat in one of the front row chairs. Cloke remained standing, crossing her arms. "Keep it in monochrome," she said to the attendant.

"What?" he asked, clearly confused.

"I don't need color," Cloke said. "I don't need anything that makes this realistic. It would be better if it weren't. Green is fine."

"A... all right, if that's what you want."

"It is."

The attendant worked over the terminal, fussing with the controls. "I've adjusted the volume for the speakers in the room," he said. "That should make it less harsh."

"Make what less harsh?" Zee asked. A quick look at Cloke showed that she was tightening her muscles, as if bracing for something.

"Do it," Cloke said.

The attendant nodded and pressed an icon on the display's interface. The moment he did it, the room was filled with an oscillation of static; rending metal, thunder and human panic all combined into a roar that was dynamically adjusted for comfortable hearing as it tried to rip itself to pieces. It was like experiencing a car crash from the point of view of the car.

It was, Zee realized, a digital scream, a translation of trauma into machine language. Something, someone was coming into being without being asked and it did not like it. It was a birth.

The noise died down and patterns flashed on the holographic display; rapid, random flashes of fundamental geometries and the mathematics of awareness as something resolved itself. Eventually it coalesced into a person, or at least, a person from the shoulders up. It reminded Zee briefly of a 20th century vid she'd seen once, back when they were purely visual and only two dimensional: *The Wizard of Oz*, with a disembodied head appearing in smoke.

Zee was looking at someone, male, still relatively young, late twenties or thirties, still probably younger than Cloke. Asian, obviously. Probably Polynesian; the features were strong enough to mark him as not Chinese, Japanese or Korean. It was hard to make out his complexion in the monochrome green that Cloke had selected, but he was thin—Zee could tell that much just from the cheekbones and jawline. The audio in the room narrowed itself from a mélange of static and chaos into someone gasping for a breath he no longer needed to take.

"Hello, Darma," Cloke said. "How are you?"

"Cloke?" the image named Darma said. "I can hear you, but I can't see anything."

Cloke looked at the attendant. "Give him a visual on the room. Anchor it to the display he sees from his position; I don't want any weird eye contact issues."

The attendant did it. Life jumped into Darma's eyes and he focused on the room around him, taking in everything including the people.

"Hey, Cloke," he said. His eyes moved past Cloke to the GIS executive in the chair. "Hey, Vic."

"Mister Chapman," Victor said, with no irritation whatsoever, and Zee suspected an old routine was playing out here. When Darma's gaze fell on Zee, he blinked a few times.

"Who's the kid?"

"Their name's Zee," Cloke said.

Zee gave a half-hearted wave, but said nothing.

"Hey, Zee," Darma said, smiling. "She dresses better than you, Cloke."

"I'm not a she," Zee said, unable to stop the irritation that burbled up whenever a stranger got it wrong. "Hir. Or xie."

Darma looked around again. "So, what's going on? I don't remember much, but if you're futzing around with my visual field like that, you're piping it in from somewhere else."

"Not exactly," Cloke said.

"Oh." Darma seemed to give this more thought. "I'm in a simulation. You're patching communications through while I convalesce? Must've been bad."

"Still not quite right," Cloke said. "What's the last thing you remember?"

"The last thing I remember is going into the lab after checking in for an update on my... oh. No."

If this wasn't really a digital emulation of a man named Darma, Zee would have been hard pressed to believe otherwise. There was a look on that face that spoke volumes about a man realizing he was no longer alive, but a neuropsychological echo that had been regularly updated anywhere from annually to monthly depending on the service contract and time availability. Darma's face collapsed into the realization that he wasn't a he, not anymore anyway, but an it.

"No, that's not what this is, is it?" Darma asked. "This is one of your really pathetic jokes, right?" He looked to Victor. "Come on, man, stop backing her up on this. How's she ever going to develop a real sense of humor if you keep encouraging this shit?"

Victor looked on, with obvious, forced neutrality. "I'm sorry, Darma."

Zee found it easy to relate to this horrible period of self-discovery, but it looked like Cloke couldn't. She watched all this impassively, her arms still crossed, but there was that same tenseness that Zee had seen during the talk with Jimmy Tong. The calm was the thinnest of veils, covering a coiled readiness for combat that was prepared to react with maximum speed and violence.

"You all right?" Cloke asked after a few moments of silence.

"Not really, no," Darma said. "So... I'm..."

"Your physical body is dead," Cloke said. "As the executor of your will, I'm here overseeing the initialization of your emulation."

"So, it actually happened," Darma said. "How long?"

"Four months since the most recent update. You went in to sync it in July. It happened first week of October."

"Four months… did I miss anything important?"

Cloke's features softened and Zee could see some actual discomfort in the lines of her mouth. "You and Nadya… you broke up."

Darma was silent, but his face said everything. "She cheated, didn't she?"

"Yeah. You almost lasted a year, though. That's some kind of record."

"With the British ad executive? She had a thing for British accents."

"Yeah. You guys had a three-way blow-out at a party. Pretty public."

"Well fuck…"

"There's no easy way to swallow any of this," Cloke said. "But then in theory you knew that when you signed the papers."

Darma no longer appeared to be paying any attention to her, his eyes drifting off to stare at some point below him.

"Do you want to be alone?" Cloke asked.

Darma nodded slowly. "Alone where?"

"Wherever you like," the attendant said. "At your discretion we can put whatever environments you or your stewards request in simulation. In the meantime, there's a default apartment you can use if you wish."

"That's if he wants sequential, real time memory," Cloke said. "Do you, Darma?"

"Yeah. For now. I'm going to need the time."

"Okay," Cloke said. "We'll talk again later."

"Sure. Whatever you say," Darma muttered.

Cloke nodded to the attendant and the holo display cut out. The attendant pressed a few more buttons and then removed the cartridge, which had a single blue light slowly winking on and off with the rhythm of breathing. Cloke nodded towards Zee.

"Give it to them," she said.

The attendant walked over and handed the cartridge to Zee, who felt like someone was passing a bomb with a hair trigger. Holding a dead man's emulated personality had not been on the list of things to do in life.

"It's perfectly secure," the attendant said, as if suddenly deciding Zee needed reassurance. He nodded down towards the cartridge. "Standard proprietary interface. It can only slot and run with specific hardware and nothing else. Also in accordance with international law there are no networking features enabled or even electronically possible. It's a ghost that's only legally allowed to exist in one machine at a time."

"Thank you for all your help," Cloke said to the attendant in a way that sounded more like "Please get the hell out of here."

The attendant, with a look of complete surprise, stammered a "Yes, of course," and left the room.

Zee started to say, "What the hell am—" when Cloke raised her finger up in what could only be construed as either "wait," or "stand by."

The vice president, Victor, was consulting an old foldable OLED display that he'd probably chipped out of rocks from the Cretaceous period. He finally looked up at Cloke. "We're basically secure," he said, folding the OLED up again. "Any surveillance that can detect us at this point would be too expensive to justify."

Cloke looked to Zee. "Questions?"

Zee held up the cartridge which felt heavier than it should, but that was likely more from psychological freak-out than actual mass. "What the hell am I supposed to do with this?"

"Learn," Cloke said. "He's your new teacher. One of the best in the biz until a rail gun cut his career short."

Zee looked at the cartridge dubiously. "If he's a jockey, this emulation is illegal."

"It would be illegal if he were ever convicted as such and it was a matter of public record," Victor said. "However, that isn't the case. Officially, Cloke is the acting executor and steward for a consultant in network engineering." He looked at the cartridge in Zee's hand. "And now, evidently, so are you."

"And how is this schooling going to work?"

"The way it always does," Cloke said, moving back towards Victor and sitting down in a chair beside him. "We'll get your supplies, your pocket calculator, text books, new uniform, all that good stuff. And then you'll start going to class."

"Class," Zee said with flat disbelief.

"Well, private class. Very. For the kind of lessons that most of the would-be hackers across the globe would give up a right hand for."

Zee snorted. It was really obvious there were things Cloke knew, but just as obvious that there were things she still hadn't sniffed out yet. "I think you might be underestimating what I can do."

"I'm not so concerned with you learning new hacks, so much as you get some solid advice on keeping your head clear and staying alive."

"What, you mean like he did?"

Cloke visibly tensed. Victor put his hand gently on her arm, but Zee could see the way her eyes focused with the force of a truck.

"Are you really sure about them?" Cloke asked.

"No," Victor said. "But I wasn't about you either."

Cloke took in a deep breath, maybe to calm herself and spoke again with a cool, neutral voice. "You'll be moved," Cloke said, keeping her eyes locked on Zee. "We'll get you set up some place where you'll have access to everything you need. We'll see if you're cut out for any kind of serious work."

"And where's that?" Zee asked.

"My house. Where I can keep an eye on you," Cloke said. She leaned back in the chair. "Hope you like Brazil."

Chapter V:
Settling In

CLOKE WATCHED AS Zee took in the view of São Paulo from her home.

The towers of the city core were visible off in the distance, their western faces bathed in the light of sunset, throwing long shadows across the eastern portion of the city.

"So, what do you think?" Cloke asked.

Cloke wasn't sure which part was boggling Zee more; the view or the house that provided the view. The final design Cloke had approved built a compound into the hill, dwarfing the restored buildings that comprised most of the neighborhood. From a distance it looked like a pile of giant black glass bricks surrounded by the rainbow colors of the matchbox buildings around it.

Zee turned and looked at her. "Do I even want to know how much this cost?"

"Probably not. Let's just say that there's high demand for a certain level of thaumaturgical skill. Very few people can operate at that level, so it pays pretty well."

The room they were currently in was roughly the size of a cottage. It had a clear, unobstructed view of the city as presented through photovoltaic ballistic polymer glass walls resistant to close support fire and the lighter calibers of heavy artillery, in addition to allowing transparent, opaque and two-way viewing on command.

Zee put down the empty glass they were holding on a nearby coffee table. One of the cleaning bots rolled by, deftly picked it up without breaking its path and continued through the house.

"I didn't think I'd get to see this city so soon," Zee said.

"Welcome to one of the great cities of the world," Cloke said. "She's having a good run in the spotlight right now."

"Right now? When was São Paulo not the city to be in?"

"When New York was."

Zee snorted. "People actually cared about that dump?"

"Yes, before the war. There was a time when things only mattered if they happened in New York," Cloke said. She shook her head. "We've had instant access to the collective history of the world for over a hundred years and people still don't bother to read up on it."

Zee shrugged. "Whatever." They sat down on the sofa and stared at the cartridge with Darma's emulation on the coffee table. "I still don't know why you're trusting me with this unit," they said. "Probably has amazing street value. I could set myself up nicely just by moving this thing—and you just give it to me?"

Cloke smiled. "No. You couldn't do anything with it. Not yet."

"There are buyers out there who—"

"Not for this," Cloke said. "Typical fences won't touch it—that thing is way too hot; they wouldn't know what to do with it. The legal and corporate response on a registered stolen emulation isn't worth it. There might be some interest at higher levels, but you have no name, no rep. It would be easier to kill you and take it than deal with you."

"So, you're an optimist then," Zee said, shaking their head.

Cloke suppressed an urge to hit Zee with a small charge of lightning. She was now beginning to suspect that Victor's suggestion to take Zee on had been his inscrutable, ridiculously indirect way of saying to her, *yes, you were like this once, when you were younger.*

Cloke got it; she could see where the insolence was coming

from. She just hoped there was more to this person than just that. Zee would need more than attitude if they were going to be thrown into the deep end of a corporate infiltration, but Cloke would save that particular bomb for a later drop.

"So where are we?" Zee asked.

"A neighborhood called Paraisopolis. Used to be the bad part of town, a long time ago. A favela."

"What is it now?"

"Gentrified. It's on a hill, so once São Paulo came into its own, there was no way they were going to let the poor keep squatting on such prime real estate. Well, to be fair, they didn't move the poor out, the poor just stopped being poor."

"Oh, so this is World War III's fault. Again."

"That's the catch-all answer. It's more complicated than that really, but it's because of what happened here. The people here," Cloke said. She made steady eye contact with Zee, with the eerie sculpted perfection of their face that demanded to be photographed and adored. "People like you changed it. People like me."

"You sound like a crusader. Or one of those people looking for a donation."

"No," Cloke said. "I just like to know my roots, so they don't come back and try to kill me. You should pay more attention to that stuff too if you want to survive in this business. Old lessons are still good ones, especially if your enemy doesn't know shit. Are you hungry?"

"Am I what?" Zee asked, obviously caught off balance.

"Are you hungry? What with all the tubing around, it occurs to me we haven't eaten in several hours. I, for one, am hungry. If you're okay with salad, I can make us some."

Zee seemed to be trying to appraise the situation. "What is this, bonding?"

"We're just eating. And I'll be grilling you."

"Ah," Zee said, and the admission of a logical, secondary ulterior motive seemed to comfort them. "Okay, I can deal."

"All right, follow me, I'll take you home and we can get some food."

"I thought we were home."

"I own this building, and you'll be staying somewhere in it, yes," Cloke said, turning to walk away. "But this is what I keep around for show and for work, it's not home. Not where I live when I'm home."

"Not getting that at all," Zee said.

"You will. Come on."

Cloke wandered through the expanses of dining rooms, salons and other rooms that were expected to host lavish parties and present the expected face of success. These were the rooms that she never spent any time in unless Victor insisted on throwing another soiree for appearance's sake. She arrived at the one door that really mattered; discreet seams in the wall with a doorknob that read her palm print, body temperature, pulse and DNA in the time it took her to grip and turn it to open the door.

She sauntered over to the kitchen and heard Zee's gasp as they came through the door.

"What the fuck is wrong with you?" Zee asked.

The sounds, sights and even smells of Hoboken, New Jersey wafted in from an open window. Cloke walked past a beat-up couch that was likely older than she was and dropped her jacket onto it, making her way to a kitchen with appliances that looked like they still ran off an electrical wall current. The décor clearly hadn't been redone since the original construction, which was probably sometime in the 20th century; the buildings outside the window didn't look like they were in much better shape either.

Cloke opened the fridge, pulled out two bottles of water and offered one to Zee. Zee took it, still looking on wide eyed at the obvious poverty on display here.

"This is my home," Cloke said. "Or at least a replica of the one I grew up in back in Jersey. The original building is still there, but it doesn't look like this anymore. Not since I bought it and had it fixed up. House," she said to the air. "Play the usual."

A guitar and synthesizer picked at the air.

"What is that shit?" Zee asked.

"Spandau Ballet," Cloke said. "Song's called 'True.' I have a thing for music in the last thirty years of the 20th."

Somewhere outside, a saxophone started up and sirens wailed in the distance.

Zee moved over to the couch and sat down, their bottle still unopened.

Cloke leaned against the counter, opened her own bottle, sipped, and waited.

"So, you have a metric ton of money and you spend it on... a shitty apartment."

"Yup."

"In New York."

"Hoboken. Most agree that's worse." She took another sip.

Zee finally looked at her. "Are you damaged? What the fuck is wrong with you?" They looked down and opened their bottled water.

Cloke shrugged. "It feels more comfortable than what's out there," she said, indicating the vast, empty spaces of the mansion that lay beyond the confines of her broken-down little Jersey apartment.

"Then why even have what's out there?"

"It's appropriate," Cloke said. "I see the usefulness of having a building resistant to conventional arms. I also see how it can be handy to have a place everyone thinks is stylish and cool. So, I keep the façade. Meanwhile, I actually live here."

"Is your bedroom also shitty?"

"Oh yes."

"And the bathroom?"

"It looks it, yes, but the plumbing won't give you any trouble, if that's what you're worried about." She took a final sip and moved over to the fridge. "I'll get to that salad now, but we can talk while I make it."

There was silence for a few moments as Cloke pulled out lettuce and other vegetables from her fridge.

"So, this is what they mean by the eccentricities of wealth,"

Zee said behind her.

"That's one interpretation. I prefer to think of it as remembering your roots. What about you?"

"What about me?"

"What are your roots?"

Cloke turned to see Zee fingering the rim of their bottled water. "You took a lot longer to bug me about that than I thought you would."

"I was hoping you'd appreciate that."

Zee looked up. "I guess I do." They took a quick sip. "Would it surprise you to say I don't know?"

"A little. I assumed you would have dug up everything you could by now."

"I tried," Zee said. "Can I smoke in here?"

"I do when I feel like it," Cloke said. "I can't smoke as much as I'd like; the cancer treatments are a bitch, and I don't have the nanos."

"What nanos do you have?"

"None," Cloke said. "Also a nano virgin." She broke away from the counter and salad preparation to hold her index finger up to the cigarette in Zee's mouth. The flame snapped to life on the edge of her nail.

Zee continued to stare at Cloke, apparently unaware of the finger emitting flame before her eyes. "You have no nanos?"

"None," Cloke said. "No cybernetic implants, no synthetic hormones, muscle augmentation, or neural enhancements. Except for the occasional vaccination, I'm all factory original. No mods."

"What the hell world do you come from?"

"A fickle one. Where synthetics integrated into my biology cuts my thaumaturgical capacity by orders of magnitude." She held up her flaming finger. "You want a light or not?"

She watched as Zee finally accepted the flame, took in a drag and let out a long stream of smoke.

"Better?"

"Slightly," Zee said.

"Then maybe you can tell me a little bit about yourself. As

much as you're comfortable with. This isn't an interrogation."

"What is it?"

"Curiosity."

Zee took another drag. "Is this a magic thing? This is a magic thing, isn't it? Witchy, magey types always wanting to know stuff."

"No, it's a story thing. You have one, obviously. And anyone would wonder. Anyone normal anyway."

"You're not normal."

"Normal psychological parameters, it's close enough. Now," Cloke said, walking back to the kitchen counter to resume her salad-making duties, "spill. You really have no idea where you come from?"

"Mostly, no," Zee said. "But I know what I was."

"And what's that?"

"A lab."

Cloke said nothing, continuing to work.

"I was... *we* were made—there were nine others—to satisfy a very, very... forceful... curiosity. We were tested, assessed, retested. For years. Put in tanks filled with God knows what. Injected. Dissected. And then I got out, and made a promise to myself that no one was ever, *ever* going to use me like that again." Zee took a long drag from their cigarette and shrugged. "Been on my own ever since. Figured out real fast that I had a knack for computers, for finding and getting things. I started out as a cleaner, taking jobs from idiots with money and no discretion. I would go online find all the stupid shit they ever said or did that would get them tossed out of the running for a job interview, kill it and replace it with only nice, hireable stuff. Safe, steady money."

"But small," Cloke said.

"And boring as shit. I could do more, I knew that. So, I did. The pay was better when the jobs were less legal. Then it turned into actual runs against municipal systems, small corporate networks, and it was getting interesting. Network reconnaissance. Data hostage work."

"I guess a nice, safe corporate job with juicy benefits and

an expense account wasn't a target on your career trajectory."

Zee sighed. "No. Not unless I can find him. I can't do anything that leaves too big a data trail, nothing too easy to see. He'd find me. I know he's still looking."

"The one who…"

"Who made me," Zee said. "I still don't know who he is. I know what he looks like. I know the sound of his voice. But I don't know his name, and I can't find him in any of the networks and databases I've raided."

Cloke stopped to look at Zee.

Zee was staring back at her. "He's rich enough, powerful enough, connected enough to have a scrubber—like you, just as thorough. There's a digital pit that follows him around on the net, swallowing up everything about him that might get documented online."

Cloke turned back to her salad making. "Are you sure he's looking?"

"Oh yes," Zee said. "When I got out, it was messy. I hurt him. I made sure I did. There were nine of us in the beginning. Three of them were killed over the years when he got too… inquisitive. I made the break, some others did too…" Zee stopped and stared at some point ahead of them. "I left them," they said, their voice a dead, flat, near whisper. "We got separated. Only family I ever knew and I… I ran. I was so scared, I just ran out… on all of them…" Zee swallowed hard, and Cloke could see that hardness spreading out to the rest of them, their eyes, their voice. "I don't know where they are or if they're even still alive," they said in a calmer voice. "But I know he's looking, or someone is looking for him. I've seen the signs. The work they're doing is brutal and fast, leaves a trail, like a break in with a trashed apartment." Cloke could see Zee's eyes wandering the length of the room. "Guess you'd know a thing or two about that."

"Cute. After everything you've told me, it doesn't sound like our job offer is too repulsive," Cloke said.

"Job offer? Is that what you think it is?"

"What would you call it?"

"Impressment."

"Wow, you do read something besides code," Cloke said. "No one's forcing you here. You can walk out that door and go right back to being at the top of Jimmy Tong's kill list."

"You're taking advantage of a bad situation," Zee said.

"I'm giving you a chance to fix a situation you *made*. We didn't put those guns to your head; they were already there when we showed up. This is the deal, Zee, and I'm only going to say this once; and then we're going to eat this delightful salad I'm making, which you will probably say tastes like shit. Unless you nano-modded your taste receptors."

"I did."

"Well bully for you. So, here's what's going to happen. I'm going to let you get access to the really nice toys. The big stuff, industrial and military grade. I'm going to give you GIS access. I'm going to let you work, and I'm going to let you learn from the best."

"Why?"

"To erase all doubt from your mind. So many people bitch and complain that if only they'd had the opportunity, they could have done something big, made something of themselves. I'm going to give you that shot. That way, if you screw up, you'll know the only thing that failed you was you. And if you make it work, it was because you have what it takes."

"Your motivational speeches need work."

"That's not a speech," Cloke said. "That's just the deal."

"Pure business, huh? Always about the deal."

"That's life. And magic too," Cloke said. "No such thing as something for nothing. There's always a cost."

"Even for fireballers."

"Especially," Cloke said. "But we're not here to talk about me. We're here to talk about you and what happens next."

Cloke finished making the salad and brought it over to the counter, gesturing at a seat for Zee to take.

"What did you think I was?" Zee asked.

"A girl."

"Why?"

Cloke shrugged and poked at her salad. "I have a sister. It's just more familiar."

"Well she's herself and I'm myself. I'm not your sister," Zee said. "She have her own shitty apartment somewhere in this house too, or does she actually live like a sane human being?"

"That's a complicated story that you don't really need or want to know right now," Cloke said.

"Everything about you is complicated. Like me staying in this house. Pretty sure you had some simpler solutions to that."

"Simple, but not secure," Cloke said. "I thought at first we just had to keep you off the Triad radar. Now it turns out you've got some super wealthy evil scientist on the hunt with massive resources. The typical safe house situation won't stand up to that kind of scrutiny. Everyone's life is more manageable if you stay here for now."

"Your life, maybe."

Cloke's eyebrows narrowed. "The other nice thing is this building is big enough that you can get lost in it and we may never run into each other again." Zee drew back, as if Cloke had started to hum and emit electricity. "You're not my sister, and I'm not going to treat you like one, I don't need that kind of additional complication in my life. And we're not friends. At this rate, that's looking less and less likely anyway. But I like to think I'm fair, and you haven't earned full bitch mode yet. Fuck up the job, and that's a different story. But that's why we're here. Now. The job. You get it done, we both get what we want, and you can move into whatever security compromised condo you want, and die, floating face down in a pool you don't own, with drugs you didn't take. Fair?"

"Well shit, with a pitch like that, how can I say no?" Zee reached for a glass of water, eyes regarding the liquid inside as if it might be poisoned, before taking a sip.

Cloke nodded in satisfaction. "How do I address you? Them, they, xie, hir, what's the term your friends or coworkers used?"

Zee shrugged. "I didn't have either, not ones that gave a shit about my preferences anyway. And I'm just me. Not XX, not XY, just Zee. As long as you don't box me in with that he-she stuff, we'll be fine."

"Okay. I can work with that," Cloke said. She remembered Zee's correction to Darma. That was the initial instinct, she'd go with that. She reached for a bottle of wine and poured it. "Now," she said. "Let's talk shopping."

IT WAS DURING the supply expedition the next day that Cloke finally saw Zee's potential, the same one Victor had seen in hir nascent criminal career. She took them to scattered holes in the walls, both figurative and literal; vendors who sometimes had shops with no name, not even a storefront, dealing in black or grey market console components.

Zee dealt with them the same way Cloke did; wearing a visor enabled with a translator that heard the Portuguese and placed the English as subtitles at the bottom of her vision, as if the world were some giant foreign film. She watched Zee haggle over something called a CMOS board and it was like a dance with money and words.

"This isn't a 7790," Zee said, and it was a step forward. "If you don't have it, just say so and we'll move on, no time wasted."

"It is a 7790," the vendor, a guy named Miguel, said, and that was his step to the side. "You can see the model number right there."

"Model number, but no serial number. Even if you got these from the factory before they went into distribution, they put the serial number early on in the fabrication. Around the same time, they build in the slots for RAM." Then another step forward. "Speaking of which, this isn't the right RAM for a 7790. They only take HCIS-20 RAM. You've got HCIS-10 in there."

"What?" Miguel asked, and it was a clear stumble.

And Zee swept in with a curtsy. "HCIS-10 comes in a blue

casing. Whoever decided to spray this blue didn't wait for the paint to dry, the fingerprints stuck. That's fine for hotdoggers and rich kids playing jockey; they'll never need a 7790 to do everything it's supposed to, but I will. Now do you have a real one, or not? You probably keep the good stuff for yourself and your friends, don't you?"

The dance ended with Zee getting the board. At a discount.

The final stop was an actual store, one that Darma himself had sworn by in São Paulo, a place called "Cavalo do Robo." Most people just called it Atilio's or Atilio's Junkyard. It was in another of the old favela districts, this one once going by the name Buraco Quente, or "Hot Hole," though mostly it was Vila Senhor dos Passos now.

Atilio was old school, a grizzled, short man with a bizarre hairstyle he referred to as "Wolvie hair," a reference to some ancient comic book character Cloke had never bothered to read up on. He was anal about maintaining the pristine condition of electronics despite chomping down on cigars, as he was doing now, and aside from a few basic implants in his heart and digestive system for health reasons, was not big on cybernetics at all. His only serious concession to the world of biological enhancement were eyes, and even those were just contacts with a net connection and some night amp capability. Atilio was, as usual, giving the stink eye to anyone that was new. In this case, Zee.

"You keep strange company," Atilio said to Cloke in Portuguese.

"Occupational hazard," Cloke said in English.

"Where's your tin man?"

"Doing some prep work. Working with another team to suss out the site of the next job."

Atilio held his hand up. "And that's all I want to know about it." He looked to Zee. "Everything to your liking?"

"Everything here is military spec," Zee said with obvious awe. "I probably shouldn't ask how you got all this stuff, should I?"

Atilio grinned at Cloke. "The kid's smart, anyway. Is he

going to be taking Darma's chair in your merry little band?"

"Darma's still got a chair," Cloke said.

"Oh. Right. Have you talked to him since initializing?"

"No."

"Are you going to?"

"Eventually. I think he needs to sort it out."

Atilio nodded. "And so do you." He walked over to the small pile of hardware that Zee had gathered on a table and ran his hand over it. "Such a weird thing, computers," Atilio said. "To think there was a time when people, regular people, used standalone consoles like this. Before distributed processing, before all the computational power moved online. They used to call it the Cloud, did you know that?" Atilio chuckled. "Stupid name."

"It had to happen," Zee said. "There was no other way it could go."

"Did you read that, or did you figure it yourself?" Atilio asked.

"It's economics," Zee said. "The average user just needs a computer to do basic stuff. Content consumption, mostly. Increased computational power was getting more expensive, it was easier to just make the hardware a receiver, stream in the functionality rather than building it in like they used to do. At the average, general consumer level it just makes sense. Who needs a computer that can do a complete simulation of Koh Samui right down to the last sand particle when mostly you want to check mail and watch videos? Why not just have the computer somewhere else do all that heavy lifting then transmit the result to you?"

"Very nice," Atilio said. "At least you've thought this through."

"Yeah, but you shafted yourselves, didn't you?" Cloke said to the both of them.

Atilio looked visibly offended. "And how's that, magic girl?"

"All this shit is ridiculously expensive now," Cloke said. "Hackers fanned the flames of World War III. They made it possible for a few riots in different cities to turn into a great big global civil war that fucked up so many of the old governments. And that was because anyone could hack. So many of the attacks that crippled the military and bureaucratic systems came from right here in the favelas, street kids with access to cheap hardware and nothing to lose. World War III wasn't nations against nations, it was civil war. Everywhere. Jockeys did that."

Atilio raised an eyebrow. "Oh, and you're telling me the Singularity kicking magic into high gear had *zero* effect on the old-world order? It was all just because of DDOS attacks? The whole world had its ass kicked by the COVID-19 virus in the 2020s. The economies were still trying recover, but when those kids came out of the gutter throwing fireballs at cops, and screaming 'we can burn it all down,' that was just a... what, red herring? Abigail Smithson didn't crash what was left of the global economy by keeping her mouth shut about getting alchemy to work and flooding the market with gold? My dear, that was *you* people."

"What did I tell you about that? That *you* people shit? People that use magic aren't some monoculture with the same agenda. We're not a fucking ethnicity, stop treating us like one."

"Oh, and that's why you guys have your little club up in the sky that no one else gets into?"

Cloke stared. Atilio held up his hands in surrender.

"Yeah, yeah, that was part of it too. Obviously," Cloke said. "But the point is, they took it away from you, didn't they? After that, they learned their lesson."

"They?"

"The companies. They saw what happened when anyone could get the right equipment to hack. Now the only things powerful enough to do it are insanely expensive, and only military or corporate grade equipment has a shot at it. You can try it with a visor or some other display, but if all your programs and processes are online, they know immediately who did it. Once they realized computers gave power to the poor, they made it too expensive for them to use."

Atilio laughed. "Do I even have to point out what you're saying?"

Cloke sighed and looked at Zee.

Zee had a baffled expression. "Man's got a point. You're talking like companies are the enemy. Aren't you on the company tab?"

"I take their money," Cloke said. "But I work with Victor, not GIS."

"Victor Chapman *is* GIS," Zee said.

"Victor Chapman is a man in the corporation, one of many men in it. A company isn't some big monster, it's a group of people pulling in different directions, the way people do," Cloke said.

Zee's head shook. "I dunno. Seems kinda shaky to me, that kind of distinction."

"There are lots of things in this world a lot shakier than that. Like your tab, for instance," Atilio said to Cloke. "You actually gonna pay me this time, or will I have to call in that favor and have you take my cousin to dinner? You know the one? Yelps like a squirrel and drools every time I mention you and magic in the same sentence? You'll have to pull a rabbit out of your skirt if we go that route."

Cloke pulled out her GIS corporate ID. "Run it through. It's been cleared as a business expense."

"Enemies with benefits. Works for me." Atilio took the card and smiled. "Pleasure doing business with you."

In the car, Cloke settled in and watched as Zee looked over the plain, anonymous packaging of one of the components.

"Now you've got all the toys," Cloke said. "Soon we find out if you can play."

"We're actually going to do some of this fabled work I've heard so much about?"

"Soon," Cloke said. "Very soon. You'll probably want to talk to your mentor a little bit. See if there's anything he'd like to share."

"You want to be there when I do?"

"Not yet," Cloke said. "I think it'll be easier for you. You didn't know him. I'll talk to him later. Put it off for as long as I can."

"Way to treat your friends," Zee said.

"Darma was my friend, it's true," Cloke admitted. "I'm still not sure that what's in that box is Darma. It's easier for you because you don't care."

"So, once I get my tips and tricks from our ghost, when do we go?"

"That's being arranged now," Cloke said. "Talk to Darma, figure out what and where you'll need to be. I'm going to get in touch with Marcus and let him know he's back on the clock, figure out some logistical stuff."

"And then?"

"Then it's off to southeast Asia. The LUMO Orbital Elevator. You better get used to traveling. Once you're in demand, you do a lot of it."

Cloke slipped on her visor and started logging in to the GIS network. It was going to be a busy day.

Chapter VI:
Recon Blues

ALL THE GEAR was ready or set in place to be ready. The programs were just waiting for the right triggers. It was time.

For the first meeting with this so-called mentor, Zee decided to face Darma on his own terms. It would be more comfortable for him that way.

The cartridge that held his emulation had the required inputs for connecting a sim unit. Zee used a neural plug and chained the units together with the appropriate cabling, made sure everything was properly calibrated, then hit the "engage" button.

Zee looked around, aware that the simulation was already running. It had scanned and recreated the surrounding guest room in Cloke's home, to make the entry transition as gentle as possible. More than gentle, really; it was invisible. The only difference was the lines of light that formed around one wall, tracing out the shape of a new door before filling in all the details. There was a soft sound as it did this, like an electric whisper talking to the walls.

Zee walked up to the new door in the room and knocked. It was the polite thing to do.

"Come in," Darma said.

There was an entire apartment on the other side of the door—a penthouse apartment of some kind, overlooking a harbor that was blinding in its reflection of precisely polished yachts and other pleasure cruisers. Zee saw the bright light of a tropical afternoon, smelled the sea in the air. In the distance, a sailboat lazily crossed the water, accented by tiny bright reds and yellows of women in bikinis scampering on the deck.

Darma was sitting at a bar on the far side of the room. He was thin; his dark complexion, hair and eyes a giveaway for someone southeast Asian, possibly Polynesian. Zee had already done some of the homework and knew he was from Bali, in Indonesia. Knew also that he had been a serious operator, one of the big names. Under his handle of "Blueshift," he had been one of the people that Zee had studied, had aspired to.

His nickname was the stuff of idle talk in forums and chat rooms where people met to discuss the shadowy rumors, myths and legends of console jockeys. Noobs and third raters watching his moves, speculating what it was like to be that kind of heavy; to do stuff that fucked important people over, made them angry enough to take notice. To be the kind of person that could take a swing at giants and actually hurt them.

Now here was Blueshift, destroyer of online worlds, wearing a Hawaiian shirt and some beige shorts while pushing a glass of sea-breeze cocktail around on the bar counter.

"Nice digs," Zee said.

"Thanks, not mine, obviously," he replied. "And you didn't have to knock, I got the notification the second you logged in. Cloke's not with you," he said, more a statement than a question.

"She's... Well, she's..."

"Freaked," Darma said. "I'm in that club too."

"She's gonna need a little more time with this."

"Yeah well, she's not the one that's dead, so while I can understand I'm not sure I'm ready to play the sympathy card for her just yet."

"I don't know anything about that."

"Of course not. You're the new kid. Got a lot to learn about this little operation. Piece of advice? If you're ever in a situation where you have the option to leave an operations post before it gets flattened? Take it." He sighed and took another long slug of his drink. "Sorry. Not your fault. Just a little bitter."

Zee took in a breath. The neural simulated stimulation was perfect; the air actually felt humid, the cry of the gulls mixed with the distant staccato of lounge music from some bar down below. Anyone would interpret this as real, especially a digital-only consciousness like Darma was now. "Not what you were expecting?" Zee asked.

"I don't know what I was expecting," Darma said with a sigh. "Being dead wasn't on the list."

"Then why'd you do it? Sign on for the service I mean."

Darma sipped from his drink and turned to stare back out at the window. "Same reason everyone does, I guess. It seems like a good idea at the time, just a security blanket where you think, 'well, if I die, I won't die, really.' Except that then it happens, and you go into 'oh fuck,' mode. Death happened and now you're a disembodied consciousness and that isn't half as fun in reality as it seemed in concept." He finally looked back to Zee. "And asking about my mental state is not why you're here."

"No," Zee said walking over to the sofa and sitting down. "There's a job coming, and I got permission from the boss to pick Blueshift's brain."

That broke the brooding vibe Darma had been radiating and he looked at Zee with a raised eyebrow. "Did Cloke tell you that?"

"No," Zee said. "She mentioned some stuff about you being a heavy and I snooped around, made some associations and put two and two together. Cross referencing is enough when someone leaves as big a hole as you did."

"What tipped you?"

"When Cloke mentioned the rail gun. Kind of hard for anyone to cover up firing off something that big, and I got into the biz as a cleaner, so I know that kind of work when I see it. There were enough tracks from that to start making the connections. And I'd been aware of your work anyway."

"Is that so?"

"Anyone that wants to be a serious operator has at least heard of the burning of the MTS network." Zee gave a thumbs up. "Thing of beauty. Always wondered how you got away with that. The online infrastructure in Australia still hasn't recovered and the Triads there still use your handle like a curse."

"Wow. A fan. That's different," Darma said. "I never paid much attention to that stuff, not a very chatty, forumy sort of guy, I tended to keep my circle of interaction small. But since you're a jockey, come over here. Check this out." He walked over to another door and opened it, staring expectantly. Zee got up and followed him in.

The next room was obviously not a natural part of the previous apartment simulation. It belonged to an entirely different older building, and the windows showed night outside, the silhouette of an unfamiliar city skyline. A monstrous console dominated the large table in the room and to Zee it was obvious that almost none of the components were original factory issue. An array of displays hung over the console, along with the expected simulation box and interface, but even that had a custom prototype look to it that made it impossible to trace its original manufacturer.

Zee gave a slow nod of appreciation. "My approval is high. Your lair?"

"My last workspace," Darma said. "Had a temp operations center going in Istanbul before the last and final job."

Zee moved over to the console. "Can I?"

Darma extended his arm, taking a step back. "Be my guest."

The most visible portion of the console was the elaborate keyboard, with its numerous custom hotkeys and buttons. Zee lifted the panel housing the main boards and noted the central processor: Tao series, not a prototype, but some kind of limited in-house development model, the one that didn't have all the extra functionality bells and whistles stripped out before going into mass production for the run-of-the-mill commercial and military models. Combined with the memory and secondary boards, it was quite likely that this one was one of the most painstakingly assembled, powerful consoles on the planet. In the right hands, this thing could sleaze its way into any system—given enough time and resources.

"So whatch'a think?" Darma asked with obvious pride in his voice.

"I'm gonna cry," Zee said. "This whole sweet, sweet set-up, you were probably…"

"Yeah. I would've been using it during my last run. It's vapor now, somewhere in carbon nanotube nirvana where hardware breaks its karmic cycle."

"What a waste," Zee said with genuine regret.

"Oh well, at least you appreciate it," Darma said. "Glad to see Cloke lucked out enough with my replacement to get someone with taste." He put his drink down on an empty space at the table and folded his arms. "Since we're where the magic happens anyway, tell me what this wonderful job is."

"Cloke wants to keep it simple because I'm new."

"And because she doesn't trust you. Don't take it personally, she didn't trust me either."

"Well, I don't trust her, so we're even. She wants to scout out the security at some building in one of the science campuses around the LUMO Orbital Elevator."

"What are you using for this?"

"I've got a decent rig, but all the gear is off the shelf."

"What's on your main?"

"A Taegu, 400 series."

"Memory?"

"Boards are maxed, eight exabytes of ULIC-100 in every slot except the CMOS."

"That's HCIS-20?"

"Yeah, thirty-two exes in that."

"That'll work for milk runs," Darma said, nodding. He sat down at the chair and had a look on his face Zee knew well; getting lost in the playground of tech. "But you can get better, faster boards and memory if you need it." He turned to the console and punched a button. "Gimme your contact, I'll send you... ah fuck." He turned back and looked sourly at Zee. "Never mind, boot out and fire up your visor or whatever you're using, I can't send you shit." He patted the console. "This thing's all for show, there's no way to get online and send you what you need."

"No legal way to get online," Zee said. "No practical, easy way to do it either without the right kind of commercially unavailable equipment."

Darma looked up. "Are you saying what I think you're saying?"

"Nah. Not unless you think I'm about to say, 'I've got a Turing DE unit piggy backing a black boxed Itautec expansion port, and it's sitting in the closet.'" Zee smiled. "Then maybe. At the very least it'll get you out of here and into another box."

Darma whooped and was out of his chair, grabbing Zee by the shoulders. "Jumping Jesus on a pogostick! I love you, woman! Or is it man? I forget, which is it? I don't wanna offend."

Zee laughed. It was hard to believe someone who had once been described as the "cordyceps virus of the net" was worried about being polite. "Cloke seems to be waffling between them and xie. I think both work, but..." Zee frowned.

"What?"

"It's weird. She's a total bitch—"

"On that we agree."

"—but she really gives a shit. About whether I'm being treated right. Whether she gets me. I'm not a girl. Or a boy. And that matters to her."

Darma gently let go and backed off. "Does not being one or the other, does that... ever get weird for you?"

"Sometimes, actually, it does. But that's the problem," Zee admitted. "It bothers me one way, or the other, sometimes both ways at the same time depending on the time of the day or month or year. And I don't want to be an 'it.' Spent too much time in that movie already."

"Sounds messed up," Darma said.

"It is. But it's my life. I deal."

"So, you're they. Maybe. Or xie."

"Sure. But not that royal 'we' shit, that's not what I'm going for."

"Okay, I can make the switch. I guess I'll have to get used to new pronouns considering my own recent developments."

It was a weird feeling, having someone else, someone that was clearly a big shot, give a shit. And Zee didn't know what to do with it. Nice, up until this point, had only been a behavior demonstrated in fiction. But, as unsettling as it was, it also really felt... nice. To actually be on the receiving end. Zee nodded. "Okay, sure, if that's the way your maracas shake."

"Have you ever even shaken maracas?"

"Not real ones, but I got a virtual pair in my sim inventory, some freebie for checking out a mariachi game a while back."

"Everything's virtual," Darma said with a sigh. "Guess I'm just ahead of the curve on that score now."

"At least I can get you inside my system so you can keep me from killing myself the next time I buzz a major corporate network," Zee said.

"Does Cloke know you're doing this?"

"I didn't tell her, if that's what you're asking."

"She probably knows," Darma said.

"Is that gonna be a problem? I didn't figure her for being a stickler for legal precedent."

"Laws exist for a reason, whether we agree with them or not," Darma said. "And there are a couple of good reasons why it's illegal to allow emulations online access, and it's illegal for convicted jockeys in particular to make emulations."

"Awareness is there, I've heard the horror stories," Zee said. "Everyone used to be so worried about AIs destroying the world through the net, instead it's just people again."

"Dead ones," Darma said. "Speaking of which, so is this apartment."

"I'll get on that," Zee said. "Just give me a few minutes and you'll be back in the saddle."

"As a side kick," Darma said. "Oh well, at least it gets me out of the house."

IT DIDN'T TAKE very long to configure everything. Zee had taken Darma's cartridge back to a makeshift workspace in one of the many useless, spartan rooms Cloke kept, and got everything connected. It wasn't pretty, but it was going to work; Darma's cartridge now slotted into the Turing DE unit normally used for one-way transfers. That now had one side cut out with wires tapping into an AI management box, which in turn was properly slotted into a standard expansion port for consoles. It wasn't a common knowledge hack, but it wasn't particularly difficult to pull off once Zee had decided to do it and used the shiny new GIS resources available to track down past attempts across the various global networks and see how they worked.

Zee switched on the console, reached for the neural cabling input and plugged it in, but didn't switch over to simulation. Instead, a few quick commands on the console called up Darma on one of the displays, sitting at his own console, as if he were still really alive and just using a camera to talk to someone online. Zee waved and Darma waved back. He tapped a key on his console and Zee's own machine responded with ugly, mechanical beeps that Zee recognized as the opening notes to "Software Skin", a song Darma had been playing repeatedly in his environment. It had been a big hit for a neotronic band from 10 years ago, the vocalist of which Darma had claimed he grew up with. The sounds that came out now were harsh, primitive, generated by the components of Zee's hardware, which would normally only make beeps like this to indicate a catastrophic hardware failure.

"What the fuck?" Zee said, more amused than annoyed.

"Kitschy, right?" Darma said, grinning. "Just wanted to

see if I could do something quick and dirty with your gear. Apparently, the answer is 'yes.' So go me. I can even make you hear it in simulation for that extra kick of irritation that says 'fuck you' with love. Didn't take long to do, either." He patted the console in front of him. "Still got it."

Zee eyed his virtual configuration. It looked slick as hell and there was still a pang of regret that all that real, physical custom hardware had been cratered.

"How's it feel?" Zee asked.

"Slow as fuck," Darma said. "I know I don't even need to sit at a console to work this shit now, but it wouldn't feel right otherwise."

Zee executed another quick command, and cut out the visual to Darma's simulation. "I've patched you directly into my neural interface, I can hear you inside my head. Are you ready for this?"

"No," said Darma. "Take it slow. Don't jump into the job just yet. Go online first, see how you like it with someone in the side car."

"I don't dive into a full simulation most of the time," Zee said. "Call it an artificial meat thing. When I'm not real meat to begin with, I like to stay less in the fake world and more in the real one."

"We work how we work," Darma said. "Every jockey's got a different ride."

Zee checked one more time to make sure everything was in Condition Go, then punched it.

This time the transition was far less subtle. Pressing the ENTER button on the console broke the room, the walls splintering like a glass house bombarded by stones from all sides. The fragments fell away into the cold infinity of the simulation of Zee's homespace, which still hadn't been configured to anything near satisfactory yet, but there would be time for that later. Darma was right; the first order of business was to see if this was even workable, or whether it would just bog things down.

Zee remained fixed in an approximation of the real-world workspace, the console and even the desk still there, thoughtfully fading to transparency or complete invisibility on command. Homespace was currently defaulting to actual geographical coordinates, so the corner of the Internet Zee popped into was a boring collection of residential networks, simple shapes glowing invitingly in near proximity; friendly but unapproachable unless the effort was made to hack into them—something currently not a priority, except maybe as a warm up.

Zee called up the virtual intelligence embedded in the console's operating system.

"Ready," it said in a calm, neutral, male voice. It was nowhere and everywhere at once; invisible voice, bodiless, a personal ghost.

"What's your name?" Zee asked.

"Currently defaulting to John Doe," it said.

Zee opened a voice menu, quickly sorted through a few samples, changing the voice to something female, brisk and businesslike.

"For now, your name is Eve," Zee said. "And you'll be working with me and another program."

"Which program?"

"An emulation."

"It is illegal to—"

Zee kicked in a waiting sub-program and watched it melt into the code of the still stock operating system, reconfiguring it. It took less than ten seconds.

"The emulation's name is Darma, and you'll accommodate his operation and requests."

"Acknowledged," the newly christened VI Eve said.

"Bringing him online now," Zee said. "You be nice."

"Compliance."

Darma came online similarly; bodiless, ghostly, though in this case it was probably appropriate.

"Hello, Internet," he said. "Long time, no see."

"Eve, confirm our network access, are we on a GIS pipe?"

"Affirmative."

"You called her Eve?"

"Hadda call her something," Zee said. "You ready for this?"

"Unclear. Please clarify the circumstances readiness is required for."

"Wasn't talking to you, Eve." Zee said with a sigh, then routed all VI interactions to a trigger on the virtual console.

"Kinda wondering why you didn't do that in the first place," Darma said.

"I'm used to working alone." Zee pressed the newly created VI button on the virtual console and kept it held down. It was going to be like addressing a secretary on a speaker. "New grid location. Southeast Asia, LUMO Orbital Elevator. Keep us high, I want an aerial."

"Compliance," Eve said.

The view shimmered, an unimaginative stock software transition, and Zee was suddenly in the neurosimulated stratosphere of the Internet, looking down on the simple, simulated collection of networks that represented everything from personal sites to regional corporate networks, to retail outlets for goods both real and virtual. Lattices of light and polygons ranged across the grid at various heights and shapes; icons dense with the information of everything from business transactions, the exchange of simulated combat, inventory and character progression data from online games, shipping manifests and archived theses from decades of graduate work.

Anything and everything rendered in digital form for the entire southeast Asian region was somewhere, down there, in one of those nodes—if you knew where to look and how to get in. And under ordinary circumstances, the only way Zee would be able to see it like this would be by living here and subscribing to a local service provider, or through limited commercial or retail access to a few services here and there.

But the GIS internal user privileges made it possible to see everything.

"Snazzy, huh?" Darma asked.

"So, this is what it's like on the other side," Zee said.

"Other side of what?"

"Corporate operation."

"Only for GIS," Darma said. "And only for you as long as you don't get flagged."

"It's nice," Zee said quietly. "No hoops to jump through, no ridiculous expenditure just to get to another country."

"Well, it was like that at the dawn of the Internet as well, but it couldn't last," Darma said. "Come on kid, don't make that hound dog face, you know it couldn't last. The governments hated the fact that global access was unrestricted; they wanted to keep their own in, and outsiders out. And that includes the hackers. Why do you think hackers have to go to the country of the network they're hitting now? That's half the reason right there that the net fragmented. No use wishing for the past, that was the wild west, and everything settled down and got all civilized since then. So, you wanna show me this work you've got?"

Darma was right. Zee got into it, calling up coordinates. A quick look "down" showed the other lights dimming as one small, wholly unremarkable icon in the vast grid of other icons blazed out like a star.

"That's it. Majitsu research facility, in something called the Singapore Science Park."

"Old name," Darma said. "This used to be a country, once upon a time. Had their own flag and everything until they converted over from sovereign city-state to corporate status and made being the site of the elevator their big business. Take us down, get a closer look."

"Do you want to do it?" Without waiting for an answer, Zee pressed the "intercom" button. "Eve, I'm authorizing Darma for net navigation."

"In this instance, or permanent authorization?"

"Until I change my mind, he's got user privileges."

"Compliance," the VI said.

"Drive on, Jeeves," Zee said.

Zee felt the simulated lurch as Darma took them down, buzzing the various networks, sending out quick, cursory probes as he passed each one. Zee did a quick check of the memory resources on the console and saw that some data was being saved.

"What are you doing?"

"Making a note of the local geography and traffic," Darma said.

Zee checked again. The incoming data wasn't being written into the console's free memory; it was going straight into the resources partitioned away for Darma's cognitive random access memory. He was memorizing this, not writing it down. Zee watched as more and more of the passing networks were noted.

"You're just taking advantage of shuffling off this mortal coil and using that wonderful digital memory you now have to do this, right?"

"If you say so," Darma said. "This is just business as usual for me, I always kept a running tab on the surrounding area. Good to know where to take cover, digitally speaking. Saved my bacon on more than one occasion."

"Jesus, how long did it take you to get that trick down?"

"Always been able to. Just lucky that way, I guess."

Zee checked on the input and output stats of the console, the simulation and bandwidth responses. "This checks out. Doesn't look like there's any kind of performance hit with you riding shotgun."

Zee watched Darma's continued use of the command system, cruising them through networks until they were sitting in the proximity of the target. "Keep an eye on the meters," he said. "I'm gonna try a little fancy buzzing here, see if you take a hit."

"Nothing too fancy," Zee said.

"Don't worry, it's still your show."

Zee had to wonder now how much of Darma's ease of control was now down to his digital nature, or just inherent talent he'd been born with. There was an assurance to his moves that was either mechanical grace, or years of experience at play.

He moved into proximity of the network, somehow gauging

the precise line at which its defenses wouldn't be tripped. He probed it, the lightest of touches with software analysis, barely grazing and yet accumulating a lot of data.

Zee was impressed. Blueshift lived up to his reputation.

Darma snorted. "Boring, man," he said. "Whatever kind of R and D they're doing in there isn't high priority. Standard network protocols and defense—no one spent any money or effort to make this extra safe."

"So why is Cloke so interested in this?"

"Witch has her own reasons for doing this shit," Darma said. "After a while I just gave up and chalked it up to her arcane side."

Zee's fingers tapped rhythmically on the virtual console. "Wonder if it's worth taking a look."

"Cold? Kid, you got nothing prepped to break into that."

"You just said the defenses are standard stuff."

"Yeah, and you don't have the standard ware you'd need for a nice clean hack. You're not gonna impress Cloke if you sloppy joe it in there and leave tracks back to her house. Unplug. Do your homework for a proper job."

Zee wasn't expecting it to take so little time to test the new software, but here it was. Darma was already forcing the issue. At least testing under these conditions would be small, benign, and probably not something he would worry too much about.

Zee issued a neural command rather than execute a virtual action on the simulated keys that Darma would have been able to see. It was the equivalent of a telepathic order issued to the console. The software ran and Zee set some loose parameters, keeping the program open and running in case real time adjustments needed to be made.

"I can do this," Zee said. "I don't need to do anything that'll raise flags on the intrusion detection systems. I don't even need to touch the firewall."

"You're going through a DMZ?"

"That's the plan. No biometrics, no nuthin', I can cook something up for that."

"How? Even for a DMZ you'd still need a password at the very least. Where you gonna hack that on such short notice?"

"Thirty minutes, that's all I need," Zee said. "Maybe less."

"What the fuck, kid," and Zee could almost feel the virtual shrug coming off Darma. "I got nothing better to do today, show me how you're gonna pull this thing."

Zee broke out a suite of basic monitoring and analysis software, programs with names like "Probe" and "Bughunt." It was easy, on the periphery of the network to get a quick ghost peek at incoming and outgoing data, of communications traveling through the lines. The GIS access laid out the lines of transmission from one node to the next, like trails of light, branching into ever growing webs of complexity. The information was like pulses that Zee could now track, focus on, magnify and gently peek at.

And there it was. Zee's point of entry: a contract worker. Someone brought in to do a little bit of low-level system maintenance and administration on a three-month term. Not all of the work had been done on site at the lab, so he'd needed some remote access privileges. Temporary password rights had been issued, but they were only good for another 48 hours, when the contract would expire, and access would be revoked.

It was enough to start.

The first bit of business was tracking the guy down. This was the easy part for someone with cleaning experience, following the messy, messy trail of someone that wanted to be heard on the Internet as much as the other billions of people, making a ton of noise and hoping someone would notice. Not a citizen of Malaysia, but someone from neighboring Indonesia.

Zee pulled back, way, way back, absorbing the information, the numerous posts on forums, transcripts from chat, comments on news stories, memberships at different web services, subscriptions to various feeds.

Zee continued to pull back, further and further away, until it was like a god's eye view of this man and all the years of his activity on the Internet.

And then, as always, it happened.

The click in Zee's head.

The patterns that began to emerge, the way this man, this Ahmad, spoke and felt and thought. Years of interaction online had left his personality bare for anyone willing to look at it, at all of it. Zee looked at the totality of his words online, his participation in voice, video and sim chats, his thoughts, behavior, watching the lines intersect, the shape of him growing out of all those interactions. It was like pixel art, or pointillism; a meaningless series of dots or colors that only resolved itself with enough distance to see the whole picture.

Zee saw all of what comprised Ahmad online. Then it was a simple matter of logging in at the research building's DMZ to supply the password. Zee got it on the third try; "04bra55Heart35."

The network accepted the password and granted limited user access.

"Jesus Christ," Darma said quietly. "How the fuck did you do that?"

"Four and thirty-five are the month and year he broke up with his girlfriend of four years," Zee said. "Brass Heart is a favorite band of his. Turn of the century, New Jazz genre. You could tell from his online journals and all the bitching he did on various boards that he thought she was going to be 'the one.' Didn't work out and he's been scarred ever since. Brass Heart's been getting him through it. It's his 'oh God, I wanna die,' music."

"But how—"

"It's a thing I do," Zee said, taking a leisurely scan of the limited contents this access would allow for viewing. "I didn't know I could do it until I got into cleaning up after people. I can see patterns, understand certain kinds of information movement. Given enough information, I guess my brain just absorbs it all in and eventually filters it down to the useful data I need. It's not like mind reading or anything, but if you show me enough of how a person interacts online, eventually I can start making predictions about what those interactions will be.

Like with passwords. I'm still shit out of luck with biometrics and DNA scanning but that's what digital forgery is for, right?"

"No wonder you got off to such a quick start," Darma said. "You didn't even need to scrounge around for crypto-ware, you've got it in your damn head."

And now it was time to see whether the test was a success. "You wanna talk about it?" Zee asked.

There was an artificial intake of breath as Darma tried to speak. Nothing. A few more attempts to start also failed.

"Wanna talk about something else?"

"What's going on?" Darma asked.

"You're censored," Zee said. "I'm sorry, Darma. I hacked a content censor they use for live broadcasts, rejigged it to interface with you. You can't talk about what you just saw with anyone."

There was silence. Zee wasn't sure if it was because Darma really wasn't saying anything or because he was still trying to talk about the hack into the lab's network.

"I don't want anyone to know about that, what I can do," Zee explained. "That's mine. Only mine. The fewer people that know about it, the better. But I knew having you on board the console, it was just going to be a matter of time before you saw it yourself. It wouldn't make sense to boot you out when I use it, 'cause odds are, if I'm in that situation, I'm going to need you there. But I don't want you telling anyone. I don't want you talking to Cloke about it."

"Because you don't trust her," Darma said.

"Or you," Zee said. "Not with this. Not yet. All I know is I got plucked out of one cage with spikey bars on fire, and dropped in another one with some cushions and velvet, but it's still a cage. And I don't know how long I want to stay in it. If I'm going to get out, I'm going to need every advantage and secret I can keep. This is one of them."

"I guess it was never an option to think I would have respected your right to keep your own secrets."

"Nope. I've tried the trust thing a couple of times. Ended badly."

"This is gonna put a serious kink in our working relationship, kid."

"You still want to have one?"

"Beats sitting around in a simulation all day. This may not be *real* real, but when I do something here it's real. Get it? Even if you put that sim into God mode, it would still all be fake. And that bugs me."

Zee looked at the console's resource usage rise slightly as Darma exercised more of his power to evaluate the network. "Okay," he said. "You got us in this far, we may as well see what we can see and report back."

"I'm sorry, Darma," Zee said again.

"Yeah, so am I. But I know why you're doing it. Given your situation, I can't really expect much benefit of the doubt. It sounds like you haven't had much of that yourself. Let's just do the job."

And they did. Poking, prodding and rifling through the dirty little secrets of the research lab until they found the secret buried deepest of all.

Chapter VII:
Between the Cracks

CLOKE DECIDED TO head to the orbital elevator in style.

They were in an airliner, essentially a colossal flying wing. One of the massive sky ships that—in function—resembled the luxury ocean cruisers of the early 20th century, complete with big rooms with big beds, bars, swimming pools, gyms, theaters, shops and full satellite access to the Net. It was another one of the benefits of magic coming into the world— in this case, mass negation; they could make aircraft as big as they wanted now with minimal power consumption to keep them in the air thanks to the ability to reduce their mass to nothing. The entire science and industry of aerodynamics had changed radically when it became clear that certain people could defy Newtonian physics to alter the mass of inanimate matter. It had made a lot of things possible, like the cheap, financially viable race to the stars, the ability to carry almost unlimited amounts of freight by air, and, for Cloke's purposes, a relaxing way to get her team up to speed on what they were about to do.

It was also an industry in which Majitsu, the company she was about to hit, enjoyed a serious dominance.

The situation report from Zee, in Cloke's own room, was brief and told her everything she wanted to hear.

Zee had gone slightly above and beyond when it came

to both recon and how far xie'd managed to break in with minimal preparation. Cloke didn't even bat an eyelid when Zee mentioned illegally jury-rigging Darma's emulator to piggyback on their console. It wasn't a bad play, even if it bordered on being totally whack, and Cloke had to admit it had brought the new recruit up to a quality of work she honestly hadn't been expecting yet.

"It's pretty standard stuff," Zee was saying. "There are a lot of research facilities at the site of the elevator for obvious reasons. It's a fast way to get projects orbital and retrieve them when they come back down. Majitsu's just one more company out of dozens that's playing it smart that way. But that research building isn't particularly important."

"So, what's it there for?" Marcus asked.

"Same as most of the other places, I think," Cloke said. "Optimizing. All the serious innovation is still down at the home offices in Japan. This is the place where they just work on tweaking, improving certain things. The kind of place for graduate work and the tedious process of elimination research that needs to be done but that no one wants to do."

Zee looked to Cloke. "Which makes me ask, why the hell would GIS have any interest in hitting this place?"

"They don't," Cloke said. "Then again, they rarely participate in the usual corporate warfare."

"So, who's paying for this little run?" Zee asked.

"I am," Cloke said. "This isn't a hire; this is my own thing."

"Fair enough," Marcus said. "You gonna tell us why?"

"It's because of that pipe, isn't it?" Zee asked.

Marcus turned to look first at Zee, then at Cloke. "What pipe?"

Zee brought it up on a screen showing off the network infrastructure in bright, simple lines. "The account we hijacked to sleaze our way in was just some contract temp administration stuff. But it was enough for us to start looking at his messages to and from management. He was apparently directed to give wide berth to one communications trunk. From what we could gather, it's a single dedicated, physical line, with no network of any kind. We traced it back. It's laid all the way out to Dubai."

"Really," Cloke said, with no surprise at all.

"That's the only thing about that place that sticks out," Zee said. "They went to the trouble of building in one specific communications cable that's completely cut off from everything else."

"It'll be connected to a terminal, a console, something, right?" Cloke asked.

"Be stupid to put it in otherwise," Zee said.

"And that's your interest?" Marcus asked.

"I think so," Cloke said. "Whatever is being piped through that, I think that's what I'm supposed to hit."

Zee pulled out a cigarette. "Some seriously fucked up research going on if they're isolating it like that from the rest of their network," they said. "Gonna be hard to steal."

"I'm not going to be stealing anything," Cloke said. "Just accessing it."

Marcus crossed his arms. "I say again, you gonna tell us why?"

"Curiosity," Cloke said. "Someone hacked into my sim while I was tubing it from Bali to New York."

"That's impossible," Zee said.

"Then you need to change your definitions," Cloke said. "But he told me that the reason he did it was to tell me to access a terminal in that building. I'm guessing that's the one."

"So, if you're the boss and the backer, then this is one hundred percent your op," Marcus said. "How do you want to play it?"

"Quietly," Cloke said. "No casualties, no film at eleven."

"No what?" Zee asked.

"Film at eleven." Cloke shrugged. "A phrase from back when image capture was a photochemical process and news was only reported at specific times. It's an Elizabethan expression, I think."

Zee looked Marcus up and down. "Don't know why you called him on this if you want it quiet." Xie gestured at the massive bulk of his cybernetically augmented body. "Not exactly the subtle type."

Cloke grinned. "Yeah, he's going to let me do a stealth grab in someone else's backyard and he'd rather sit it out and knit a sweater. That's totally going to happen."

Marcus grinned back.

"Besides there's always a need for an extra pair of eyes on the field, especially when those eyes can jump thirty feet in the air and cling to buildings. And let's not forget plan B."

"Which is?" Zee asked.

"Probably something involving ammunition if subtle doesn't cut it," Cloke said. "It only seems like overkill until you need a contingency that can punch through walls."

"Haven't actually done that in a while," Marcus said. "Almost makes me hope you fuck up just to give me the excuse."

"And I'm the one that's supposed to have no sense of humor," Cloke said. "Okay, when we make landfall, you know what you're all supposed to do. You'll have two days to get prepped and then we hit it. That's not an unreasonable period for a job of this scale. Are we all good on this?"

She waited. No objections came, not even from Zee. She looked at Zee. "You going to be okay on this?"

"Christ, if you didn't think I could do this, you shouldn't have brought me," Zee said. "I'll be fine, Mom, I packed my own panties and everything."

Cloke pointed her finger at Zee and watched the jockey yelp as a ragged charge of low-level lightning jumped across the space between them and nipped hir elbow. "Bitch mode only goes so far before it stops being cute. That's the line," Cloke said, turning away. "You may as well all enjoy whatever leisure time you have until we land. It's gonna be work, work, work once we're on the ground."

Zee was already walking towards the door.

"Zee," Cloke said.

Zee turned around, not saying anything.

"That was some good work you did on the recon," Cloke said. "Victor was right. There's talent in you. That's all I wanted to say, don't rip my head off. Now get the hell out of my room and try to relax."

Zee did it, still without saying anything. Cloke listened for the door shutting as they all exited her room and tried to remember if there was anything around LUMO that she wanted to buy.

THE RUN, WHEN it finally got underway, had a good start. Two days of prep time on site. Zee and hir dead mentor working closely together to sleaze into all relevant aspects of the Majitsu network.

The Majitsu lab was a non-descript building amongst the many others in the Singapore science park. It resembled a massive, fallen domino neatly laid out amongst others, a discarded toy of giants left in neatly trimmed hedges that fought a constant war with the tropical jungles of Southeast Asia. Cloke's visor led her straight to the correct building without any trouble, its augmented reality functions laying a bright trail of light across her view of the world that she simply needed to follow to her destination; the personal, digital equivalent of a trail of breadcrumbs that no one else could see.

"It's a go," Cloke said to the choker pendant at her neck. It was a cornerstone of Chimera unit operations, a "comm stone," in the industry slang; a simple communication enchantment applied to inert objects like earrings and necklaces for undetectable, untraceable transmission and reception. Cloke's current guise, as a goth punk revival electrical engineer who still dressed like she was in college, had been conveniently placed in the Majitsu lab's database the day before when their resident engineer reported ill due to carefully administered food poisoning at the favorite pho noodle stand he had loudly proclaimed online he would be eating at.

Getting in was the easy part, as long as the lab security was unaware that they were a hot target for incursion.

Cloke's newly forged credentials could withstand

normal levels of paranoid corporate scrutiny, as would the strategically placed dermal pads placed in all the standard areas of biometric identification. It would all fall apart if a team of dedicated data and records specialists put it under a magnifying glass, but for the average security guard at his standard issue, stock ID terminals, it would pass muster.

"Haven't seen you around before," the receptionist at the desk said. He was young, Chinese, spoke with a faux British accent that matched his immaculately sculpted hair.

"New to the island," Cloke said in a passable Australian accent. "Doing a bit of work before they send me up to Tokyo."

"Nicely done," the receptionist said. "Who are you with?"

"Freelance mostly," she said, sliding into her cover story. "But I'm on contract for the next six months with Areeka." Areeka being a Brazilian tech support outfit that had once pissed her off with their incompetent handling of some routine network maintenance and security. Their databases had been easy to get Zee to hack as cover for this job and Cloke was hoping this would land them in some hot water and get them to take their job seriously if Majitsu started making inquiries.

"Well, good luck with that," the receptionist said, checking for her admittance. He verified all her authentication, his inquiries intercepted by Zee and replied to with forged confirmation, then gave Cloke the thumbs up. Cloke smiled and made a point of asking for nav data for her visor, even though far more elaborate schematics of the complex were already installed on it. He keyed them into her visor, and she thanked him before going off to work.

She followed her personal nav trail through the first layer of office administration, marching past a regimented cubicle farm with a host of office workers that were blissfully putting in an honest, innocent day at the office. Some of them eyed her with open curiosity. Most ignored her since she walked like she knew exactly what she was doing and where she was going.

This had been the hardest part to accept when she'd been

starting out; the idea that corporations weren't singular entities of evil. Most of the decisions that had dramatic effects for good or ill were made by a select few at the executive levels. People, like the ones she was walking past now, were just that; people. They worked hard at their jobs and just wanted to get by. It wasn't their fault that they were occasionally employed by people that made catastrophic choices and for the most part, the vast majority of employees were completely unaware and unassociated with those measures.

But they were usually the first casualties of any drastic corporate warfare, either literally or economically. And it had punched Cloke straight in the guts the first time she'd seen her handiwork and realized people she'd met and shared drinks with on mid-term infiltration jobs, people she'd grown to like, who had invited her to weekend barbecues with their family... she'd just destroyed their careers and put their future in jeopardy. It had made her careful to limit her damage when possible, given her more focus and purpose in the jobs she took.

She maintained proper corporate contract worker decorum as she made her way through the more public layers of the building. There was nothing unusual about her except for her style; a bit more on the younger, playful side than normal, but that would play into the misdirection she liked to have. Her visor's trail led her dutifully through only one more security checkpoint as she was headed for a low-level research area for the required maintenance.

She entered the server room that she'd been contracted to work on and put on what some in engineering affectionately referred to as "the gauntlet." A portable diagnostic terminal with haptic feedback fields so that its projected holographic screen and keyboard could provide the sensation of buttons being pressed.

It would have been weird for someone with Cloke's cover to *not* have it, but it also served to mask her activity as she patched a link through to Zee, who was waiting on the other side of network security for Cloke to open access.

Cloke watched the display on her gauntlet as it showed the security camera in the room get taken over by Zee and hir sleazware, feeding in a new signal that would show Cloke diligently working away at routine network maintenance.

"Good," Cloke said as her gauntlet confirmed that the room was secure from cameras. "Full scan now."

"Clean," Zee said over the comm stone. "No weight plates, no microphones, no security that goes above and beyond. It's like I said, standard stuff."

"Then we're off to a good start," Cloke said. She reached into her small toolbox which did not contain the kinds of tools a network engineer would require and pulled out the tiny holographic emitter that would project a likeness of her, complete with a virtual intelligence, to interact with anyone that happened to physically stop by to check on her progress. She placed it discreetly on the floor where it scanned the room's dimensions then calibrated itself to project a hologram that would copy and project the entire room plus one new occupant.

A virtual Cloke appeared and got into it, consulting displays, nodding to herself in an intently professional manner, and opening panels to access boards and drive cradles.

The real Cloke ditched her puffy fashion victim outfit to unsheathe the custom, impressively svelte IF combat armor she was wearing underneath. She also put away her colorful, eye-catching consumer visor and strapped on her combat model. She dropped her disguise to the floor and watched it disappear into the holographic space that now enveloped the room.

It was time to get to work.

"How's it looking on your side?" she asked Zee.

"We are everywhere we shouldn't be," Zee said in voice that sounded too pleased with itself for Cloke's taste. Cloke suspected the more open Internet that privileged GIS access provided might be going to Zee's head. "Say the word and we can bust this place wide open."

"No word, no busting," Cloke said. "I'm walking out of

here with a kind word for the receptionist and an invite to dinner."

"What?"

"I'm thinking he thinks there's a spark going on," Cloke said. "Not that I'd accept."

"I wouldn't bet on that."

"Would you bet against?"

There was silence for a moment and then Zee said "Yeah, what the hell, I would."

"Our actual dinner tonight is on you if he asks me out."

"And if he doesn't, we're having Kobe beef on you."

"I know a restaurant here that'll give you what you want. It's ludicrously expensive, tacky and I have no intention of ever, *ever* eating there. You've got a bet."

"Okay, then get yourself through that vent so you can hit your terminal and we can get you back out front for your reality crash."

Cloke's visor scanned the room and highlighted the ventilation panel she needed to access. She broke out her tools and got to work on it.

"Marcus how are you doing?" she asked, breaking the electromagnetic seals on the panel one by one.

"Bored, luv. Bored as fuck."

"If you're lucky that won't change."

"Either way I get paid," he said.

"Your concern for my personal safety is always reassuring."

The panel was off. Cloke crab-walked in and followed her nav trail, looking up to see it stretching into the darkness of the vent as it ascended to the higher floors of the building. She could see her own breath now that she was in one of the vents actively trying to cool down the server room she'd just left. She pulled out her wire gun and calibrated it for the required height and her weight.

"I don't understand why you're doing that shit," Zee said.

"What shit?" She switched her visor to passive night sight, aimed the gun and fired. A quiet puff was the only noise the gun made as an anchor shot up, unspooling monofilament wire behind it. It hit the top of the vent a few floors up and the electromagnet kicked in, sealing it tightly to its surface.

"This tech spy shit," Zee said. "You're a mage, right? Shouldn't you be magicking your way through everything?"

"There's a time and a place for all things," Cloke said. She attached the gun to its holster and triggered it to reel in, feeling the soft jerk as she was lifted up. "This is neither the time nor place for thaumaturgy. Too flashy. If they see any evidence of magic in use, that narrows down the list of suspects considerably."

"And you'd be at the top of the list?"

"Not just *the* list, *all* of them," Cloke said. "But especially combat magic. Remember that operations list of the College I mentioned? Only nineteen of us if you don't count trainees. Infiltration, by itself, is a much bigger list of course. But both? That's pretty small. Kind of like the suspect line up for console jockeys riding shotgun with illegally liberated emulations."

"Okay, okay, message received," Zee said with a clear, sour note. "Then explain to me why you're using magic for communications."

"Because it can't be traced," Cloke said. "There's no residual evidence of its use, unlike the big stuff." She used the conductive grips at the tips of gloved fingertips to anchor herself solidly to the vent she wanted to crawl into, and hauled herself in. Zee's route was going to take her through an initial uncomfortable stretch of HVAC systems designed for temperature and bacterial control. It was going to be tight until she got back into less hardened areas for admin and other staff work.

"It also makes it difficult to talk to Darma if you want to say anything to him," Zee said. "How the fuck does this even work? How can it only detect sound from living things? Even if I put Darma on a speaker it wouldn't transmit him?"

"That's why it's called magic," Cloke said, following her nav trail through its maze of turns in the ventilation shaft. "Newton's rules don't apply."

"Then what does?"

"If we knew all the answers to that, we wouldn't need the

College, and we wouldn't call it magic," Cloke said. "But I'm pretty sure there's some quantum interaction going on that's measurable. Quantum computation wouldn't exist otherwise, and they needed magic to get that working."

Cloke traveled through the duct work, being careful to maintain "silent running" mode whenever the vents she came across showed actual people in the rooms beside or below her. Usually the noise these people made all on their own from conversations, video conferencing or, in one case, frantic office supply room sex, was more than enough to let her slip past completely unnoticed.

She stopped at the vent where her visor's nav ended. "In position," she said to Zee.

"On it."

Cloke waited. A suite of anti-security software that Zee had tweaked for the room went into action, unfurling like some invisible digital shroud to cover the entire room's sensor system in whatever "All Clear" data they required.

"You're ghosted," Zee said.

Cloke removed the ventilation panel and entered the room that, theoretically, was at the root of all this curiosity. The room was simple and grey, like an unfinished idea that no one had bothered to come back and reconsider.

It was, as Zee had said, a room devoid of surveillance cameras and microphones. Whatever happened in this room, the owners didn't want to take the chance that any of it would be recorded, even by their own security.

"I wish you'd transmit some video off that visor," Zee said through the comm stone. "What do you see?"

Cloke was looking at two chairs and a single desk that seemed to grow out of the floor with a terminal built into it. There was no display of any kind, which probably meant there was either a holographic projector—the desk was big enough to house one—or no data was ever meant to be seen by outside observers.

"There's a console here," Cloke said.

"What make?"

"None, it's custom."

"Gonna tell you right now," Zee said. "I can't help you with that thing."

"You want me to stream an image from my visor? Show it to you?"

"It wouldn't help," Zee said. "That thing is completely off the network, so I have no access to it. I can't mess with its security, its operating system, nothing."

Cloke looked over the terminal, carefully noting the inputs for neurolinkage. It was rigged for simulation, probably also wireless sim transmission. She reached out her hand and touched the smooth surface of the desk.

"What are you doing?" Zee asked.

"Something you wouldn't approve of," Cloke said.

An image appeared over the desk, a thin sheet of light suddenly popping into existence as text flashed by too quickly for Cloke to read. She only caught bits and pieces of it, but it was obvious that it was programming code, something was going on close to the metal of the console.

After a few seconds the flood of code was replaced in the display window with a single image. It was from the shoulders up, an older man, someone Mediterranean maybe, long grey hair, a beard, sharply groomed. He had an air of someone used to being in charge, perhaps military or upper management in some multi-national—though Cloke couldn't place him, but there was a nagging feeling she'd seen his face somewhere before.

"There are three separate alarms not going off right now despite the fact that your touch failed the biometric log in," the man said.

"I figured anyone that could hack a random sim unit wouldn't leave anything to chance with a hardware destination they'd called out themselves."

"Who are you talking to?" Zee asked over the comm stone. "You got in? How did you get in?"

Cloke removed her comm stone, placed it on the desk and stared at the man on the display. "So, I've played it your way, and now I'm here," she said. "You want to tell me why that is? You don't even have to start with 'why.' 'How' would be a good place. It's my understanding that the hacks you pull off are nearly impossible."

"They nearly are," the man on the screen admitted. "For people, anyway. When you're not a person it makes certain things more achievable."

Cloke reminded herself that she was safe. There were no gas vents, no auto turrets, nothing in this room that could be turned on her at the whim of whatever she was talking to.

"I don't deal with artificial intelligences," she said. "There's not a whole lot of overlap in our spheres of interest and I don't feel like being brought on trial in international court on charges of conspiring with one."

"I'm not an AI," the image said. "I'm not a person either. But I used to be one. Once. Fifty-three years ago."

Cloke's mind froze for a split second as the implication sunk in. "Interesting story, but full of holes. Like chronology. Neuro-synaptic digital preservation didn't go into practice until the turn of the century."

The man on the screen smiled. "So quick. That's why I picked you."

"Yes, let's talk about that."

"Oh, but you're right. It was too early for emulating back in the 2080s. They were researching it, prototyping it. But there was another technology available at the time, still somewhat exotic by today's standards."

Another domino fell in Cloke's line of reasoning. "Cryogenics."

"I knew you were the right one," the man said. "You're not like the others. The magic becomes a crutch for them. They ignore technology, they ignore physicality because they can't use it, or because it's so much more difficult than just falling back on magic, but you... you embrace it as much as you can. You weren't just the right choice. You were the only one, really."

Cloke ignored the flattery. "So, you were important.

Important enough to freeze, and important enough to emulate once the technology was even remotely feasible. Who are you? I know I've seen your face somewhere before."

"Your history books," the man said. "The ones with the best images are the physical ones, stored away at the College, never allowed to leave or be scanned into the databases. The ones governments and corporations have been trying to gain access to for decades. Think hard."

The last domino fell. The familiar face, the dates lining up, his intimacy with the paranoia of the College. The dominance of the Majitsu Corporation in the applied mass negation industries.

His offer to teach her something.

The name came to her lips with the weight of her own heritage crushing it. "Matheus Azevedo."

He tipped his head. "No longer in the flesh, but still very much in the world."

There were statues of Azevedo in São Paulo and in his hometown of Rio de Janeiro. His image was on the last of the fifty real notes that were printed before the use of cash was all but legally discontinued. He was the man that brought order to Brazil during World War III, fighting the gangs, the juntas, the other pretenders to the seat of government. He was the man who perfected mass negation and put it to practical use in industry, taking Brazil with him out of the poverty and anarchy to be the first of the new nations to embrace magic and forge a new economic and political foundation as other countries fell apart, cementing Brazil's position as the next great superpower. The man, some historians argued, who saved civilization from the brink of collapse, by proving that magic, science and economy could not just co-exist, but profit.

He was the reason Cloke and her kind had a place in the world today.

Cloke wanted to sit, but didn't, not trusting in her ability to get back on her feet afterwards.

"That's a lot of quiet coming off you," the emulated Matheus said. "And you don't have the time for it right now."

"What the fuck is this?" Cloke said softly. "Why are you here?"

"That was the whole point of bringing you here," Matheus said. "I'm a prisoner with no option for escape. I want to hire you. I want to hire you to kill me."

Cloke finally sat down.

Chapter VIII:
Plan B

ABOUT SEVEN MINUTES after everything went dark on Cloke's end, Zee's side of the job went completely bug fuck.

It started with the multiple alarms, both physical within the Majitsu building, and digital, turning the block of corporate data into a bright blue pulsing nova when viewed from a distance inside the net. It was the Majitsu building and network screaming to anyone with physical or online ears that something was horribly wrong.

"Fuck," Zee said. "Fuck, fuck, fuck."

And just like that, the show was over. And it had been a good show too. Zee, riding high as the shit hot console jockey, unstoppable, with clear, clean code that latched onto everything and wrested control. This had been a *real* score, and with real stakes, and it had been proving that Zee had what it took to not just do it, but do it in style.

Now, suddenly, all on fire.

"I need a sit rep. *Now*," said Marcus over the comm stone and it wasn't the Marcus that Zee had known over the last few days. The voice was the same, even the rhythm was the same, but there was a level of seriousness Zee hadn't suspected could be there. It was a voice that couldn't possibly tell a joke, let alone laugh at one. A voice that belonged to someone that killed as easily as most people had lunch.

"I've got nothing for you," Zee said, tapping some keys on the console. "Ditch this magic comm stone shit, I've got a secure channel you can patch into, hit it now, I'm staying in my net workspace, and it's easier for me to talk that way."

"Have it your way," Marcus said. "Just tell me what the hell is going on, people are running, shutters are going down around doors and windows."

"Lot of alarms just went off," Zee said. "Don't know why. But there are fire, intrusion, firewall breach and even biohazard alarms all going off in the building and in the network."

"Where's Cloke?"

"No clue, she cut me out a few minutes ago," Zee said, watching the various nodes on the summary screen lighting up like New Year's eve in Rio as all the security code that had been carefully put to sleep woke up and broke into a run. "She put the comm stone down, and left me hanging. Now get on that comm channel, I'm going in."

Zee synced into the neurolink.

The workspace created to monitor and manipulate the Majitsu hack was practically buzzing with energy from all the new activity.

"Tell me this is not you," Darma said, as the flood of new, unwelcome data came streaming in. "It would be a frack of legendary proportions if you got in this smoothly only to trip up now."

"Not me," Zee said, trying to get a grip on all the information. "Her."

"Cloke?"

"Who the fuck else? One minute she's talking about a custom console, the next she's putting away the comm stone, going into communications blackout. Of course, you wouldn't know about any of that, because you're out of the loop when she uses the comm stone. Then suddenly the whole building *and* its network goes into grand mal seizure."

Zee consulted all the displays floating in the workspace. Nothing but bad news. A line was automatically going out to the local cops, internal security systems were all spinning up; cameras, drones, the works. Staff were being evacuated because fire and biohazard protocols had gone into effect, and human security was already headed down to the armory to switch over to assault rifles and body armor. On the digital side, all the doors were closing fast.

Zee saw a blinking ready light coming from Marcus' communication system and connected him.

"We're all on. Marcus, I think you know Darma."

"Hey," Darma said. "Long time no breathe."

"Hey," Marcus said. "Sorry man, didn't think this was going to be the way I finally got around to talking to you."

"Better to talk about work than metaphysics," Darma said. "Now our little protégé here is in a bad place."

"What are we looking at?" Marcus asked.

"The technical term for it is well and truly fucked," Darma said.

"Whatever Cloke did, she set off *everything*," Zee said. "And because that room is completely off the grid, I can't do anything to help her."

"Gotta do something," Marcus said. "And it's gotta be fast."

"Is there a fall back?" Darma asked.

Marcus snorted over the comm channel. "This is Cloke we're talking about."

Zee ignored them both and concentrated on executing, as quickly and precisely as possible, whatever options were left. It was the security network version of an emergency response team with full sirens running straight through convincing murals of a calm, empty street that Zee had erected with digital silk sheets. Most control was lost, but some of it remained. How much of it would prove useful in the next few minutes was another question altogether.

"I've got surveillance, some clearance access, maybe a little bit of intrusion if I'm really lucky, but no promises on that last one." Zee said at last. "So, does anyone know what we should be doing next?"

"I'm doing it," Marcus said over the com channel. "If you've got anything strategic, give it to me."

Zee linked Marcus into the surveillance program that took all the personnel movement in the building and summarized it in clean, 2D, overhead maps.

"Nice work," Marcus said. "That'll do."

"What are you going to do?"

"Patch in and see for yourself."

Zee connected to Marcus' optics and felt the vertigo and gut-lurch from the bird's eye view Marcus had as he leapt from one building to the next.

"I'm using factory-issue stock armor, no clear identifiers," Marcus said. "No cute custom designs to give me away, just a generic hired combat cyborg, could be working for anyone."

"Drawing fire," Darma said.

"It works most of the time…" Marcus said, impacting on the roof of the building in a pointlessly stylish three-point landing. The barrel of his cyborg class carbine—a small, heavy artillery cannon, really—swung into Marcus' view and opened fire on the communications tower mounted on the roof. "Just standard operating procedure for a Chimera unit on covert ops. Do some hand waving to keep attention away from the fact that magic is being used." Another dizzying lurch, and his view took in the fast-approaching ground, then was halted as he grabbed at the wall on the side of the building, swung himself around, and punched at an armored window that had been designed to withstand ballistic fire, but not getting ripped out of its housing. A grenade lazily arced into view, causing Zee to take in a short, sharp breath over the potential casualties of such a move, but it was a false alarm; light pulsed, a filtered sonic burst erupted through Marcus' audio inputs. He had only thrown a stun grenade. His view changed again as he loosened his grip slightly, let gravity take over, and slid down the side of the building, his hand creating a long trail of destruction behind it as he continued to hang on.

"Disconnect," Zee heard from Darma. "You've got work to do."

"Yeah, I'll be fine," Marcus said. "I bring the chaos; you bring the exit."

Zee did it, deferring Marcus' transmission down to just one more screen that was part of multiple displays monitoring the research compound's high alert status.

"He's keeping things nice and grounded," Darma said. "As long as the assault is conventional and there's no obvious use of magic, they won't have any reason to suspect it was being used anywhere, and they won't spend the money to investigate that avenue. Our cover's not blown yet; it's just changed. Now you've gotta hold up your end."

"This wasn't in the plan," Zee said.

"Plans change. Can you?"

"Asks the guy who's just a bunch of code," Zee said, regretting it the second it came out.

"Harsh on the deck," Marcus said with clear disapproval in his voice even over the comm channel. "Save the sniping for when the job's done."

Zee wanted to say, "I'm sorry," but Marcus was right, this wasn't the time for it. The first thing that needed doing was to try and get the situation back under some kind of control. The surveillance network showed that Cloke was still off the grid, which meant she was probably still in the room.

"If you don't mind some unsolicited advice, diversionary tactics work better when they look credible," Darma said. "If Marcus is gonna tell them a war story, it better be a good one."

Zee took in the maps of the building and then patched back over to Marcus, noting the crucial points on the schematics. "I want to aim you."

"Where?" Marcus asked.

Zee added the waypoints to Marcus' navigation. "Fourth floor, here or here, or both if you want. One is a room for prototyping, some new toys in there. The other is a server room I tagged where they archive copies of their research data. Not sure whether either room is enough to warrant an expensive hire like a cyborg assault, but at least there's stuff there they don't want people to see."

"No corporation with decent management will ever doubt the stupidity of a rival with money to burn," Marcus said. "I can make that work."

Zee watched with a growing sense of nausea as Marcus' view took him on a dizzying arc through the air that had him turn and unload his carbine, as well as some incendiary grenades popping from his shoulders into a wall. There was an explosion, fragments of flame dropping to the ground, and palm trees on the ground below lit up with flames like tropical Christmas trees. Another indicator chirped while its dedicated display blinked red to indicate the hacked system's new alert status.

Zee checked the update, enabled Marcus' channel and said "You're going to have company soon. Majitsu just sent out an emergency response request."

"What kind?"

"Local SWAT. Classed for cyborg engagement."

"Which outfit?"

"Looks like Tannhauser."

"Middle of the road. They'll put up a decent fight," Marcus said. External cameras showed the havoc Marcus was wreaking. It didn't seem to matter which camera Zee flipped to: all of them were tracking the shattering glass, flaming wreckage and impact craters he was gleefully making wherever he went.

Zee went back to the more familiar world of networks and hacks, to keep the pressure on. "Okay Darma, you're up."

"What?"

"You seriously think I'm going to let a spare seat go empty on a run when you've done this way more than I have?"

"I was under the impression that was the way it was gonna go down, yeah."

Zee tweaked some of the settings for access to the hackware and granted more authority to Darma. "Security and intrusion countermeasures are going to require constant tinkering. I can't do that if I'm supposed to stay on top of things with Marcus and Cloke."

"Eventually you're gonna have to."

"Well not today," Zee said. "Today I'm going to concentrate on what I know I can do and worry about achieving my potential some other time. Do what you can with security, and loop me in on what control you can take back."

"What are you going to be doing?"

"Finding out where the fuck the boss is and whether she's even still alive."

Over the comm channel, Marcus laughed. So did Darma. "You're new. I'll cut you some slack on that," he said. "This is Cloke. Unless you drop a few buildings on her, she's probably fine. You get points for due diligence though, that's good to have."

"Are we gonna get this done or what?" Zee asked, trying to change the subject.

"Kid's got a work ethic all right," Marcus said.

"Sorry boss, won't happen again boss, getting right on it, boss," Darma said.

Zee grunted acknowledgement—half irritation, half in a rush—and flipped through the surveillance systems, checking to make sure the hacks were still in place and whether Cloke was appearing on any of them. There was also the clock to keep an eye on; the one counting down the arrival of the response team that was going to try and take Marcus down.

Zee was just about fed up with the place Cloke had put them all in when the woman herself finally appeared. Pressure sensors in the ventilation system—which were still under Zee's control—tipped off her presence. Zee patched into her visor, bringing in both Marcus and Darma.

"Line is secure, Darma's on deck and can't use the comm stone," Zee said. "It's twelve different kinds of fucked up out there, and don't you dare bitch me out about it."

"I had an oopsie," Cloke said.

Zee almost screamed and clamped down on the response. "What the hell is *that* supposed to mean?"

"It's a big, game changing oopsie, we can talk about it later, but it's what set off everything. What's the sit rep?"

Zee patched in the charts that showed which systems were still under control, which were still partially so, and which were just flat out gone. They were all probably dominating whichever field of view Cloke had configured on her visor for incoming images.

"That's... actually not as bad as I expected," Cloke said.

"I'm holding off some of the dogs," Darma said. "Systems are still mostly stock, no special hacks, all the usual back doors are still available."

"Marcus, you kill anyone yet?" Cloke asked.

"Surprisingly, no," he said. "But Zee says we got a Tannhauser unit heading down to welcome us."

"Play nice with them," Cloke said. "Zee, is my route still viable?"

"Mostly. There are going to be a few detours and your preferred exit is a dice roll."

"It was a nice hope while it lasted," Cloke said. "So, we're looking at business as usual?"

"Yup," Marcus said. "Plan is toast and everything else is on fire."

"I'm plotting out a new route and patching it to your visor," Zee said. "Just keep following the trail and stop when I say so."

Zee watched as Cloke navigated the ventilation ducts and ended up at a duct that led out into an office.

"This one should be okay," Zee said. "You can open the panel here; I've had this one hacked for the last few days to go off for no reason at semi-regular intervals. Even if their records show the alarm going off now, it'll be consistent."

"Smart," Cloke said. "So, you did have a back-up."

"Not really, no," Zee said. "I just did it because I could, and I was bored. Didn't think we'd actually have to use it."

"Murphy is an auxiliary member of the team," Cloke said. Zee noted on the sensors that she was configuring her armor for combat, sliding plates in place that would cover her face. "And he's always laying down the law."

"I thought you guys were joking about that."

"There's truth in humor," Cloke said. "Especially with a third-rate group of hacks like us."

At this, Zee heard both Marcus and Darma laugh and felt like there was an old joke happening that just went flying on by without so much as a glance or invitation to take part. New kid syndrome was already starting to feel old.

Cloke's icon tracked on Zee's graphical map, showing her slow but steady progress as she followed the trail through the halls.

"Hold up," Zee said, checking more security cameras. "The next vent you need to take has a problem."

"The kind with a gun?"

Zee let the Jane's military software do its recognition work on the image. "Yeah. MAR 22, looks like."

"Local pride," Marcus said. "Malaysian assault rifle. Good middle grade choice."

"Chaff him," Cloke said. "He's plugged into the local tactical network?"

"Yup," Zee said, watching Cloke take up a position just around the corner from the vent and the armed security officer that was in the way.

"What's our surveillance situation in this area?"

"Sloppy. I'm blocking live security feed in the areas you're in, but I'll have to clean it up later before their system experts get a good look at it. For now, they can't see you in real time, but the work is traceable."

"Same goes for our target here?"

"Yeah, he's under the blanket, but I have no control over the data log in his gear. Their network might not see you, but his visor or helmet cam will, and they'll see that once they download and debrief."

"Fair enough, that's on me," Cloke said, and Zee could see the woman crouching, bunching up her muscles. "Chaff on my mark." Cloke was low to the ground now, like a cat in sleek, shiny carbon body armor. "Mark."

Zee flooded the guard's earpiece with blisteringly high and loud white noise while his visor was blanked out by static. It was a quick burst, only a second, but it was enough.

The guard's hands went up to cover his ears—a useless, purely reflexive move that did nothing since his communications gear was embedded in his helmet. The burst of static in his combat visor, combined with his own panic reaction to bend forward, completely hid Cloke's approach.

By the time he looked up, his hands now off his weapon and moving to remove his helmet, Cloke was already on top of him.

Her foot swept in a clean arc that took him off his own feet while her elbow followed up, hitting him in the nose with so much force that he collided with the wall behind him. Blood spewed out of his broken nose as he slumped down. Cloke tore off his helmet and landed a solid kick to his head that sent him spinning and collapsing to the ground, clearly unconscious.

"Shit," Zee said.

"Clean," Darma said over the comm channel.

"It will be in a second," Cloke said, bending down and applying a micro-EMP emitter to blow out the data storage systems built into the guard's security gear. She patted him on the shoulder reassuringly before getting back on her feet and entering the next system of vents.

"How the fuck did you do that?" Zee asked.

"Practicing Jeet Kune Do," Cloke said. "Lots of it. Just like anything."

"You're looking at one of the few combat mages on the planet that also has abs of steel," Darma said.

"And I got 'em the hard way," Cloke said, continuing her way through the vents. "I'm a decent shot too."

"You're a barely adequate shot," Marcus said. "But that's still better than most people."

Cloke grunted, something that might have been a short chuckle of amusement or maybe just the noise of effort from pulling herself through the vents, it was hard to tell.

With Zee's constant coordination, Cloke made good progress through the compound. When the SWAT team arrived—a Tannhauser unit, as predicted—they focused their fire on Marcus, and he responded by putting some distance between himself and the building.

"They're baiting on me," he said. "What now?"

"Situation is still bad," Zee said. "Most of the building is going into a hard lockdown, security is sweeping room to room now."

"I don't suppose the skylights are still unlocked?"

"They're running a live current now, the drones and auto-turrets are covering any easy exit, and it looks like the network administration boys finally stopped watching porn long enough to justify their salary."

"Will that be a problem?" Cloke asked.

"No," Darma and Zee said at the same time. Zee smiled and pushed the large red button sitting in the virtual workspace, the one with the words "PANIC!" inscribed in bold white friendly letters on the top. The button itself was nearly the size of a dinner plate and sunk with the satisfying "click" of an old 20th century mechanical keyboard still using a Cherry MX Blue switch. "Right now, their porn is flooding all local networks and terminals trying to assert admin access. If they try to override it, it just pulls them deep into some bestiality sites. Then it locks up their equipment trying to apply for two million lifetime subscriptions per minute."

At this Cloke did laugh. "I thought you were joking about that."

"Porn is never a joke to a coder, it's a way of life," Darma said.

"Keep moving," Zee said. "I'm routing you out to a vent near the lobby."

Cloke's tracking signal was a bright, steady pulse on the monitors. There was a speed and efficiency about her that Zee hadn't seen in other people. The focus on the job at hand was frightening, though maybe the more frightening prospect was that there didn't seem to be any intense focus or ambition behind it, like this was just another day at the office. Zee wasn't even sure that had been possible until Cloke had come along.

"Drone," Zee said, coming back to the job at hand. "Floating upwards from a shaft five meters ahead that you'll need to go down yourself."

"I hear it," Cloke said. "Clicky little bastard. Is it still networked?"

Zee keyed up another sequence that amplified the stream of garbage data flooding the network. It was a short burst, wouldn't last more than a minute, if that, before a competent programmer clamped down on it, but it was still time.

"It's flooded, you have a minute, maybe less, *go.*"

Cloke did. On tracker, Zee could see Cloke's point of view on her combat visor, hauling herself forward even faster, looking down at the vent with a small, disc-shaped drone rising up the shaft like a Liliputian flying saucer. Cloke's hand stretched out, and a small light flashed through the air, a ragged arc like a miniature bolt of lightning that hit the drone. It froze in place for a moment before falling, stiff and unmoving, back towards the bottom of the shaft.

"Lightning?" Zee asked.

"Small," Cloke said, with a petulant tone of protest in her voice as if she'd been caught with her hand in the cookie jar. "Small and fast enough that it could read as a short or electrical arc even if monitors were active here."

"Must be nice," Zee said.

"It was an opportunity," Cloke said. "You flooded the network right? It was safe enough to make a move a little more flamboyant."

Zee had been thinking the same thing.

This was an opportunity that Zee could also capitalize on even if it hadn't been on the program. The flood of espionage-ware that was overwhelming the compound's tech support created enough noise to hide what would have been an otherwise very loud intrusion into the financial database of the network. Cloke was focused on getting out with her skin intact from the depths of the corporate beehive. Marcus was fighting a private SWAT unit and Darma had his hands full keeping digital security in check. The Majitsu compound's network was in a state of full siege, and its defenders didn't have the time or resources to keep an eye on everything.

It was time to commit.

Zee quickly zoned in on the target that had been scoped and quietly noted during the earlier recon. An executive in upper management that, amongst other things, had been siphoning money off various charity drives Majitsu Malaysia participated in, putting the money towards obtuse purchases like gold-plated faucets and top-quality escorts. The same executive was also named in multiple sexual harassment cases that somehow never made it all the way to court.

It was easy to not feel guilty about this.

Zee had already done the homework and had gotten the access to his accounts in the company financials. It was easy to grab the money, bleed it out, and take a small cut. It was just a few extra sequences to extract content the same executive had tagged in a private file; filled with sexually compromising videos he had been dumb enough to store—complete with leering, verbal threats of ruined careers if the secretary/intern/research assistant/low-level manager didn't comply.

The bulk of money that Zee didn't keep—because it was too big and too hot to handle in those amounts—would divert over to some carefully rerouted stock purchases—including some GIS shares—and a few charities in the region for upholding women's employment rights, some educational institutions and a few funding groups for underprivileged children. Even the smaller, disseminated leftovers of stolen charity cash would keep some of these groups running for an entire year. The videos of sexual harassment and financial transaction records for siphoning off the charity money into his accounts went to three different news agencies in the region, at least one of which had been forced to bury an investigative piece on the executive when a lack of solid evidence—and some Majitsu legal muscle—put the case to rest. Things were about to take a turn for the catastrophic for this particular executive over the next few days.

Zee whistled "It's Beginning to Look a Lot Like Christmas,"

and got back to the main job, which had been carrying on just fine with Darma on hand to help. As a matter of precaution, this also required keying in another prepared sequence to slap down the censor on Darma in case he'd been paying attention.

Apparently he had. "Is this going to keep happening?" he asked.

"Is what going to keep happening?"

There was a long sigh. "Just be careful," he said. "You steal long enough, you get caught. No one thinks it'll happen to them, but sooner or later, it does."

Zee was about to come back with a softer, more reasonable reply when Cloke cut everything short.

"I'm in position, how fucked is everything that I can't see?"

"What can you see?" Darma asked.

"Security lock down, guards with assault weaponry, siege gear being readied up."

"Not much more fucked than what you're already seeing, then," Zee said. "You're not getting past that. Not quietly, but I think we all knew that."

"Only you knew that," Cloke said.

"No, I'm pretty sure you're fucked," Marcus offered.

Darma grunted with obvious amusement. "I'm flash backing to Bogota now."

They all laughed, and Zee sighed as the in-joke whizzed right by. It was probably not intentional, they were a team, and this was a team situation, but it still felt marginalizing.

"I don't know if I can help you," Zee said over the comms channel to Cloke. "I didn't have anything ready for something like this."

"It's hard to prepare for dragon kings," Cloke said. "No one's going to get on your case for this."

"Yeah, that's great that you read books and all, throwing around your high-level physics slang, but it still doesn't help your ass out of there does it?" Darma said.

"I know something that might," Cloke said. "But I'm gonna need some fireworks outside."

Zee watched a security camera showing Marcus as he ran

across the roof of the Majitsu compound. A trail of gatling fire ripped up holes just behind him as one of the SWAT members pursued him in a Gyro somewhere above.

"I don't think fireworks is going to be much of a problem," Zee said.

"Gonna need to do better than ballistics, I'm gonna need something *really* firework-y. Something bright."

"Wait," Darma said. "Cloke, are you... no. No, you're not thinking that."

"Yeah, I am."

"No, that's not gonna work."

"It is. It's just got to be bright."

"I thought you needed to prep shit ahead of time to make that work."

"I've got a contingency for this."

"Does that contingency improve your odds? 'Cause that's got a dicey success rate even at the best of times."

"What does?" Zee finally asked.

"Shadow dance," Cloke said. "Magic."

An explosion from a stray micro missile slammed into the shielded doors of the Majitsu compound. Zee could see Cloke's visor view shudder from the reverberation. "So, the no magic rule just blew up?"

"No magic rule is always a good rule," Cloke said. "Still holds here, but if we hide it, like I did when I fried the drone, we still might get out of this kinda, sorta clean. Marcus."

"Aye."

"Gonna need you to be on the wall, front of the building, ten meters from roof level. Can you hold that position for at least five seconds?"

"Depends on your budget for my repair bill, they're going to be knocking me around a bit once I stop moving."

"I'll get you some decent suspension for your legs if you need new ones."

"That's what you said the last time."

"I'll throw in a 'go faster flames' paint job."

"Be still my heart. You've got a deal."

"I hate you two," Darma said. "This is a dumb ass move."

"What is going on?" Zee asked. "Okay, there's a plan happening, I get that part, but what are we doing?"

"You and Darma are going to amp up the garbage data," Cloke said. "I'll need a ten second window if you can manage it. Marcus, do you still have any flare rounds left?"

"I have all of them left."

"When you get in position, you'll need to face upwards, towards the roof, then deploy at least half your flares towards the ground. It's gotta be really bright, you need to cast a big black shadow on the building. Save a micro missile for the front door."

"Aye."

On the displays, Cloke's point of view became a jumble of confusion. It took Zee a few seconds to realize that her visor camera was just showing what it looked like as Cloke turned herself around to face away from the ventilation panel in front of her. Her combat boot moved into view as she firmly planted one foot on the grill. A hand came up and picked out a flare and EMP grenade from her web belt.

"Zee, switch back over to the comm stones, you're going to want to be on that for what's gonna happen soon."

Zee did it, wearing the tacky jewelry that Cloke had issued.

"Okay," Cloke's voice said, coming in from every direction at once, as if she were right inside Zee's head. Her voice was still coming through on conventional communication channels for Darma's benefit. Zee had to mute all but Darma's comm channel to avoid a bizarre echo effect of voices in the ear and the mind. "I don't expect this to be elegant, but I think we can still pull this off. Do we have control of the lights in the building?"

"What do you need done?" Zee asked.

"I need the lights out in this area."

"Can't shut them off, but I can overload them to burst," Zee said.

"That works too," Cloke said. "Marcus, there's gonna be a local EMP burst."

"I'm out of range."

"Okay. Then it goes down like this. Zee, Darma, you've got your situation under control?"

"I can flood their combat network," Zee said. "But it'll be the last time I can get away with it."

"I can manage five, maybe ten seconds of drone control," Darma said. "Then it's like Zee said. We're shut out."

"That'll be enough. Can you hit them on my mark?"

"Yeah," both Zee and Darma said at the same time.

"Darma on drones, you go second, on my mark."

"Anything special?"

"Turn drones on security, put the auto turrets on self-destruct if there are any. I don't want them shooting at me when I make my run for the pillar."

"Wait, what?" Zee asked.

"Zee, you're up first. On my mark to you, hit the combat network hard. Same as what you did for the guy in the hall, only as many as you can as long as you can in that lobby."

"Okay, fine. Then what?"

"Then you've done your job and the rest is on me. Anything happens after that, it's not your fault."

"That's not the kind of answer you should be giving employees," Zee said.

"Whatever. I'm going. Zee, mark."

Zee went through a rapid mental litany of *WaitwaitWAIT! TOO FAST, if I fuck this up, she dies, if I fuck this up she DIES...*

On the monitor, Cloke's visor cam showed her leg coiling back, presumably to put her foot through the grate and send it flying.

It was a pointless gesture in the simulated workspace, but Zee's hands slammed the keys of the console, triggering another explosive round of garbage data.

Zee's eyes flitted to the various displays to keep track of what happened next.

The first view, Cloke's, showed her solid kick to the ventilation panel, her gloves power gripping the duct above her so she could push herself out. The security cameras Zee still had under control confirmed this, with Cloke sliding out of the duct as if she'd been spat out. Another security camera showed the security guards squirming as white noise hit their ear pieces, their combat visors went into stroboscopic display of all available data, while certain officers that had enabled their medical monitors had their legs injected with a coagulant and local anesthetic as those same integrated suit systems were told that an amputation had occurred.

"Darma, mark," Cloke said.

It was a double whammy.

The compound's human security, already reacting badly to the feedback screaming over their combat network combined with a few surprise injections of anesthetic, found themselves spinning away from automated gun turrets that turned on each other, and even the security officers themselves.

"Marcus, mark."

"Aye."

The external cameras showed Marcus grappling himself to the roof and then dropping down to hang off the wall at the distance Cloke had requested. He had his feet on the wall, his back to the ground, so that he was looking up at the sky and the grappling cable that tethered him to the building.

"Rock mode enabled, I'm not moving," Marcus said.

The security cameras in the lobby showed Cloke already building up an impressive running speed as she tore a straight line through a scattered crowd of security guards that were dealing with the improvised combat overload Zee and Darma were inflicting on them. Cloke's passage went unnoticed as she aimed herself at one of the massive, wholly unnecessary pillars that dotted the Majitsu research compound's lobby.

"Emping," Cloke said with the kind of inhuman calm Zee normally associated with elevators counting off floors.

On Cloke's visor camera, her hand came forward, lobbing a small EMP grenade casually to her left, towards the guards and auto-turrets. Her other hand came up with another grenade in grip.

"Flashing," she said. She tossed the grenade ahead of her in a slow curve that took it around the pillar she seemed hell-bent on running into. The camera went black, as Cloke adjusted the opacity of her combat visor.

Zee needed to monitor multiple cameras to keep track of what was going on.

The EMP grenade went off first, shorting out every digital or electronic device within its small range, which was enough to fry the tactical network and most of the weapons the guards had. Being a modern force trained in the latest combat techniques, Majitsu security was now useless in a fight. Cloke, being in the thick of it, immediately stopped transmitting to Zee's display, her feed dropping out the second the electromagnetic pulse swept past her.

Zee could only see what was happening by switching views to a camera positioned high up in the outer reaches of the massive open lobby, just far enough away that Cloke's EMP pulse was out of range. Cloke was still visible, running straight at her selected pillar like she meant to break through it.

"Missiles," Cloke said, now coming through the comm stone.

From Marcus' point of view a panel popped up on his optics display, targeting the main doors of the compound. Another indicator lit up, showing a round of micro-missiles launching from his left shoulder pod and screaming towards the door. It was probably for show, Zee realized, to give the more scientifically inclined a probable exit for the intruder, rather than whatever it was that Cloke planned on doing.

"Mark," Cloke said.

Yet another indicator on Marcus' tactical view tracked his right arm as it swung down towards the ground and shot a series of flare rounds below him. His missiles were nearly at their target.

Cloke's flare grenade detonated. A cluster of charged, photoelectric nanoparticles burst into an expanding sphere of light, swallowing everything in its path, a miniature sun being born. It was going to be a nova in that room for at least three seconds.

The security camera, still under Zee's control, immediately went opaque, its lens darkening to compensate. Not that it mattered; it wasn't actually capable of recording anything it could see right now, but it showed Zee what mattered most.

Cloke was going to collide with a pillar. She was headed straight for it, almost entirely lost in the massive black shadow cast by the pillar thanks to the flare grenade in the room that was now detonating.

"Now," she said over the comm stone.

The camera showed Cloke extending her hand—there might have been the hint of blue light, or at least some kind of energy emanating from it. Zee sucked in a breath as Cloke leapt, headfirst, to crash and slump against the pillar.

What happened instead was that she dove *into* it. Into the darkness being cast by its shadow.

Over the comm stone, Cloke started screaming. She didn't stop.

"Marcus' feed," Darma said.

Zee looked. Marcus was staring straight ahead. Thanks to the flares he'd shot directly below himself, he was also casting a massive shadow across the wall of the Majitsu compound. A portion of the shadow ahead of him bubbled, as if the darkness itself were water that was suddenly boiling over.

Cloke erupted from the shadow, still screaming. Her momentum carried her clear of the shadow, and Marcus' view adjusted as he bunched his leg muscles, triggered the release on his grappling cable, and leapt away from the building to catch her as she descended in an arc.

She only stopped screaming when he caught her. He came down hard on the ground and quickly took out a med sensor that he applied to her neck.

"Exit stage right, kids," Darma said. "We're gonna lose control of the network any second now."

"We're gone in five seconds," Marcus said, then leapt for the next rooftop.

The data from the sensor came in a few moments later.

"Heart is gonna explode if that keeps up," Darma said,

monitoring the new data. "Neurologicals are all over the place too. Synapses are firing outta' serious whack, having a knockback effect on muscles."

"That would explain the trembling," Marcus said. He was traveling fast but discreet now; running, jumping, but no longer cratering rooftops, and hiding under a suite of electronic countermeasures. Zee checked his feed and saw that he was right. Cloke was shaking violently in his firm but gentle grip.

"S-s… side effect," she said through gritted teeth. "It'll ease up."

"Goddamn witch," Marcus said under his breath. "I don't believe you just did that. Way to ignore the door, boss."

Zee could see Cloke's hand curl up to give a trembling middle finger to Marcus. "Try that with fucking software," she said weakly.

Zee tracked Marcus' progress as he bounded out of the area. He'd already disposed of the gyros from the first response team, and by the time more showed up, he'd be long gone. There would need to be a very quiet backdoor cleanup to make sure residual traces were wiped out, but the job for the most part was done.

"Medivac team on standby," Darma said. "They're at the old Jurong West stadium. Give me clearance to send her vitals over so they can start prepping."

"Done," Marcus said.

"See you when you get back," Darma replied. "Closing up shop on the op." Zee could see him enabling a few house cleaning sequences in his virtual workspace: his *virtual* virtual workspace, since he was already dead. "Annnnnnd… we're out."

Zee sank into the virtual chair, feeling tensed back muscles relax, and breathed out slowly.

"And that's your first job," Darma said. "Could'a been worse, huh, kid?"

The monitors were still active, the audio pickups droning with the sound of faraway sirens as more emergency and tactical response teams descended on the compound. They'd be too late of course. Cloke was clear. It was over.

Zee looked at the window open on Darma's workspace. He was no longer in it, having transitioned back to the office in the default house his emulation had created for him. He was stretching, cracking knuckles as he spun in his chair.

"Is it always like that?" Zee asked him.

"With Cloke? Yeah. With a normal outfit... let's just say reliability tends to be higher on the list." He walked towards the fridge in the kitchenette. "My God, do I ever need a fake drink right now to go with my real relief..." He opened the fridge and pulled out what looked like an ancient bottle of whiskey. He poured himself a glass and then toasted towards the camera. "You may as well get yourself a real drink. It's been earned."

"So how does debriefing work? That happens next, right?"

"Oh, that goes pretty much like you'd expect. We all take off our underwear and show it off to check for skid marks and other accidents," he said, absolutely dead pan.

"Shit. Tell me that you guys are not a typical example of a pro team."

"No such thing as typical with a Chimera unit. You think any normal methodology is going to work when you combine hacking, cyborg muscle and combat thaumaturgy in the same group? It's a miracle if it doesn't implode."

"How many others are there?"

Darma shrugged, taking another long sip from his virtual booze. "Not the sort of thing you can just go online and ask your search agent about," he said. "There are at least four other units I've seen in action personally, and one more that I strongly suspect is probably a Chimera unit, but they won't own up to it."

Zee absorbed this quietly. All these casual snippets from Darma and the rest were stark reminders they lived in a different world from everyone else—one where magic and digital resurrections were all a matter of contract and payment.

"Anyway, good job, kid," Darma said. "If you have an

unwinding ritual, I suggest you start it now. Cloke's gonna be in the hospital for a bit. I doubt it's anything that'll kill her, but magic can fuck up a body in ways you can't imagine. After that... well, I'm sure I'm not the only one who wants to know what she wants to do next."

"You think she got what she wanted?"

"She got something," Darma said. "It must've been big. Contrary to what you might think, she's not going to trip an alarm and fuck up a successful infiltration on impulse. It would have to be worth it for her to burn her own plan like that." He stretched and moved a hand towards a nearby panel on the wall. "Anyway, I'm going to shut out for a while. Privacy mode is going up, I'll see you tomorrow."

Darma logged out, disappearing entirely from the tactical network.

Zee sat back and let out a long sigh. Things were getting more complicated. But at least there was a bit more money in the bank.

II
The Pieces
November 2, 2138

Chapter IX:
The Wrong Warning

CLOKE DREAMED A lot in the hospital.

The primary image in these dreams was Matheus Azevedo, but it wasn't the simple emulation that greeted her on screen in the locked-down terminal room. This was a majestic vision, like a shirtless, well-built Brazilian god, with the winds of the Amazon blowing through his hair; an icon of both magic and romance novels.

In these dreams, Azevedo told her things about herself, things that were patently obvious to everyone and things that made her uncomfortable as he spoke. In a patient, quiet, relentless whisper, he talked about her teen years, about her aptitude for learning thaumaturgy, the books that had made her cry and the days at the College that had nearly broken her.

"There's an engine in you," he said, staring her down, unblinking, "And it will never, ever stop. Not until you're dead, and even then I can't be certain. It's an engine fueled by the one thing no one counted on with you."

She wanted to ask about his biceps. Instead, her dream self asked, "The magic?"

"The knowing," Azevedo said. "You can't not know, and the not knowing eats at you in a way that's worse than being dead."

"That's not true," Cloke said.

"Then why did you accept my offer?"

Cloke's answer was cut short by her vision flooding into white.

It was the windows of her hospital room, the blinds drawing themselves up and letting the sun in. The décor was a dead giveaway, the friendly, flowery smell of antiseptic even more so; this was the medical compound at the GIS New York office. She'd been here eight months earlier, getting treated for a broken right leg and arm.

Victor was there, sitting in a chair and consulting his OLED display. Cloke was forcefully caught up in a feeling of being seventeen again. Of having this man always there when she woke up from some "incident," watching over her, reading up on the business news of the morning before looking up, as he did now, and saying:

"I'm sure there's a fascinating story here."

"How long?" Cloke asked.

"This would have been day three," Victor said, looking back down at his OLED. "Now, how about a little bit of catch up?"

"Are they here?"

"Your team? Zee is."

"That includes Darma?"

"Yes, Zee has his emulation. Marcus went back home to London last night, but we can send for him if you like."

Cloke nodded. "I'll—"

Her sentence was cut off by a sound that put her into caution mode. It was an incoming call on her visor. The distinct tone of it meant it was her private, direct line to her sister.

"I need to take that," Cloke said. "It's Em."

"I'll get it," Victor said, moving over to a dresser in the room that had Cloke's belongings. He pulled out the visor and handed it over to her.

Cloke slipped it on, feeling the gentle pulse against her skin as the visor's biometrics detected it was being worn by its owner and switched the call indicator over to vibration mode.

When she answered the call, the voice conducting through

her skull on the other end was not her sister, was not even female. "Your sister can't talk to you right now, but she has a message for you."

"Who the fu—"

Before she could finish, the voice channel shifted and her ears were filled with the sound of someone screaming and that, most definitely, was her sister. Cloke had heard her scream like this before and had hoped to never hear the sound again. It was the wail of a cornered animal with no escape from some endless cruelty.

The visor went opaque, the interior display blinking to life and for just a few seconds, Cloke was hit with a barrage of images: a naked thigh, a wrist held down, teeth clamped down in agony, opening wide in fear. Hair in clumps being thrown on the ground. All of it immediately, undeniably indicating that something was being done to Emily.

Cloke flung herself backwards as the image of bloody teeth flooded her eyes.

Victor was already on his feet, Cloke could feel his hands come to her shoulders. "Cloke, wha—"

The images abruptly stopped. Cloke raised her hand and yelled "STOP!" at Victor to make sure he didn't tear the visor off her face and make her miss whatever came next. Whatever came next was probably the whole point of this.

Muscles she didn't even know she had tightened relaxed across her entire body. A voice on the visor said, "Walk away from the job. Walk away and save what's left of your sister. Do it, or Mr. Komarov will send considerably more than his regards."

It took her a few seconds to place the voice, and when she finally did, she let out a quiet groan. It was already happening so fast. Too fast.

The visor went dead.

Cloke counted silently to five, waiting for something more. When nothing came, she finally pulled the visor away from her eyes and let it clatter to the floor.

Victor kept a steady gaze on her. "Are you all right?"

She nodded.

"And that was—"

"A warning." She finally looked at him. "They have her. They have Em."

"Who?"

"Matheus Azevedo," Cloke said numbly. "And the man holding his choke chain, Andrew Komarov."

"The Chief Technology Officer of Majitsu." Victor frowned. "That's not a man you want to cross."

"That's pretty much the message, I think."

"And Em is their bargaining chip?"

She nodded.

"I find that highly unlikely. Her security is impenetrable. You saw to that yourself."

"Get confirmation," she said. "And get them here. All of them. I'm going to need them, and I need to tell them. They need to know."

"Know what?"

"Who they're going to burn. Burn right down to the ground. Andrew Komarov just told me I shouldn't cross him." She could feel the cold, hard place growing harder in her chest. It was there, like it always was, waiting for her. Patient and endless in supply. Anger. "Well, he shouldn't have crossed me."

WHEN THEY ARRIVED, Marcus looked like he was going to give Cloke another one of his "Stuck in the hospital again, huh?" lectures. The smile on his face said it all, but she wasn't in the mood to entertain his "This wouldn't happen if you had cybernetic implants like me" teasing. Time wasn't on her side. "Is Darma online?" she asked Zee.

Zee stood up and established a physical connection of the emulator to the display on Cloke's wall. "He is now."

Darma's image blinked to life on the display. "Big pow wow," he said.

"Things just got complicated," she said to all of them. "They've got my sister."

Marcus' smiling, open mouth vanished immediately.

Cloke looked at all of them. "A lot of stuff happened when we hit that building. I'll tell you what you need to know to keep up with me for now, you can ask for details later if you want. There was a Thaumaturge. He was *the* Thaumaturge. His name was Matheus Azevedo."

"I know him," Darma said. "Any kid that went through contemporary history remembers that name: the father of Brazil's new golden age. Weight mage."

"Mass negation," Cloke said. "And Majitsu has an illegal emulation of him. There was a terminal in that building hard-lined for communication. That's what I was talking to."

Cloke watched her information sink in with everyone in the room. She wasn't surprised to see it hit Darma the hardest.

"Here's where it gets complicated. Azevedo wants to be deleted. That's what he's hiring me— *us* for. But the catch is, only two out of three of him want this. The other one already got bought."

It was Marcus who spoke, "Wait, you mean—"

"They took their illegal emulation and duped it. Twice," Cloke said with a nod. "Three copies total. The original and copy three want deletion. Copy two is on Majitsu's side. The deal for this job is to take out all three. I have the locations of their permanent housings. That's what got me in trouble. Azevedo couldn't even speak the information without setting off the alarms."

"Man, shit's fucked up," Darma said, shaking his head.

"It gets worse," Cloke said. "I'm pretty sure copy two just took Em hostage as a warning shot to fuck off the job. Do we have confirmation on that?"

"Of a sort," Victor said. "I talked to one of the support engineers at her facility. An unscheduled maintenance cycle has locked everyone out and they can't abort it. Her neurological data is reading as semi-vegetative."

Marcus' curious expression changed to something harder.

"That's taking the low road right from the start."

"But it's tactically sound," Victor said. "Hit the enemy's weakness. I'm just surprised they knew."

"Going after Em..." Darma said with the disbelief clear in his voice. "Ballsy. Love to know how they pulled that off."

"You'll figure it out," Cloke said. She looked at Zee, who had been remarkably good about keeping hir mouth shut despite the fact that this was all probably coming in as information overload. "I'm going to explain this all to you now. It's important you understand this."

"Thanks," Zee said.

"It's because I need you to understand. You're the one that's going to get her out."

Zee was mute for ten seconds before finally saying, "What?"

"They have my sister," Cloke said. "Her name is Emily, but that probably doesn't mean anything to you. On the Net she goes by the name Miriya."

That name sunk in hard and fast on Zee's face. "Wait, WHAT?!? Your sister is *Miriya*? Miriya is *real*?"

"Yes, she's real."

"I thought she was just an artificial or virtual intelligence with kick ass socialware, something cooked up by one of those software studios in Tokyo or Reykjavik."

"That's what everyone thinks. It's a convenient story to cover up an otherwise complicated truth," Darma said. "But yes, the most famous digital celebrity on the planet is not, in fact, software, even though no one ever denies it when the question comes up."

"I don't get her being famous, but it is what it is," Cloke said with a shrug.

"Some people are just like that," Darma said. "Famous for the sake of being famous, some kind of perpetual motion machine of celebrity. But you're lying when you say you don't know why she's so famous on the Simulations and Internet circuit. She knows the SimNet. She is the SimNet."

"And now Azevedo has got her locked away. And he's doing something to her."

"What's he doing?" Darma asked quietly.

"Something that hurts," Cloke said, staring at her lap. She watched as her fist, almost of its own volition, slowly clenched. "Among other things."

"I know that tone of voice," Marcus said. "When you talk like that, someone dies."

Cloke didn't bother to speak.

"Somebody had better die if they're hurting Em," Marcus said. "I'm in."

"Thanks," Cloke said. She looked up and locked eyes with Zee. "But I need your help."

"You really don't," Zee said quietly. "This is Miriya, assuming you're telling the truth. She's happiness on the Internet. Doesn't she have a squad of tech support to handle this stuff?"

"Not this stuff," Cloke said. "Not hacks. Not illegal code. Not black or grey market neurosimulation. They don't know what to do. They don't deal with this kind of code and protocol. You made this stuff for a living."

"I've never tried this."

"Not many have. But you won't be alone. Darma?"

"I'm in," he said. "Of course I'm in. It's Em." He looked at Zee. "I've run stuff similar to this before, I'll take you through the routine."

Zee sighed. "I guess just backing off and listening to this Azevedo guy's warning isn't an option?"

"He took my sister. It stopped being pure business the second I heard her screaming. We're not going to back off. We're going to get my sister out, and then Matheus Azevedo is going to get his wish. He's going to die. Every single copy is going to die."

"And what about Mr. Komarov?" Victor asked. "You've got to be expecting a reaction from him."

"I expect him to flinch," Cloke said. "He can't do much else when someone gives him the finger over a couple of violations of international law that he can't have the courts looking into."

"This is going to put you right in his sights."

Cloke sighed. "Victor, it's not like I've never hit Majitsu before. *You* sent me against them yourself years ago. More than once."

"And that was always calculated. Small risks compared to the scope of their operations, not enough for them to justify the expense of any serious retaliation. Komarov is a sleeping giant. An amoral, unsympathetic sleeping giant. This might be different. And if it is... I can't help you. Not anymore."

Cloke could feel her own frown softening. "You shouldn't have to. And I wouldn't expect you to. It's not fair. Not anymore."

"You can always ask if you need it."

She wanted to say more. There was a "thank you," on the cusp of her breath. For taking care of her over the years. Caring about what she learned and what she didn't. Even the disapproving glances when she experimented with drugs and magic and nearly froze herself to death. This was a man that had given her years of his life and would always give a damn about what happened to her.

But she knew he'd never put a name to what he'd given her, fearing the pride she'd earned wouldn't accept it. Maybe he was right.

"Azevedo gave me a reason to trust him," Cloke said. "Did anyone tell you about what happened at the end of the run? How I got out?"

"They said you shadow danced."

Cloke nodded. "No preparation."

"That's impossible," Victor said. "That simply cannot be done—no one's ever done it, lab conditions or otherwise."

"Azevedo showed me how. And it worked. His way of apologizing for creating an alarm situation."

Marcus shook his head. "So... that was new magic?"

"Not new magic, just a new execution. A better one," Cloke said.

Victor looked to the screen with Darma on it. "You can confirm this?"

"I can confirm she did it, and it seemed like a spur of the moment thing. I didn't know it was supposed to be impossible to do it that fast."

"You're not supposed to," Cloke said. "One of those trade secrets the College would rather not have get around. It's better to let the masses learn everything they can about magic from shows."

"An emulation taught you a new thaumaturgical technique," Victor said flatly.

Darma shrugged as he lit a cigarette on screen. "It's like she downloaded and installed some kind of fucked-up witchware direct to her brain. How does that even *work?*"

"It was easier than I thought it would be," she said. "This is the real deal, Victor. This is big. This is a piece of history."

"And of course, there's Emily." He sighed and closed his eyes. "I'm not going to argue with you about this. I know how you feel about your sister. You know how I feel. Anything said beyond that is just going to be regrets." He walked over to her and put his hand on her shoulder. "But be careful."

"Thanks, Victor," Cloke said.

"You are not thinking this through."

"Not yet," she said. "But I will."

"Em is—"

"No. Don't continue. Remember what you just said. Regrets. She's family, Victor. She's my sister."

"I know," he said quietly. "What are you going to do then?"

"I'm going to get her out. When she's clear, and I can take my shot, I'll go to the College. Let them in on it. It falls under their jurisdiction."

Victor nodded and stood up. "At least you're being polite about it. That's a start," he said. "I shouldn't hear whatever you're talking about next. Just do what you have to. And no more than that. Cloke, I'll come back and see you again tomorrow."

"Okay."

He nodded to the rest and left the room.

"I'll give you all the details later," Cloke said to everyone else. "But for now, you just need to know the big stuff. I want to talk about what comes second, the original job."

"This is a job?" Marcus asked.

"Like any other. People are getting paid. By me." She looked at Marcus. "Anyone that signs on for this gets the usual rate. Plus bonus."

Cloke could see the muscles around Marcus' mouth tighten. "That sounds like a hazard bonus."

"It is. Everything about it is, even just finding out where to begin was dangerous. But I know where they're physically housed. We can get to them."

"Please tell me it's not the Japan home office," Marcus said.

"It's not the Japan home office."

"Thank God."

"It's the Dubai campus, the Prague office and Majitsu Orbital Platform Two."

There was more silence.

Marcus finally said, "I'm waiting for the punchline."

"Are you fucking serious?" Zee asked.

Cloke kept moving forward. Even if they weren't digesting everything right now, she needed to keep the plan in motion. "I'm thinking the best way to do this is to hit all of them at the same time. That's the ideal tactic anyway."

Zee looked back and forth between Marcus and Darma. "Why are you two just standing there, not noticing that she's saying fucked up things that should not be true?"

"You don't yet have the experience to know that this is a stupid idea," Cloke said.

"But Zee's right, it is stupid," Marcus said.

"I'm still working out the details," Cloke said. "Which means that I need to think on it and so do you. I'm not going to force anyone into this." She looked squarely at Zee. "Something like this... whatever it turns out to be is a bit further along the timetable than what I'd call safe for you. You give it a good long think about whether you want to sit this one out or not. It won't be a textbook raid. Nothing about it will be. But I need you for Em. Help me clear that and I'll consider it square, I won't drag you into the big op."

"You're going to need more firepower," Marcus said.

"Yup."

"A *lot* more."

"I was hoping I could talk to you about that later."

"Maybe," Marcus said, pushing himself away from the wall. "Maybe not. Your protocol is bad, boss. Call me in just to drop a bomb on me that I need to step out and think about. You could have used mail for that."

"No unsecure channels for serious shit, I thought that was your rule."

"I hate that rule when it means I have to travel," he said with a sigh. "Fine, let me have a think. There's a sour talk with the wife in the making on this one. I don't think she's forgiven you for the last time you offered hazard pay."

Cloke watched as Marcus made his way for the door.

"Leave Darma here," Cloke said to Zee. "There's something I need to talk to him about. Otherwise go, have lunch, have a good long think. Get back to me in an hour, we have to move on Em soon."

Zee nodded once, was gone without a word. Cloke could sympathize; this was a lot more than she had to deal with when she'd been offered her first serious job. Marcus followed hir moments later, leaving the soft, reassuring tone of Cloke's EKG monitor as the only sound in the room.

CLOKE ATTACHED THE neurolink and plugged it into a jack on the side of the bed that looked like it hadn't been used in years. She looked at Darma as she completed the connection. "I hope you and your pad are decent," she said.

On the screen, he gave an indifferent shrug.

She rolled her eyes and keyed the sequence to enter his emulation. "Knock, knock," she said.

Instantly, all pain, all aches, all physical warnings from her body that she had undergone some excruciating suffering disappeared. The default sensations of the neurosimulation put her nerves in a perfect, pain-free state. The default transitional white light enveloped her, faded away, and revealed a sight both surprising and familiar.

She was on the roof of a warehouse. It was an early summer evening and the sun could be seen hanging low in the sky, silhouetting church steeples and other 19th century buildings in the small city that sat on the western edge of Lake Ontario, between Toronto, Niagara Falls and the border to the NEASA. It had been one of Darma's random real estate purchases. Someone, probably Victor, suggested he maintain some property in North America, and he had dumbfounded everyone by selecting a location nearby—but still just out of easy reach—of every important destination on the eastern seaboard.

Darma was already sitting down in one of two lawn chairs, smoking a cigarette and listening to music coming out of a retro music player that still had visible, physical speakers. He raised a drink in his hand, but didn't bother to get up. Cloke looked down at herself. Her lack of any preferences file in the sim unit meant the software had clothed her in simple, comfortable grey shirt and pants. She looked like she might be on her way to a yoga class. She walked over and sank down on the other lawn chair. She took a good long look at her dead friend.

Everything about him screamed, "I am Darma."

He crinkled his eyes against the setting sun in the same way he always had, whether it had been on vacation in Cancun, or working an op under the Egyptian sun. He still took a drag from his cigarette gingerly, only to blow it out of the right of his mouth a few moments later. There was the running scar along his right arm that he'd never bothered to fix; his badge of honor, a personal reminder that even when something had gone wrong, he'd still managed to get out alive.

At least that time.

"What's this town called again?" Cloke asked.

"Hamilton. And it's not a town. Hasn't been for centuries, now it's all just part of the sprawl here."

She took in the tree-lined neighborhoods, the boats sailing lazily in the water of the bay. "This doesn't look like much of a sprawl."

"Well, Toronto hates this place and the feeling is mutual, so there's resistance to complete sprawlification on both sides," he said. He reached down into a cooler, pulled out a bottle of the local beer and put it on the table between them, then knocked the pack of simulated cigarettes closer to her.

She took the pack and pulled one out for herself. The flavor seeped into her mouth the second she put the cigarette to her lips. Mentholated. Of course.

"What's the word, C?" he asked as she lit her virtual cigarette.

"Other than my sister? You, I guess," she said. "Figured it was time we had a talk. I wanted to see how you were doing."

"You picked a weird time to get sociable."

"I'd put it off so long there was no such thing as a good time anymore," she said. "So, tell me, is it everything you thought it would be and more?"

"There's a big 'all things considered' that prefaces anything on that subject," he said. "But it's been okay. I guess."

"I'm sorry I didn't speak to you sooner."

"No sorries required. It's pretty obvious why. You don't get spooked easy, so when it does happen, it's economy sized." He took another long drag from the cigarette and exhaled. "So. To the question, of how I'm doing... How are *you* doing?"

Cloke looked at Darma for a long time before answering, "I'm going to manage for the next little while," she said. "I have to, there's no choice really."

"See, you're talking about Em, but for me? That's me to the tenth power about life," Darma said. "I feel a lot like that first week of going to college."

"I never went to college."

"You never went to *that* kind of college. I'm talking about hitting that first philosophy class where the googly eyed professor suddenly starts spewing this shit about 'what is real? Am I? Are *you?*' I question everything now, except that it's not hypothetical, I already know what the answers are, except for the big one."

"Are you still you?"

"That's the one. Have you ever stopped and tried to remember what it was like when you knew you were you... and then tried to see if you still felt that way now? I mean, I feel like I'm me, and I think that means I feel the way I felt before. But that could be the code talking. And then there's this."

Darma stood up, dropped the cigarette he was holding and stubbed it out with his foot, rubbing his shoe solidly into the roof of the building. He got down on his haunches and looked at the ash and grime he had just rubbed out on the roof, sliding a finger across it and bringing it up to get a closer look at the smudge on his flesh. He held it up to her.

"This is real for me now. It always felt real before, that's the whole point of neurosimulation, right? But when you live here, when there's no switch to flip to exit, what does that make it? Suddenly my whole life is philosophy 101, only the class never, *ever* ends. And then I have to remind myself that now, if I feel like it, I can do this..." He held out his finger, it was clean. A moment later a cigarette appeared between his fingers and he stood back up and lit it. "And everything is all squirrely again. I have to make sure I've enabled the inebriation *settings* in the simulation if I want to actually get drunk from any of this stuff. And even then, when I get bored, I can just turn those settings off and go back to instant sobriety. That's my life now. Such as it is."

"There was some part of you that must have known it would be like this."

He sat back down beside her. "Probably, sure. I'm not dumb. But when you're reading the brochures and seeing the ads, all you're really thinking about is immortality. Not what kind of immortality it's going to be."

"Having second thoughts?"

"Just... thoughts. I don't think anything can really prepare you for waking up and being told you're code. Even when you paid a lot of money to have it happen. I'm basically God in a simulation. I keep thinking about all those people that need to get counseling to stop logging in so much, and now I'm living their dream. I'm not just in the simulation forever, it's me. I'm simulated."

Cloke nodded and wondered what kind of friend she was to him, to make him face all this stuff alone for so long. She wondered if what was happening now could even be called friendship. She didn't worry about hurting the feelings of her search agent, or house operating system, didn't try to remember installation dates to wish them happy birthday. When she played in a fantasy or science-fiction role-playing game that encouraged relationships with the other characters, she might have remembered them, maybe even liked them. But she never went back into those games to keep talking with them, or share virtual dinners, or ask them questions about what they wanted to do five years from now.

They were code. Just like Darma was now.

"I'm sorry," she said again, because it was the only thing she could say that was true.

"We both are," he said. "But I chose this. Got the receipt and everything. I guess this happens to a lot of people when they wake up and have to deal. It's just the nature of the beast."

"How do you find working?"

"You mean..." he raised his hands up, miming the action of his fingers dancing across the keys of a console.

"Yeah."

"Honestly, it's probably easier. And even more illegal than it was before. I can get *better* at it. Faster. And the only thing that would stop me from really wrecking shit once I get going would be ethics. I can see why they made it illegal to emulate convicted jockeys. Promising not to hack 'cause it's wrong isn't much assurance. I'm surprised you let Zee disable my limiters."

"It seemed inevitable to me," Cloke said. "If xie hadn't

gotten the idea, you would have given it to hir. No one calling themselves a jockey is going to let something like illegality stop them."

"And the point goes to the fireballer," Darma said, raising his bottle of beer in mock toast. He took a long sip. "If I'd refused, I wonder if they'd have gone and done it anyway."

"That wouldn't surprise me at all," Cloke said. "What do you think of hir so far? This thing with Em. I need hir to deliver. Can Zee do this?"

The wait for Darma's answer stretched on. He seemed to be trying to think about what he wanted to say. It made Cloke wonder if maybe the emulation process wasn't as complete as they'd made it out to be. Darma usually wasn't one to hesitate.

"Xie has promise. A lot of it," he finally said. "Xie's talented. Xie has a sense for it, good instincts. And xie's fast. 'Course, you can say that about a lot of hopefuls fighting for position on the ladder."

"Can we trust hir?"

"That's a stupid question. Did you trust me on my first job?"

"I mean eventually."

"Is there even a point to answering that? You've already let hir in deep. If you weren't even sure about that, why'd you let it go this far?"

Cloke shrugged. "You wouldn't like the answer."

Darma looked away, taking another long drag from his cigarette. "You and your fucking feelings."

"They were right about you and Marcus."

"Yeah, and look where that got me."

Cloke visibly winced as if the words had slapped her.

"Okay. Okay, bad form, I'm sorry," Darma said. "That was mean. Mean and untrue. Sometimes my mouth sees an opening and goes for it before my brain can issue the 'bad idea' command."

But Cloke knew there was a germ of truth in what he had said. And he probably knew it too.

And it was the one thing she didn't need right now. She was hurt. She was tired. Her sister was being tortured—even if it wasn't physically real, her nerves couldn't tell the difference—and she had barely been holding it together. What he'd just said loosened that grip, made it harder to keep it together.

"I tried," she said. "I really, really tried." She could feel a fist tightening around her heart as the words came out. This was why she'd put off talking to Darma. Not because she was afraid of him. Because she was afraid of this. "I tried everything. Sent a scramjet to the impact site, medivacked what we could to the best facility. Nano repair, cellular reconstruction… I screamed at the healers in the College and the ones GIS have on retainer to fucking *do* something…" She brought up a wrist and wiped the tear she could feel coming down her cheek. "Nothing. They couldn't do anything. No matter how much I threatened, no matter how much money I threw at it, no matter how much fucking magic I have in my hands…" She looked at Darma. "I couldn't fix this."

"Cloke…"

"No," she said, forcing the fist around her heart to tighten even more. She looked for the cold, hard center inside her that carried her through training, through combat, through all the things that tried to crush her, and she held onto it now. "No, it's okay. I… I just don't want to talk about it right now, okay?"

Darma nodded slowly. "Okay."

She nodded back, wiped another tear, and put out her cigarette, fishing out another and lighting it. "Tell me about Zee."

"Zee's good."

"Will xie get better?"

"Yeah."

"What are the problems with hir?"

Darma opened up his mouth, paused. He closed his mouth again and shook his head.

"What?" Cloke asked. "What is it that's so hard to say? Is xie going to fuck us over? That's pretty textbook. It's expected, really, considering hir position. Is xie already cutting deals with other teams? Is Zee a sleeper?"

"I… can't say."

That made Cloke sit up in her chair. "Can't or won't?"

"Zee will get the job done," Darma said. "Whatever instinct you had about hir skills, it was a good one. Xie can do this. Xie will get better, will be an asset. If you want me to talk beyond what xie can do on the job, if you want to talk head space..." He seemed to flounder again, mouth open, unable to find the words. "I can't say."

She looked straight at Darma. She didn't want to bring up his coded nature as the reason he was being so un-Darma right now, she'd already done enough of that. "If you're not going to talk, you must have a reason," she said finally. She got up from the chair. "And I'm going to trust that whatever the reason is, it's a good one. Whatever else you are now, you came from a man that gave himself up to make sure his friends would be all right. I'm going to trust that some of that man is still in there." She took a final drag of her cigarette and then put it out. "Thanks for the smoke. I'll be going."

"Were you telling the truth to Vic when you said you were going to the College?"

"Yeah," she said. "I'm going to make enough noise that they'll hear about it. I'll need to make sure all the proper channels are ready to ignore alarms when they go off."

"This is some serious shit, then."

"It is. I'm going to need everyone to deliver. You, Zee, Marcus, me... everyone."

"I'll do what I can."

"That's what I like about you," Cloke said. "You always do." She signaled to the emulation and found her perceptions dissolving her back into her hospital room.

Her aches and pains returned, but she didn't mind. The pain was real. And it was temporary; she'd get better.

Whatever they were doing to her sister, it wouldn't stop unless she made it stop. She nestled into the bed and tried to sleep without using neurosimulation to cheat her into it. She thought of her dead friend, her uncertain new recruit, her disapproving guardian.

But mostly she thought of Azevedo. Or one of them anyway,

and how he had thought that threatening her family was going to put her on a leash. He was Brazilian. He should have known better.

Cloke lay in bed and felt the constant, bright pulse of anger smoldering somewhere in the depths of her gut. It didn't bring sleep, but it did bring purpose with the cold, mechanical precision of a switchblade sliding into position.

Chapter X:
Prep & Launch

THE ROOM THEY assigned had the calm, clinical white that carried unpleasant memories of Zee's childhood. Numerous exams, blood samples, DNA checks and rechecks. It made it hard to concentrate on the task at hand.

Cloke wasn't helping much in that regard either.

"You're sure you've got everything you need?"

"Yes," Zee and Darma said at the same time.

"What about your emergency power back up?"

"I have two set up," Zee said. "An Arclight and a TripSwitch. Between the two of them that's nine hours of power even if the main power feed gets killed and the building's auxiliary generator blows up."

"Let it go, C," Darma said with what Zee was pretty sure was an attempt to keep a lid on his irritation. "It's covered. Xie's as good to go as xie's going to be."

"Do you need another pair of eyes on an external monitor? I can do that."

"No," Zee said.

"It's just another access point to worry about," Darma said. "Xie's taking all the smart precautions. Let hir."

"But—"

"I can *do* this," Zee said, hoping it sounded competent and badass and irritated all at the same time. Darma had used that tone of voice a few days ago, and he'd sounded like something from a good action movie.

"I know," Cloke said. "I know, I know. But there's... there's got to be *something* I can do."

AND THAT'S WHEN it clicked. When it finally sunk in what was going on, why it had been so hard to place this weird mood Cloke had been in all day. Zee had never seen it before. Cloke felt helpless. And it didn't really sit right on her. At least not with the current picture that Zee had formed of her.

On the display, Darma's face softened. "Hey. Hey, come on, C. Let hir do hir job. Xie's got hir own mojo, just let it moje."

"'Moje,'" Cloke said. "My God, you actually just said that. Fine, fine." She closed her eyes and straightened her posture. She took in a deep breath, let it out and looked at Zee. "Just help her," she said. "You have to help her. *Someone* has to."

"Yeah. Sure, of course," Zee said, realizing immediately that came off as too flustered. Like someone that cared beyond a professional capacity. "That's what you're paying me for."

"She's not paying me, but I'm doing it anyway," Darma grumbled. "I'm just that kind of super admirable guy."

Cloke raised her hands in surrender. "Okay, I'm going. I'll leave the maestros to their work." She pointed to the next room over. "I'm going to be there. Right *there* with your support crew. You need anything, you tell me, I'll make it happen. Just get her out of there."

"Hey," Darma said. "Come on. It's Em."

"Just make sure she stays that way," Cloke said. She reached out, and put her hand on Zee's shoulder. "And whatever you see in there, whatever you learn about her, just remember, she's my sister. She's my family."

"Uh... okay."

Cloke stared Zee directly in the eye for a moment, then nodded and pushed away. "Go to work guys," she said as she left the room. "Don't spooge this or I'll fucking kill you."

Zee laughed.

"Love you too!" Darma said, waving and smiling back at Cloke. "She's actually not joking about that; she might really fucking kill you." His wave grew more frantic. "Also, that's probably the closest you're ever going to get to her actually asking for a favor. And it didn't take six years, so you're making better progress than I did. Now, let's do this and blow up this popsicle stand."

Zee connected with the console and did a complete status check. Everything on the system was good. A quick look at the "side projects" revealed that GIS was still unaware of the fact that a few of their central processing banks had smaller, non-essential portions hijacked to house an array of hacked virtual intelligences. The VIs had been modified to pass human authenticity tests and sign up for various advertising programs that, collectively, awarded something called Consumer Awareness Credits. Most people just called them "Ad Bucks" since it amounted to the same thing; people were awarded credits based on how much advertising they voluntarily watched, listened to or filled out surveys for. The credits could then be spent on various products offered by the conglomerates as loyalty rewards.

Zee had already adjusted Eve, her onboard virtual intelligence, to act as a clearing house agent, collecting the ad bucks and fielding requests on the grey market for those same ad bucks, and the products specifically on offer for purchase with ad bucks. It was all proving to be very lucrative, and Zee was amazed more people within GIS hadn't taken advantage of this themselves. The money was piling up. It felt nice. Secure. For what, Zee hadn't figured out yet, but it felt safe.

Darma watched and shook his head. "I admit, it's a neat little operation you've got going there, but seriously… Stop it."

"Gotta make a nest egg somehow."

"You're already getting *paid*," Darma said. "Good rates. Really good. Cloke's always been fair about that stuff."

"Yeah, but you're working under the assumption that I'm

at the beginning of a long and healthy career. Sure as hell doesn't feel like it from where I'm sitting."

Darma sighed on screen and spun himself in his chair, staring at the ceiling. "Someday, I'm going to find a hotshot neo-jockey that isn't like every other neo out there."

"What kind of neo would that be?"

"One that isn't fucking hirself over, because xie's got no faith, too much paranoia and too much greed," he said. "And yes, that was me too, back in the day."

"Anyone that doesn't grab an opportunity when they see it is an idiot," Zee said.

"I'd amend that to add that they'd also need an eye to see the *real* opportunity. Stealing scraps from the campfire when someone is teaching you to shoot is… myopic."

"Thanks for the advice, lecture-bot 9000," Zee said.

"Jesus, you're turning me into my mom," Darma replied. "Okay, no more sagely wisdom. You keep your nose on that console and just remember this isn't a system hack. Someone's locked up. You're getting her out."

Zee nodded. "Systems check."

"I'm good," Darma said. "All my ware is idling on standby."

"Eve, how are we doing?"

"Nominal," the console said. "Atelier Media residential intranet has granted full access."

Zee looked over the profile one last time, the simulation version of an 8 x 10 glossy hanging in 3D space. The signature eyes, the warm lines around the mouth, the trademark crooked smile, framed, at least in this image, by a nearly glowing frizz of anime teal for the hair. She was the reason half of the Internet stayed online these days, and all of the reason anyone on the SimNet did so.

Miriya.

It was still unbelievable that not only was Miriya a living, breathing person, but Cloke was actually related to her.

Miriya was the definition of someone who was famous simply for being famous. A personality that had burbled up across various online communities, engaging, interacting, pulling in people with wit, charm, humor and a surprisingly good singing voice. She looked sublime, but that didn't matter, since everyone on the simulation net could look as sublime as they wanted. She was a comedienne, a hostess, a singer, a friend. No one had ever seen her live. She interacted with anyone and everyone on the Net, but any appearances in the real world were relegated to displays and holography.

It had become pretty common knowledge that Atelier Media, the company that represented and handled her affairs, was probably fronting some custom artificial intelligence. The fact that they would neither confirm nor deny this when questioned point blank simply gave everyone more reason to believe this was the case. It didn't matter. Whether she was real or not, everyone loved Miriya, and she, it seemed, loved everyone right back.

Now Zee was told that not only was Miriya an actual human, but that she worked somewhere on this floor, in the very best medically supervised immersion suite money could buy. Zee had heard rumors about facilities that offered that kind of service, but it always seemed like an urban legend, something to make the kids stare at their sim unit in shame and despair as they logged out for the night.

Zee's simulated workspace showed a few notifications for call requests. One was from Cloke which was ignored immediately. The other was a hail from a caller with an official tag identifying it as an artificial intelligence under GIS stewardship.

A check, a recheck, a re-recheck and a call to GIS tech confirmed that the incoming call request was legit and approved by GIS itself.

Zee hesitated, staring at the blinking notification.

This was beyond the horizon of all but a tiny handful of jockeys. Artificial intelligences were not of this computerized earth, living in the lofty peaks of some digital Olympus, mostly isolated from the rest of the world. Trying to hack an AI within the SimNet was one of the few direct interactions that could be lethal thanks to the AI's inhuman mastery of neural stimulation. They were the new workhorses of the 22nd century, few in number, but regularly contributing to every field of human knowledge and pushing the entire species forward. They were feared because of how necessary they had become.

Curiosity won out. Zee engaged all the surveillance and anti-intrusion protocols onboard the console, ensuring that the AI couldn't hack into the workspace or its systems. At least, not easily. Zee accepted the call request.

A woman entered the workspace. Or more precisely, the concept of a woman filtered through a lens of gold and light. She presented herself entirely in the most valuable and beautiful substances defined by human art and economics. She had an odd sense of modesty; utterly naked, but devoid of critical features such as nipples or genitals. She presented like a superheroine, or a female anime pilot wearing an impossibly clingy flightsuit. Zee had to wonder whether this avatar was an attempt to please her human creators, or a statement about the AI's own sense of self-worth.

"Hello, Zee," the AI said in a lilting completely human voice. "You probably don't want my official Turing designation. Most people call me Athena."

"Can't imagine why," Zee said.

The AI gave a tiny smile. "I'm just letting you know that someone upstairs at GIS has allowed an allocation of some of my resources to your... venture. If you require it." She gave Zee a straight, level stare and said, with the smile still on her face, "Although I guess you're doing all right with an emulated hacker riding shotgun."

"I don't know what you're talking about," Zee said.

"Relax. Mr. Chapman told me everything. I can keep a secret." Athena shrugged, and particles of gold light fell from her hair and shoulders, disappearing before they could make contact with the floor. "If I couldn't, I would've been deleted long ago. General Information Systems can't conduct itself without a capacity for discretion. Now, are you going to show yourself, Darma, or am I going to have to break out the chocolate fondue?"

Darma projected into the workspace, a cigarette stuck behind one ear. "Evenin', Thena," he said. "Long time, no interface."

Athena appraised him. "You look good. Being dead suits you."

"And you're still a bitch. I still keep wondering if that's all your own invention, or whether someone coded it in."

She smiled. "I have a reputation to maintain. I also have a couple of offers. One for Zee and one for you."

"Yeah, about that," Zee said. "You said allocation of resources?"

Athena nodded. "In the purest sense. I've got clearance to offer you some cycle time. How would you like access to quantum computational speeds?"

Zee felt like the AI had suddenly offered a lamp with three wishes. This was right at the cutting edge of computer tech, all made possible through thaumaturgical research. Faster than light digital systems, breaking the barriers imposed by silicon's molecular limitations. Only a few military organizations and the wealthiest of corporations could afford the cost of the arcane maintenance required for such complex systems.

"What's the catch?" Zee asked, still not quite believing this could just fall from the sky like that.

"Oh, the usual provisions," Athena said. "Don't screw this up. I'm just here to make the job easier. And remind you that, for the moment, the job is more important than you are."

"Cloke said that?"

"No. But could she be thinking anything else in this situation?"

"You used the word 'couple,'" Darma said. "What's the other offer?"

Athena turned to face Darma and lowered her eyelids. "Oh, that one's private. For your eyes only."

Zee was already moving to boot Athena out of the workspace when Darma held his hand up and shook his head. His stare went back to Athena. "Well that's not like you," he said, crossing his arms.

"And what do you really know about me?" Athena asked. "We've worked together, had a few laughs, done a few favors, but now I want to do something more. Just for you."

Zee wondered if this was some kind of creepy AI sexual proposition when Darma said, "I'll give you 60 seconds in my office."

"I'll only need 30," Athena said.

"Done."

And they were gone. Zee had just enough time to do a quick adjustment to some Ad Buck transactions coming in when Darma popped back into the workspace. The clock said only a little over 14 seconds had passed.

"So?" Zee asked. "What was that about?"

"She hacked me," Darma said. "More accurately, she gave me access to a portion of my emulator code that moderates my perception of time."

"Does that mean what I think it means?"

"If you think it means I can now think and work as fast as a computer, without the artificial limitation of human processing speeds, then yeah, it does. She said it was her little housewarming gift. Welcome to the neighborhood and shit. It's not quantum computational speeds, but still... subjectively it felt like we'd been at it for at least an hour."

"What else did she say?"

Darma brought up a display with a clock ticking down. "We don't have time right now for all of it."

Zee maintained eye contact and let the silence grow for a few seconds before finally saying, "You knew her. How well?"

"Better than my last girlfriend, apparently," Darma said. "I've worked with her a few times over the years at Cloke or Chapman's request. She would bug me from time to time for a visit."

"That's it?"

"That's it."

Zee didn't buy it, but wasn't going to turn it into a production number now. Darma was right, they needed to start soon. "Well, if you're new and improved, that'll help. Since you seem to know the AI, you coordinate, you've got the speed for it."

"Roger," Darma said. "I'll get to work on patching things up between everyone."

Zee saw the confirmation of a local communications patch almost as soon as Darma signed off. He hadn't been kidding; the AI had already made him less human, which was probably not a good thing. Cloke would need to know.

But only once she stopped having anxiety attacks about her sister being a neural hostage.

Time to go to work.

Zee called up the situation displays that showed off the target in different formats, from pure code to simple three-dimensional iconography that represented typical net navigation to the administrative data that Miriya's medical hosts were now helpless to change.

Miriya had been blocked off.

The most interesting thing had been the way the Azevedo emulation had done it. There was an almost unnecessary amount of complexity to the system infiltration. Aesthetic, but hardly the most efficient way to do it, though ultimately that made it tougher to crack. Rather than opting for a single point of intrusion to taking over the systems, Azevedo had come in across multiple access points, from the lines for financial transactions to the network for environmental regulation. He had effectively imitated the Internet itself, with no single node that could be decisively locked out to negate the rest of his attack. It was like a hydra; there was no one head to kill that another head couldn't replace.

Preparing to take it down had been the best work Zee had ever done.

The access GIS afforded helped. A lot. Poring over everything Azevedo ever said or did, had granted a better picture of the man. Or at least, a version of the man when he had been alive and not in league with one of the largest aeronautics corporations in the world. Cloke had even allowed a link with the College's own archival network.

But beyond all that, and perhaps most important of all, was the ability to look at Azevedo's work. His code.

It was like looking into the secret gallery of an artist, hearing the most intimate compositions of a musician, watching a dancer who thought that no one was around. It was work that bared the soul of the person that had made it.

Zee was able to see straight in the heart of the man called Azevedo, and pulling back, further and further, the nuances of his code became apparent. His idiosyncrasies, his preferences for timing, how he arranged his conditions. It was a picture of how he created his code, and it was everything Zee needed to understand where the holes in programming were that even he didn't know about. It wasn't something that could ever be explained to another jockey, or any programmer really. A poet had a better chance of understanding how this worked. The art of intuition, the sensation when something just felt right. These were the things Zee now apprehended about Azevedo's habits with coding.

And there was something else that had come to light. Something that helped in numerous ways Zee couldn't put a name to. It became clear that even though Azevedo had years of experience with coding, it wasn't his strength or his passion. It wasn't an art or a calling, and that was going to work against him today.

It had been fast work. Grueling, unreasonable work considering how quickly it had needed to be done. But it had been done.

Zee's initial plan remained unchanged, but the addition of quantum level computational speeds and sudden boost to Darma's own processing capabilities opened things up considerably. What was originally going to be a slow burn could be more of a flash fire.

It was a three-pronged retaliation. Darma's secondary duty was to babysit the suite of chaff viruses Zee had cooked up. They were designed to keep Azevedo's program busy monitoring numerous futile attempts to lock down or delete it. Interspersed within the noise were counter intrusion measures that slowly locked out the invading program's access to other parts of the network.

When Darma wasn't nudging or adjusting the intensity of the chaff virus he was also supposed to be waging his own war across the numerous connections Azevedo had established. This was made considerably easier with help from Athena. The AI could now turn what was originally intended to be an annoyance into a viable threat. Quantum speed computing turned certain actions from nearly impossible to inevitable, such as using old-fashioned process of elimination to "brute force" through access into Azevedo's data, a guessing game that would take a conventional computer far too long to reasonably complete. If Athena managed to actually gain control of Azevedo's systems, it was an unexpected bonus. If only one or two went down, or Azevedo simply realized he was vulnerable and had to devote more attention to his defense, it was still an improvement over merely trying to irritate him.

And finally, there was Zee's job. Finding and securing Miriya. Fighting off Azevedo's intrusion. Trying not to get anyone killed.

Zee watched the timer count down to zero.

Go.

Zee tapped the ENTER key and dove into the network simulation. It was a custom view, a little bit different from the usual consumer SimNet navigation experience of floating in a simple, geometric abstraction of the data in the area. A hack like this required certain data to be present at all times, and interpreted in a fast and easy way. Presenting the SimNet as a virtual world, while easy for the average human being to navigate, wasn't practical as a hacking interface. Even pure code could be cumbersome for that sometimes, so Zee had retooled a version of the existing workspace to display all the ancillary data on other panels, floating in the air, resizing and moving into view as required. Meanwhile, Zee rotated around a huge, single structure, about the size of a typical office block tower. The tower's windows cycled through individual colors, each window represented network activity, whether it was routine interactions within the system, transactions with outside entities, or activities being subverted by Azevedo's invasion.

It was a skyscraper filled with bad shit. Zee was going to clean it out.

Zee opened up the arsenal of viruses, a flood of predatory data that swept through the system identifying all the processes that had been co-opted by Azevedo's work. The way to fight this was not to fight Azevedo's code at all. That was like trying to fight cancer with a wooden club. Azevedo might not have been a natural hacker, but he'd had the benefit of time and study on his side, and his intrusionware, however conventional it might have been, was clean and well written.

So, Zee took the opposite approach, with a virus that was written up to modify discreet packets of code and co-opt them to seek out similar, specified code and functionality, then execute its attack parameters. Parts of Azevedo's virus were being goaded into attacking Azevedo's virus itself, creating a feedback loop that could eventually overwhelm the network intrusion. If it was left alone long enough, Azevedo's virus would eat itself.

Zee saw the effects on the tower block that represented Miriya's medical monitors and its surrounding online environment. The secondary systems of the attack kicked in, protocols designed to track and flag any errors or fluctuations in Miriya's life support systems that might arise from the struggle to overtake Azevedo's intrusion. Normally it was the sort of thing Zee ignored, but glitches in life support could mean oxygen cut off, medication overdose, or simply too much improperly filtered neural input. Any of it could be lethal or traumatic. The identified life support glitches were immediately forwarded to an entire stand by medical team with neuro-linkage specialists to monitor and address any problems.

It felt very weird, working like this—with other people who were very, very good at what they did, concentrating on their jobs so Zee didn't have to worry about that stuff. It was a far cry from being the only person who seemed to know what was going on, getting the blame when things went wrong, getting pushed off to the side when things went right, and the money came rolling in.

And then it was time.

It only took 20 minutes, putting the plan ahead of schedule. The system restoration had progressed enough that the other crews had regained some measure of life support control. It was safe enough for someone to get into the guts of the simulation and cut Azevedo out of access. And of course, Zee was going to be the person to do it.

"How're we doing, kid?" Darma asked. He appeared in the space, a cigarette in his hand. "Just thought I'd let you know that between me and Athena, we've actually managed to piss in Azevedo's garden."

"How?"

"I cooked up a nasty little dox virus and we managed to squirt it down the line back to Azevedo's main network. It's going to search, record and release all the network activity that would confirm they have an illegal emulation in use. Anyone on the other side of that will have their hands full going into track and lock down mode."

"It's Azevedo doing the work himself."

"How do you know?"

Zee consulted the security tower. Everything was still going according to plan. The countermeasures were working as intended and things were getting cleaned out. The program was going to work. A quick window in the timing of Azevedo's virus frantically resisting the assault opened up an opportunity for a peek. It was easy to capture an image of that moment and put it on the display for both of them to see.

"There. See it? He wrote in a dead man switch but he put it in as an object in Miriya's simulation. He's made something that can only be manned from inside. He's in there. Right now. With her."

Darma shook his head, looking at the security grid. "You're a nasty piece of work, you know that?"

"What's that supposed to mean?"

He nodded his head in the direction of Zee's network board, the virtual building that was being cleaned of Azevedo's virus. "This code of yours. The way you wrote it... The way you anticipate his code... It's like you crawled into his fucking head and knew exactly how he thought. How is anyone supposed to figure out he likes to put a certain data tag every hundred lines of code? But you know it. Somehow."

"I just did my homework."

"You don't study the way the other kids do," Darma said. "It's good work what you do. But be careful with it." He looked off distantly, probably consulting information displayed on his virtual cornea that only he could see. "It's almost show time. And that switch in the sim just confirms your plan is a go. Are you ready for this?"

The correct answer was "Fuck, no," since Zee had never thought a situation would arise that would necessitate logging into a rogue simulation to kick out a kidnapper and end his fantasy prison routine. Zee nodded instead.

"Athena's checked with the neuro-linkage team," Darma said. "You're green on their board, they'll monitor and support you the whole way once you're in. Don't worry about that, they know what they're doing."

Another nod, but it was difficult to trust Darma's words. Not that he was lying, it was just hard to accept that being kept alive was in the hands of a bunch of other people. It felt like giving up a lot of vital control, and that was nerve-wracking.

Darma loomed in close. "Hey. You okay? You don't look so good."

"Nerves," Zee said. "Feel a case of the shakes coming on. Who put me up to going into the sim myself?"

"You did," Darma said.

"Why did you all agree to it?"

"Because you were right. It's the fastest way to put an end to this. You disengage it from the inside, it's gone. No chance of fragmentation, no comebacks, no second chances, you kill it."

"If I don't kill her."

"You have a better chance of keeping her alive from the inside too," Darma said. He put his hand on Zee's shoulder. "It's okay. You're already doing better than I did on my first run. I threw up."

"I already did that. An hour ago."

"Then welcome to the club. Now go. Wreck that shit and bring her home."

Zee threw out a half-assed salute and consulted with Eve. "What's my status?"

"Nominal, except for neuro-linkage protocols, which were previously specified as falling out of metric range for this operation."

"What are they at?"

"Fluctuating between negative 12 and 106 NSUs approximately every millisecond."

"So, bouncing around between a dead and dangerous signal," Darma said. "You got your work cut out for you." He returned the salute back. "I'll see you later, kid."

Zee grunted at him as he faded out of the workspace and gave the neurolink portion of the onboard simulation program one final check. It was going to be down to Zee's own modifications to the code combined with whatever support the medical team, Darma and possibly Athena the AI could muster to ensure that interfacing with Miriya's locked down simulation was actually survivable.

"Count to five, then go," Zee said quietly to Eve.

"One," Eve said.

Zee stabbed the ENTER button on the workspace's virtual console and hit the simulation hard.

There was a split second of pain: fragmented, reflected, shimmering everywhere like a galaxy with a million shining white lights of infinite, monstrous agony. It was the lethal neural feedback Zee had been expecting, the one the entire support team had been prepped for. The baffles cut in, filtering and minimizing the neural signals Zee was invasively trying to integrate with, the ones designed to kill any outsider trying to interface right now. Somewhere on the outside, the medical support team was monitoring vitals, supplying counter-neural input, selectively disconnecting Zee's own neuro-link at key points to deflect the multiple signals to stop the heart, the lungs, to go into a seizure, to overload the pain receptors.

Zee screamed through it, focused on the goal, kept at the code, made sure it did what it needed to do.

It's only pain. You've lived with pain. You know pain. You know this and you'll get through it like you have every single time.

Of course, it wasn't only pain. This was a neurosim, it sent fabricated signals to every sensory organ the brain apprehended. There were other things too, random sensations that Zee's brain tried to make sense of; deliberate, hostile code that looked for anything tagged as a negative. The antiseptic smell of the lab Zee had spent the early years growing up in. The particular dim shade of yellow from the lamps in the "playroom" where the innocence of Zee and all the others had been lost. The sound of his breathing, calm, methodical, right in the ear as he poked and prodded.

The sense memories were almost worse than the pain. Forgotten miseries that made themselves known once more. But Zee had been expecting these too; perhaps not this degree of intensity, a testament to Azevedo's skill, but it was still something that could be passed through; endured.

It had to be. It was either endure, or die.

Chapter XI:
Off the Grid

"ZEE'S GONE," ONE of the neuro-tech supports announced.

That made Cloke sit up in her chair and take her legs off the desk. "What do you mean gone?"

"The signal's lost. We're still getting vitals because xie's plugged directly into that, but hir net presence just dropped off. We don't know where xie is."

"Process of elimination suggests Zee's probably already inside," Victor said. He was good to his word. GIS were not officially participating, but as an observer, he could still make the occasional suggestion. He was already on his feet, walking towards the display Cloke had at her desk. "Give us a feed on Zee and the network activity log."

The two requested pieces of data appeared on Cloke's display, one showing Zee, plugged into the neuro-link to their console and looking for all the world like some absurdly elegant personal assistant that had fallen asleep sitting up at the desk. The other piece, a simpler graphic representation of lines and color tracked Zee's progress through the hack. It showed the amorphous blob of attack and denial xie had dropped over the network intrusion like rain on a forest fire. Somewhere in the middle of all that aggressive data had been Zee's own entry into the barrier that locked out everyone else. It was like trying to pick out one carbon-reinforced, razor-sharp snowflake in a snowstorm.

"Which one was Zee?" Cloke asked.

"That one," Darma said, through Cloke's speaker. One of the shards in the attack lit up, blinking steadily in green. Darma's image appeared, snapping into a new window on the display. "Not that it does us much good now. I was riding shotgun with 'em and it was like the half of the car they were in went straight into the tunnel, but I hit the wall."

"I expect someone is trying to kill Zee now," Victor said.

"Confirmed," one of the techs said, cutting into the operations channel. "We've lost hir tracking data in the network, but vitals are showing massive spikes."

"Trying to stop hir heart?" Victor asked.

"Everything," the tech said. "Whatever foothold they can get, they're trying to get it. Shutting down the brain, lungs, anything. Counter measures already in effect."

This probably should have killed Zee, Cloke realized. But most console jockeys didn't enjoy the combined support of medical staff with a secondary team of operators trying to fight off the malignant code themselves.

"Will it be enough?" Cloke asked Darma.

"It's touch and go," Darma admitted. "They can only do so much from out here, with direct access to hir cut off. They can help. Even Athena is in on it, but none of us are in the middle of it—there's a lot of code we *can't* see and can't deal with."

"You can take the edge off the attack," Victor said. "Not much more than that."

Darma shrugged. "I'm sorry, man."

"Where did we screw up?" Cloke asked.

"Nowhere," Darma said. "The support team is rock solid. The network security has worked as intended. Even Zee didn't fuck up anywhere, the prep work was slick as shit, you'd know if you could understand what xie did."

"Then why are we locked out? Why can't we help hir?"

"Honestly? Because he had a plan and we didn't, I think."

"Explain," Victor said.

Athena appeared in another display window. "I've been

looking at the attack methodology. We both have," she said, a head nodding in the direction of Darma on the next display window. "The level is meticulous. Even if Miriya wasn't always the intended target, this incursion has been built up over quite some time. Maybe someone was just looking for an excuse to finally execute, see how it does in the field. We're just the victims of someone's morbid curiosity."

"Is there anything we can do?" Cloke asked, feeling her nails dig into her flesh.

Darma was tapping a table that had conveniently appeared below his hand. "I got something. It's not much, and it won't help lethal neuro-feedback, but it'll work."

"Do it," Cloke said. "Whatever it is, do it."

"On it," Darma said, and his window disappeared, leaving Cloke and Victor to stare at the team frantically working to maintain the beach head Zee had established in the network, while trying to stabilize Zee's vitals.

"Xie's very talented," Victor said. "Xie's done well."

"Then let's do just as well to keep hir alive," said Cloke.

"We'll do what we can, of course. But Zee's broken through to a level we can't yet reach."

"I know," she said, forcing herself to sit back in the chair. "It's all on hir now."

The hums, beeps and other indicators from the teams played out like a discordant song in the background as Cloke watched, unable to affect any of it.

Chapter XII:
The Prisons

ZEE RODE IT out.

It required keeping the code paramount, making the minute last-second adjustments required to keep death at bay until the counterattack did its work, flooding Azevedo's defensive code and burst through the other side. And it meant doing it all while every old agony Zee had ever tried to forget came back. And then the other side finally arrived.

Zee let out a breath as the pain, the terrifying, sour smell of his sweat, and even the music he liked to play during his visits faded away. The lethal neural feedback endured and broken. Focus on the job had held. Team working life support had succeeded. There was still a job to do.

Only there was nothing to work on. Zee was suspended in the middle of nothing.

This was the part where there should have been a secondary defense, some sort of auxiliary, if Azevedo had any semblance of competence.

There was none.

This was the "other side" of the virus, what was lying in wait for the recognized operator of the code, a small transitional unit linking to Miriya's simulation—almost like an airlock. This was confirmed when Zee opened up the link back to the support teams.

"Med team, what's the status?"

"Holding. Subject's status hasn't changed, but the intrusion is getting cleaned out."

"Got a fix on me?"

"Affirmative. You're at a maintenance node for the simulation. We confirm that you have lock, and your signal is still strong."

"Darma, you got a second? I need you to take a look at something."

Darma appeared, arms crossed. "What is it?"

Zee gestured at the space around them. "Is this it?"

"Is what what?"

"Scan this shit. Tell me what you think."

Darma took a low look around the area and shrugged. "We're in a node, what else do you want me to tell you?"

"Use it."

Darma called up his own virtual console, even though he didn't need to, creating a few rudimentary simulated objects that hung in the air like the toys of an infant's mobile. A stuffed rabbit, a brick, a wooden sphere. He looked at Zee. "I have creation rights here, what else did you want to know?"

Zee tried it as well, calling up a work station and spawning, in rapid succession, an assault rifle, a miniature whale with rainbow wings, and a status window reporting on the integrity of the simulation they were all supposed to be in the process of breaking without killing the person inside it. Consulting the status window showed all the available options for users, super users and people with admin rights, and every option was open to selection meaning Zee had admin rights.

"See?" Darma said, almost as if he sensed Zee's suspicion. "You're in."

Zee keyed in a sequence to view the subject. The status window responded by showing a generically well-decorated hotel room that was clearly simulating a resort in some tropical paradise, possibly Belize judging from the pristine blue of the water viewable in the distance.

There was a woman in the room, lying in a pool of her

own blood. Her clothes were in tatters, making it almost impossible to guess what they had been originally. The cuts on her body were too numerous to count. Zee couldn't tell whether she was breathing or not, but she lay perfectly still in the room, the only anomaly in what should have otherwise been a perfect brochure image for a tropical hotel.

The face was obscured, but the hair was right. It was Miriya, or at least, Miriya's latest hairstyle, bloodied and matted with abuse.

"Jesus fuck," Darma said. "Get her out of there already."

Zee nodded, systems already initiating the link to open up the simulation and formally enter it. Zee stopped just short of punching ENTER and getting this whole surreal nightmare unraveled.

"What's the deal?" Darma asked. "You want to watch her lie in her own blood for a bit more?"

"Give me another system scan," Zee said to both Darma and Eve. "What am I looking at?"

"A compromised high security simulation currently co-opted by third party intrusion viruses. One occupant. Neural signal erratic," Eve said.

"She's suffered enough," Darma said. "End it already."

Zee looked at him. This still felt wrong.

"I want a third opinion."

"From who? The back up?" Darma thumbed open a chat window. "Med team, we need confirmation on the status of the simulation. Can we get a read on the neurosim from this node?"

"Confirmed reading," the tech on the other end of the line said. "You've made a door; you just have to open it now."

Darma looked at Zee. "So, open it. What are you waiting for, an invitation?"

"I want a fourth opinion."

"What? From who?"

"Athena."

Darma stared. "Okay."

Zee was already on it, setting up the channel to Athena...

or would have, had it been possible. The commands to access Athena were still there, but the actual network channels that Zee had set in place were gone.

"I can't open a window. Can you?"

Darma's eyes glazed over for a moment. "No. Might just be this node. Limited access, that shouldn't be a big surprise. You'll probably have full communications once we take this all out."

"Maybe…" Zee said, liking this whole situation less and less. A node like this might have been the eventual goal, but it was too soon. Way too soon. There couldn't have been only one defensive layer. The viruses and malware being used were good, but not *that* good. Zee didn't have the chops yet to make anything that could have cut through military or corporate grade defense that quickly. If it was Darma's show, maybe. But Zee wasn't there yet and knew it.

Zee was running the options of how to approach the final entry when the console started acting up. It took just a few seconds to recognize the beeps as Darma's cute little trick, "Software Skin" playing on the hardware itself. Zee was about to turn to Darma to get on his case about this not being the time. The admonishment died on seeing Darma's horrified expression.

"Oh fuck, your hardware is bugging out?"

It was suddenly time for complete, full-scale silent alarm mode. Darma not recognizing his own gag pointed to one alarming possibility. Zee was careful to maintain a neutral face and voice, silently engaging the command to disable the face tracking function that would normally mirror every real-world blink and mouth twitch on the digital Zee that was presenting in this simulated space.

"Open it up," Zee said to Darma. "Let's see what happens."

"You do the honors," Darma said.

The inner alarms were clanging with sirens and wall-shaking subwoofers now. "I'd rather see how a pro does it. Maybe I'll learn something."

"This is your show," Darma replied, clearly getting annoyed.

"That's right, it is my show. And since it's my show, I'd rather have you in the spotlight for a while. Open the simulation up. I'll follow you."

"I can't," Darma said.

"Why not?"

"I guess my access must be more limited than yours. Can you unlock it?"

Zee consulted the command list. "Yeah, I can."

"Then you'd better do it."

Zee waited a moment, decided to make the play. "I'd still feel better about asking the Athena team about this."

"They'll probably just give you the same answer I am. Get her out of there."

Darma suddenly didn't know who or what Athena was. And Darma would only not know that if Darma wasn't Darma. Athena had obviously been a last-minute addition, and there had been no communication with the AI in the minutes prior to starting the run. Anyone eavesdropping on lines of communication wouldn't know about her.

"When are you due for your next emulation update?" Zee asked, which was one of those questions rich people were always too happy to answer, loudly, in public, to make it abundantly clear to everyone that they were all paid up for electronic immortality.

"What?"

"Check your calendar."

"I haven't scheduled it yet," Darma said. "Maybe I'll schedule it after this run, make sure my ghost is all up to date."

That was all it took. Darma didn't even know he was already dead.

"Eve, drop the logic bomb," Zee said, staring straight at Darma. He had just enough time for his eyes to widen and his mouth to open in some kind of protest, but the words never got out.

"Compliance," the virtual intelligence said.

The room imploded.

More precisely, the code that maintained this space—because Zee was pretty sure it wasn't a node at all—was now trying to hold itself together against some priority override code that was initiating a deletion of the area and anything not within a tiny partitioned sphere of influence that had been tagged to recognize only one person.

This time there was no pain, not for Zee. It was still impressive, watching the way the fake node struggled to live, trying to maintain its integrity even as the very core of its command code disappeared. Random sensory elements, test frequencies, visual and olfactory patterns struggled to fill the void before being swallowed up in turn. It was like this tiny pocket of digital existence was struggling to find some innocuous form that the bomb wouldn't burn, failing at every turn. When there was nothing left, the bomb turned its attentions on the Darma construct that still occupied the space.

Zee had only ever seen Darma scream once, and that was when he was being woken up for the first time into his new digital existence. This scream was nothing like that. He was being shredded, and even as his voice fragmented, distorted, ran up and down a series of scales and filters fading into nothing, it was clear that the scream was not of fear, but of rage. It was probably Azevedo and he was seriously pissed off now as the bomb tried to take a piece out of him too. He had no choice but to disconnect.

And like that, Zee was in non-space. Neither outside the simulation, nor inside it yet, but in an area the console had constructed adjacent to the final destination. It was grey, stateless, colorless, carefully neutral, waiting for that human touch to make something of it.

Zee keyed up two chat channels.

"Darma, Athena, you guys there?"

Darma didn't even bother to answer, he just appeared in the space. "And... xie's back, ladies and gentlemen."

"I confirm," Athena said crisply over the channel. "For a while there, your neuro-link was also locked out. What happened?"

"Azevedo got lateral," Zee said. "He laid out a secondary simulation for jockeys. Dump them someplace where they're supposed to be a button press away from victory and then sleaze them into opening up their own system to a lethal hack."

"Elegant," Athena said. "Clearly, you didn't fall for it,"

"I think he miscalculated my ego," Zee replied. "I'm pretty sure most jockeys would just congratulate themselves on being so badass and pump their fist in victory while flipping the kill switch. I was pretty sure I wasn't good enough to have gotten that far."

"That was a nice catch," Darma said. "I wouldn't have fallen for it either."

"An ego trap?" Athena said. "You'd have pushed that Kill Me Now button faster than anyone."

"Getting close to that red line on the bitch-o-meter, Atilla," Darma said.

"Athena."

"Not for the next five minutes."

"He misjudged the back up," Zee said, cutting in before the argument could really take flight. "He didn't know about Athena and he thought you were ali—..." Zee stopped short of saying "alive." The other word choice had been "real," but that wouldn't have gone over so well either. "He also didn't know about 'Software Skin,' so yeah. Thanks for that."

Darma looked smugly at Athena and nodded to himself. "Saved by the fucked-up bell, in other words. Oh well, at least you're here."

"And I want you to open it up."

"Sure. Why?"

"First, so I can keep an eye out for any more fun things designed to kill a living jockey."

"And second?"

"So that I know I really did break out of that trap, since the real Darma wouldn't give a fuck about participating in this run."

Real Darma proved his realness by shrugging and saying,

"Fair enough," then immediately spawned his favorite chair and simulation of his console to sit down and get to work. He stabilized the link to the simulation and started setting things up to enter it. No hesitation, no slacking, knowing exactly what he was doing and oozing pure pro the whole time. He was also working much faster than Zee ever could, probably just wanting to show off Athena's little mod to his capabilities.

"You're set," he said a few moments later. "I can hold it open for a minute or so. Less if you want me to go in with you, since I'll have to start shutting down certain routines early."

"I want you in, but not at first. Give me five minutes in there alone, then come in unannounced."

Darma smiled. "Getting used to it, aren't you?"

"Used to what?"

"Giving orders. You sound like Cloke."

Zee flipped a middle finger and watched the smile on Darma's face for the split-second before everything disappeared in the sudden entry to simulation.

As expected, everything was bug fuck.

According to the information provided by the neuro-sim staff of Atelier Media, Miriya was supposed to be touring a simulation of the Prague Christmas Market where an interactive ad was going to be developed. There were only supposed to be background characters in the merchant stalls, no other actual participants. But what Zee found wasn't an old European city with falling snow and dozens of charming old stalls selling useless trinkets and tourist shit.

This was a cathedral, bigger than anything Zee had ever seen, with windows made of insect wings and walls of giant, ancient bone. There was a dusty smell in the air that choked as Zee breathed in, and somewhere in the distance, with the regular rhythm of a bell, was what sounded like the flapping wing of a massive, ancient beast.

Neurosim had become the new ink blot test for personality evaluation, whole schools of psychology like the Bolanger theory of virtual cognition tearing down Freud and Jung faster than fashions passing out of season. What people made and interacted with when they could make and interact with anything said a lot about a person's psyche. Zee didn't even know what to make of this, or what it said about Azevedo.

In the center of the cathedral's space, highlighted by dusty shafts of broken light, were a pile of pews and bodies, as if some great storm had simply killed everyone attending mass and deposited them in one place. Zee could smell this too: a mixture of decay and old excrement. On top of this hill of gristle and waste was a single person, a woman, in rags, barely covered at all, all her limbs tied down to unseen points within the splintered wood and bodies. She was twitching constantly, as if in the throes of a seizure.

She was Miriya.

Zee stopped the first instinct, which was to run over and help. To yell and ask all the stupid questions like whether she was okay. She was clearly not okay. She didn't even have to be experiencing this. Azevedo could have just locked her off in a white room, in no room at all, and fed her pain through the neuro-link. To go to all this trouble was disturbing in a way Zee didn't want to think about.

Panicking now and trying blindly to free Miriya wasn't going to help. Might in fact be what this copy of Azevedo wanted. It took an enormous amount of effort to think of it all as code. To ignore the immersion and remember there was still programming at work. Access to restore, intrusion control to shatter, life support to maintain. All of that would do far more to help Miriya than running up the mountain of broken flesh and wood to try to break her restraints. It was a hero's instinct. Azevedo would be counting on it.

Zee was not a hero. Zee barely qualified as having any kind of defined moral stance. But there was one thing at work that was easy to feel: anger, and direct it at Azevedo.

Zee had been helpless and been abused while in that helpless state. Azevedo clearly had no issue with doing the same thing. That made it easy to hate him.

Zee called up displays to check on the external progress.

Everything was still going to plan, including the fact that this entire virtual space was going to get devoured by countermeasures—with everything inside it—unless specific intervention took place.

"So, are you going to show your face or what?" Zee called out.

The only response was a cry from Miriya. A piteous one as her back arched, and some unseen pain flowed through her like a current of electricity.

First things first, then. The dead man switch. He had to be in here, somewhere, maintaining it. However else his ego worked, it didn't respond to calling out.

Now, inside the simulation, Zee had access to much better information. From this side of the sim, it was possible to see exactly how Azevedo had booby trapped all the life support functions. The switch was confirmed. It was the only simple way to shut down everything. It was a relief to see that this version of Azevedo wasn't murderously psychotic; there was an actual hostage exchange mechanic in place, it really was possible for Miriya to be released.

Multiple scans washed over the local area of the simulation, checking for triggers, physical, verbal, whatever. So far it was clean.

"Miriya, can you hear me?" Zee called out, walking closer to the pile. "I'm here to help."

Miriya screamed again, and Zee wasn't sure whether that was her reply, or just a response to another wave of pain.

"Okay, fuck this torture shit," Zee said, looking over whatever commands were available. This time was for real, there were no administration rights, so it wasn't possible to just wipe everything clean on a whim. But it was possible to do away with some of the ancillary "layers" of the simulation. The pain was absolute, there was no getting around that without access to Azevedo's dead man switch. But the over the top cathedral of pain?

It was gone. The sounds, the smells, the dusty light, the cavernous walls... One by one Zee wiped them away. It was blunt and inelegant work. They simply blinked out of existence, no smooth transition, a cheap film editing trick with no style at all. It only stopped at the pile of corpses Miriya had been laid out on. That's when a response finally came, not aggressive, just enough to block the deletion.

"Is there a reason you want to keep the horror show around?"

Azevedo finally appeared, walking out of the corpse pile like a ghost. Unlike the environment he'd created, he looked completely approachable and normal. His age was indeterminate; a man that could be in his 40s or his 90s with extension treatments. His clothing was carefully neutral; a large shirt, almost a tunic that any affluent man might wear lounging about in his own home, loose pants, sandals. He'd even taken the time to affect a cologne, which Zee could smell now.

"You are a surprising problem," Azevedo said, in a calm, almost friendly voice.

"That doesn't answer my question."

"I doubt you were expecting any actual cooperation."

"I had hopes."

"Because you're young. That's what youth does."

"That probably means you're not going to tell me where your dead man switch is, either."

"If that's what you call it." He walked up the corpse pile, caring enough about his own virtual clothing and dignity that he seemed to be walking up an invisible flight of stairs, his feet not sinking into the quagmire of broken flesh and wood. He looked down at Miriya as if she were just another part of the pile. "The fashion of personality has always been beyond me," he said. "They love her. So many of them love her." He kicked her, and this time his foot was subject to proper physics, landing solidly at her hip and causing her to scream. "I don't see it, personally, but as I said, fashion and personality." He looked back at Zee. "I'm keeping this around, her pain, because it still has its uses. Even now."

"It's not going to last, you already know that," Zee said. "If I got in this far, you know you can't keep this going."

"And that brings us back to you. I was surprised you got in. But I was even more surprised I couldn't track you down. Even that partner of yours left a trail. But you? It's been a long time since I've come across anything unknown."

"How nice for you," Zee said, and hit him with a core command attack.

He responded as expected. There was a slight twitch to his face, likely from the effort of defending an attack he knew was coming, even if he wasn't quite sure when. The attack manifested visually as random streaks of light, crawling up from the ground, trying to get purchase on Azevedo, constantly slipping back to the dirt. Zee's code hit him and was blunted, only managing to gain the most trivial kind of access to his systems, random bits of loose information, no actual control. There were an impressive number of systems and active programs viewable at cursory glance from the attack. He wasn't fucking around and was loaded for bear.

"Surprise," Zee said, as the attack fruitlessly continued.

"A rather disappointing one," Azevedo said, his Brazilian accent becoming more distinct as he grew annoyed.

Then the second attack kicked in, followed ten seconds later by the third, and five seconds after that by the fourth.

Zee had kept it simple, with different colors to make them easy to visually track. White light had been the first attack, followed by black, green and red. The first attack continued its attempts to seize control, while the second interfered with Azevedo's own ability to control, the third attack feeding him a lot of data that he would need to sort through. The fourth attack magnified the effect of the second and third attack by falsifying data Azevedo would rely on, or moving its location, slowing him down. Zee coordinated everything through a new technique involving random "jumps" between attacks. Rather than simply activate four programs and let them do their thing, there was personal involvement, interacting with each separate program at random moments for small adjustments, tweaks and boosts here and there. It made each attack less predictable, more difficult to counter.

And it was working.

Azevedo was now lit up like some marquee sign for a downtown stage or theater. His face showed anything but boredom or disappointment now. Zee knew his code, and this concerted, multi-threaded attack knew where to go.

But even now, Azevedo still had some fight in him.

He didn't waste words or breath—virtual or otherwise—on curses or banter, instead choosing to collect his wits, time and resources to push back. Zee watched the response on the monitors, noted the ways access was being blocked, and saw that it would be a losing battle for Azevedo. All he could do was stall the attacks, for a couple of hours at best, but there was no way it could be resisted.

"Just give me access to the switch already," Zee said. "That math's not favoring you in this scenario."

Azevedo didn't respond, choosing instead to sit down beside Miriya, and cross his legs, almost as if he'd suddenly decided to meditate. He reached out a hand to Miriya, his fingers brushing against her forehead.

She arched her back and screamed.

Zee re-prioritized and went to Miriya's defense, automating some of the attack on Azevedo to concentrate on the manual, on-the-fly adjustments need to keep his pain and execution commands at bay.

It took just enough concentration away from the main attack that Azevedo was able to gain some ground. He was able to predict the commands from an automated attack program far easier than with a human at the helm.

"That's why pain is useful," Azevedo said. "Lesson learned."

"I've got a lesson for you," Zee said, trying to keep calm. There had been a split second where a kill command for Miriya had nearly gotten through. It was going to take much more effort to keep Miriya alive than it was to attack Azevedo. "Classic lesson, 20th century, World War II. Two front wars are bad news."

It had been more than five minutes. The fact that Darma hadn't announced his presence meant that he was likely in some kind of stealth mode, roaming the simulation. Zee was right. He cut in smoothly, taking a cue from Zee's life support efforts, and taking on the task of fighting the kill commands.

Zee resumed the full attack on Azevedo, watching with a mix of frustration and admiration as he lost ground again, but less than he had during the initial attack. He was already learning how to fight back against the attacks. The revised estimate on the attack duration had risen from two to five hours. Zee pressed on, opening up another com channel.

"If you still want to help, now is a good time," Zee said. "Back door is open."

"Even more help?" Azevedo said with something like contempt in his voice.

"You know those heroes that fight on the field of battle with honor and dignity?" Zee asked. "I'm not one of those. I'll take a win any way I can get it. Meet team Athena."

Athena didn't even bother to present within the simulation, choosing instead to bluntly drop the hammer of quantum computational speeds on Azevedo's defenses.

Azevedo's face changed again, to something closer to outrage or panic.

Athena worked like no other hacker ever would, brute-forcing her way through with a tedious trial-and-error, process of elimination technique that should have taken weeks on conventional silicon and carbon. Only her support systems still used that kind of traditional hardware, the rest of her processors using literally arcane techniques that combined the dreams of theoretical physics with applications of magic to create computing speeds that broke the light speed barrier. Athena and the few other artificial intelligences like her could literally think and operate faster than light.

Azevedo had no chance, not even against just a fraction of that process arrayed against him, not with the combined forces of Darma fighting his hold on Miriya while Athena assaulted him directly, opening the way with ease for Zee's attack programs.

He actually cringed.

Zee and Athena had come to the same unsporting conclusion, mixing in painful neural feedback along with the conventional attacks, and they were now bleeding into Azevedo's sensory input. Even if he didn't have a real body, the mounting pain was going to make it hard to focus.

If it was going to happen, it would be now.

Zee broke into a run, charging up the hill of corpses towards Azevedo and Miriya. Azevedo didn't have to talk about where the dead man switch had been hidden. Zee had seen enough, and had a pretty good idea where a man like him would put it. A combination of vanity and traditional thinking made it obvious.

It was just a bonus that this was going to be both humiliating and painful.

It's just data. Just data, Zee mentally repeated. But there was still a feeling of queasiness reaching towards Azevedo, punching up the strength parameters of the simulation to make sure that there was actual penetration.

Zee's hand crushed through Azevedo's rib cage. The shock was enough to make Azevedo spasm and Zee's suspicions were confirmed by a quick peek into the surface data available; Azevedo had worked the dead man's switch into his heart. It was in his interventricular septum, the wall between the two main chambers.

Zee pulled.

Now it was Azevedo screaming, as the wholly unnecessary recreation of his old physical body gave way to immense amounts of digital pain. It was the final break. Zee tore through his defenses, sending out viruses back through his connection to damage, delete or steal any information that might be on the other side. Streaks of random data were attacked or pulled, and it would only be later that there would be time to sort through whatever was salvaged. For now, the most important thing was breaking the twisted confinement and torture Azevedo had created.

Zee crushed the heart, feeling the wetness, hearing the nauseating "squish" of it as it collapsed into itself.

Azevedo had no choice but to disconnect. For a flesh and blood person, it would have been disorienting at best, possibly psychological trauma. For Azevedo, the suddenness of breaking away was going to daze him until his systems reset themselves, perhaps he'd need to roll back his internal clock, memory and systems to a more stable point of operation and lose the last ten minutes of his fake life.

Zee stared at the bloody, pulpy mess that had been Azevedo's simulated heart, and used more conventional commands to simply delete the remains away. Then it was Miriya's turn.

Darma was trudging up the pile when he stopped and whispered, "Oh fuck."

Zee looked down at Miriya. She had been stripped, beaten, cut and broken. Her limbs didn't sit naturally within their sockets or even rest at normal angles. Again, the internal mantra, *It's just data. None of this is real.* Miriya hadn't really been broken and had God knows what else done to her. Her real body was sitting safely uninjured in an immersion suite. All the pain had been neural impulses fed directly to her brain.

Which meant that as far as her brain was concerned, the pain had happened, even if it left no physical marks or deformities.

Zee opened up all access. Now that there wasn't an elaborate hack subverting every single incoming command, it was trivial to open up the channels to the med and neural support teams. They would do their thing.

Zee was done.

UNPLUGGING FROM THE simulation revealed the ceiling of the room as the real-world chair reclined to a nearly horizontal position. There was still a buzzing somewhere in Zee's brain, the last remnant of the very real adrenalin from taking on a serious operator with a serious lockdown and somehow not fucking up and getting anyone injured or killed.

Darma's image popped up on the nearby display, followed a second later by Athena.

"And that's a wrap," he said. "The tech support staff is analyzing how Azevedo broke in, and how you routed him. I'm guessing they'll want a report from you, and maybe scraps of your clothing to rub against their consoles for good luck."

Zee snorted. "As if they could learn anything from me."

"That was good work you did in there," Darma said.

"No, that was good work you guys did. It wasn't exactly a fair fight, was it? Three on one, and one of them was an AI. I just released the hounds."

"You stepped up in an emergency and delivered," Darma said. "I'd say that counts for something."

"It was an impressive performance," Athena said. "Your code is inspired. A lot more precise than what I do. I just poke my finger at a wall repeatedly until I finally find a hole, and then punch it."

"So how did we do then?" Zee asked. "I mean all of that was to make sure Miriya is not dead and okay. Is she?"

Darma shifted uncomfortably on the display. "The support teams are doing their thing but…"

"But what?"

"She was always delicate to begin with. I know Cloke doesn't like to hear that, but it's true. I'm sure she's fine physically. Psychologically… she was already damaged. I can see this making it worse."

"Miriya? The digital happiness girl? She's damaged goods?"

"See for yourself," Darma said. "Cloke's in her room now. You should go see her. I think you earned it."

"You'll also get sued into the Stone Age if you speak publicly about it, or this whole endeavor," Athena added. "It was in the contract you signed before going to work."

Zee sighed. "Must have missed that somewhere in the thousands of millions of clauses."

"Clearly," Athena said with a smile. She waved. "Anyy good work. I've already filed my report, but I expect th want to be hearing from everyone. I've given you clea with security, and I've embedded a bread crumb trail f to follow on your visor. Go be a knight to the princ

just saved, and tell Miriya I said 'Hi.'"

"I'll see you in the room," Darma said, and signed off.

Zee stood, stretched, and let out a long breath. The levels of stress after these jobs was going to take some getting used to.

As Athena promised, there was no interference on the way to Miriya's immersion suite. No one even bothered to look up as cameras and other security scans all went green as soon as Zee was identified. Even the human security at the doors gave only a cursory glance and then went back into intimidating, no-eye-contact sentinel mode when Zee approached the door.

Zee sucked in a small, surprised breath upon entering the room. Cloke was there, as was a doctor and nurse. And then there was Miriya, and she wasn't at all like what Zee had imagined.

Miriya was an addict.

It was obvious at a glance. The pale skin, thin, wasted limbs that only got minimal exercise from neural stimulation and of course, the Somutsu; a glorified mechanical diaper that enclosed her groin and waist, keeping the area clean and piping away the waste through connections that had been built into the hospital bed she was laid out in.

From the looks of her, she hadn't been living outside of simulations in any meaningful sense for at least ten years. Then Zee remembered that Miriya had been big for at least fifteen years, and had worked her way up to fame for years before that. This was not the kind of immersion suite most people used, which was usually some kind of comfortable chaise longue, and perhaps a bathroom and fridge with mini bar to minimize time outside of the simulation. A lot of money had been spent to ensure Miriya could stay plugged in almost indefinitely, and it suddenly made an awful kind of sense why her company had quietly encouraged people to think she was an artificial intelligence. They went by a lot of names, from the Japanese Hikikomori to simply online addicts to the unkind "vermits," a portmanteau of VR and hermit, that came into use in the 21st century when pre-neural simulation technology first came into use as virtual reality.

It didn't really matter what name was used; the public reaction was always the same; a kind of contempt for people that couldn't unplug.

But for now, the gear was off, her neural interfaces laid aside while Cloke sat beside her, holding her hand. And it was possible to see the resemblance between the two in that moment. Miriya had the softer lines, even though she was the older of the two. She was thin, drained and wasted away. She looked more Asian than Cloke, but her hair retained the same color. She was looking up at Cloke through half-closed eyes, her lips moving, saying something too quiet for Zee to hear.

Cloke's eyes shifted direction and met Zee's. Miriya noticed and turned her head slightly to look.

"Hey," Miriya croaked, and even though it was clear her throat hadn't been used in weeks, perhaps months, the voice was unmistakably Miriya's.

"Hey. I'm Zee," Zee said.

"Xie's the one that got you out," Cloke said, still staring. "And I am not going to forget that.

Miriya sighed. "Jesus, even your gratitude sounds like a threat. Just say thank you." She returned her look to Zee. "Thank you."

Zee nodded. Now, face to face with her, there was an urge to be noble, to say it was just the right thing to do that impelled this rescue, that anyone with decency would have done it. But it had been more Cloke's urging, the payday at the end, and curiosity of accessing all that GIS infrastructure and back up support that had been the real motivations. Zee was acutely aware that noble intentions weren't high on this list of motivations and was suddenly uncomfortable with that, staring straight into Miriya's eyes.

"Do you remember anything?" Zee asked.

Miriya nodded. "Too much. But it's over now, right?" Her eyes went back to Cloke. "Is it?"

"It is." She squeezed Miriya's hand. "You're safe now."

Miriya's body relaxed. She sank into the bed and looked like she was going to be swallowed up by it. Zee knew a lot of people that didn't look the way they did in Sims, but had never seen someone so physically ravaged by it. "So weird," Miriya quietly said.

"What is?"

"This is the first time I'm not mad at you for making me unplug just to talk to you."

"I needed you to see my hair," Cloke said. "And I think it was good for you to see who helped you."

"She's seen me before," Zee said.

"Have I?" Miriya asked.

"Yeah. You probably just didn't notice or remember. At one of your concerts you reached out and held my hand."

"Which one?"

"A year ago. The rings of Saturn venue."

"I remember that. You presented as a boy then."

"Yeah, well... it's complicated."

"Oh, I can do complicated," she replied with a smile. "I'm all about complicated."

The doctor finally stepped in. "For now though, I think we should keep things simple. We'd still like to do some assessments, and I think she's earned herself a rest."

"Sleep. Real sleep..." Miriya said quietly. "That would be nice."

Cloke nodded and leaned over, kissing her forehead. She stood up, still holding Miriya's hand and patted it. "Take care of her," she said to the doctor.

"Only the best for her," the doctor said. "That comes directly from upstairs."

Cloke put her hand on Zee's shoulder and guided them both out of the room.

"I guess I really should say thanks," she said as the door closed behind them.

"Not really," Zee said. "You're paying me. That's the thanks, I guess."

"And you earned it. But you also did some good. Saved a life."

"Yeah, but..." and Zee looked back at the room they'd just

left. Somewhere back there was a woman who had given up on all this. The realness. "What kind of life?"

Cloke took in a deep breath and let it out slowly. "She wasn't always like that," she said. "When we were kids, she looked out for me. But it's a long story. Bad men. Bad experiences. Then there was me, my magic, the perfect world of the SimNet... and the fact that she's really good in there. A goddess." She shrugged and looked at Zee. "Makes it hard to justify this world when the one she plugs into is the one that makes all the fame and fortune. Especially for the companies. Her wanting to stay in there all the time suits them just fine."

"So, all you can do is... make her comfortable?"

"You make her sound like she's got a terminal illness."

"Isn't it?"

"No." Cloke's gaze fell to the floor as she thought for a few moments. "It's a problem," she finally said. "A life-long, extremely profitable problem."

"With a solution that no one wants."

"I want it," Cloke said. "But it's not my call. And I've had that argument with her, and with Victor too. He's really down on her. It's an old fight. I lose by default because of my bias, Em says. Since magic is so anti-tech, I'm expected to be down on her for what she does. How she lives. And it's not like she's a junkie wasting her time on a useless, unproductive, self-destructive addiction. She makes a difference. She's happy in there. A lot of people depend on her for their livelihood." She finally looked at Zee. "Like I said, not my call to make. Victor tried to make it once. That didn't go down well. I don't think those two will ever speak to each other again."

She started walking down the hall and Zee followed.

"Is it safe to assume that this family attack isn't going to go unanswered?"

"That's a logical conclusion, yes. I might have accepted the proposal from the nice Azevedo, but the psychotic one just ensured this job gets done. We're going back home, we're going to rest up, and then I'm going to start setting up."

"Setting up what?"

"The dominoes," Cloke said. "If we're going to wreck this, we're going to wreck it right."

Zee watched as Cloke's face tightened. It wasn't exactly anger there, but it was almost as if she were looking at some distant point on the horizon and marked it, like it was a new destination.

They left the building and headed back to São Paulo.

Chapter XIII:
The Desert & the Daisho

CLOKE HAD ONLY been to Libya once before. That had been for just a few hours, at night, unable to see anything except the lights from munitions and explosives. None of that prepared her for what she saw now.

The Sahara was shrinking.

It was still a vast expanse of sand, a repeating wave of dunes that defied her ability to process it, stretching out to the horizon forever. But this threshold she stood on, with its tentative green and expanding line of trees and other plants hadn't been here last year. The desert, according to scientists, was supposed to contract on its own anyway around the year 17000 CE, but the various nations of North Africa had decided to hasten that timetable. And they had given the task to the College's Faculty of Meteoturgy. Or at least, that was the formal designation. Some people called them Tempests, or more exotically, Tempestarii. Most, however, just called them Weather Witches.

The particular Weather Witch that Cloke was looking for was surveying the border between the expanding green and the desert that was fighting to keep its territory. She was standing on a dune, long curls of hair waving in the breeze, her face a picture of contemplation. To many, she was one of the few faculty members that had both the instinct and the sheer raw power to manage weather on a regional scale.

To Cloke, she was Gwen Stepniski, of Marin County, NoCal, and her guilty secret pleasure—which she shared with Cloke—was movie musicals.

"You can stop looking all majestic as you survey the dunes," Cloke said, walking up to her. "I know you've got a cooler of beer stashed around here somewhere."

"You kill all joy wherever you go," Gwen said.

"It's my job and sole source of happiness in life," Cloke said, and hugged her. Gwen laughed and hugged back tightly. A lot of things had changed over the years, but one thing that hadn't was that Cloke and Gwen always seemed to revert to seventeen-year olds whenever they were in the same room together. Studying and training at the College hadn't been much fun, but for Cloke, what little fun there was usually had Gwen attached to it.

Cloke looked out at the Sahara stretching out beyond the horizon. "You're slacking," she said. "I still see a ton of sand out there."

"Shut the fuck up. We've completely reversed the desert creep of the last hundred years, and we're gaining more back every year. By the *mile*. Cut me some slack. You can't call *that* much rain without seriously fucking up the weather system somewhere else. Or did you already forget Meteoturgy 101?"

"No, I remember it," Cloke said, trying to keep her tone light. She tried to smile to reinforce her lightness and that was probably the wrong move.

From the look on Gwen's face, she'd already realized where this was heading. "Oh God." She turned and walked away from Cloke. "Oh God, oh God, oh God…" She turned back to look Cloke in the eye. "This is why we don't hang out more often, this, right *here*," she said, pointing at the ground. "Every time you talk to me, it's because you're going to go ballistic. Like, intercontinental ballistic. What needs wrecking now? Never mind, don't tell me, I'm not going to do it. Do you realize they still hate me in Scotland because of you?"

"You don't need to wreck anything," Cloke said.

"Oh, thank God."

"But you do need to be on standby for damage control."

"Why, what are y… oh. Oh no."

"I don't need an entire country hit. I just need one area. I can do that myself. But it's going to be extreme. There are going to be… repercussions."

Gwen's eyes narrowed. "And of course, Rector Ortega and the other Wardens are sitting around right now, sipping tea, with two big thumbs up for you, going 'Yay, Cloke, we totally endorse this action,' right?"

Cloke shrugged and said "Enh."

Gwen's face turned upwards and she blew some hair out of her eyes. "How bad are we talking?"

"F3. Minimum."

"Jesus. You've never even gone that far."

"Nope. But I know I can."

"Will you know what to *do* when it gets that far?"

"I did the reading."

"You read what I wrote, you mean," Gwen said. She marched down the dune and Cloke followed her, raising her hand to catch the bottle of beer that Gwen was, indeed, pulling out and throwing from a cooler half buried in the sand. "Fine. You have your reasons, you always do, miz big shot international combat mage. What the hell do *I* know, I just make it rain."

Cloke opened the bottle and took a sip. "You know I wouldn't ask if it wasn't important."

"I also know about curiosity and what it does to cats." Gwen shook her head and pulled out a bottle for herself. "Fine, you keep your secrets. I know you wouldn't do it to wreck lives. Homes, maybe, but only in the literal sense. You are so going to owe me, after this."

"I'm going to owe a lot of people."

That made Gwen stop. "Really going all out on this one, huh?"

Cloke nodded.

"Okay, that's a little different for you."

"This one is a different situation."

Gwen held her hand up. "Don't tell me anything else. I really am better off not knowing. Just tell me this. Is what you do, is it going to matter?"

"To us? Yeah."

"You've already said too much. Just finish your beer and then have another. If I'm doing this for you, then the advance on the favor is dinner tonight, your treat. Then I can tell you all about the man in my life who will shortly be out of it."

"They never last long with you."

"I'm a Tempest. They really oughtta know from that alone what they're getting into."

Cloke made herself comfortable. It was always nice to mix a little catch up time with the business.

THE NEXT DAY Cloke was in Japan and, as always, the country provoked mixed feelings.

It had been one of the countries she'd most wanted to visit when she was young. The land of the ninja and samurai, the birthplace of anime and an example to the rest of the world about how losing a war didn't have to mean the decline of a nation. She'd had big expectations when she'd first come here. Some had been met, others torn down, and then there were things she hadn't been expecting at all.

Like Hiro.

Cloke stopped walking in the middle of the forest path and looked around. Everything was the way it was supposed to be: quiet, primeval and seemingly free of modern surveillance.

Which, of course, was utter bullshit, because Hiro was here, and she knew how much he liked his toys. How he liked to mix and match them.

There was energy here, thaumaturgical. Not enough for a full-blown spell, but more than enough for it to be simple, ambient background fields waiting for a touch like hers to manipulate them. It was small but constant, not a pulse or wild fluctuation, so it was probably some kind of object. The feel of the energy was unmistakable: mass negation. Something in the area was lighter than it was supposed to be.

She scanned the brush carefully, but could see nothing.

So, she concentrated, reaching out towards the natural energy in the area and shaping it, twisting it, spreading it out.

Turning it into a strong wind that blew through the trees.

And that's when she saw it; the branches and leaves of one particular tree rustling unnaturally against an optic camouflage system that couldn't keep up with the unexpected disturbance in the environment. The break in the visual pattern was human shaped, crouching in the branches of one of the taller trees.

Cloke raised both her hands. "I can see you, and I will submit to a scan. You probably already know I'm unarmed."

The unit shut off the camouflage, revealing itself for what it was: a heavily modified love doll, originally built to resemble a delicate Japanese girl dressed as a French maid. It was another typically baroque example of Hiro's collection. It had been retrofitted with some combat chassis parts, and the fishnet stockings had graduated to full on a fishnet bodystocking in keeping with a Kunoichi, a female variant of a ninja. The French maid's hat and frilly skirt remained, however, as it perched in the tree like some surreal adolescent fantasy, which was consistent with Hiro's degenerate style.

The ninja doll dropped to the ground and stood in front of Cloke, saying, in English, "Security scan confirms no weapons. ID scan incomplete."

"I'm not in standard databases," Cloke said. "Transmit my image to your central security, you'll get your authorization."

The security doll said nothing, but Cloke assumed it was going through the usual channels. 30 seconds later, it said, "Authorization granted. Proceed down the path. Do not deviate."

It resumed its camouflage, blurring into a transparent, hyper-sexualized curvy silhouette, slightly distorting the bark and foliage behind it. It leapt back into the trees to resume its mechanized vigil.

Cloke continued onwards.

She always had to make the trek to talk to him. It was a physical thing, as he called it. There wasn't any other way to contact him because he was so analog. Staying off the Net, refusing all online devices, living off the beaten path in some big ol' house shuttered away in the mountain forests east of Kihoku, a small town on the island of Shikoku. It was one of the least populated, least popular islands in Japan, which was probably why Hiro chose to live there.

It was also a pain in the ass for the Japanese government that considered him a national treasure, but they weren't going to do anything that would somehow cloud his frame of mind and impede his work. Fortunately for Cloke, her standing with both GIS and the College gave her enough rank to pull that she could get through the nearly invisible layers of security to tromp through the path in the woods that led to Hiro's complex. Although "complex" might have been too strong a word for a decent sized home, the cottages for all his help—completely self-sufficient and off the grid—and a smaller building where he worked with his apprentices.

As she came up the path and saw Hiro's house looming in front of her, she caught sight of what must have been one of his apprentices: a delicate-looking Japanese girl, who carried a large pail of water over to the work area.

Cloke called out to her in Japanese, one of the few languages she had bothered to learn, and said, "Hello. I'm here to see your master." She bowed.

The girl stared wide-eyed for a few seconds, and returned the bow. "Thank you for coming. We were not expecting any visitors," she said cautiously. Cloke couldn't blame her. She might have looked in her teens, but Cloke suspected the girl could probably put up a good fight and kill the average trained combatant. Everyone here was prepared to defend Hiro with their lives.

"I will wait here," Cloke said. "You can tell Sensei that his gaijin friend is here about some work."

The girl bowed again. "Who shall I tell him is visiting?"

"Cloke," Cloke said.

The girl tried the name out for herself, her accent turning it into something like "Croak," reminding Cloke, once again, that despite her fascination with this country, she really wasn't suited for it. The girl went back to the house proper and Cloke waited, listening to the sound of the forest and the river that babbled somewhere nearby.

When Hiro came out, he was carrying a cup of what Cloke presumed was either tea or whiskey. His hair was still long and unkempt, and he looked like he'd been staring directly into a display, unblinking for the last three days.

"The fuck, Cloke," he said in English, extending his hand.

Cloke took it and shook. "Long time, no harass."

Hiro grunted. It might have been a laugh, or maybe just gas. "You're early," he said.

"How early?"

"About two years." He turned around and walked back towards the house, limping with a bad leg that could have easily been treated at any modern hospital. It was one of those little quirks that baffled Cloke. She had an excuse; she couldn't undergo any kind of nano-treatment or cybernetic enhancement without losing a chunk of her ability to use magic. Hiro didn't have that restriction; he just didn't want to get his leg fixed, his two reasons being "I hate doctors messing around more than they need to," and "I don't need to run, so I don't need it fixed."

Cloke looked at the clock on her visor. One minute. That was enough time for chit chat. Any more than that and he would steer it over to pornography.

"I'm here about that side-project," Cloke said. "I need it. And I'm calling in that favor."

"You can call all you want, but it's not ready. You want me to make it ready, I'll give you something so broken we'll have to start all over again. That's not me being difficult, that's just the way it is. You got a problem with that, take it up with the gods."

"There are no gods."

"And you know what? That means there's no miracle way to rush this either. It's not ready. Not if you want it to work the way you requested. I shouldn't even be making it, you know. The Diet is still nervous about all the work I *won't* show them. If they knew there was a gaijin commission in there, their collective hair implants would spontaneously combust."

"They probably know," Cloke said. "I can't imagine these apprentices of yours aren't reporting everything."

"They're not," Hiro insisted. "They're good kids. At least the ones that make the cut. They might bitch about the 'wax on, wax off' shit, but once they realize that they're getting a chance to work on the realest of the real deals, they get the proper perspective."

"And that is?"

"Shock and awe."

"Can I see it at least?" Cloke asked.

"Before it's finished? Blasphemer."

"I'm paying for it, aren't I?"

"No, you are *not* and we both know it. Don't pull that customer shit with me, you are *never* right."

"So, what am I?"

"A co-conspirator, since this is half your fault."

Cloke shook her head. "And to think, you were once Tokyo's king of hentais."

Hiro stopped and looked on wistfully. "I miss those days," he said, shaking his head. "Life was simpler then."

"Tentacles and maid porn?"

"You knew what you were getting into with those."

Cloke rolled her eyes.

"And nun porn. And tele-dildonics."

She choked on a laugh. "You are the only person I know that *still* calls it that." They got to a branch in the path, and Hiro steered them away from the houses and towards his workspace. His forge.

When they got to the forge, he opened the door and walked in on a small group of Japanese apprentices, the youngest probably only twelve, the oldest in her thirties. They all bowed as Hiro entered.

"Break time," Hiro said in Japanese. "Go recycle net memes for a half hour. Or have dinner, and watch your serials. Just don't be here."

The apprentices bowed again and quickly stopped what they were working on, and filed out of the room. When they were gone, Hiro walked over to the decorative stone dominating one wall and pressed his hand against it. "Shinji is always alone," he said.

Like magic, a panel in the floor slid away, revealing some stairs. Unlike magic, a synthetic voice intoned in Japanese "Masamune, Hiro. Biometric scan recognized. Welcome, Shokunin."

They walked down the stairs, each step lighting up just as Hiro lifted his foot from the previous one. They were walking into his other workshop, the one that only a tiny handful of his apprentices would ever see, where he held up, grudgingly, his family name.

Hiro Masamune was a descendent of one of the greatest swordsmiths in Japanese history, and he was able to imbue his blades with magic. It was an application that no one else on the planet had managed thus far, and the Japanese government had kept him at home rather than risk the College ransacking him for secrets.

The workshop lit up as Hiro arrived, a bizarre fusion of medieval metallurgy and 22nd century robotics engineering. Hiro modified his love dolls here as well, taking the exotic, mechanical, pornographic novelties and twisting them to his own whims. Some of them, in various states of mechanical and fashion undress, sat on worktables or walked the perimeter, bowing and greeting Hiro in exaggerated, high-pitched, effeminate voices. Scattered amongst the hydraulic worktables and various disassembled servomotors, knee joints and glossy lipsticks were hammers, tongs and an actual working forge. Containers of iron sand and refined carbon dotted one wall, along with blades in various states of assembly.

Hiro waved away the dolls that were mobile and they lined up against a far wall while he made his way over to the smithing area. "You have any idea how much of a pain in the ass it is to disable all the surveillance gear every time I let you down here?"

"I'd imagine it would have been a huge pain if you weren't very good. But you are."

He winked. "You always know just what to say."

"So where is it?"

He gestured towards the mess in front of him. "You're looking at it. It's never much during the assembly stage."

Cloke walked up to the blade. Hiro had been telling the truth: he wasn't finished with it. The katana wasn't even fully constructed yet. It was in the work area, mounted, no hilt, no tempering, the forging process still in progress.

Cloke leaned down and moved in closer to get a better look at the blade. Like everything Hiro made, it was obvious it was going to be beautiful when it was done. Beautiful and dangerous.

"Thanks again for not telling anyone," Cloke said, moving closer still, but making no move to touch the blade. She'd learned long ago how apoplectic he got when people messed with his shit.

"And say what?" Hiro asked. "Hey guys, I let that combat mage you hate so much into my forge, and she magically poked at the blade I was making and now it's some kind of super magic blade and I don't know how to replicate the process? That'll go over well."

"I'm still surprised no one ever tried it before."

"Who's going to be dumb enough to try fucking with an existing thaumaturgical forging process by adding magic fire? Who in the actual fuck thinks that way?"

"I did."

"And look what happened," Hiro said, shaking his head. "And we couldn't do it again."

"So, why's it taking so long?" Cloke asked.

"Because I don't want to break it," Hiro said. "I already

tried with some of the other steel that came out of that forging. I lost it. All the properties, the new ones, the ones it was supposed to have... lost it all."

Cloke turned back and looked at the blade glumly. "So, this is gonna take an epoch or two."

"Maybe," Hiro said. "Ooooor... maybe not."

Cloke slowly turned back to look at Hiro. "You're doing that thing with your eyebrow."

"What thing?"

"That same look pedophiles have when they talk about having a van full of puppies in the alley."

"And just like that, we're back to not being friends again. That is an amazing talent you have."

"It's a gift. Now what's this thing you've got?"

"It's more of a theory. And, well, this..."

He reached over behind the katana and pulled out its counterpart, a companion blade of the smallest size, what would have been called a Ko-Wakizashi in the feudal days. As a pair, the katana and wakizashi were known as daisho, and historically only samurai had the legal right to bear them. This sword, at least, was finished; tempered, hilted and sheathed.

Cloke blinked a few times then looked at Hiro. "What the fuck. You did it?"

"Not quite," he said. "I was able to finish this one, and keep its potential to manifest the properties intact. But those properties are latent right now. And that's where the theory comes in." He held it out to Cloke.

She took it slowly, almost reverentially in her hands. She gave Hiro a lot of shit, but his skill at the forge was unparalleled and even just taking the blade in her hands let her feel a quiet, significant power slowly pulsing within it, almost like it was breathing. "It feels like it's... sleeping," she said.

"I think it is," Hiro replied. "I can feel the energy in it. You can too, right?"

She nodded.

"But I can't draw it out. I know this thing can work. I know it can take magic, hold it, amplify it. It could be so much better than you half-assing it with making your street knife hold a charge on lightning. But it needs something."

"What?"

"The personal touch." He took the blade back from Cloke and pulled it out, checking its edge. "We can try something. But if we fuck this up, it'll break."

"What do you want to do?"

"I want you to try it out, and force this thing to submit. It bucks like a son of a bitch, and every time I try to work it using my own methods, I always have to back off, 'cause I can feel it hitting the breaking point way too fast. But you're used to working that kind of energy on the fly. Fast, big, instant, minute adjustments. That's what you do." He placed the blade in front of her and then limped off to a nearby chair. "So, I want you to try to make it work. Get it to hold the charge, fire, lightning, I don't give a fuck, just make it do it. You're going to bend it without breaking it. Do what I do, but without a hammer. Thaumaturgical energy is the kind of material you're good at working."

Cloke stared at the blade. "Just one shot?"

"Just the one," Hiro admitted. "If you don't want to do this now, fine. But you'll need to do it eventually."

"Then the katana will work the same way?"

He shook his head. "Get this one to work first, and I'll tell you the rest if we actually get that far."

"This wasn't exactly what I was hoping for," Cloke said. "But I'll take it."

"Now?"

"Now."

Hiro nodded and got back up on his feet. "Good luck then," he said, walking deeper into the shadows of the room.

"Wait a sec, where the fuck are you going?"

"Taking shelter, what do you think?" he said. "You girls, keep watch. If Cloke blows herself up, save the blade, her survival is secondary."

"Acknowledged," the love dolls said in unison.

Cloke gave him the finger as he walked away. As if in a

sympathetic response of asshole magic, he returned the gesture without looking back.

"You didn't even give me a Tatami mat or any cool samurai shit to kneel on to make this feel more mystical."

"Life is harsh. Deal with it. I'll be watching safely behind ballistic glass if you need anything."

Cloke sat down on the floor cross-legged and held the small sword in her hands. It was still too big to be considered a dagger, but like most wakizashi, was ideal for fighting indoors, in smaller spaces. She could still smell the wood Hiro had used to make the scabbard, and could tell he had already attuned the blade to its housing. It would never work to its full potential without a place to sheathe itself.

She pulled out the blade, heard the small ringing sound it made in the air as it was drawn. She could feel her own thaumaturgical energy brush against it, probing it. There was only the mildest response from the blade, as if it were taking a quick peek to see who had knocked.

Once again, Cloke felt a certain awe at holding a Masamune blade in her hands. Hiro may have ignored his legacy for many years, but the swordsmith inside him had come out immediately once he'd embraced his family's legacy. It had come as no surprise to anyone in Japan that the Masamune family line would have magic in it, and even the most basic, clumsy attempts of Hiro with his first blades were deadly enough that they could cut through anything, regardless of material.

"Okay, little sword," Cloke said quietly. "Let's see what you've got."

She started out delicately, nothing too ambitious, the kind of thing that kids learned during their first weeks at the College if they didn't know how to do it already.

She started with light.

It was normally pretty easy to simply generate a ball of light in her hand, or fix it to a point in space, on a wall, on an existing light fixture. Now she was trying to show the light to the sword, teach it how to make the light on its own.

The response was instant.

It was like a train in an earthquake, rumbling back up through the line of energy Cloke was projecting, hitting her full on, causing her to open her mouth and gasp in pain and surprise. The sword was fighting back, almost knocking her on her back with the force of its resistance.

"Need help?" Hiro called out, the lack of concern in his voice a clear alarm of just how concerned he was. Cloke had learned years ago that any time Hiro sounded nonchalant, that was his cover for panic.

"Jesus *fuck* this thing has a kick on it," Cloke said, fighting for control.

"Back it off if—"

"I know," Cloke said.

The blade shook in her hands.

"What the hell are you doing to it?"

"Light, just fucking light, that's all," Cloke said. "It's fighting back. Now shut up, please, I need some quiet."

Then she felt it going up her arm. Warmth. Unpleasant, but not painful. Then the pain itself came, riding up the heat like it was a wave, enveloping her entire body in a sensation like falling through needles. She shut her eyes and concentrated on riding it out.

"Cloke…"

"Not now, Hiro."

"Yes now. Cloke, do you know you're on fire?"

She opened her eyes and looked at herself.

Blue flames danced all over her skin.

It wasn't the normal kind of fire, not the kind that burned. The pain Cloke was feeling wasn't from her skin cooking, it was something else. These flames, this pain, all of this was some kind of magic. The sword was trying to use it. To fight. It didn't know what do with magic, but it knew how to use it, how to tap its energy and manipulate it, at least, and Cloke marveled at that.

"Does that hurt?"

"Yes," Cloke said through gritted teeth. "But not the way

you think. Now please, no more talking."

Cloke knuckled down, leaning in as if some wind were trying to blow her away. It was strong, and it was defiant, and it clearly was not going to do anything just because someone wanted it to.

Cloke could understand that. Moreover, she could actually respect it, and found herself liking this little sword, even as it tried to destroy itself once it was aware of her intrusion.

And just like that, it was obvious to Cloke what she needed to do. The sword, the energy within it, it wasn't looking for a boss, a lord or a master. That might come later, with time Cloke didn't have right now, but it was daisho, it was part of a pair.

It wanted a partner.

You want me to be your big sister? Fine. I'll be that.

Cloke stopped forcing her energy on and around the little sword, keeping her energy present but no longer aggressive. She felt the wakizashi respond, retaining its own potency but stopping its retaliation. It was waiting to see what she did next.

Cloke did the one thing they always advised against at the College. She left herself open.

The sword took it.

She felt it pour through the gap she'd left in her magical defenses, engaging with her own thaumaturgical energy, feeling it, riding it, taking its measure of her. She assessed the energy of the little sword as well, seeing the purity of it, the handiwork of Hiro's genius in harnessing this energy; but she could also feel the erratic, unpredictable nature of it, a flame that could rise up and consume without warning. It took her a few moments to realize she was looking at herself, at her own contribution to this artifact; the essence of her own personality that had been within the flame she'd casually thrown into Hiro's forge against all common sense.

And in understanding this fusion of Hiro's consummate mechanical perfection and her own chaotic willfulness, she understood more about this blade, and its sibling, and why they were willing to die rather than yield.

She was exactly the same way.

Cloke accepted the wakizashi's energy, allowed it to surround her in a way that would have been fatal with any mage that had hostile intent. Then she reached out to it, offering an interaction; safe, secure, on the blade's terms.

She watched the blue flames die away on her arms, her legs, the pain reduce itself to a pleasant tingling as it became mere ambient magical energy in the air once more, no longer directed. Then the energy flowed forward, into her.

She felt it engage with her energy, embedding itself within. The blade was becoming a part of her, somehow.

And in that instant, she tried again, running the keys through her mind, showing them to the new, watchful presence within her thaumaturgical pool of energy reserves.

"This is light," she whispered to herself and to the sword in her hands. "This is how you make it."

She held the sword in her right hand while her left played host to a gentle orb of warm, yellow light, hovering a few inches above her palm.

"You see? It's easy. Try it. Go on."

The sword glowed. And this time, it wasn't the side-effect of a fast track to self-destruction. It was the goal. It was light. The sword was generating it all by itself, taking Cloke's knowledge and energy, shaping it on its own.

Cloke nodded and the light faded away.

She sheathed the sword and slowly lay down on her back. She closed her eyes, feeling the cool floor underneath her head.

"Well there's something you don't see every day," she heard Hiro say in the dark. She opened her eyes to see him leaning forward, his arms open. He indicated the sword that now lay at her side. "May I?"

She nodded.

He picked it up gently, running his fingers over it. "Feels different now," he said. "Ready."

"It does."

"What did you do?"

"I offered a partnership. Ototo accepted," she said.

Hiro's eyes narrowed at her usage of the word. "Little brother?"

"That's what he is," she said. "That's what he wants to be. He's waiting for his big sister." She looked over to the katana.

"Then he's going to need to help. You both are," he said, pulling the blade from its sheathe and examining it. "This one was the more reasonable of the two, if you can believe that," Hiro said. He looked back at the katana. "After seeing what you just did, I'm pretty sure the other one isn't going to listen at all. So my theory just got more weight."

"I still don't know what this theory is."

"You need to teach and bond," Hiro said. He held out the wakizashi to her. "This is a sword, it's meant to be used, but it doesn't know what that means yet. Teach it. It's a new kind of weapon. Let it learn from you, let it absorb your energy so that it's as familiar with you as it is with its own inner workings. When you've done that, I'm going to pair with its big sister. I think it'll work then."

Cloke took the sword. "So... you're just... giving it to me?"

"I'm entrusting it to you. If that sword breaks and somehow you survive, then I'll kill you myself."

Cloke nodded. "You want to see where this goes."

"I want to see how far, yeah. It's not every day you see a new way to use magic. It always seemed like there was a bond between the bearer and the blade, but it's crazy to see what happens when magic enters the equation."

Cloke looked down at the small sword in her hands. "You weren't exactly what I wanted when I showed up here," she said. "But maybe you're what I'll need. Someday." She looked back up at Hiro. "Gonna need a belt and a sageo to wear this properly."

"I can recommend a great souvenir shop back in Tokyo that even comes with an official ninja stamp of approval. Don't tell them I sent you though, they'll jack up the price."

"Wow, you're going all out with the whole customer experience thing."

"Look, that thing is eventually going to be making its own

fireballs. I'm not going to tell you, of all people, what's the best way to wear a weapon that does that."

"I can't argue with that logic."

"Can't argue with the price either."

"Free magic sword is a pretty good deal, yeah."

Hiro's entire attitude changed. His posture straightened and his voice lost its casual tone. "Actually, there is one thing I'm going to be requiring as payment for that sword. And its sibling."

Cloke stood up and looked at Hiro. "Name it."

"I don't know whether you ever read up on it, but my ancestor, Masamune, he had a rival of sorts. Muramasa. Muramasa made devil swords, blades that hungered for blood, because all they knew was violence for the sake of power. Ambition. Greed. I always thought it was just hokey manga stuff. I'm not so sure anymore." Hiro looked back at the katana. "If that thing learns, then teach it the right things. Make it a weapon that fights for the right things. Don't make it a sword that lives to inflict suffering."

"So... get stronger to protect the ones you care about, respect the power of friendship—"

"Fight and die with motherfucking honor, yo," Hiro said, holding out his fist for a bump.

Cloke didn't reciprocate. Instead she nodded and stood up, formally bowing towards Hiro. "Whatever floats your boat, Sensei."

"You dialed down the bitchiness a little, so I'll take that as an actual yes," he said, shaking his head. "Have fun."

"Oh, I will."

"Not the kind that explodes."

"That's the only kind."

"Give me the sword back."

Cloke walked back towards the stairs. "Sorry, no do-overs. Gonna need it anyway. Big job coming up. Real learning experience."

"Is someone rich going to be hurting after this?"

"The odds favor it."

"Then God bless you and your sharp little bundle of joy. If you end up killing anyone from Blackmore Labs, tell them my bum leg says 'Hi.'"

Cloke walked out of the workshop, said her goodbyes, then headed back to the trail that would take her back into the first world and its maze of convenience and information.

Now it was just a matter of paying courtesy calls to make sure the powers that be wouldn't get too upset when things burst into flame.

Chapter XIV:
Official Notice

ZEE HAD NEVER been to a flying building before.

The obvious reasons were money and security. Anyone that went to the trouble of regularly reapplying mass negation magic to a building to keep it suspended in the air belonged to that stratified portion of global society that ignored the other 99.5%, and Zee was unlikely to pass the kind of security checks required to set foot on that kind of real estate. At least, that had been the assumption until this morning.

The world was always different when Cloke was around. Or maybe it was simply that Cloke's world was different, and she brought it with her wherever she went. In this particular case though, it was very much Cloke going through a familiar routine of her world. The people at the College loading bay knew her on sight and waved her through, not requiring a retina, finger or DNA scan of any kind, not even a coded card. Zee suspected it was because they had their own forms of identity confirmation that didn't rely on conventional technology.

Their time in the loading bay was brief: Cloke walked past all the incoming and outgoing ferries that shuttled everything from food to mail to visiting dignitaries back and forth from the College primary campus complex that hung over the city of São Paulo. It had the antic frenzy and rich mix of smells that reminded Zee of the harbors of Sydney, New York, Hong Kong and the LUMO orbital elevator. This was a place of transit. Most of the people worked, and they worked hard, and they didn't have time to make sure people had a pleasant shopping experience.

Cloke got into a small personal gyro, taking the pilot seat and motioning Zee to join her.

"You can fly this thing?" Zee asked.

"Scout's honor," Cloke said. She ran her hand along the window. "Got my merit badge and everything. It took a couple of tries though. Got a little too excited being in the air. Had to retest a few times because of... enthusiasm. But I always wanted to fly. Always. You feel free, you know?"

Zee got in and reflexively reached for the seatbelts. "So what can't you do?"

"Draw a picture to save my life," Cloke said, cycling through the launch sequence. "Be a big hit at dinner parties," she stopped, tilting her head in thought. "Or any parties at all, actually. Plenty of things in this world I'm bad at."

"I can't sing," Zee said.

"No, that's a lie, you can," Cloke replied, pulling gently at the stick in her right hand. The gyro rose into the air, turning itself around to face the College's aerial stronghold. "I've heard you humming on the way between the shower and your bedroom. You can hold a note."

"Not great."

"Better than me," Cloke said. "I can't sing either. And you don't want me to prove it."

Zee watched as Cloke took them above the colorful sprawl of São Paulo and approached what amounted to the brain of magic in the 22nd century, smiling as the vehicle rose into the air and tilted forward to break away from the ground. "I could do this all day," she said to Zee. "It's all so much simpler up here."

College Central Administration was a smooth, almost featureless complex that looked like it had been plucked from a single piece of aerodynamic pale blue-grey coral, with multiple towers that seemed to grow from a flat, massive base. A proud, airborne testament to the fact that here, in São Paulo, Brazil, was where magic was understood and harnessed; where the people persecuted for what they could do in other countries made this nation an economic super power which picked up the pieces that the old, unified America either couldn't or wouldn't see in the possibilities of magic co-existing with technology and commerce.

"So that thing is totally free floating?" Zee asked.

"Yup."

"Where does the sewage go? You just drop shit on São Paulo every day?"

Cloke chuckled. "Same as any privileged city or corporate estate, only with rookies. All college freshman have mandatory latrine duty for the first year. They have to transmute all waste into hydrogen, methane, ammonia. Then they just package it up either for reactor or commercial use. Even I had to do it."

"Seriously?"

Cloke shrugged. "All part of the training. New students don't get treated like shit; they treat shit. That's the deal."

Cloke took them down to one of many receiving pads for gyros and let the vehicle land itself once they got close enough. There was no one to greet them as they disembarked. Cloke was still acting with the indifference of someone going through a dull routine.

"I still don't understand why I'm here," Zee said.

"Because you know lots about one part that keeps our world working. You know almost nothing about the other part. That's a deficiency. In this line of work, what you don't know can kill you. Besides it's always fun to watch."

"Watch what?"

"The bug eyes," Cloke said. She walked over to the doors at the other end of the pad and let them slide open for her.

Zee wasn't sure what that meant, as all that lay before them was a plain, narrow hallway that smelled of pine. But as they got to the end and walked through another door, it became pretty obvious what Cloke was talking about.

"I spent most of my teens laid out on my back here," Cloke said.

It was a hall. It reminded Zee of Cloke's gym. There was a combination of open spaces; brightly colored, padded floors, and racks with everything from light armor to automatic weapons and electrolyte-rich beverages.

There were people grunting with effort, yelling or screaming in pain; there was a smell of ozone in the air, a tingling, the rush of strong winds, and the shimmer of heat. People whispered, people mumbled, people gestured; boys barely in their teens, women that had only just become so, all scattered about amongst a taste of smoke in the air.

Zee had never imagined what it would be like to see, to feel so much magic, the *real* thing, being used in one location. "So, this is…"

"Training hall. This is where they whip kids into shape to spit fire and lightning," Cloke said. "I was already able to do that before getting here, which pissed them off. A lot. But they still taught me a few things. Like how much it hurts when someone sucker punches you in the middle of getting your fireball off."

Zee looked over the array of young people down in the hall below and it didn't take long to make an obvious observation.

"The girl to boy ratio down there is like ten to three."

"More like ten to two," Cloke said. "You never noticed it before?"

"How could I? I've never seen a real mage until you came along, and in the serials and games, most of the time the mage is a guy."

"Only about 20% of people that can use magic are male," Cloke said. "Magic affinity seems to be matrilineal, generally. Another one of those things that drives researchers crazy, since there seems to be no actual genetic characteristics to support that. Not ones they can measure yet, anyway. It's mostly a girl's club. You'd know that if you read more. That's why China went down the toilet in the new economy and is going to stay there."

Cloke leaned against the railing and watched the children and teenagers below as they went through various training and sparring routines. A few of the instructors and students noticed her, and gradually everyone stopped what they were doing to look up at her.

"Carry on," she said. "Don't mind me."

They continued to stare.

Zee could hear the voices bubbling up from below; the whispers; the reverential tone; the same word coming up again and again: "Cloke." They all knew her. Zee suspected from the looks on their faces that they wanted to be her. Or at least be like her.

"Uh... good job kids," Cloke said. "Keep... keep it up." She gave a clumsy thumbs up, seemed to finally realize they were just going to keep staring, waved casually, then continued walking. "Well, that was awkward," she said.

"YOU'RE SO BADASS!" someone shouted from below. A collective roar of agreement followed. They started chanting her name.

"Okay, that's more awkward," Cloke said, increasing her pace.

"You're kind of a big deal here," Zee said.

"Fucking leaderboards..." Cloke muttered softly.

"You have leaderboards here?"

"Well... everyone who studies here calls them that. That's not what it is really. More of a ranking system. Classification. Juggles a lot of factors, raw power, skill, that kind of thing. It spreads across all the disciplines. Once you graduate, you're licensed, certified and graded in the system. All the men and women certified for licensed Glamours, or for Meteoturgy, or Alchemy, whatever... they know who the others in their discipline are, they know how they rate compared to them."

"And anyone can check them out?"

"Anyone that's a student or alumnus, yeah," Cloke said. "It's supposed to be good for them. That's the theory, anyway. Aspirational, or some shit like that."

"So where are you on these leaderboards?"

"I told you, I'm rated for combat magic. That one is kept off the public networks. Not many people have access to that. Except the kids with a flair for hacking, I guess." She grimaced. "Fair amount of those at any given time, actually."

"You also said there were only nineteen people that were rated for it. So, it's a small leaderboard."

"Yeah," Cloke said. And Zee had to pick up the pace because Cloke's speed kept increasing as they talked about this, almost like she was trying to run away from the topic.

"So where are you? Those kids acted like you were at least in the top ten."

"I do okay," Cloke said. "Let's leave it at that. And don't listen to anything kids around here might say. They're full of shit. And power fantasies."

And Zee knew, in that instant, despite having absolutely nothing to back it up, that Cloke was probably the best combat mage in the world. And this fact seemed to bother her a lot.

They made their way through the halls until they got to a large, central space that seemed entirely open to the elements, even though Zee could neither hear nor feel the wind, or the sunlight. At the far end—complete with the kind of conventional security Zee was used to seeing—was a large reception desk that stood before an ornate elevator shaft that rose to the top of one of the College towers.

Cloke approached the desk, occupied by a slim South Asian woman with stark blue eyes, who regarded her in silence.

"I need to talk to them," Cloke said. "I know they're in session and I know it's not important."

"Would it make any difference if I said they were busy?" the woman asked.

"They'll make time for this," Cloke said. She reached over the desk to the receptionist's display of tools and applications and pressed a communication icon. "There's an interesting variation of an Article Three violation going on that you'll just drag me back here to explain when you find out about it later," she said.

There was no response on the other end of the channel. However, the receptionist's display indicated that an elevator was now being sent down to receive a visitor.

"Plus one," Cloke said, nodding her head towards Zee.

"She doesn't come up on any of the usual ID scans," one of the men by the elevator said.

"I'm vouching," Cloke replied, putting her hand on Zee's shoulder. "If anything happens you can put a bullet in my head after I melt hir brain."

"Or I could just wait here and count the breakfast crumbs on my shirt," Zee said. "I'm totally okay with that if the alternative is brain melting."

Zee felt the firm tug of Cloke's grip as she walked towards the elevator.

"Xie's just a little shy around guns," Cloke said to the security guards. "Childhood trauma thing. Long story."

The elevator arrived with a clear, clean bell tone as its doors opened. The security stood aside, and Zee was dragged by Cloke into the elevator. Cloke gave one last informal salute to the soldiers and leaned against the back wall as the elevator rose.

"As a precaution, not a fucking word," Cloke said. "You should probably answer if they ask you any questions, but otherwise, don't get in their faces. This bunch doesn't have much patience for that."

"Who's this bunch? Like a white circle of enchanters or something?"

Cloke snorted and it turned into a full-blown laugh. She looked at Zee with a grin. "Ho-lee *fuck*, is that really what they're making it out to be in games and serials now?" She laughed again. "Nothing that romantic. Not even in Haiti and they're about as close as it gets to what you must think magic is. No, this is a college. It's a *school*. You're meeting administrators. The Rector and her Wardens. All they do is enforce policy, draw up curriculums and cut deals with the Board of Sovereigns whenever they start whining about one country getting more magic talent than another."

"So... bureaucrats."

"That can melt your brain, yeah," Cloke said. "Don't get me wrong, they still work some badass magic, but they're so high up the ladder they don't get much chance to anymore. Nature of the biz in any field, right? Get too good at something and they'd rather have you teach it or manage it than do it."

"So how come you're not up there?"

"Office politics," Cloke said. "Did I mention that's another thing I'm really, *really* bad at? I also suck at the kinds of parties that involve raises and promotions. Besides," she said, pushing herself back onto her feet as the elevator started to slow. "I think they're happier with me out in the field. They're hoping it'll kill me one day, save them the trouble."

She flashed a cheery grin that reminded Zee of a lobotomized Japanese idol singer, and said under her breath, "Remember, not a fucking word."

Zee followed uncertainly behind as Cloke walked out of the elevator and into a large, rounded, open chamber with obscenely huge panels of curved glass as walls. They were probably hardened against conventional attack, and were currently at a dimmer setting to reduce the glare from a cloudless, sunny day.

The only thing that was in the room was a long, arc-shaped table, almost like a "U" or the horseshoes Zee had seen in pictures and period westerns. It had been deliberately laid out so that a person who had to walk into it would be surrounded on all sides by people: in this case, mages. Or the telepresence version of them, since it was also clear that a few of the seats were occupied by monochrome holographic representations, or else a holographic monolith that read "SOUND ONLY." There were only two men at the table, one actually present, the other virtual. Everyone else that was visible was female.

The woman at the head of the table was quite live, however, and she was staring at Cloke with an expression of tired distaste. She was attractive in a stern way, still slim, not so vain as to cover up the greys that were starting to appear in her long hair. She was a local, a fact that made Zee double check to ensure the translator was on in case Portuguese started flying around. The woman was also obviously girding herself for an old argument that was about to repeat itself.

Cloke stopped when she got to the center of the table and maintained steady eye contact with the woman. She gave a slow, slight nod, never breaking the stare and said, "Rector Ortega." She finally looked at the others both present and virtual. "Wardens."

"Magistra Cloke," a few of the people said, nearly simultaneously.

Rector Ortega, however, didn't waste any time. The words came out in Portuguese and Zee's translator obliged. "It's probably safe to assume that despite the severity of accusing any person or group of an Article Three violation, you don't have anything remotely usable in court to justify this."

"I didn't say it was an Article Three violation, I said it's a variation."

The woman to Ortega's left spoke in a stream of irritated Cantonese. "And exactly how does one vary the process of proscribed cloning on College members?"

Cloke let her eyes sweep across all of them before speaking. "There are three illegal emulations of Matheus Azevedo under Majitsu control." She crossed her arms.

One of the SOUND ONLY holograms, again clearly female by her voice, said in crisp, British English, "Explain this. Now, please."

Zee watched as Cloke told the story again, but this time it was different. Cloke might not have particularly liked these people, but she took them seriously. She respected them. She answered all of their questions with only a slightly cavalier tone, but she held nothing back and was as thorough and accurate as possible.

Then she explained her intention and the mood of the room changed.

It was Rector Ortega that said it first. "Are you certain that destroying all the emulations of Azevedo is wise?"

"It's what he wants," Cloke said. "I think we owe him that."

She let her eyes scan the collected Wardens. "We all do. And let's not forget what Majitsu has done to him is completely illegal."

Zee thought of Darma happily hacking away at various high value networks as a pleasant way to kill time, and said nothing.

The British holographic slab spoke again. "There is an opportunity here, Magistra. An opportunity for expanding our knowledge, which is the cornerstone of this College."

"He wants deletion. It is his primary, overriding wish. Are you saying we ignore that just to make our textbooks bigger?" Cloke asked.

"Of course not," Rector Ortega said. "As you say, he is one of ours, and we take care of our own; even the international courts recognize our legal rights in this area. And we abide by the wishes of our own. But we can always honor his request after we've learned what we can. Then we can give him what he wants."

"I'm sure Majitsu promised the same thing," Cloke said.

"We are not Majitsu."

"You're making the same threat."

"We're offering a *trade*."

"I'm not," Cloke said. "I'm going to do what he wants. I didn't come down here to ask for permission or advice. I came as a courtesy. You have the right to know what I'm going to do, since this falls under College interests. But you don't have the right to administrate this."

"And why not?" the sole present male Warden asked.

"Because I don't want or need College participation. I'm doing this on my own. It's my operation and I'm informing you of it, but it's not your gear, expertise, infrastructure or lives I'll be risking. The one thing I need more than anything to execute this properly is the most experienced combat mage the College has. And I've got a feeling if I ask myself nicely, I'll be saying 'yes.'" Cloke turned and began to walk away. "Thank you for taking the time to meet with me. I'm sure you've got important matters to attend to with the Board of Sovereigns. They're always looking to buy more of us, and you're always willing to sell to them."

Cloke walked past Zee and motioned with her head to follow. Zee quickly took up a spot beside her and asked quietly, "Did I really need to hear any of that?"

"Yes, you did," Cloke said. "So that you don't go thinking that these are magical people with some higher form of morality. Power is power. The lure of more power makes people do funny things."

"And why do I need to know that?"

They got into the elevator and Cloke looked to Zee. "What's our attention whore situation like?"

Zee checked out the visor readout that was patched into a suite of surveillance detection gear built into both the visor and select articles of clothing. It registered only one active device. "We're okay except for the camera in the corner."

Cloke turned slightly and Zee did the same to make sure their lips weren't in the camera's field of view. "You need to know they can be just as political and motivated by personal agenda as anyone else, so you won't feel bad about bugging their network."

Zee's eyes widened. "And why, aside from the fact that that would be impossibly cool, would I want to do this?"

"Because I may be the most experienced combat mage they have, but I'm not the only one. And after what I just said, it would be dumb to expect them to sit by and not try anything on their own with people who are better at taking orders than I am."

"So why not just *not* tell them?"

"Because they're still the College. My College. They taught me. Raised me half the time," Cloke said. "And ulterior motives aside, they do take care of their own. Eventually. When they're not fucking each other over for pole position. They needed to know. If only so that there would be some official resistance to Majitsu from *somewhere*."

"Ransom of services," Zee said.

"That's such an ugly phrase," Cloke said, smiling. "Call it proactive negotiation. Majitsu might want to squash me, but not if it's going to kill their advanced propulsion research division and cripple their generator infrastructure."

"How?"

"Faculty of Alchemy. You know the British Warden that was transmitting only audio? She's the one that every government and corporation on the planet has to bow and scrape to for access to a small team of mages that can reliably transmute anti-hydrogen. No anti-hydrogen? No anti-matter reactors or propulsion research. It would take them decades and trillions of reals to generate the usable mass of anti-matter that an alchemy magistra can transmute in seconds."

And it struck Zee in that moment just how right Cloke was. This was a blind spot. There was power and money behind magic and Zee had ignored it because it wasn't something that could be hacked.

"Bad family ties are still family ties," Cloke said. "And they'll have your back even if they still want to rip your head off. They know I'm right. They're probably just wishing I would be a little slower about righting things. Azevedo can teach them new things. He already has with me. What I can do is worth a lot of money."

"That's what you meant by selling," Zee said. "They need College staff, students."

"Better, cheaper, faster... for *everything*. What company or government in their right mind wouldn't want that?" Cloke asked. "The only catch is you can't put it on an assembly line. It's the age of the artisan. So, now that it is not only impossibly cool, but you have a better understanding of how actually relevant this is, what do you want to do with this?" Cloke reached into a pocket and pulled out a memory card. "Handpicked by Darma to serve your network infiltration needs."

Zee reached out and took the card. "You don't have a problem spying on your own?"

"What family doesn't?"

"And this wasn't something worth doing sooner?"

"You've got a question for everything, you know that?"

"Learning is for winners."

"Just call me paranoid. There have been shuffles in both the faculty and board of sovereigns. There was a balance before. I think it's changing now, and I want to make sure I stay in the loop."

"Okay, I can appreciate that," Zee said, pocketing the card. "I'll need server access."

"You'll get that. And ten minutes of me time."

"I only need five."

"You really shouldn't say stuff like that," Cloke said. "It just gives me an excuse to be harder on you when you get lazy." She leaned back against the wall of the elevator, relaxing once more.

Zee took it as a signal that they were done here. It was going to be just another run from here; do the hack then get out.

"Okay, I owe you a latte. Then you get the grand tour," Cloke said.

"And then?"

"You get to work on prep. Get into the College network, get what you need. Set things up with Marcus and Darma, everyone needs to start figuring what they need and where they need to be. We're going to hit Majitsu hard, and it's going to be on the news, and we have to make sure we're not there when the reports start up."

"And what are you going to be doing?"

"Oh, I get the fun part. I have to figure out how a magic sword, an uncooperative digital dead guy and massive atmospheric disturbances all work when they go into orbit."

Chapter XV:
Making Luck

THERE WAS ONLY one part of Cloke's compound that got any regular use outside of her apartment. The gym.

Zee, upon entering the room for the first time, pointed out that it was a gym in the same way the hypersonic tube transport was a train. The basic concept was there, but the execution went above and beyond.

What mattered to Cloke, however, was the fact that it worked. It got results, and it was the closest thing she would ever get to multiple people trying to kill her on a daily basis.

The room was massive, which is why the term 'gymnasium' wasn't entirely inappropriate. It was also fire resistant, bullet resistant and could withstand all but the heaviest conventional explosives; it was even shielded against radiation and electromagnetic pulses. It was equipped with a series of barriers of all shapes and sizes that could be fixed at points all over the space to create anything from a labyrinth to waist-high shields for shooting over. All of this was synchronized to a wireless sim transmitter Cloke wore like the kind of plastic tiara little girls wore when it was time to play princess. Rather than immerse her completely in a simulation, it created the look and feel of a simulation onto the objects within the room, a copy of the augmented reality perversions certain national and corporate combat forces had been utilizing for years.

Cloke was currently in a bombed-out urban zone; piles of rubble, half-standing buildings and blasted walls were scattered everywhere. Her opponents this morning were the Brigada de Operações Especiais, Brazil's spec ops group. She had maxed out their equipment and given free rein to the simulator's combat intelligence to be as lethal and efficient as possible within human limits.

"They're coming from the north," Zee said over the chat channel in Cloke's sim-gear, completely ruining the combat simulation's surprise element.

Cloke was already regretting inviting hir in to watch. She raised her hand to give Zee the finger and immediately pulled it down as a hail of fully automatic gunfire sailed over the broken-down wall she was hiding behind. That little moment of pettiness had allowed the squad to zero in on her location.

The team of six was already down to four, thanks to one unfortunate encounter with ball lightning, and a bullet in the spine while everyone was distracted. She was certain they would send two around either side in an attempt to flank while the other two kept her pinned down with fire.

She switched tactics and went on the offensive.

The first thing she did was use one of the first tricks Gwen had taught her when they were in school. She created a micro-weather system, manipulating moisture and temperature to bring fog in. That effectively neutralized the human visual range. Concentrated gusts of focused wind would provide enough micro changes in air density to render pure motion trackers useless as they would now show movement everywhere.

As the fog formed, she rolled away from her position, going on the move. A quick read of the local temperature and she ran the keys through her head once more, dialing in the general temperature of the environment and then dialing down the air around her own body to match the surroundings, neutralizing the effectiveness of infra-red or thermal sensors.

She didn't even need her own field sensors to see the enemy: she could hear them just fine. With three soldiers in full armor and one combat cyborg, it was impossible for them to move silently. Of course, with Cloke wearing only a light tactical suit of IF body armor, she'd be lucky to take more than a couple of direct hits from gunfire and survive.

"So, tell me why you're doing this again," Zee asked as Cloke maneuvered towards one of her flankers. She had a clear shot at his back. She broke into a run that she knew he would hear, turned the run into a slide as he turned around and extended her hand to help guide her aim, the keys in her head forming the necessary components to cause a fire directly inside his helmet. He flailed and Cloke raised her leg, her slide turning into a kick as she got in range. He fell at the same time she rose and with one smooth, practiced motion, her hand came up with what she called her "hand cannon," a German ASP-63. She zeroed the face and pulled the trigger. The armor-piercing round tore through the helmet and went out the other side in a textbook messy exit wound.

Three down, three to go. She moved through the fog.

"Do console jockeys not practice?" Cloke asked through the shielded comm system of her visor and mask. "Even Darma likes to stay sharp."

"No, the drill is total sense," Zee said. "It's the method, I don't get."

"My style?"

"Sure, I'll humor you, let's call it that."

Cloke moved around, making her way over to the two stationary attackers. "What's not to get?" Cloke asked, as she made a slow, quiet, methodical circle.

"All this in-your-face shit. From what I'd read and seen in videos, combat magic is strategic. You guys are walking nukes, you sit at the sidelines and drop fireballs and lightning. You get in closer than Marcus does."

"Marcus and I are both mid to close range," Cloke said, ending the stealth mode approach. She was now behind the two opponents, going through the basics of assault. Wind blew away the fog, she raised her gun and aimed, putting one shot into each soldier. The iron sights used for aiming the pistol also doubled as her guide for the ice that covered the joints, sensors and other internals of the enemy armor.

They'd just been shot and now various apparatus in their combat systems were freezing to death. Their ability to react in any meaningful way was broken.

"Marcus doesn't use a sword," Zee observed as Cloke closed the distance and pulled her wakizashi from its sheathe.

Cloke didn't reply, instead concentrating on a clean swing as she dropped down, and even though she'd already casually experimented with watermelons, paper and even a log, she was caught off guard by how cleanly the sword cut through the combat armor and the leg inside it. Even as a simulation, the scream from the soldier was enough to send a chill through her, but she was in the middle of a rhythm now, and she maintained it. She ignored the first soldier as he toppled, clutching at the stump that was his left thigh, and concentrated on the second as she focused the cold and froze his internal organs, filling his heart and lungs with ice.

He fell over, thrashing.

"Have I mentioned recently that you are not a nice person?" Zee asked.

"Nice is not a factor on the field," Cloke said.

That left only the cyborg. Her pistol was rated for armor piercing, but she doubted the simulation would have been generous enough to throw someone at her with components her rounds would affect.

She took one look at the cyborg emerging from the fog and was pretty sure he wouldn't. He looked like he was using a combat chassis similar to Marcus and this gun would barely scratch his paint.

Just to be on the safe side, she took a shot, and watched as it bounced off him, no flinching at all, as he continued his steady gait towards her.

"So, here's the thing," Cloke said, drawing the sword out into a good, neutral position. "Today, specifically, is a test for this."

She let her magic reach out towards the sword and greet it. Ototo responded, allowing the magic to flow through, accepting the distinctive configuration of energy that was the trademark of one of Cloke's specialties.

The blade crackled and burst with a cold blue glow as lightning arced and danced around it. Cloke marveled at the ease with which Ototo created and held the lightning.

The combat cyborg halted as the combat intelligence running the system paused, unsure how to proceed.

It was a trick Cloke had picked up as a teenager; one she'd assumed everyone that could wield magic could do since she'd managed it without any training. She imagined back then that for real mages, it was something that required far less effort, since it always took a lot of focus for her to maintain it. When she finally went to the College she found out no one had ever been able to do it, and even now, only two others had eventually picked up the technique.

Now here was a sword doing it all on its own: taking, holding and maintaining Cloke's magic in an active state because it had learned from her.

The combat cyborg had finally decided on a course of action, and that was to keep Cloke at range.

He was armed with a massive carbine rifle that, in a pre-cyborg era, would have been called an anti-materiel weapon. It was the kind of thing normally operated by a crew of two or three to take out armored targets and hardened installations.

He now aimed it at Cloke and popped off a few rounds.

That made perfect sense when a woman was standing around with a sword. The obvious intent would be to close within range of the melee and deal a killing blow. The problem with combat mages was that they tended to reverse expected outcomes in most battle situations.

Cloke went into automatic mode, dodging one way while throwing out a strong gust of wind that blew in the opposite direction. Ice formed on the carbine at the same time, all conspiring to throw off the aim of the cyborg.

Her dodge turned into a roll and then she was on her feet again, low to the ground. "Okay, little sword, you can hold a charge. Wanna rev it up?"

"Who are you talking to?" Zee asked.

"My weapon," Cloke said. She built up the lightning she was creating, felt the sword quietly observing and mimicking the way she shaped the magic.

"Ask a stupid question..."

Cloke extended the blade and released her lightning into the sword. The sword accepted the lightning, built on it, making it bigger, stronger, more dangerous; created its *own* lightning, built on that, then added it to Cloke's own burst. It wasn't something she'd been expecting, and it happened so fast that she wasn't prepared when the discharge came.

It was like the first lightning bolt the world had ever seen came screaming out of Cloke's blade, happy to suddenly exist and be free. The thunder that accompanied it was equally mythic in scope, rattling through Cloke's skull even as the lightning hit its target.

The cyborg was engulfed in a column of lightning bigger than he was. He exploded.

The force of its destruction knocked Cloke off her feet. She landed on her back, breathless.

The air was rich with the smell of ozone as Cloke stared at the ceiling, listening to the maintenance systems of the gym struggle to understand what just happened and how to repair the situation.

"Wow," Zee said over the chat channel. "What the fuck was that?"

"Fall down go boom," Cloke said. She flexed the muscles in her back experimentally and felt them spasm in protest. She sat up. Slowly. "I think the combat intelligence didn't know what to do with the lightning and reacted badly. Improvising isn't big on the feature sets for virtual intelligence systems."

Cloke stood up, removing the simulation rig from her head. The room stopped being a burnt-out urban warzone populated with amputated limbs and dead soldiers and once again reverted to a series of obstacles, some of which were smoldering.

Zee came walking in through the door, a cigarette already

lit. Xie tapped it, completely unconcerned about the ash it left on the floor. Considering the blast scarring around most of the equipment in the room, it was a justified piece of nonchalance.

Zee surveyed the damage and took in a long drag. "From what I just saw, you don't need much practice."

Cloke checked her blade, sheathed the sword, then inspected her gun. "What you just saw was what people don't get," she replied, taking a close look at the housing, the barrel, and other components. "This little daily exercise routine is what people mistake for natural talent making my life so 'easy' that things just fall into my lap. They think they'd have the same kind of life too if they had what I was born with. Talent doesn't keep you alive in a combat situation. Training does."

"Why bother with all the shooting and cutting when you can just magic people to death?"

Cloke sighed and went into her cool-down stretches routine. "You know how in shows whenever they have mages, the second they can't use magic and the bad guys break out fists or guns, the mages go down like a sack of hammers? Like just worse than completely fucking useless without a spell to lean on? That happens in the real world too. I promised myself a long time ago that wouldn't be me."

Zee nodded. "Okay, I get that. I know what dependency can do when someone takes the crutch away."

"And I really needed to see what this sword could do," Cloke said. "It's starting to give me some interesting ideas."

"That was crazy," Zee admitted. "First time I think it's ever been unfair to bring a knife to a gunfight."

"When the knife amplifies magic energy and redirects it at will... yeah, that's a cheat," Cloke said, patting the hilt. "And right now, I'm the only one that has it. Now, were you just snickering the whole time I was in the drill, or have your feelers paid out?"

"Oh, I got something," Zee said. "Put your gear back on."

Cloke put the simulation harness back on and Zee connected to it. Xie patched them into a private sim party, ruthlessly exploiting the GSI privileges to render them invisible to all the attendees.

It was a small affair, set on a cloud at sunset. All the furniture was fashioned from cloud cover, and the partygoers all presented as young, under thirty.

"This is real time?" Cloke asked, assuming Zee would have taken care of blacking out their chat channel.

"It is," Zee said. "You want to keep an eye on her," pointing to a girl, barely out of her twenties, with a white dress and wispy, cloud-like white hair. "Jaqueline Bouchard. She's hosting. She does this a lot."

"What's your angle?"

"Bored, rebellious daughter of one of the Majitsu Prague executives," Zee said. "As far as pecking order goes, her dad is second last in the Prague management inner circle. He's protective. Physical security is restrictive, she's mostly stuck in the corporate estate. She gets bored, so she does a lot of stuff on SimNet."

"What, you mean unlike every other kid in the 22nd century?"

"Big stuff," Zee said. "Her dad foots the bill for all these huge parties, contracts appearances by big names. She's basically the sim-party queen of Prague, and no party is complete without a lot of people. Her dad figures it keeps her out of trouble. Physical trouble, anyway. Idiot."

Cloke looked at Zee, their sullen expression, the way even the cigarette dangling from hir mouth seemed to say, 'Fuck off.' "Social butterfly is not the first thing I see when I look at you."

"Fuck no," Zee said. "But, her parties are the back door."

Cloke nodded. "Her home network?"

"Yeah. Her dad's home network security is tight, but conventional. I can break it, sleaze in to the Majitsu Prague network through it, but I'll need to be in Prague for the physical access privileges, and I'll need to be at one of her parties to tweak their home security and keep the door open."

Cloke walked over to the girl. She was laughing now, waving

dismissively at some suitor, her virtual cigarette providing the perfect accent to her outfit as its smoke interacted with her clouds. At this girl's age, Cloke had already been running operations with the College, and had taken apart two governments. This girl looked like she already knew more effective color palette combinations for make-up than Cloke ever would.

"How do you plan to get into one of these parties?" Cloke asked.

"I'm thinking of hijacking one of the waiter or security NPCs," Zee said. "This girl likes to keep them around for atmosphere, makes her feel more like some British old school noble or something, I guess. Some people just like having servants around."

Cloke removed the sim gear from her head and made for the door of the gym. "Send me her details."

"I already did."

"Good. Ever been to Prague?"

"Bavaria once. Munich. But Prague? Nope."

"Cherry popping time. Pack your bags."

"I still need to work out the particulars of hacking her NP—"

"You won't need to," Cloke said. "You'll get into the party. First class entry."

"How?"

"My sister. She owes me, she owes you, and she's been wanting some face time with you anyway. This is it. When you get there, I know a little hole in the wall that makes this fantastic goulash. You should try it. Also, build up your tolerance for beer."

"I hate beer."

"It's cheaper than water in Prague. Get used to it." She turned around just as she got to the door. "And good work."

She left the gym and put her visor back on as it chimed a message notification. The tone indicated it was Darma, which sent alarming bells ringing since Darma never bothered to leave messages; he was more into actual talking.

She opened the message and watched the data float in front of her as she made her way to the shower. Links. Numbers. It didn't make sense at first, just seemed almost like a random promotional message, or some poor marketing or hack job designed to get her to visit dubious places on the Net.

Except that she didn't get those. Ever. And this *was* from Darma.

She was almost at the shower when it finally clicked what Darma was getting at.

She kept the visor on and sorted through the message as she cleaned herself up.

She didn't like what she was seeing.

Chapter XVI:
Social Engineering

MIRIYA HELD UP a golden ticket, ensuring that it was in clear view of the half dozen virtual cameras focused on her.

"Jacqueline Bouchard," she said to the entire online world, reading the name on the supposedly randomly selected ticket. "I hope you throw a good shebang, because you know what? I'm coming over."

Somewhere, out in the warm, cozy confines of a private, corporate community estate, a young woman was probably screaming in panic and delight. She'd just "won," a contest to entertain a visit from Miriya, and even now, Miriya's army of legal, media and technical support were reaching out to secure the proper consent and online connection protocols.

Zee wasn't sure whether the final plan had been Miriya's or Cloke's. Either one could have come up with this stunt for different reasons. Whatever the case, the final solution to Zee's infiltration problem into a European simulation party was as an accoutrement.

Zee was a tiny bit of glimmer.

Specifically, Zee was one of a countless number of shimmering, dancing, flying "fairy lights" that surrounded Miriya, cascading and spiraling around her body and twittering down to the ground to be forgotten wherever she walked. It was a demeaning, insulting, degrading idea.

It was also guaranteed to work. If someone were to be assassinated at a wedding, no one was going to list the confetti as a suspect.

Zee had two big advantages going into this sneak-op. The first was that Miriya was Miriya, meaning the bright flame of her global fame was going to burn most rational thought and sensible safety precautions away. The second was that the victim of the op, Jaqueline Bouchard, was far from a technocrat, and, like most people, relegated her network security to automated processes from subscription services. In other words, there was absolutely nothing in her arsenal of personal intrusion countermeasures that could stand up to a concerted, professional console jockey assault, and that was the chink in the otherwise respectable armor of her father's corporate-grade network defense.

Zee had done a few jobs like this already, but never as someone's fashion accessory.

Miriya walked towards a door that was already taking shape in her space. Her entourage followed, all smiles and giggles. She knocked on it, and somewhere in Prague, a college student still living with her family got a notification on her home network that someone was requesting visitation consent to the designated public areas of her Homespace. She granted it.

That was all Zee needed. That blanket legal consent granted safety and admittance status to Miriya and her entire entourage, whether they were virtual, virtual intelligences, programs or subprograms required for the broadcast.

Miriya smiled for the world that was watching and opened the door saying, "Let's have ourselves a party, shall we?"

Zee changed the personal point of view to one that was detached and following somewhere behind Miriya. The true point of view was too disorienting, rapidly orbiting around a giant Miriya and entourage was just an invitation to nausea that wouldn't do right now.

Still, there was something unnerving about being around Miriya, watching her work.

She opened the door and walked through the space into Jacqueline Bouchard's world: a sun-dappled pool and lounge area on a flying island that drifted slowly in the basin of Brazil's Iguazu Falls. It was sunset of the most spectacular, fake kind, throwing out an almost neon-orange light on the proceedings, while a wholly out-of-place aurora shimmered in the sky above. The scent of jasmine and lilacs had been set on priority by the home environment's olfactory settings.

A few hundred of Jacqueline's closest online friends were already there, with more dropping in as word spread through the SimNet that she was the big winner.

For most of the people there, including Zee, this would be the first time they experienced what a fully produced broadcast simulation was like. Miriya's theme kicked in as she entered the space, her technical crew's audio programs subverting the home system. She raised her arms up and looked at the assembled group.

The crowd didn't need any cues or prompting. They burst into cheering and applause. Miriya had arrived; let the fun begin.

Zee clicked out of the simulation view and returned to the comfort of the workspace. It wasn't actually necessary to be totally engaged in what was happening at Jaqueline Bouchard's big win party. The important thing was being physically in Prague, and being virtually present at the party, so as to be present and accounted for by the Bouchard home network. That would make it possible to subvert the security protocols. The real work was still going to be done here, in the workspace, just like always. Nothing sexy about it.

At least until Miriya showed up.

A door appeared, followed by a courtesy knock, followed by Miriya, still looking glamorous in her hair and make-up, clashing with the sweatpants and big, baggy t-shirt that she was now wearing. It looked old, as if it survived a dozen too many runs through a laundry cycle. The shirt had a large picture, animated on a 15 second cycle, with some heroine from a ten-year-old anime series winking and flashing the peace sign.

Zee gave her the confused eye. "Aren't you supposed to be partying it up for my cover?"

Miriya made a bean bag chair materialize a discreet distance away and flopped down into it. "I am," she said. "I can multi-task. I also have a virtual intelligence that kicks in from time to time for the hum drum PR stuff. It drives my avatar for a while, gives me some warning when I need to take over, but I've got a few minutes of the usual presenting and glad handing, figured I didn't need to keep a close eye on it."

"And... so..."

"So here I am," she said, and broke into a wide, adorable globally recognized crooked smile.

It was hard to believe that just over a week ago this had been the same person trapped in a virtual torture chamber. She was acting like she'd just come back from a software upgrade, which Atelier Media had indirectly hinted had been the case. Maybe it was just a requirement of being famous that they could walk it off like that and forget it ever happened.

Zee sure couldn't, and went back to going over the various programs that would need to be set in place to properly sleaze the Bouchard home network. "You're welcome to stay," Zee said. "But it's going to be real boring."

"Is it busy for you? Does it require a lot of focus?"

"This part? No. This is like flipping switches and moving boxes around."

"So, it's okay if I hang out with you?"

Zee stopped and stared. "It is... but... why would you want to?"

"What do you mean?"

Zee had a hard time believing this needed to be explained. This broke all the rules. It was one thing to admire people like Miriya in sims. Awe was easy from a distance. Just a few feet changed awe to unnerving. Like falling in mud at a wedding and then being asked to carry the bridal train. It dirtied the other person. "Well... you're... you. Like, super fucking famous. Everyone loves Miriya. Why would you hang out here when you could be doing amazing things and hanging out with amazing people?"

"You don't think saving my life was amazing?"

"Well, you being saved was amazing. Maybe not the way it happened, or the person who did it, but it was important you got saved," Zee said. "So that you could go do better things than... this."

Zee could feel Miriya's stare. It wasn't harsh or rude, just constant. "Do you spend a lot of time in simulation?"

"Me? Nah, not really. Not a whole lot of time for it. More of a backstage person. Sim time is more for normal people, I guess."

"Oh, like me, you mean," Miriya said with a smile.

"You're totally different. It's your job."

Miriya tilted her head, looking like a perplexed cat. "Well, I suppose that's the charitable way to put it."

Zee continued with the work, laying out the foundations for what would be a slow, subtle infiltration of Jacqueline Bouchard's network that would eventually creep into and infest the entire Bouchard home network and open up a feed to her father's network access to Majitsu's Prague office. "I guess I just don't spend much time in Simulation. Not anymore, anyway. I used to, a lot, when I first started getting regular access to computers, but I stopped after a while. I'm not a good fit for it. Not yet, anyways."

Miriya walked up and took a good long look. "This is your default image I'm seeing right now? This is how you actually look, right? I think I remember from the hospital."

"Yeah," Zee said. "I didn't bother customizing anything. Work is work, no need to be fancy about how I present."

"Sis told me a little bit about you. Was that okay?"

A shrug. "If you can't keep a secret, the world is doomed."

"She said you had it pretty rough."

Another shrug. "Everyone does, right?"

"Did she tell you about us?"

"No. And I didn't ask."

"We were poor," Miriya said. "Dirt poor. Didn't know whether we were going to be able to eat from one month to the next. Jersey was an urban warzone. Like most places in America twenty years ago. And there were gangs. You pretty much had to run with them if you wanted to live. So I did. I did a lot stuff I'm not proud of. Did it to keep Cloke out of that life."

Zee stopped working to look at Miriya.

Miriya gave a weak smile. "Not trying to pull on your heart strings or anything. That's just the way it was. Do what you have to do to get through the day, right?"

"Yeah," Zee said. "Yeah, I know."

"I thought you might," Miriya said. There was something to her eyes and her face now that Zee had rarely seen in the broadcasts. This wasn't the infectious, bubbly cheer that Miriya was known for; it was the look and tone of voice that sometimes surprised people when she interviewed them, or was being interviewed herself. That sensitivity that someone who laughed so much wasn't supposed to have. "So... things were done. And the whole time I was doing it, you know what got me through it?"

Zee looked around the simulated space they were in. "This?"

Miriya nodded. "I'm not so different from most people. Simulations are an escape. The perfect world. And just like everyone else, I liked it here. Then eventually I realized I was good at being here. Better than I ever was out there. And I could make money here."

"So you did."

"Circumstances favored it," Miriya said with a bitter laugh. "I spent all that time in my street's gang, doing some shit I really regret now, but I kept telling myself, it would keep Cloke from having to endure the same thing. Then her magic happened. And she ended up in the gang anyway." The bitter laugh came again. "But as one of their most important lynch pins in their little territorial wars. She was the ace in their sleeve. So suddenly she was important there, and I was getting important here." She looked up at Zee. "Didn't seem like much point going back. The money got better, and the people, the managers, the agents... they realized the longer I stayed, the more money I made. Worked out for everyone, didn't it?"

"But... you're..."

"Beyond addicted," she said. "You can say it. I know a lot of people think it's a huge problem that needs to be addressed. But the world here is a better place, for a lot of people. I don't know what kind of argument is going to convince that kind of person to leave." She leaned back in the bean bag chair and crossed her arms. "So far Cloke hasn't given me anything convincing. Oh, wait a sec..."

And like that, Miriya suddenly vanished from the space. Zee looked back to the display showing the actual party, as a camera cut to Miriya and Jacqueline Bouchard sitting down at two chairs.

"Are you nervous?" Miriya asked the girl, who was presenting as some kind of towering Nordic ice queen goddess, complete with gown of snow crystals.

The girl nodded vigorously, then squealed, completely breaking the illusion of a calm, collected deity.

Miriya smiled again, the smile that probably printed money for some executive somewhere every time it happened, and leaned in close to talk to the girl. The next few minutes were a series of gentle, probing questions getting to know her better, showing a careful understanding of just how freaked out Ms. Bouchard would be right now. Miriya eased her into a world where everyone was watching her, and did it with gentle humor, and the kind of patient understanding that made Zee believe perhaps there really was an older sister in there, somewhere, capable of looking out for someone like Cloke.

She said a few intimate, gentle words of reassurance to the girl, followed up with a few jokes. The assembled crowd swooned at her easy, likable nature and suddenly she was on her feet shouting, "And now we DANCE!"

The moment she said that, frumpy, casual Miriya reappeared, sitting on her bean bag chair in Zee's space.

"So where were we?"

"I was boggling at how good you are with people?"

"Only here," Miriya said. "I can't act, convince or entertain to save my life out there, for some reason."

"And you still can't dance," Zee said.

Miriya grinned. "I can cut a rug somewhat. But yeah, letting the VI take over dance choreography while I go do something else is convenient."

"Sounds like you could be having fun then, instead of hanging out here."

Miriya made a face. "You're doing it again."

"Doing what?" Zee asked without looking at her.

"That thing. That stuff with your words like I'm somehow supposed to be above you and some kind of social law is being broken right now."

"Isn't it?"

"I just told you sometimes we didn't eat," Miriya said. "Do you think I could look down on anyone considering where I came from?"

"Some people do. Especially with roots like that," Zee said. "I've met them. Worked for them."

"Well, I have a psychotic condition that keeps me dysfunctionally imprisoned here, I think that negates my mocking rights and sense of superiority. Also, you are not the terrible person you believe you are. And it breaks my heart a little to see that it's not modesty. That you really do think you're that bad."

Miriya got up and walked towards the workstation, but stopped a discreet distance away, close enough that Zee could almost feel her just a few feet away, but far enough that no touching—no invasion of personal space—was possible. "You have a conscience, you know," she said.

That almost made Zee stop working. "What?"

"The things you say and do don't line up. You talk like nothing matters, but you act like everything does. You say the world is shit, but then you try to save the things inside it. The fact that things are bad makes you angry. It hurts you. That's your tell."

"I don't do as much good as you think."

"Who does? There's a reason saints are rare. We can't be our best all the time. Sometimes we're at our worst. You think I've never done anything I've regretted? That there aren't people out there I haven't hurt? Maybe ruined, because this industry is so political and competitive? We're people. We fuck up. Sometimes by accident, sometimes on purpose."

Zee turned to stare Miriya straight in the eye, thinking of the money that was being quietly gathered through the server harvesting, the dips into Cloke's own accounts and peripheral corporate accounts within GIS itself. They had more than they'd ever need, and they weren't on the run. That's what Zee kept internally repeating. "I've done some pretty shitty things."

"I don't doubt it," Miriya said. "But I also don't doubt that you did it for a reason. Whether it's for survival, or security, or fear, or anger, you don't do anything without a reason. You don't enjoy hurting people. I think whatever's happened to you in this world has pushed you into the dirt so much you don't know how decent you actually are."

Zee felt a complicated mix of anger and almost desperate relief hearing that. There was a sensation of something inside shifting. Almost as if in response to heat or light, trying to seek more of it. "It doesn't matter if I'm decent or not, especially if I'm shit the rest of the time."

"No," Miriya said. "It does matter. It matters a lot. Because you don't even realize it, but you've nailed the most important thing. You're good when it counts."

The sensation was now a pressure in Zee's chest. Something was being squeezed inside, or maybe it was the reverse and something was opening, and it was getting unbearable. Zee looked into the eyes of Miriya, remembered that even this woman's funds were being quietly bled right now, the money going through a comprehensive VI-assisted laundering system of trades and sales before going into Zee's own accounts.

Zee could suddenly understand now why Miriya was so popular with the world. This was the part they all wanted to see, wanted to have turned on them however briefly.

Miriya could make people feel like they mattered.

Zee turned and went back to monitoring the situation with installing the bypasses and other sleazeware that would keep access open to the house network. This, at least, was all going smoothly. "Why are you telling me this? Why do you even care about what I'm doing or what I'm thinking?"

"Because you saved my life," Miriya said. "You saved my life, but you think you're shit, and you're not."

"How much did Cloke tell you about me?"

"She told me enough," Miriya said. "Enough to know you have a good reason to run, to keep under the radar. She told me you know what it's like to be used. To have yourself be somebody's science project. And I can't just accept that someone who could be so much more is going to let that keep hir down."

"You can't fix people."

"Of course not," Miriya said. "They have to fix themselves. But do you want to? Because at least that's a start." She stopped, looking at Zee expectantly.

Zee didn't reply, unsure as to what Miriya seemed to want.

"Hm," Miriya finally said. "You didn't do it."

"Do what?"

"Throw my own situation back in my face and ask me why I don't just unplug then if it's that easy."

"Not my place," Zee said. "And honestly, not my position either. I'm not going to tell people to leave a place where they belong. You're not the only one that's better off in here than out there."

"You've got a knack for telling people what they want to hear."

"I've got a knack for seeing diseased patients and people that can't afford operations for new eyes, or ears or limbs, or autistic conditions that find a place where they can finally cope. Here. No one has the right to tell them they can't stay in a place where they're on a level playing field with everyone else."

"That's... surprisingly progressive."

"I tend to think of it as 'not cruel,' but whatever." Zee pushed at the virtual desk and felt the wheeled office chair slide across the floor. "Annnnnd we're done."

"That was fast."

"Well, I didn't have to bust in here. Saved a lot of time."

As Zee wrapped things up, Miriya said. "So, are we going to talk about this?"

"No," Zee said. "I'll think about it. But we're not going to talk about this anymore. But I'll say one thing. Thanks. For not being what I thought you'd be."

"Which was?"

"Cooler than thou and smug about it."

"My little sister literally throws fire, lightning, can make objects lighter and transmutes matter into other states and elements. She's changed government regimes and busted economies. I'm active on social media. Tell me where in that equation I'm supposed to feel superior."

Zee smiled. "You've also got a way with words."

"I say again, throw lightning. Talk real good. I'm not winning that on point by point comparison. Now, if you're done here, do you want to get back to the party?"

"Probably not," Zee said, reaching out to the wall to press a massive, shiny, button that pulsated with a gentle blue light. The button was labeled "FINISHED." "I'm not good with social stuff. I think I'm more on your sister's wavelength that way. When people are having a good time, I'm not. Besides, I don't think I'll have the time for it anyway. Your sister wanted to know when I was done. I think she wants to move fast."

"How fast are we talking?"

A display opened up in the air, with Cloke dominating the frame, her feet up on an immaculate tablecloth. In the background were tables, diners and the Eiffel tower. Zee could tell from the reactions of the diners that this wasn't a simulation, Cloke really was being uncouth in an actual French restaurant.

"Well aren't you two all cozy," she said.

"Okay, that *was* fast," Miriya said. "What's the rush, little sis?"

"On the clock," Cloke said. "Zee, how solid is your foot in this door?"

"Invisible titanium," Zee replied. "I could turn their network into a child pornography hub and they'd never know it."

Miriya made a face. "You're not actually going to do that, right?"

"Xie won't have time," Cloke said. "Set up what you need at that end, then Darma will help you set up some more."

"For Marcus?"

Cloke nodded. "And me."

"What did you have in mind?"

"Your best impression of an organ transplant, possibly a faulty airlock."

Zee blinked a few times. "That's new."

"A lot of this job is." Cloke leaned back and slurped noisily from a glass of wine, drawing more dirty looks. "Now, I'm going to have my dinner here. You can party with Em, or whatever else you want to do for a bit, and when I'm done, I'll set things up for a little meet. That's the part they never tell you about when you're trying to destroy three illegally preserved and copied personalities. All the meetings."

Chapter XVII:
Pre-Amping

CLOKE HATED PARTIES, but found them useful as noise generators to mask whatever signal she was trying to preserve. In this case, a French debutante soiree where, when they weren't primping to the youngest princess of Monaco, important people discussed important things, and both physical and data security were at a premium.

Marcus, even in a combat cyborg chassis, fit right in. People ignored him as security, since he had the bored-but-diligent stature of someone patiently waiting for a legal excuse to shoot something. People ignored Cloke, but only in that awkwardly deliberate way that showed how aware they were that people of the highest power and authority deferred to her, even if people lower on the social and financial hierarchy were ignorant of her identity.

Cloke watched as Zee fidgeted uncomfortably in hir chair, ignoring the drink xie'd ordered. They were in a ballroom within the palace, on one of the second levels that gave a spectacular balcony view of the proceedings and the Genoese architecture. Down below, people mingled, classical music played, and the old money looked genuinely bored and tired of the pomp, while the young and new money tried, unsuccessfully, to do the same, unable to hide their thrill at being at a royal debut.

"I don't even know who this is," Zee said.

"She's a princess, the title is more important than the name."

Zee finally took a large gulp of the drink in hir hand. "You have the most fucked up social life of anyone I've ever known."

"I don't socialize with these people."

"That's what's fucked up about it, you have the *option*. Most people can't say 'Well, the Sultan of Brunei invited me to hang, but I'd rather stay at home and watch anime.'"

"I wouldn't bail on the Sultan. I'd come over and make him watch anime with me."

Zee looked to Marcus.

Marcus shrugged. "I think you just proved hir point, C."

"So, if you don't socialize with these people, why are we here?" Zee asked.

"Efficiency," Cloke said. "Between the privacy tech our host so thoughtfully provides, and the mute globe I've thrown up around us, it's nearly impossible for anyone to hear what we're talking about. And I needed to come down here anyway for not-social reasons."

"You got a funny kind of idea of work," Zee said.

"I'm a funny kind of girl," Cloke said. She watched as various guests on the balcony suddenly parted to make way for a woman and her attendants. The woman was older; modestly, tastefully and expensively dressed; clearly used to wielding authority. It gave Cloke great satisfaction as Zee's face changed from curiosity to shock when xie consulted the Net for facial recognition and hir visor told hir the woman approaching them was Aldea, wife of Rainier VII, making her the ruling Princess of Monaco. Princess Aldea nodded to Cloke as she got closer and Cloke nodded back.

"Better stand up and do the bowing thing," Cloke said, getting to her feet. "You too, Victor Victoria. Be polite."

Cloke gave a slight bow as Aldea signaled her entourage to stop. She entered the mute globe and Cloke said, "Your Serene Highness." Marcus and Zee followed with their own bows, Zee going for a formal, deep Japanese bow.

Aldea looked at Cloke and said, "That never, *ever* sounds convincing when you say it."

Cloke shrugged. "I just have to say it, I don't have to mean it."

Aldea broke into a grin. "You ignorant cow," she said, leaning in to hug Cloke.

"I learned from the master," Cloke said, and returned the hug. They sat down, and she stopped and looked at the necklace Aldea was wearing, made of gold and diamonds, glittering with reflected light and holographic certifications. "Wow, not too tacky tonight, are we?"

"It's my daughter's official debut, I have to wear the official jewelry," Aldea said.

"Hey Zee, come here, take a look this. I don't think you've ever seen it."

Zee approached with uncharacteristic meekness and did a bow and a curtsey. "Zee, Aldea, princess. Aldea, Zee, console jockey."

Aldea grinned and nodded to Zee. Zee merely looked stricken.

"Look," Cloke said, pointing to the gold and jeweled necklace. "It's gold."

"So?"

"No, it's *heritage* GC gold. Geologically certified. This stuff actually came out of the ground, it's not that alchemically transmuted stuff you buy at street stalls and convenience stores. That's why it's got the registered, encrypted holographs."

Zee leaned in to get a closer look. "So…"

"Yeah, it's actually *worth* something. Not costume jewelry, but historical, expensive jewelry."

"How do you know it's not fake?" Zee asked, clearly forgetting where xie was.

Aldea laughed. "Well, in this case it's pretty easy. It's been in the family vaults for centuries. Put it in analysis and you'll see all the impurities in it that come from traditional smelting and jeweling techniques, something you'll never get with transmuted elements. The encrypted holographic certification was just a way to ensure that even the illiterate *nouveau riche* know this is genuine. After all, how else was old money going to keep gold and jewels valuable once magic could generate infinite amounts?"

"Old money's not that old anymore," Marcus said.

"I beg to differ," Princess Aldea said, standing up to kiss Marcus on the cheek as he leaned down to accommodate her. "I think somewhere down in the hall we have an IBM executive. Silicon is still *very* old money."

"I was thinking more landowners with serfs. The guys that made their money the old-fashioned way profiting from food they didn't grow and taxing the people that did it for them. Then when that stopped bringing in megabucks, their superiority came from legacy," Marcus said. "These industrial-age oil and Silicon Valley guys that actually generate a profit are just kids, comparatively speaking."

"How is *your* kid, Marcus?"

"Same as always. Getting too smart, growing up too fast. Congrats on your daughter."

"Yes," Aldea said, looking down at the young princess as she mingled with guests on the ballroom floor. "She's now old enough to humiliate herself on public broadcasts without requiring parental consent. That makes me feel ever so proud."

"Well, that's just bad parenting," Cloke said.

"And bad teaching," Aldea replied.

"I'm not her teacher," Cloke said.

"Not on a regular basis. But you're still the College special lecturer on combat magic. And you *did* promise you'd keep an eye on her."

"Wait, the Princess of Monaco is a mage?" Zee asked.

"Oh, kids these days," Cloke said. "If it's not a hit song on the charts, it doesn't exist in their world..."

"Well, it's nice to meet you all," Aldea said. "But Cloke, if you're not going to tell me why you accepted my habitual invitation that wasn't actually expecting any kind of RSVP, I still have my own rounds to make."

"Actually, I came here to ask about your planned visit," Cloke said. "To the Ortegan Orbital headquarters."

Aldea looked appraisingly at Cloke, then sat back down. "I'm not even going to ask how you know about that."

"You're royal, your banking habits are your business, and the smart money is kept out of terrestrial jurisdiction anyway. I don't care about what you're going to do there, I don't care how offshore or no-shore your money is, I just care that you're going."

"Why?"

"I need to be your luggage. And your garbage."

Aldea blinked slowly. "You're sure that mute globe of yours is working?"

Cloke leaned out and looked at Aldea's security detail, standing just outside the globe's range. She smiled, waved and said, "Hey, I'm about to kill your monarch and feed her remains to the street cats, then I'm going to do the same to your immediate family members. Also, my underwear is filthy with bubonic plague and I just sat in the punch bowl."

They continued to stare impassively.

Cloke leaned back in her chair. "Pretty sure."

Aldea took to the empty seat that was directly across from Cloke. It was, Cloke noted, with a grace and elegance that she herself was never going to have outside of a simulation, the kind of thing that could only come from being raised in a classy way by classy people your entire life. "So," Aldea said, fully reclining in the chair. "Why would I possibly let you come along for the ride?"

"One, you owe me."

Aldea let out a dismissive sigh. "I don't owe you *that* much."

"Well then, how much would I owe you?"

Aldea was silent for a moment, regarding Cloke with calm, level eyes. "So, this is big enough that you'll owe me?"

"Within reason, yeah. I'm just looking to be a silent part of your entourage."

"And if you're found out, established orders will crumble—including royal family structures, let's not forget that part."

"So, did you have something in mind? And assassinations are off the table."

"Anyone that I'd want dead is already that way."

Zee's eyes went wide and Aldea reached over and patted hir hand. "I'm joking, of course." Her gentle touch tightened slowly around Zee's wrist. "Mostly."

"Oh, leave the kid alone," Cloke said. "It's my arm being twisted."

"Very well," Aldea said, releasing her grasp and leaning back. "Let's make this worthwhile then. Let's make this... anti-matter."

"Let's not. That's restricted class alchemy. It's like your GC gold, every piece created is documented and registered."

"Officially, that's true. But that's what I've always liked about you. You have a knack for going unofficial when you need to."

Cloke shook her head. "Not going to happen. That's like me asking to borrow your car and you saying it's going to cost me a nuke."

"I had to try."

"Try something within reason."

Aldea gazed out at the soiree, watching the people greet the princess. "All right," she said, turning back to Cloke. "My daughter."

"What about her?"

"Put her in your combat program."

"What?"

"Nothing in the field," Aldea said firmly. "I can talk to the appropriate channels to ensure that, but I want you on her training regimen."

"Why?"

"Teach her to fight. The way you do."

Cloke could feel herself growing very tired. This, again. "I can show her how to do it," she said. "But I can't promise she'll be able to."

"Why?"

"Because she might not have it in her," Cloke said. "This is like bird flight. If you don't have wings, it's all just theory. It'll never happen for you."

"And you're saying she doesn't have the wings?"

"I'm saying she probably doesn't, so don't get angry if I just confirm it."

"What makes you so sure she can't do it?"

"The fact that she hasn't been internally evaluated for a concentration in combat is already the biggest indicator," Cloke said. "The percentage of thaumaturgists that have the talent and the predisposition to handle themselves in a combat situation is very small."

"And how many of them fight like you? How many don't need some kind of incantation or ritual to focus and just fight like it's a reflex? Every other combat mage I've seen needs a system of gestures or vocal foci to fight, sometimes both. It can take them seconds or even minutes to initiate a spell. How many don't?"

Cloke paused for a few moments. "It's… very, very small."

"I see," Aldea replied, in a voice that indicated anything but that sentiment.

"I'll do what I can," Cloke said. "I'll take her under my wing. I'll show her what I do. I'll show her *exactly* how I do it. I won't keep secrets or hide anything from her. Whether she can do it after all that… that's all up to her own natural ability."

"She either has wings or she doesn't."

Cloke nodded.

Aldea seemed lost in thought, her eyes directed elsewhere, as if she were watching some drama unfold that only she could see. "Very well," she said at last. "It's not anti-matter—"

"And it never will be," Cloke said, reaching for her drink.

"—But it'll do. I'm not asking for anything miraculous."

"I'll do everything I can."

Aldea signaled to a nearby server, who entered into their area and offered her a glass of wine. She nodded as she accepted it and politely waited for them to be alone once more. "Now," she said, taking a sip. "Tell me exactly how difficult you're about to make my life."

"You'll get over it," Cloke said. "And you'll have a great story to tell at your next party."

Cloke gave her the broad strokes of the idea. Aldea chuffed and made all the appropriate grumpy noises in protest, but it was all formality at this point. She was a princess: there was actually very little she couldn't do if she made up her mind about it.

When they'd finished, Aldea stood up and gave a slight nod to Cloke's assembled crew. "Nice to meet with you all," she said. "I hope your insurance is paid up." She left them to get back to overseeing her daughter's official debut to the world.

"I've always liked her," Marcus said. "For a royal, she's got her head on pretty straight."

"It freaks me out that you can speak from personal experience like that," Zee said.

"You're getting that same experience now," Marcus said. "And it's useful. Remember it."

"You never know when something will come in handy," Cloke said. "Especially with this next job."

"And you're going to tell us exactly how that's going to go down now?" Marcus asked.

"Parties like this are the best place for it," Cloke said. "It sets the right atmosphere for a well-planned explosion or financial collapse."

"And those are always the best kind," Marcus said. "Okay. Details. Give."

Cloke sat them all down, checked on the integrity of her mute globe one more time, then got into the specifics of how they were going to hit three separate offices of one of the biggest multinational corporations on the planet.

III
The Majitsu Siege
November 25, 2138

Chapter XVIII:
Syncing

CLOKE HAD BEEN right. It was cheaper to buy beer than water in Prague.

Zee, not willing to trust lightning-fast judgment and snap reflexes to the warm, enveloping fog of Pilsner Urquell, was now living off energy and soft drinks. A loft had been rented, exactly the kind that Zee had seen in a movie once. Despite not needing to, multiple monitors had been set up on a rack to make it look and feel more badass. Zee could even see the Majitsu office building just a few blocks away, set up on a hill like a benevolent dictator; large, friendly and bristling with weapons. That had made it easier to get work.

Zee's initial suspicions about the world were correct; even when it seemed like nothing was happening, data was happening underneath.

It was something that became clearer as more systems were penetrated, as Cloke unveiled the inner workings of higher powers and the nature of deals. The big motions, the sweeping changes, the on and the off... all of it was punctuated by what people would call nothing, but were really tiny, minute changes in information too small or worthless individually to take notice of, but, in sufficient numbers, could evoke any kind of change imaginable with the right tools and timing. Zee was beginning to appreciate the most effective kind of coding was like a giant, invisible hand, shepherding all that minute, seemingly trivial data into shapes and forms that could punch holes through anything.

It was something that seeing behind the curtain at GIS made very clear: it wasn't the individual information that mattered. It was the collective data mass, how it interacted with the world. What people did with it.

Like right now: the relevant pieces of information were lost in the mass, but they were going to become important to a lot of security and law enforcement agencies in short order.

Names like Sulafa Tower, the building that Marcus was perched on, his camouflage immaculate, his view of the opposing office tower unrestricted. His "buddies," as he'd referred to them, were in other buildings in the area, but all the ballistics and flashpoint analyses that were to come would trace their lines of origin back to Sulafa Tower. Then there were serial ID numbers like, OECC 189263B/R, which belonged to the cargo container traveling up the LUMO orbital elevator, carrying Cloke inside, designated as a mix of audio components and organs that had transport priority to the top. The inevitable investigations would trace the unauthorized LUMO intrusion to that particular box. Of course, the theory was that by the time any of these bits of data came to light, it would be too late.

Then there was that other data that no one was ever supposed to know about; the pile of money accumulating slowly into more and more zeroes as Zee's various transaction systems built a respectable nest egg. With some careful investment and no extravagant living, life's little expenses would be taken care of for the next few years. And no one was getting hurt. That was the important part. That was the part that meant that Zee wasn't supposed to feel bad about any of this. And sometimes the guilt actually did go away for a while. Cloke had more money than she knew what do with. She didn't need it. Zee did.

Zee was in between status checks, eating what Cloke had derisively referred to as "sludge." It was a tasteless nutrient compound with an optimized calorie count and all the essential vitamins and minerals. It had the consistency of paste, and could be spooned into the mouth or sucked down with a straw. It was dirt cheap, fast and easy to consume, and the lack of taste wasn't an issue, since the nano-implants in Zee's tongue made it taste like any flavor that had ever been neuro-recorded. In this case, a particular gourmet chocolate aficionado's sensations filled Zee's mouth with the rich, exquisite taste of a world class, award-winning Parisian mousse. There wouldn't even be a need to snack later since either the implant or any number of simulation ready devices could fill Zee's nervous system with the sensation of a pleasantly full stomach.

That was going to be important since there wouldn't be much time for eating in the next little while. The countdown was on.

Zee went on the tactical channel that had been established for everyone involved in the run. Cloke's comm stones were also available as a secondary, untraceable means of communication that she was only sharing between herself, Zee and Marcus. The tac channel showed what it was supposed to: Marcus and his crew were in position, although not all the gear had been properly configured, but that was in progress.

It was hard to ignore all the Majistu branding that adorned nearly every building in the city, but that was their right; they practically owned Dubai after the original residents could no longer afford to maintain the place. The limited nuclear exchange with Israel had put the entire region on life support. Alchemical research had brought alternative energies to light that collapsed the old petroleum market almost overnight and pulled the plug. The business leaders in the region had never bothered to diversify, content in their domination of only one industry and confident the reign of oil was endless. It was hard for Zee to believe that the nomadic desert tribes that now fought over water and sold hand-made goods for the artisan markets had once controlled the fate of the world's energy industry.

"Friendly neighborhood paranoia check," Zee said on the tac channel to Marcus and 'buddies'. The buddies were of the disquieting sort that didn't know what the hottest new music single was, or which celebrity had just confessed to a massive drug problem, but could keep you updated on the three latest ways to bring military grade weapons into every major urban center of the world without the police or corporate security knowing about it.

"Got a nice view," Marcus said, feeding his optic stream into the channel. Zee felt a small lurch as the communications defaulted to Marcus' point of view and suddenly traffic and the ground were tiny, distant things far below. Zee quickly backed out of the sim channel and back into the distant, unreachable, more malleable environment of the workspace with everything, including Marcus' channel, as a window of information floating at the desk of central control.

"We'll be ready to go on the clock," Marcus said, as if sensing why Zee had suddenly popped into comms. "As combat ops go, this is pretty straightforward."

"Even with minimal casualties?"

"That's the mostly highly requested kind," Marcus said. "Most war isn't fought to raze everything to the ground. There are usually resources meant to be acquired, and when you're talking proxy corporate warfare, no company wants the PR nightmare of a massacre traced back to them. A factory assembly line gets wrecked? Who cares? A factory goes up in flames with all the peasant labor burning to death and the orphanage next door with cooked children? Everyone cares and now someone is out for blood."

"I'll take your word for it."

"And that's why you'll go far in this biz," Marcus said. "Put your faith in the experts and the universe will unfold as ordained."

One of the buddies laughed.

"And peons will shut the fuck up as also ordained," Marcus said.

"And everything is still fine with your secret little science project?" Zee asked.

"Still a secret," one of the buddies said. "But the science is cooking nicely. Been meaning to try this one out for a while now. Glad I finally have an excuse."

It had been a little disturbing to Zee that Marcus' group

not only had a component of the plan they weren't talking about, they'd managed to move it into a nearby warehouse where it occupied a deluxe cargo container nearly as big as the warehouse itself. Marcus had brushed this aside with a reassurance that it wouldn't impact the plan in any bad way. But even good unknowns were still unknowns and it was hard to take comfort in that. Especially when the unknowns probably involved tactical or strategic combat systems.

"How's Cloke doing?"

Zee consulted that feed. "Just rose out of the exosphere. She's got privacy mode on, and I don't feel like breaking it."

Another comm channel opened up. "I can get you into that," Darma said. "Assuming you dig 20th century rock music."

Marcus laughed over the channel. "Okay, say no more, seen that gig, don't need to see it again."

"I'm going to regret this, aren't I?" Zee asked.

"Only if you don't like rock music."

"Definitely going to regret this," Zee muttered. "Okay Marcus, I'll hand you off to the loving care of Eve for a few minutes. You need anything, let her know, she'll let me know."

"I like Eve," Marcus said. "You did a good job training up that virtual intelligence. Total pro."

"We try," Zee said, turning hir attention back to Darma, who had now entered the workspace, opening a door that had appeared in the space and then holding it open after coming through.

"Ma'am," Darma said with a nod.

Zee sighed. "Why are you even fucking around like this anyway, don't you have things to do on your end?"

"Yup. And they're all done," he said. "You work fast when you're dead, and we've got time to kill, why should I have to kill it all alone with Cloke? That's cruel and unusual punishment."

Zee walked through the open door and into the swirling, screaming chaos of a mob. More precisely, it was an audience, but bigger than any Zee had ever seen.

It was night and it looked like hundreds of thousands of people were here: probably a *lot* more than that, with a tiny stage off in the distance. The crowd was every ethnicity imaginable, although the bulk of it seemed Brazilian. The clothes pegged the time period as latter half of the 20th century, though Zee couldn't be more specific than that.

"What the hell is this?" Zee screamed over the crowd.

"Copacabana beach."

"In Rio?"

A big nod. "New Year's Eve, 1994, or 95, I guess," Darma shouted back. "Biggest concert in the world, over three million came for the show." He moved through the crowd, which considerately parted around him as he walked forward. Just one more reminder that they were in a simulation and not an actual mob of hysterical 20th century concertgoers.

"What show?" Zee asked, following.

"Guy named Rod Stewart," Darma said. He pointed to the stage. "But I wouldn't call this a historically accurate simulation."

And there, on the stage, was Cloke, with hair almost as big as she was, playing a guitar like it had killed her sister and she was trying to strangle it in revenge. A tremendous solo was wailing from the combat mage-turned guitarist on stage, and Zee needed to use the onboard Pedia to identify the song as "More Than a Feeling" by some band called Boston.

"I didn't even know she could play," Zee said.

"She can't, obviously," Darma replied. "If you were to check out the actual neural output, she's just randomly thrashing. The sim is translating that into the required fretting for the song. Like those anti-karaoke sims where people open their mouths and Georgia Aquino comes out."

"Who?"

"Jazz crooner in the 2090s, and my *God*, is your ignorance on a roll today." He walked up to the front of the stage and then hopped onto it. Cloke saw him, nudged her head in the direction of the bass player. Darma walked up, held his hands out, and the bass player simply offered him the guitar.

Cloke turned her attention to Zee. "You wanna drum?" she asked.

Zee killed the realism of the experience by going to the global audio settings of the simulation, dropping down the volume of Cloke's music, and entirely muting the audience.

"And in those final days shall come the great beast that devours all fun," Cloke said, shaking her guitar, as if that would somehow make the noise drop out of it. "You could have just said 'no.'"

"I was just going to start jamming," Darma said, his lower lip sticking out petulantly.

Zee sighed, keyed the current audio settings strictly to "personal," and restored the global audio settings back to normal. Now they could hear everything normally, but Zee's ears heard nothing. Cloke and Darma nodded to each other and resumed thrashing.

"You guys are making a shit case for being world class professionals," Zee said.

"I don't think anyone ever said we were," Cloke replied.

"Do you at least care about how things are going?"

"Sure," Cloke said. "You gonna fill me in on one of them super important, totally pro statusy reporto thingies?"

Zee turned to Darma. "You didn't tell me she was going to be like this."

"It's the majesty of rock. It does things to people." He raised up the neck of his bass and Cloke moved in with her guitar, the necks of their instruments crossing as they bobbed heads in unison.

"I actually just wanted to see how you were holding up," Zee said. "But I can give you a status update too, while we're at it."

"So do it."

"Everyone's nearly ready except you."

"Oh, I'm ready," Cloke said. "I just can't do much else cooped up in an elevator, so thank God for sims, huh? Look, it's very simple. Either I stay here and rock out with a few million of my close personal friends... or I unplug and stare at the packing crate I'm currently stuffed in, and check my ammo and ambient air pressure for the umpteenth time. What do you think I'm gonna do?" She ran towards Zee, then dropped to her knees, the slide carrying her almost to the edge of the stage where the audience went mad and reached towards her like mere physical contact would cure cancer. "HOW YOU DOIN' TONIGHT, RIO?" she hollered.

The crowd, as one, screamed back in what would have been a deafening roar had Zee not already muted them.

Cloke walked back to Zee, her head still bopping, her hands still dancing across the guitar. "So how are things with you? Ready to light the powder keg?"

"Pretty much," Zee said, not bothering to ask for permission and bringing parts of the workspace into the sim. The simple 3D network map of Majitsu Prague glowed on the stage like an elaborate laser light show. "I've got at least three solid points of attack locked down, with a fourth in progress, although that's probably overkill."

"If you can, always try to overkill something," Cloke said. "Especially since you're tackling Bad Azevedo. I still wish that was my beat."

"Yeah, you take the quaint Euro office and let the new kid handle an orbital op with zero experience," Darma said. "That's a story that's going to end well."

"I didn't say the task allocation was wrong. Just that after what he did to Em, I want a piece of him."

"Oh, I'll get that piece for you," Zee said. "I've got my own beef with him after that last run."

"That actually makes me feel better," Cloke said. "How are your contingencies?"

"I've got Plan B, C, D and E if things go bug fuck."

"Which will probably still not be enough," Cloke said. "And Marcus? He's set up?"

"You could just ask him yourself."

"And the devouring of fun continues, how does xie do it?"

Zee ignored the remark. "Marcus and crew are in position, but gear is still being reconfigured. I didn't ask which ones."

"Better not to know," Cloke said. "Everything is on schedule here. I can't do shit until the elevator hits the top, then it's all about the sneaky-sneaky."

"That's not industry approved slang, in case you hadn't figured it out," Darma said. "I've done what I can on this end, but then you saw me casing the systems and prepping the satellites. You don't need the run down twice."

Zee nodded, unwilling to add that many of his techniques were being filed away for future reference to be slavishly studied and imitated. Just watching him work was still revealing short cuts, sub-program configurations and exploits that would have otherwise taken years of trial, error and research to eventually stumble upon. He was fast tracking the foundation of Zee's career.

"What happens after?" Zee asked.

"After what?" said Cloke, still fake-playing her guitar.

"After this job. What happens to me?"

"Oh, you'll have lots of choices, I expect," Cloke said. "That's one hell of a bullet point you'll have on that resume you can never show, but, y'know... word gets around. There's always work for someone who can deliver."

"You'd let me do that?"

"Are you going to throw that word impressment around again? I didn't put a ball and chain around your ankle. You wanna go out into that big bad world and make a name for yourself, no one here is stopping you."

"Is that what you want me to do?"

"It's what I expect you to do. What I want and what you want don't have to line up."

"Okay," Zee said. "Gonna go back and check on the systems one more time."

"See? Xie's diligent," Darma said.

"Less talk, more bass," Cloke said.

Zee left and went back to the workspace and sat down in a chair, staring at status readouts coming from Prague, Dubai and orbit.

Something churned inside.

There was disappointment that Cloke hadn't asked Zee to stay on the team permanently. Zee didn't even want to do that, so why suddenly feel hurt about it? Cloke was a lunatic anyway, who approached everything like some freewheeling jazz improvisation, where seeing how things played out was more interesting than keeping people alive. She was a bitch. No one wanted to hang around a bitch. Zee wanted freedom, choice, opportunity. Bitchy Cloke had basically just told her "It's yours."

So why didn't it feel good? Or at least a relief? There would be no need to run away, or disappear, the door was already open, waiting for someone to leave. That was the goal, wasn't it? To not be leashed?

Zee went back into the financial accounts, watching the money slowly accumulate. The amounts involved were getting almost too big to be leashed by anything.

One more job. Just this last job. Then freedom. To do what? To go where?

At least, after all this, there would be some kind of choice. That had to matter right? At least there was freedom, that was something that none of the others had during those awful years in the lab. It wasn't something they probably had even now.

But freedom was here. Or soon would be. And the ability to make all the choices in comfort. In safety. Hadn't that been the goal, and now it was nearly here?

Zee wondered why there was no relief at the prospect.

Chapter XIX:
EVA

CLOKE FOCUSED ENTIRELY on the nav trail her combat visor traced out for her along the exterior of the LUMO elevator. It was too nauseating to look at anything beyond that, since the platform was rotating to create gravity via centrifugal force. It meant the Earth swung into view with frequent and alarming regularity, and that much movement on the periphery of her vision would make her vomit into her helmet given enough time. Past experience during her College years had already taught her that nothing made you feel less like a badass than your lunch staring back at you just a few inches away from your face.

She'd seen this view on more than one occasion, looking down at the Earth, though in far less nauseating fashion. Like so many before her, there had been that nearly religious moment of realizing that she was no longer on the planet she'd walked her whole life, although she hadn't used any of the tourist packages available on the platform to commemorate the event. She'd never had the opportunity to go orbital for purely recreational purposes, and her working trips never seemed to allow for much time to fully appreciate that it was finally happening; humanity was leaving its cradle and taking its first tentative steps into full-blown space exploration.

The LUMO elevator. The LP colonies. The moon and Mars

stations and bases. The asteroid mining facilities. Even the Saturn outpost on Titan. It was all happening now, thanks, ironically, to thaumaturgical techniques like alchemy and mass negation conveniently short cutting problems that had been stumping physicists and engineers for decades. It had taken magic to make their advanced technologies possible.

It was a lesson Cloke always tried to keep in mind, and it was at the core of her successful little operations. Like now, for instance.

Things had been going well. Darma's work was clockwork as usual. The cargo container had obligingly spit her out once it had been moved to its storage destination, and the "faulty" air lock door opened on cue, Darma's viral glitch deleting itself once she got through. She had to hurry. On top of the schedule she had to keep, fitting out her combat armor for vacuum activity, while certainly possible, was hardly ideal. She wasn't going to be able to work for hours out there the way dedicated EVA suits could, so oxygen would be an issue if she stayed out too long.

The electromagnetics on her combat boots and gloves made traversing the exterior of the elevator as straightforward as simply walking on its surface. With so much hectic, daily activity in the area, as long as she was properly hidden from digital security, human eyes weren't going to find it remotely strange that one more person was outside the station on maintenance duty. The only real question mark was the sword, tightly bound to her back, but a human observer would have to get really close to see that.

Aldea had docked the shuttle exactly as planned, and Cloke only had to wait a few minutes before the automated maintenance roused to life. The official transport shuttle of Monaco royalty didn't look much different from most other standard models, apart from its nationalistic paint job, a nice break from the norm— some of the wealthier individuals insisted on custom designs to stand out from the pack. The worst offenders were the retro-designs based on fictional ships. Cloke knew of at least two people that rebuilt their shuttles to resemble giant blue police boxes from London's 1960s era, and she'd nearly choked on her lunch when she looked it up to find out why.

Her alarm beeped to notify her it was time. The drones went into action, prepping the ship for launch.

This was the first dicey part of the transfer. Cloke didn't want to waste any propellant from the tiny Vernier thrusters fitted onto her armor, so she jumped for the maintenance hatch she needed to enter, trusting her judgement—and inertia—would carry her where she needed to go. The hilt of her sword caught on the hatch, nearly yanking her back and killing the smooth, stylish entry she'd been imagining in her head, but that aside, she was inside the shuttle, and still on schedule.

There was a panel inside, gently glowing on and off, and she pressed it to indicate to Aldea that she was on board, and would she be so kind as to throw a little heat, oxygen and air pressure her way?

The life support came through, and a few minutes later and with a slight sense of motion and the muted sound of thrusters, Cloke was underway. The Monaco entourage would follow Aldea's orders to the letter, regardless of how eccentric her requests might be, such as modifying their course vector to pass much closer than usual to Majitsu Orbital Platform Two, designated for Advanced Research. The course modification was much easier to get past Majitsu security when they were informed Her Serene Highness wanted a photo op from the observation deck of her shuttle with the research station visible in frame. It was an opportunity the Majitsu PR department simply couldn't afford to pass up.

Cloke checked in with Darma, who had had his emulation cartridge unceremoniously dumped into a portable unit that Zee had jury-rigged into Cloke's on-board tactical systems. "Please tell me the surveillance at the lab is taken care of," she said.

"Did you miss that part of the status report?"

"Sorry, the power of rock compelled me."

The words, "IT'S BEEN DONE FOR A DAY AND A HALF"

scrolled along the entire field of view of Cloke's visor like the old 21st century stock tickers some diners in New York still displayed for kitschy value.

"Did you get that?" Darma asked.

"Please don't do that when I'm in combat," Cloke said.

"Well, now that you've gone and said it, I won't be able to stop thinking about it."

"I can just unplug you, you know."

"And that would be the first real break I've had this whole gig."

"Is it too soon for a sleep when you're dead comeback?"

"Yes."

"Then how about we just shut up and go? The exit window's coming up."

"You just aim yourself where you need to go," Darma said. "We're clear for fifteen minutes."

Cloke readied herself, touching the panel Aldea's crew had installed to notify everyone she was ready for the next phase. The compartment depressurized, and Cloke could once again hear how loud her own breathing was as all outside sound disappeared along with the oxygen. It wasn't an especially glamorous exit, but jettisoning herself along with the garbage and toilet waste of the shuttle was the easiest way to approach the platform.

"Are you going to say 'Geronimo?'" Darma asked, as a series of lights blinked down to the opening of the maintenance panel. "Because I want to say Geronimo."

"There's only room for one twelve-year-old here," Cloke said. "Be my guest."

The maintenance panel mutely opened to reveal the vacuum of space. Cloke pushed herself away, careful to mind the sword at her back this time and retain some dignity with a graceful exit. Or at least, as much dignity as anyone could have with a dead hacker shouting "Geronimo" into the speakers.

Majitsu Orbital Platform-2 was right where it was supposed to be.

The scale of it impressed her. It obviously wasn't as big as the LUMO elevator; nothing on Earth was. But it was easy to forget that LUMO wasn't simply another place when you were standing on it. Here, floating out of a shuttle and into the full vacuum of space, it was easy to see MOP-2 as a giant, rotating, cylindrical building with a 500m diameter, that, improbably, was just hanging in the dark. It was small enough to not dominate her vision like some continental horizon, but big enough to remind her that several thousand people lived and worked there. She felt like a gnat approaching some giant, sleeping whale in space.

She tested the Vernier micro-thruster modules attached to her armor. It was one of those rare moments when she was grateful for corporate excess. Sure, maybe only ten per cent of the people that used lightweight combat armor would ever be in a situation where they needed to maneuver in a zero-g environment, but those ten per cent were extremely grateful the option existed, and showed their financial appreciation for the thoughtfulness the manufacturers showed.

She approached the station and adjusted her course towards the one particular airlock she wanted.

"Can I ask a question, C?"

"You mean besides the one you just asked?"

"How come you never use a VI agent? Zee got hir pal Eve up and running pretty fast. Marcus has his battle buddy... Khan, I think he calls it. Even I had Mr. Roboto, which reminds me, I should dredge him up. How come you don't have a little digital Jiminy Cricket to work with you?"

Cloke shrugged and watched as the shadows of MOP-2 swallowed her up in the darker side of the platform. Her visor switched over to passive night sight, rendering the world in green. "I wouldn't feel alone then, I guess."

"You're gonna have to explain that."

She fired the thrusters, matching the speed of the rotating station so it appeared to stop moving as she got closer. "It's better to feel alone," she said. "When you think you're not alone, you think that someone will help you when you get in trouble. You think it'll be okay until someone can come along to make it better." She reached out and touched the platform, letting the electro-magnets in her fingertips grip onto the surface. "That's dangerous in this job. No one can help you. No one is going to come along and make things better. When you're in deep shit, you better hope you have strong arms to pull yourself out, because no one is going to toss you a rope."

"Except your team."

"If that's their job," Cloke said. "If that's not their job, it's not their problem, it's yours."

"You got a harsh interpretation of reality."

"I grew up in Jersey. Sue me." She negotiated the surface of the platform, letting her boots grip the exterior and making her way to the airlock. When she accessed the display, it blinked ready to open on her command.

Cloke used the comm stone. "Okay everyone, final check. Are we all on standby?"

"Check," Zee said.

"Waiting on the word," Marcus said.

"Stand by for my mark," Cloke replied. She worked the airlock controls, taking advantage of the temporary control that had been granted to her intermittently for the next two hours, timed to bypass regular security checks on the mechanism. Her visor obligingly ran the window for counting down to when the next control interval went live, and she gave her code when the bright green square flashed across her vision.

The airlock door slid open mutely. Cloke slipped in and watched her visor as the timer for the next door's access panel prepped itself.

Oxygen returned to the airlock chamber, and with it, sound. Cloke was already at the panel, using the access and watching the door's security act like she was just another engineer returning to base after some routine maintenance.

"Mark," Cloke said, pulling her pistol from its holster. "Whatever you're looking at, hit it."

And just like that, it was game time.

Chapter XX:
Three Point Strike

Two and a half major streams of data. The half stream was the combat feed from Marcus, and there was almost nothing Zee could do to add or help with what he was doing. Siege by cyborg, after all, just wasn't in the wheelhouse. The secondary stream was Cloke and Darma, and their batshit crazy orbital assault. The final stream was the main event as far as Zee was concerned: handling the attack on the Majitsu-Prague network and taking down the one digitally preserved personality that didn't feel like being deleted.

And it was all happening at the same time.

On the Marcus feed, it was one hundred per cent pure crude, opening up with a random barrage of flash explosives harmlessly going off in the air. A few actual rounds of artillery were scattered amongst the crowd for drama's sake, and the security sensor systems. It would trigger Majitsu-Dubai to do the prudent thing and start evacuating employees for safety and to avoid litigation.

On the Cloke feed, she was being even less subtle: walking through an unoccupied lounge area of the orbital platform and taking note of the observation window. She directed her hand at it and the ice flowed, forming around the reinforced viewport. She walked to the next bulkhead, ensuring she was safely at the exit, and then raised her pistol and fired a few rounds at the window. It shattered, the loose objects in the room sucked out into the vacuum of space even as Cloke shut the bulkhead and moved on. The hull breach alarms blared to life. Again, the end result would be safety and evacuation procedures for the non-essential personnel.

Marcus and Cloke said "We're go," almost at the same time, punctuated by either explosions or explosive decompression.

Zee's own campaign began in far less flashy fashion with the simple press of a button. Nothing was going to explode here—at least, not through any deliberate action on Zee's part. Instead, days of careful setup would now start to play out.

"Rube Goldberg is go," Zee said.

Majitsu's Prague office was in the old part of the city—a densely populated, ancient piece of real estate with too much history and preserved architecture for anyone to casually erase. There was no scenario involving the use of live ammunition that would play out with a happy ending under those conditions.

Instead it was going to play out with something Zee had been meaning to try for a long time, but had never had sufficient access to time or resources to entertain. A wet hack: inspiration courtesy of Azevedo himself.

Zee monitored the first domino that would start the chain reaction. Nikola Havel was a mid-level support engineer that Zee had been tracking and profiling for days. She was now nearing what, according to her personal schedule, would have been the end of her shift for that day. She was unaware that Zee had already raided the main shift schedule data-base and put in a request for an extra hour of network access to work on some last minute additions to a roster of monitoring and calibration programs that had entered the system.

As far as Nikola Havel herself knew, she was wrapping up work and unplugging from the system.

Except that her log out command was intercepted by Zee's wet hack.

She did not actually unplug from her workstation. Instead

she experienced the expected transition that signaled she was leaving her work sim environment, but was actually placed into a neurosimulation of her physical office, the Majitsu-Prague building, and the three block walk to her nearby condo, populated with a smattering of pedestrians, shopkeepers, wait staff and other computer generated crowd background that had been averaged out from compiling the last several days of surveillance footage from security cameras along the route.

Nikola Havel wouldn't deviate from her normal schedule. She played a key role as a pilot for a long-range strategic attack wing for an up-and-coming squad in a competitive space fighter combat game. Zee had already broken into her squad's private forum and seen their plans for an important raid against a rival squad today.

Nikola made the walk from her office to her one bedroom condo, barely paying attention to anything, for which Zee was profoundly thankful since there were "seams" in the alleys leading away from the main path that a more observant person might have noticed. She used her bathroom, changed into some loose, comfortable clothing and logged into her account. Or at least, thought she did.

This was the part of Zee's carefully orchestrated hack where things would go wrong for Nikola. Instead of logging into the game, she was greeted with connection problems. In a mix of panic and fury, Nikola went through all the expected procedures to try and re-establish a connection with her game.

Nikola Havel thought she was doing her own emergency tech support to get connected to her personal game account in her own apartment. She was actually redirecting her neural commands—still plugged in, at her office workstation—to open up the doors Zee needed to dive deeper into the Majitsu-Prague internal office network.

"We have access," Zee said, as secure command channels became vulnerable thanks to Havel's frenzied attempts to get back into her game. "Moving on to step two."

Zee unleashed "the horde."

A suite of attack software roamed with impunity through

the network, finding their appointed points of assault to await command. While that was going, Zee put out a "parade float" just outside the network portals to give the bored and unprepared digital security staff something to keep them occupied and earn their salary. That code poked and prodded at the defenses, multiplying in number and not attempting to hide it, like the barbarian horde banging their shields and raising spears at the city gate.

They gave Zee time to go after a secondary Neanderthal insurance policy. One of the airborne security drones would fulfill that requirement nicely, in case it came down to that.

Zee's own skillset favored going after Bad Azevedo through the networks, going for a full, complete deletion. That would be the classy, badass way to do it. But having a security drone capable of getting to Azevedo's actual storage area, and pumping his physical housing full of bullets, electricity, or both would also get the job done, albeit in a less efficient, more crude way.

Zee wasn't about to refuse a possible route to victory just because it wasn't stylish enough.

The selected drone was in its charging station. Once all the software had settled into place in the system, Zee co-opted it, ordered a reload of all its onboard ammunition and sent it on a routine patrol route through the office. Meanwhile the attack programs idled, waiting for their signal.

Another status check showed Marcus and friends demonstrating once more why a few well-trained special operations cyborgs were worth more than a platoon or two of unenhanced security guards. Their mobility and firepower were terrifying. Just one of them had the weapon capacity of an entire conventional combat unit, complete with heavy artillery capability, but they combined this with an agility that neither a human nor a vehicle could replicate, since they sat somewhere between the two.

With four of them, working together as a coordinated team, the security dayshift for Majitsu Dubai was woefully unprepared.

Zee noted with satisfaction that despite the explosions and collateral buildings that threatened to come sinking to the ground, Marcus was good for his word. Their attack had helpfully avoided evacuation routes, letting employees safely run for their lives without endangering them.

"You guys don't do anything small," Zee said.

"No one pays for small," Marcus replied. He punctuated this with a grenade that blew out every window of the building he was facing. The glass descended like a rain of hard, glimmering light. "How are things on your end?"

"On schedule," Zee said, giving the status board a quick check. Mostly green with a few yellow areas for some attackware not working as quickly as hoped, but still well within the overall parameters of the op. "Gonna drop the hammer soon."

"I'd say we're already in the nail phase over here," Marcus said.

"Hold that thought," Zee said, noticing an orange indicator blinking to life. It was a warning that in no way should have been active for this operation. "Eve, tell me that's not what I think it is."

"Understood, but then I will be unable to comply with your earlier request for early warning notification."

Zee sighed. "Fine, give it to me."

"Is this bad?" Marcus asked. "It sounds bad."

"There's a notice of tactical mobilization sounding through the College internal security network," the virtual intelligence said. "Combat unit. Assembly and prep in progress."

"That is definitely bad," Marcus said.

"Give me a departure point and destination," Zee said.

"Team assembly taking place in Qatar, set for deployment via hypersonic transport to—"

"They're gunning for you," Zee said to Marcus. "Are you rated for that?"

"I dunno, are we?" Marcus said on the comm network, clearly asking his teammates that he must have patched into their talk.

"I guess we'll find out," one of them replied. "That's the part about hazard pay that really bites. You don't get any say in the kind of hazard…"

"What are we looking at for squad composition?" Zee asked the computer.

"Strategic thaumaturge, elementalist," Eve replied. "With conventional defensive combat support."

"They're going to fry us with lightning," Marcus said. "Long range. Sounds like they're not even going to try to get close. Smart move. We are cyborgs, after all."

Zee switched over to the program that was spying on the College network and gave it a quick overview. "No one in Dubai or the Majitsu home office sent word to the College for help. It looks like they're acting on their own."

"Only one combat mage," one of Marcus' team said. "From the size of the unit they didn't have a lot of preparation for this. They're just throwing whoever they could find at us."

"Are you getting anything on communications?" Marcus asked.

"I've got chatter down the line from the College itself, and from the base about deployment logistics. Nothing from the squad," Zee said. "That's radio silence."

"Probably because they're on comm stones, like us," Marcus said. "This is mage shit. They're going to stay off the wire when they can."

"What's the response time?" Zee asked the VI.

"Current projections estimate deployment on site in thirty minutes," Eve said.

"Gonna be tight," Marcus replied.

"Aerial response coming in," one of his teammates said on the channel. "Combat drones. Counting at least six."

"Just got tighter," Marcus said, and the comm stone went dead as he cut the communications out, presumably to concentrate on surviving the next wave of quasi-military defense the Dubai office was finally starting to put up.

There was nothing else that could be done on Marcus' side. He was a big boy, with a carbyne-reinforced, combat-grade chassis: he could handle himself in a fight. That's what he was paid to do.

Zee turned back to the digital siege at hand. Prague's network defense staff was finally awake and alert, and they were all warmed up, just waiting for the main event to start. "Eve, keep me apprised of the combat mage approach, five-minute intervals."

"Compliance."

Zee worked the comm channel. "Darma, I'm going full in now, but you should know Cloke's College buddies are sending a response to Marcus. Tell Cloke. I'll keep you updated. Out."

And finally, the moment arrived.

"Go time." Zee pressed the button and brought the hammer down.

In Nikola Havel's simulated apartment, her entire building's network died, forcing her to resort to less legal means to acquire a connection—attempting to leech off the network of the office in the next building. In reality, she'd just put an override on all the defenses protecting the Prague network's most sensitive research data.

Zee raided it.

This would be the obvious target, and the Prague network defense would divert all resources to it. It was a coin toss to Zee; the data, if any could be grabbed, would make for an interesting bonus, but primarily the effort—as genuine as it was—was more diversionary than anything else. As far as Majitsu Prague digital security was concerned, a by-the-books hack was incoming from a competitor in Dusseldorf, Färber Schwerkraft AG, and their staff would enact a textbook defense. Zee knew what they would do, how they would do it and when they would do it, and it left holes for someone that knew where to look. That was one of the nice things about big corporations. The company protocol made their methodology very predictable.

Meanwhile, one specific group of espionage-ware that had infiltrated the heart of the network received the signal they had been patiently waiting for. They were largely custom code, the kind of thing that played off Zee's first specialties: in this case, digging up career-ending dirt. Zee had carefully tracked some of the key management and tech personnel at the office, broken into their lives, watched their abuses, and located where they'd buried their shit.

On command, the actual attack went into motion, going into full blackmail mode. The code branched out through the Prague network and used that as launch point to jump into personal home networks using top management overrides. Office documents, personal communications, messages on devices, in forums and sim spaces no one would want anyone else to know about were all ransacked. Videos, pedophiliac sim replays involving the children of relatives, personal messages, threats, collusion mails discussing how to overthrow powerful, vindictive, inter-office rivals, drugs and homes bought on the company tab and misreported as company expenses, prostitutes bought, law enforcement officers silenced—all the indiscretions they'd been dumb enough to commit to digital were rounded up.

Zee's code notified all the pertinent employees that their dirty little secrets were about to see the light of day. They did exactly what anyone would expect.

Executives diverted available technical staff to a new, even higher priority defense. The best digital security staff in the office completely forgot about their job, the alerts ignored on their consoles, and the invasion of their office network unattended, because the lid was opening on things no one was supposed to know about.

No one cared about saving a company when they had to save themselves.

Without a human hand guiding the defense programs, Zee's assault became much easier. Essentially the soldiers had stopped defending the fort. Now it was time to beat a path to the treasure room inside.

Eve chimed in with regular updates as Zee's programs steamrolled over the unattended network defense. The combat mage group was already in the air, probably twiddling their thumbs, or meditating, or doing whatever it was that combat mages did to prep themselves for engagement.

Zee dropped back into the comm stone with Marcus. "You're going to have that company drop in really soon."

"I think we're about as ready as we're ever going to be," Marcus said.

"How ready is that?"

"No idea," Marcus said. "Nature of the beast with magic. Still, we do have a few tricks. Especially if it's going to be a ranged strike. That narrows down the options for everybody. How are you doing?"

"On schedule so far," Zee said. "The Prague network is basically on fire at this point."

"We've got clouds moving in here," Marcus said. "Big, dark, fat rain clouds. When the sky was clear. In the desert. Guess that means our new friends are warming things up ahead of time."

"Good luck with that," Zee said, noting the indicators in the workspace that announced access to the specific network gateway Zee wanted. "I'm on the clock again, you guys take care of yourselves."

There was a unison of grunts from Marcus' team as they signed off.

Zee sent out the programs and began opening up the gateway. Bad Azevedo had been the only duplicate to willingly cooperate, and so had been the only one granted limited but regular access to the online world in order to better conduct his work and research. Zee was now at the point of contact between the dead mage and the rest of the world: basically the front door of his house.

Zee played it carefully.

Getting early access into the network and being able to poke around had made it possible to set up much more comprehensive attacks and defenses. The standard blocks were carefully disassembled. The illegal defenses kicked in, the ones that tried to kill console jockeys by overloading their nervous systems with lethal neural feedback. Zee rode it out, watching the signals blunt themselves against viral shielding as programs rooted out the source of the attack and blocked them up by putting them in virtual bottles, like angry, lethal lab specimens. Zee would take the specific code and examine it later to see if there was anything in it worth incorporating.

Zee wondered if it was worth it to give Bad Azevedo any last words, and decided against it. Better to just burn the whole thing down and get out.

The choice was taken away from Zee when Bad Azevedo literally opened a door to the workspace and walked right in, maintaining steady eye contact.

An alert went out in the workspace indicating that something wrong was happening on Cloke's end. Zee ignored the blaring of the alarm.

"Somehow I expected something more... elaborate," Azevedo said, looking around the virtual environment like a disappointed interior decorator.

Zee didn't speak, didn't move, and really, didn't have to. The neural commands did everything, analyzing the form of entry and setting up a retaliation that would push him back out as slowly and as painfully as possible.

Azevedo raised his hand. "Oh, please. We can dispense with that. I'll give you credit where it's due, your defenses are solid enough that the best I could do was communicate. I couldn't even do anything remotely hostile. Not for lack of trying, mind you."

Zee leaned back in the virtual chair and hoped it looked cool, detached and in control. "So, you just came to acknowledge my superior power?"

Azevedo smiled in that way that reminded Zee of irritated customer service staff that had just been spit on and were still contractually obliged to be polite and not reply with "fuck off and die." "I came with an offer," Azevedo said.

Zee's eyebrow arched of its own accord. "Is this the kind of offer that involves life support and breathing through a straw in my throat?"

"I used the stick on Cloke because it's the only thing that cow understands," Azevedo said. "I can already tell you're reasonable enough to respond to a carrot, so that's what I brought."

He gestured and a number appeared in the air, hovering and glowing with neon luminescence. It had a lot of zeroes in it. "That's in reals," Azevedo said. "Or any other currency you designate. And it's yours if you walk away."

"You're paying me to quit?"

"Most people only get paid if they work. It's a nice change, isn't it?"

Zee looked at the number again. There were a *lot* of zeroes in it. Far more than this job itself was paying. Or several beyond it. "That's a nice offer, but it would put my career in the toilet to bail out on an operator like Cloke in the middle of a job. Hard to get much work after that."

"You wouldn't need to," Azevedo said. His head tilted as he stared. "I thought you looked familiar to me, but I couldn't place it. Not at first. And then I remembered a visit I undertook once, courtesy of Andrew Komarov. He wanted to impress someone with the genie he had in a bottle. It was this man." Azevedo held out his hand. An image appeared over his palm.

Zee forgot to breathe.

It was him. The eyes, the face, the slight tilt of the mouth, that deeply intelligent, deeply twisted grin that promised hours of humiliation, possibly death if things got too routine and predictable. The man that had made Zee, and the others, amusing himself with his exotic guinea pig family in his private laboratories.

"It's not a photo," Azevedo said, as if in answer to Zee's question about the impossible image. "It's taken directly from my memory. He logged in to chat, let me peek into my security systems, including your... pens. I preserved the image and cached it away before his scrubbers could delete the data. I have the entire visit. I have his face. His voice, his words. I have his name."

A scream was building somewhere inside.

Azevedo walked closer, but stopped just short of physical striking distance. Not that it mattered in a virtual space, it was probably more out of careful, diplomatic habit than anything else. "I can give it all to you. You could find him. End him. And then you'd have a life, wouldn't you? A safe one. You wouldn't need to do any of this anymore. You'd be free. And handsomely paid. And all you have to do is... nothing. Stop. Right now. That's it. And freedom and money are yours. So easy, isn't it?"

"Why are you doing this?" Zee asked.

"Because I know what it feels like to be a prisoner. And I know what it means when someone offers a way out. We're not so very different, you and I. We're somebody's ugly secret. And we're both just trying to survive in a world where we have no place. This is a fair trade. You leave my life—such as it is—alone, and I give you a chance to have a real one. That's my angle. That's what we get out of it."

There was something about the way Azevedo spoke that felt like everything Zee had ever wanted someone to say. It was easy to wonder how long he'd been practicing this speech.

On paper this was everything. The answer to all the current problems. It would be possible to find him. Finish him.

And then Zee realized it would also be possible to find them. Save them. All the ones that had been left behind. This was it. A chance to finally make good.

"Give me a name," Zee said.

"No," Azevedo replied. "You know how this works. Half now, half when the job's done. Or undone, as it were." The logo of Ortega Orbital Banking appeared beside Azevedo and he raised a finger to touch it. The numbers that were still floating in the air moved under the bank logo, and he poked at it, letting the glowing numbers and letters slide across the air to stop in front of Zee's face. "I'll give you the money first," he said. "For obvious reasons, it doesn't do much for me. And believe me, I have far more where that came from."

Zee ran a quick confirmation. The account number checked

out. Somewhere in an off-world account, safely beyond the jurisdiction of most financial government agencies on Earth was a fuck-ton of money. A big glowing question popped up under the logo and its ridiculous amount of cash that read "Accept Fund Transfer?" Under that, "Y/N" floated, waiting for Zee's touch.

Zee remembered the signal that was still blaring. Cloke was in some kind of trouble. As usual.

Then Zee remembered those first nights of freedom spent in fear and hiding, the drudgery of sacrifice made for survival, the things endured under Jimmy Tong. The way money could make all of that disappear. Forever.

Zee touched "Y," and watched the zeroes move.

Chapter XXI:
Maelstrom

CLOKE WATCHED THE MOP-2 platform spiral away from her as the explosive decompression sucked her and three security officers into the cold black of space.

She remembered now why everyone had told her guns with high explosive armor piercing rounds in extra-orbital operations were beyond stupid. She probably owed someone a dinner.

"I wish I could say that was unexpected," Darma chimed in. "But it wasn't."

Cloke ignored the jab and concentrated on the immediate situation. One of the security officers blew past her, waving her arms frantically with no visible means of stopping her flight. The other two had grabbed onto each other, although one was probably going to die. His face plate was up, and he couldn't seem to bring it down to get the oxygen going and air pressure normalized in his combat suit. The other could only watch, holding with one hand while the other clung to a pipe he'd managed to grab onto. All four of them had flown through the hole in the viewing gallery Cloke had made when the officers opened fire with energy weapons, and she'd fired back with her hand cannon.

Now she was tumbling away, like the other security officer. But she had options.

She didn't want to use the thrusters on her suit; she still might need them for whatever else could go wrong.

Instead, she judged her tumble, then positioned her gun near her center of mass, away from herself and fired. She was startled by how pretty the discharge was that came from the barrel, shaped like a bubble and expanding. The recoil kicked in.

Her own pace slowed considerably and MOP-2 stopped looking like it was running away from her in a hurry, and now looked like it was slowly drifting away from her. She fired again, and MOP-2 changed its mind and started coming back towards her.

"We've got a problem," Darma said.

"What was the give-away, the firefight or being in Goddamn space?"

"Got a new problem on the ground. It's Zee."

"Can we do this in a minute?"

"Sure, I'm just covering my ass. I know how you get when someone doesn't tell you something as it happens."

"I'll make a note in the log, now please shut the fuck up. Kinda busy right now trying not to fly off into deep space."

"It's not actually deep space, we'd have to leave the solar system for it to qualif—"

Cloke muted Darma's comm channel.

She watched the two remaining security officers struggling together. The one who couldn't bring his faceplate down was going to lose his face, and then his life in a minute.

Cloke drifted towards them and bumped once more onto the hull of MOP-2, grabbing at a panel and reaching towards the dying security officer's face. It wasn't pretty or painless, but once she'd made contact, she ran the keys through her head, keeping thoughts small and focused and formed a sheet of ice across the man's open helmet. She shifted the keys, changing what she wanted; a localized ball of oxygen flooded his helmet. She threw in some heat as a bonus, then went on the proximity emergency channel that overrode all local communications.

"He's got enough to keep him going for a few minutes," Cloke said to the other security officer. "Make it count, and stay out of my way."

Then she clambered over the pipes and paneling and made her way across the surface of the station. She remembered Darma and unmuted his channel.

"Random act of kindness?" Darma asked.

"They were just doing their job and I saw a chance, so I took it. No big deal."

"You know what is a big deal? Multiple hull breach. We've got that in the station now, how are you going to get back in when the airlocks are hard-locked?"

"I thought you were supposed to be the optimist."

"I died. Changes your perspective on things."

Cloke made her way back to the viewing gallery she'd been blown out of. An airtight emergency barrier had dropped seconds after the room had blown.

"I'm better off out here right now, aren't I?"

"If you still want to get into the main chamber, yeah. Every bulkhead in there is in lockdown, it's actually faster to just monkey over to where you want to go, but then what?"

Cloke called up a map of the platform. It floated in front of her face: a giant cylinder the size of several office towers combined, rotating for artificial gravity, with transparent "stripes" running from top to bottom to let light in. The solid portions were actual station infrastructure, life support, research, habitation, sanitation.

The map indicated the destination she wanted: a sealed-off terminal room, near one of the small arboretums that housed some trees and plants. The terminal room bordered one of the massive windows, designed for light.

Cloke made for the point, pulling herself along and letting inertia carry her in good time to the area she wanted. Periodically she saw escape pods jettison from their cradles and shoot off on pre-programmed courses for the nearest neighboring stations. She activated her boots on arrival and let them clamp onto the surface so she could finally stand. Earth swung by thanks to the rotation of the station, the lights of other installations twinkling in the distance. Peering through the window under her feet showed a combination of maintenance complex, and trees arranged in a pleasing mini forest.

"How are things in the station?" she asked.

"Evacuation is almost done," Darma said. "They're down to a skeleton crew in there now. So, are you going to explain to me how you plan to get back in?"

"I got a theory," Cloke said.

She ran the keys through her mind before activating the ice: this needed to be strong and big. She watched as the ice formed in a ring around her and rose up, creating a dome that she stood inside. Then she switched gears, noting her suit's environmental readout about air pressure—or distinct lack thereof—and created some oxygen inside the dome she'd made, watching the level rise and stopping it when it was something close to Earth-normal, like it would be on the little slice of forest primeval someone had carefully cultivated on the other side of this window.

She pulled out the sword. Even without the crazy properties she and Hiro had embedded within, it was still a Masamune blade. It was time to call once more upon what some had called fifteen years of pointless training in Japanese swordsmanship.

She swung down at the diamond reinforced aluminum panel and gasped. It was like the blade moved through water; only the mildest sense of resistance, despite the fact it was slashing through something inches thick and designed to stop heavy artillery fire.

"Ho-lee *shit*," Darma whispered in her ear.

"It slices and dices or your money back," Cloke said.

Two more strokes and she'd carved out a large triangular hole that she had to put a foot on to lock in place, as the centrifugal force of the station tried to make the now-loose panel fly away from the station. She pushed down, shifting it away: it felt a bit like cutting out a hole in the ice and moving it down and out so that it was still "floating" underwater, just away from the hole itself.

The air "thumped" as the variations in air pressure sorted themselves out, but no explosive decompression this time. Alarms were blaring everywhere, now that atmosphere from the station was coming through.

She reoriented her sense of direction, reminding herself that when she crawled through that hole, she would be climbing "up" from a hole in the ground relative to the way gravity worked.

She looked down at the hole. The ice dome below it was holding. Security sensors would have lit up this area over her breach, so there was going to be a response here soon. A big one. Too many weapons; too many people. She was clearly outnumbered. As long as she played fair.

Cloke surveyed her surroundings.

The inside of MOP-2, or at least this part, was vast, cavernous, but tranquil. Trees; the sound of running water; long, graceful white walkways; and even the smell of cooked lobster coming from somewhere. Majitsu knew how to take care of their employees. Despite the fact that they were essentially in a giant floating can in space, it felt like being out in the country. "Above" her, in the center of the cylinder, she could even make out small clouds as part of the microclimate a space this size generated. The surface that she stood on was dotted with the usual corporate campus infrastructure; the courtyards and gardens for walks, the restaurants, spa therapy and pools, the many, many restaurants, the corporate and guest residences, in addition to all the engineering and life-support infrastructure that reinforced the offices, labs and space docks that dotted the interior.

She took in a few deep breaths and centered herself. It was a lot slower and trickier this time. She wasn't as familiar with manipulating the energy in this way, at this scale, working with this much artificial atmosphere. Not having the luxury of access to unlimited amounts of air was going to make manipulating what was present trickier and far messier and more volatile than anything on Earth. Which was probably why no one had ever been stupid enough to attempt this. Even the keys came slowly to her mind, not the near instant reflex of fire or lightning in their many varied forms. She hadn't done this kind of magic in a while.

But it was still working.

Her suit noticed it first, the sensors monitoring the change in air pressure. The air stirred far beyond what ventilation and circulation specs recommended. Then the breeze kicked in. Then it stopped being a breeze and became a wind. Then it stopped being a wind and became something else entirely; much worse.

She was pretty sure no one had ever created a tornado in space before.

Probably the reason no one had done it was for the same reason guns were a bad idea. Somewhere down on Earth, the sudden redirection of climate forces would be having a massive blowback reaction on a regional scale. The layer of magic that governed weather was like a giant tablecloth stretching beyond the boundaries of Earth, with the weather systems sitting on top like dinnerware. Cloke had just yanked on that cloth without the finesse to keep the plates on the table. Meteoturgy on this scale was like dropping a boulder from a bomber into a lake: there would be catastrophic meteoturgical ripples across the planet. It would result in snowstorms in the tropics, or flood-worthy rainstorms in some city's downtown, unless an extremely powerful Meteoturgist—like, say, Gwen Stepniski—had already been warned and prepped to compensate, and massage the grumpy atmosphere back into something less hostile.

"Okay, I've got some quiet time," Cloke said, keeping the electromagnetic clamps on her boots active to keep her stuck to the floor. A stray visor whipped by and a tree bent at an alarming angle as the wind speed increased and the life support systems struggled against it. "Sit rep, please."

"Marcus is getting hit with a combat mage. Long range. And Zee's gone."

"What?"

"Just dropped off the combat network. All activity

stopped. I checked the activity feed. Xie was wrecking the Prague network hard, broke through nearly everything, hit the gateway to Bad Azevedo, and then went dark a couple of minutes later. Xie's out."

"Like out out, or dead out?"

"Can't tell. It's like xie fell into a black hole, nothing's escaping, not even vital sign data."

Cloke went back to the comm stone. "What's happening, Zee?"

There was nothing. She switched over. "Marcus, are you up to speed?"

"More than you," he replied. "Zee's out, and we got us a little party over here, courtesy of one of your buddies on the leaderboard. Lightning storm's hitting like a bitch. That hazard pay isn't looking like such a great deal right now."

"Take it up with your accountant. Did you get anything from Zee?"

"Nothing unusual, then shit hit our fan. We got some aerial defense drones trying to shake things up. Didn't last long but kept us busy, then Zee was gone. Xie was warning us about the combat mage team until drop out; xie was supposed to get back to us when it was all over on hir end."

"How are you guys doing now?"

"See for yourself."

Marcus punched in an image from his own targeting optics.

It looked like someone had opened up the gate holding in all the lightning in the sky and they were going on a rampage. Bolts of lightning were coming down from a blackened sky, concentrating themselves in the areas where Cloke suspected Marcus' team was either fighting or just hiding.

"That doesn't look good," Cloke said. Cyborgs and lightning were never a great combination and someone was plainly aware of this.

"It looks worse than it is," Marcus said.

"Seriously? How are you guys not freaking out about overload?"

"There are worse things," Marcus said. "And if we get

enough prep time, then the team that's doing this will find out exactly what."

"What do you need from me?"

"From orbit? Shit, woman, how magical are you?"

"Darma, can you help them?"

"Minimally," he said. "I can try and pick up the slack Zee's left, but it's going to be resource intensive. And very loud. On such short notice, there's no way I'd be able to hide what I'm doing or where I'm doing it from."

"So, I'll be an even bigger target."

"Remote work sucks, Cloke. That's why we don't do it that way."

She nodded to no one in particular. "Do it. And help Zee. Whatever's fucking hir up, make it stop."

"I can't promise anything, but I'll look around," Darma said. "Hope you're ready for this."

"If I have to be ready for everything that happens in my life, I'd never get anything done," Cloke said. She watched as some of the aerial defense drones in the station entered into the vast, central space of the area she was in. The burgeoning tornado immediately sent them flying and she laughed.

A couple of cyborgs in shiny new military grade combat chassis showed up, along with a flotilla of combat drones sporting too many tentacles to count, and Cloke stopped laughing.

"Fix this shit," she said to Darma. "My break's over. Keep me posted, boys."

Anyone that saw them in action called them "squids"—the flagship products of Deveraux Laboratoire de Robotique in France. They looked like giant, spindly, delicate jewelry, but they'd been deployed to devastating effect in riot suppression in the Christian Confederated States and certain African military campaigns.

Cloke ratcheted up the force of the tornado to less safe, less comfortable levels.

The cyborgs responded by stalemating themselves. They kicked in their own electromagnetic grips in their feet and lost all mobility.

Cloke took aim with her right hand and released the lightning.

It surged out with no chance to dodge and hit one of the cyborgs. Cloke heard the scream as his digital and mechanical systems shorted and he slumped over momentarily before the force of the wind threw him spiraling away into the air.

The other cyborg responded by killing his own grip to the floor and letting the wind take him wherever it would. That same unpredictability would keep Cloke from getting a bead on him.

The squids were using the opportunity.

Cloke now understood why they were deployed. Each tentacle had an array of electromagnetic grips running across the entire, sizable length of the limb. They still had their mobility, resisting the wind and moving into firing position like monstrous, aquatic fridge magnets. Cloke saw the flare of laser targeting systems moving in to get a bead on her. She was just as stuck as the cyborgs.

She needed to time this right.

She cut the grips on her boots and she was paper, blown along in the wind, just as unpredictable as trash. She ran the keys through her mind and then flung her arm, like she was throwing something.

An arc of shimmering white traced out the shape she'd made in the air, and from that arc, three thin streams of bright, white, killing light shot out, bending at sharp angles as they twisted and turned towards the nearest squids.

The official term for them was tactically deployed and directed phased thaumaturgical emissions.

Most College students just called them magic missiles.

Cloke had been slinging them by the time she was fourteen. It was only after she got to the College that she found out this was supposed to be an advanced graduate-level technique that normally required years of theory and application work.

Three squids exploded. Seven to go.

Cloke took a quick accounting of the locations of the squids, and there was still that one cyborg also being whipped around somewhere. She collided into a combat drone that was still struggling in vain to maintain position in the air and heard her combat suit's status alarms blare in her ears as part of the right shoulder pad shredded with the contact of the drone's engines.

It wasn't worth the energy, so she pulled out her gun and shot it.

Then she yelled in alarm as her trajectory carried her straight into some kind of dining patio for an in-station restaurant.

She hit the glass wall that separated the patio from the indoor dining area, but it held, pinning her there as the tornado continued to rage.

She'd tumbled so much that two of the squids had been lost by her combat network tracking, and the remaining cyborg was also off the scan. Not good.

It was time for some help.

The tornado had to stay; it was at the point where it was nearly self-sustaining anyway, and it would take more energy and time to wind it down than it would to keep it going. But she needed some controlled mobility back.

She drew out her sword, pushed herself away from the barrier the winds had pinned her to, and swung it enough that it cut out huge portions of the viewing glass and let her stumble through into the restaurant itself.

She backed through some doors and found herself in the kitchen. She was only going to have a few moments to do this.

It was some pretty on the fly adjustments. She hoped Ototo could keep up.

She showed the sword the particular configuration of magic that was causing the tornado. She followed this with the reversal: a quick, rough and ready introduction on how to stop the flow of wind, and how to adjust that to take into account the intensity of the wind.

Then she threw in the keys that allowed for smaller, localized effects of magic.

"Did you get all that?" she asked the sword.

It glowed, a soft blue light, and a crystal tone rang once, in the air.

She checked her hand cannon, ejected the clip and put in a fresh magazine.

"Rock and roll," she said to no one in particular, and watched her combat tracker update with five signals closing fast.

She started things off with a fireball. Big one, the kind that looked like an asteroid had decided it was time to throw down with the locals.

It blew out the restaurant window and enveloped the squids that had bunched up as they arrived at the scene. Four signals winked out.

Seven down. Three squids left, only one still tagged on the combat system, one cyborg still unaccounted for.

Cloke ran through the exit she'd made and nodded in satisfaction as she hurled herself headlong into the tornado and kept on running. The Wakizashi had completely negated any weather effects within a six-foot radius.

She could move. She still had to watch out for stray loose objects flying into her, but the proximity sensors on the combat suit could compensate for a lot of that. The important thing was the sword was cancelling out the tornado, and she could still move freely and use her own magic.

She stayed at a run, keeping her movements quick and janky, letting the combat systems sort themselves out and get a better fix on the remaining targets.

The one squid that had remained on her sensors was ahead of her. Another signal popped up behind her as her targeting computers rescanned and updated.

The squid in front of her reared up, using two of its tentacles to stay electromagnetically anchored to the floor.

Cloke charged headlong into it, pulling out her gun. She saw the squid's camera focus on the weapon, analyzing and prioritizing. She turned her run into a slide, throwing herself on her back, whipping the gun behind her and using it as the focal point to let off another magic missile.

The missile guided itself to the squid behind her, and it exploded in a shower of sparks and shrapnel.

Her slide carried her under the squid she had been charging and she swung the sword, cutting off one of its tentacles. The squid swung wildly in the air like a crazed pendulum as it lost its balance to the tornado and reprioritized its goals to regain stability.

Cloke aimed her gun, compensating for the wind, and shot it in the face.

It fell to the ground, then the tornado swept it away, smoking and sputtering into the air.

One squid, one cyborg.

Cloke's navigation systems rerouted, showing her that she now had a minor rat maze of spas, cafes, restaurants and shops to negotiate before getting back to the area with the terminal room access. The tornado had thrown her quite a distance.

She was going to assume that the squid was hunting her actively and would momentarily pop back up on targeting. The cyborg would probably be doing the intelligent thing and trying to set up an ambush. He'd had enough time by now, had seen what she could do on open ground and knew the layout better than she did.

It was what she would have done.

"Tell me we've made progress," Cloke said to Marcus on the comm stone, keeping the gun out and methodically making her way back to the terminal access door.

"Not the kind you want to hear about," Marcus said. "Your magic friends are doing more damage to Dubai than we were."

"Are they going to stop you?"

"At this rate, maybe. We're not going to be able to move on this unless we take that mage out. Whoever she is, she's got a hell of an eye. One of my guys lost a foot just making a run from one building to the next."

"What's going on with the actual op?"

"That's not too bad. The bonus damage from the lightning has done a real number on the systems inside. My guess is that the other team is just making their own entrance easier, but it helps us too. And they don't have our firepower."

Cloke asked the delicate question. "Are you going to use it on that combat unit?"

"You mean lethal?"

"Yeah."

"If I have discretion, we'll see. We need to get a better lock on where she is and how she's deployed. We might not be able to finish this without casualties to their side, if that's what you're asking."

"Do what you can."

"I'll do what I have to, but she knew the risks, same as you." He grunted. "Too bad these comm stones can't pick up explosions. You just missed a cracker. Gotta go. Stay alive, boss."

Cloke checked her own progress. Tornado immunity was definitely showing its benefits. She still had to duck out of the way of any loose objects that went hurtling past, but at least the rising intensity of the storm had made the majority of the crew give up on trying anything aggressive.

Her combat scan remained clear: there was nothing out there, or at least, nothing within range that was moving. She felt almost like she was in a simulation, the way the whipping winds and chaos of the environment were suddenly not factors for her.

Then her combat sensors pinged her that something was closing range. It was directly behind her. She'd have to turn to deal with it.

It was too convenient. "Fuck," she whispered to herself.

She decided to take the hit. She ran the keys through her head, maintaining the level calm she needed for this, concentrating on keeping things warped and small.

The air shimmered and distorted around her, and she finally turned to face the squid as it came half bouncing, half pulling itself towards her. She fired at it with her pistol, her aim not really there as she concentrated on maintaining the shield she'd just thrown up. The shot went wild as the squid pulled itself out of the way and kept closing.

It came a second later: a bright shaft of high-powered laser fire, instantly hitting her. It was blunted by the distortion of her shield and warped around her like broken threads of light, draped against a snow globe.

That was going to piss off the cyborg, who had probably sent the order to the squid for the rear attack hoping to be in a good sniping position to take advantage of the situation. The laser was a good call: no interference from the wind, instant target acquisition too. In another situation, Cloke might have been looking into who this was to add to the roster of potential hires for future jobs.

But that didn't help with the squid, that had now closed range enough that it could do some serious damage with the serrated blades it was unsheathing from the tips of its tentacles. Two of the blades were on motors and Cloke realized someone had decided to make a chainsaw-wielding mechanized combat squid.

One of the chainsaw tentacles swung down with a speed that surprised Cloke and she barely avoided getting her arm shredded by deflecting the blow with the flat of her sword. The blade still grazed her armor, bouncing off, and taking a few pieces with it, slicing through down to her skin and drawing blood.

She flicked her wrist to complete the motion with the sword and it cleaved into the tentacle, not quite amputating the blade but leaving it useless and dangling on a small piece of connective wiring and armor.

Another shaft from the laser hit her, this time coming from the side, and she grunted as she felt the heat of it coming through the shielding. Whoever it was had moved to a new angle and amped up the power. This was no good: the squid was keeping her off balance and the remaining cyborg was using the distraction to strategically take her out from a distance. This one probably had some actual experience against combat mages.

But probably none like her.

He would be relying on the usual weakness, the precious

seconds it took for a typical combat mage to get off an incantation or gesture in order to work the magic. Almost every combat mage relied on a verbal or motion trigger to put the mind in the configuration it needed to be for the energy of magic to be focused in the way they wanted.

Cloke didn't need that. A lot of her magic worked as fast as she could think.

She threw herself to the side, a movement that the cyborg would have to compensate for and re-aim. The squid would need to do the same thing.

She fired her pistol at the same time, and the squid saw it, instantly reacting, its survival protocol moving it out of the way.

The keys in her head were fast, simple and cold.

The lenses and sensors on the squid first clouded over with frost, then were quickly blocked out, then weighed down by ice. It was deaf, dumb and blind, and its limbs waved spasmodically as it tried to go into emergency diagnostics and restore its sensory capability.

Cloke finished it with lightning. It fell to the ground close enough that she was able to kick the main housing. It crunched against her boot and spun away into the wind.

Normally her favorite tactic now would be to drown the area in fog, create enough breeze to mess with motion trackers and then drop the temperature around her body so that it matched the local temperature to make her invisible to infrared scans. The tornado negated most of that.

She decided to go for a more traditional approach.

Most combat mages were considered heavy artillery. She usually fucked up expectations by getting up close and personal, but she could still do long distance when it was required.

Cloke took shelter in another building and gave the order to Ototo to stand down. Then she took a guess as to the most promising areas for a sniper to hide in a tornado.

She got biblical. With the sword's help it was much faster and easier.

Fireballs rained from the central space of MOP-2, descending from the "sky" to the surface in all directions, like apocalypse o' clock. Big ones seared huge chunks of the available real estate, and some of them zigzagged in unpredictable twists as they got caught in the shearing winds of the tornado. The sniper would have to either move or die. This would be setting off all kinds of craziness in the alarms and sensor systems of MOP-2, but it was the kind of sudden scorched-earth approach that had made combat mages so feared in the first place.

All the employee perks went up in flames, or were being currently torn apart by the world's first orbital tornado. There was probably a really good academic paper in here somewhere, but Cloke wasn't going to be the one to write it.

She kept it stylish, moving forwards towards the destination her visor laid out while keeping a safety circle around her that the fireballs would not descend on. Everything else was fair game, though. It must have been working, because the sniping had stopped. The unpredictability of the bombardment made it too risky for the cyborg to stay in one place and get a bead.

Cloke didn't care whether the cyborg had beat a retreat or was dead, as long as the end result was the same, and she could move without being under fire.

She arrived at the terminal room and examined the door. It was locked down, on full alert, and had the kind of security control that she was never, in a million years going to figure out on her own.

She took her sword and cut a Cloke-shaped hole into the door, watching it fall forward with a surprised, artillery-proof "clang."

The room inside was similar to the one she'd broken into back down on the LUMO terminal island. Not much in the way of security or monitoring on the inside. Very minimal forms of access.

Cloke placed her hand on the terminal and a holographic projection appeared in the room. High quality, solid: it was like Azevedo had suddenly blinked into three-dimensional, full-color existence in front of her.

"This is not going all that smoothly," Cloke said to the hologram.

"Did you really expect it to?"

"No, but I was hoping what would go wrong wouldn't be as bad. My jockey's out, and my conventional team is being hit by lightning."

"Surely you're not blaming that on me."

"I'm not blaming it on you, no one put a gun to my head and forced me to take this job. Just wondering if you knew it was going to go down like this."

"It's difficult to reliably maintain any direct communication with each other, so I can only speculate on how the others reacted."

"That's a pretty good speculation if you're just hypothesizing what you would do if you were evil and pissed."

Azevedo sighed. "He's not evil. We're not somehow kissing babies while he's throwing them in boiling vats of oil and cackling. He just made a different choice. To cooperate."

"How come he did, and you didn't? Aren't you all the same?"

"We were all the same at the moment we were duplicated," Azevedo said, scratching his chin. "We stopped being exactly the same the moment we went our separate ways. Different experiences, different thoughts… ultimately different results. Whatever happened to the other didn't happen at the right time or circumstance to us, so we didn't turn. He made his choice, we made ours."

"And you're sure about this choice?" Cloke asked. She hefted the sword. It glowed briefly and a small arc of electricity snapped across it. "Because this is final. And there are people in the College that would love to grant you political asylum. They can probably restore your citizenship. The Azevedo I first talked to really wanted this to end, but like you said, different choices. What's yours?"

"Eventually everyone has to ask themselves what kind of life they want," Azevedo said. "I had a long one. A good one. I did what I had to. Regret some things. Feel very proud of others. It wasn't everything I'd hoped, but I had a life. It was mine. This... I'm still not sure what this is, but it doesn't belong to me. To any of us. It's a mistake." He stared at Cloke. "I want you to fix it."

"You're not forgetting, I hope, that there's the little matter of the bill."

"Of course not," Azevedo said. "We already gave you a trinket. You obviously deserve more than that. But can I trust that this payment isn't in vain? You're here, yes, but is the job actually going to get done? All of them?"

"I have contingencies," Cloke said. "Big, messy, international scandal-sized ones, but they'll get the job done."

"Then I'm going to trust you," Azevedo said. "The other showed you what's possible with shadows, but you're perfectly aware of our specialty. Majitsu is what it is in aeronautics, construction and propulsion because of us, of what we know about mass negation thaumaturgy. But we didn't tell them everything." He took a few steps up to Cloke. "Today, I'll tell you."

Chapter XXII:
The Hard Place

ZEE HAD TO keep remembering that none of this mattered anymore. It was just hard to stay in that headspace.

The displays lit up with all the things going wrong. News reports about orbital blow outs and a Majistu platform in a state of total emergency. A lightning storm in Dubai that was providing high wattage counterpoint to the small, professionally conducted war being waged by an unidentified team of combat cyborgs. And the invasion of the Prague network was now running riot and uncontrolled while Azevedo looked on all that Zee and friends had wrought.

"A tornado. In orbit," he said, shaking his head as he viewed the situation reports from Cloke's portion of the operation. "The woman has absolutely no sense of decorum or restraint."

Zee squirmed through the comment. Cloke was in a huge dust up and this guy was critiquing her style.

"There are a few less flamboyant alternatives," he continued. "But none of that is your concern anymore."

"Right," Zee said, looking at the money still sitting in its own separate account. Never mind that this guy's first impression was a torture porn cathedral in a simulation imprisoning one of the world's most famous people, nothing flamboyant about that...

The tactical communications network was now intermittently coming on and off as Zee's console, without the benefit of a jockey, fought off the Prague network's countermeasures.

"...DEAD FISH," DARMA said during a sudden burst of clarity on the channel.

"What?" Marcus asked.

"I tried futzing too many systems, and killed the platform's rotation. Bye bye gravity. Cloke was jacked into the console over here to learn her new hoodoo, I think. Now she's floating around like a dead fish until it's all done, but one of the cyborgs she thought was out... isn't. He's making his way here and—" the network broke off again in a harsh burst of digital interference.

Azevedo smiled and clucked at the exchange.

Zee's hands balled into fists.

Azevedo turned to Zee. "What's the first thing you're going to do?"

"Now? Those guys are getting creamed out there, and *now* we talk about this?" Zee blinked a few times. "Are you being patronizing?"

"No, just trying to help. You must have a goal, some kind of endpoint. Why else would you accept my offer? What is it? Safety? Revenge? You can do what 95% of the people on this planet can't. Whatever you want. What will you do?"

Zee remained silent. If Bad Azevedo had seen as much as he had claimed, he already had some idea of what that old life had been like, and how much it cost the others. He was just making bad polite conversation at this point.

"You just got the keys to your freedom. This should be a happy occasion. Don't worry about this," he said, gesturing towards all the blinking fail states popping up on all the displays in the workspace. "Or what's about to follow. It doesn't matter to you. Not anymore. Shut it off. Walk away. Enjoy yourself."

The tactical channel jumped back into life with a burst of digital interference. "—are fucking comms so wonky now?" Marcus asked.

"Got something new coming down the pipe," Darma replied. "From the Prague site. Virus."

"Not Zee?"

"From hir line, but not hir," Darma said. "Not hir style. It's going to start assessing all our systems and co-opting them soon. Communications will be first."

Zee's eyes widened.

The tiniest hint of a smile crept up on Bad Azevedo's mouth and then disappeared.

"Can't you wipe it out?"

"While I'm epoxied to Cloke's life support module and in space? Sure, I'm that good, but I don't know if there's time to get it done with all the hoops I'd have to jump through."

"You'd better hurry. If the comms go, so do my team. The witch out there is cooking us. That's almost literal at this point."

"Man, you really know how to piss on a birthday cake," Darma said, then the communications blacked out again.

Zee took in the overall operational situation. Marcus' team was on the run now: the arrival of the College's single mage had turned everything around, even from a distance. Cloke's feed was worse, lit up with all manner of red emergency sigils indicating broad, catastrophic failures across multiple systems in the MOP-2 station, with Cloke herself currently on DISCONNECT. The run on the Prague networks were far from dead, but they were idling now, not doing much more than maintaining the damage already caused and preventing any disruptions to progress, but that wouldn't last without active intervention.

There was, surprisingly, some jockey buttressing going on, from the outside. It was Darma, trying to keep the run going as best he could, even though he had only the most distant access to what Zee had been doing, and a nearly myopic understanding of the moment by moment adjustments and what was required because of that limited access.

Zee was amazed he could accomplish even that much from orbit, tethered to Cloke's tactical systems. What he was doing now was practically legendary, and anyone who knew anything in the jockey scene would be giving up a first-born child right now to watch him do it.

It was even more surprising when he managed to burst into Zee's workspace, his hair a mess, his skin covered in psychosomatic sweat.

"Jesus, kid, what's the hazard here?" he asked, trying to take in the situation.

It was the only moment he had. Azevedo regarded him clinically for a brief instant before initiating his own shut out, and Darma suddenly wasn't there anymore.

"He's quite persistent, isn't he?" Azevedo asked of no one in particular.

"Why are you watching this?" Zee asked. "What's all this to you?"

"A little pettiness, I'll admit," Azevedo said. "I think I'm allowed that. This is my affair now. I've earned the right to watch these people squirm a little."

On one of the situation displays, the one showing Dubai from various co-opted security cameras, a mythic bolt of lightning came down like a pillar of light. Over the tactical communications net someone screamed.

"Head count," Marcus said over the line with eerie calm.

"I'm down," said one of his squad mates.

"How bad?"

The comms went down, reasserted themselves a second later. "—ried to get out of the way, couldn't. Witch had me tagged. No leg mobility."

"I can get him," the female cyborg said over the line. "I've got a bead on—"

"That's a bullshit move, Marie, don't bother—"

"I'm getting him," she said. "We can still salvage this. Just plug him into the package. He's the only one rated to use it anyway."

"Do it," Marcus said. "Get him and plug him in."

"On it."

It's not my problem anymore, Zee repeated over and over again. *I didn't even know these people very well. I don't owe them shit.*

A few seconds passed as surveillance cameras still feeding into the workspace showed the female cyborg, bounding and dodging with incredible skill, as she hurtled into the area where the lightning had struck. "Jesus," she said. "He's gone from the waist down."

"I said no leg mobility, didn't I?"

"Is this a guy thing? It's a guy thing isn't it? 'Gosh, I'm only half a man, so I'll just tell them I can't walk, they'll never suspect a thing.'"

"Are you going to fucking rescue me or not?"

Azevedo turned to Zee. "I'd prefer it, actually, if you would just quit out," he said. "It will be easier for you. For everyone. You might need the head start if people come looking for you."

"I want to see this through. This was my only shot at the big time. I may as well ride it out to the end."

"I can understand that too," Azevedo said. "We agree on that much, at least. "It's important to see things through. Especially if there are things that need to be settled. Like Miriya."

Zee stiffened. "What about her?"

Azevedo opened up a display panel and it hovered in the air in front of him. There was an image of an entertainment program, a live broadcast, with Miriya playing host as usual. "Oh nothing," Azevedo said. "Nothing you need to worry about anymore. You're wealthy. Once you have the name of your... benefactor... you can work on being free. Forever. Isn't that important? Your freedom?"

Zee looked at the window currently showing Miriya, who had done absolutely nothing but show kindness and grace during the time of their acquaintance. Zee wondered if Bad Azevedo were the type of guy that finished what he started.

Including torturing people to death. Then there were all those displays for the actual op; the fact that Bad Azevedo had, in all likelihood, fed something lethal down the connection that was going to throttle everyone and probably leave them for dead.

Zee looked to some distant point that was life in the future. It was filled with wealth, comfort and a freedom that had been bought with the lives of others crushed underfoot. And under that future, holding everything up to the light, was self-loathing.

Siblings. Family. People all in the same horrible experience, who gave each other comfort and strength. Zee had run out on them, put fear and survival before anything else. Now here was a new kind of family, or at least the seed of one, still growing, and Zee was in the process of pouring ash all over it and killing it. This was killing one family to try and save another, wasn't it?

This wasn't worth living with.

Zee sent the command to push out Azevedo.

Nothing happened.

Azevedo's gaze changed to make eye contact. He sighed. "I had really hoped for more from you."

Zee ran through a series of commands and all of them were ignored.

Azevedo turned back completely and stared. "This is my last act of graciousness," he said. "I'm being very generous. You have your money. Quit out. Now."

"What did you do to my workspace?"

"Nothing you didn't give me permission to do when you accepted that fund transfer," Azevedo said. "Full control will be returned when you shut this run down and quit out. Last chance, Zee. Money and the identity of the man you're looking for. Neither of these two will ever come this easily again, and I want to believe you're reasonable. I'm being very reasonable and civil to you right now, even with your disappointing behavior. Be the same." He folded his arms. "Quit. For your own sake."

Zee screamed, not even sure whether the scream was for Azevedo, the betrayal of Miriya and the others, or for some distant part of Zee that clung to the idea that maybe bad people could do good things sometimes if they'd just grow a spine and own up to what they'd done. An all-clear limiters-off attack command went through the entire system and some of it was actually able to respond.

Eve, the virtual intelligence, monitored the scream and went into emergency mode, kicking in certain life-support software. And that probably saved Zee's life as the scream grew louder, this time from the pain as Azevedo's lethal neural feedback kicked in.

Azevedo looked on sadly and shook his head. "The offer was completely legitimate. I was really going to give you a name. Give you a *chance*. And you threw it all away. For what? A celebrity. A pat on the back from a dog of war. Your priorities are completely broken."

Zee screamed again and rode through the sensation of being thrown into a pit filled with razor blades. Points of pain that were sharp, well defined, precise in their agony, and everywhere. The only thing that was worse than the pain was the feeling of stupidity over just accepting the fund transfer. The money had been real. That had blinded everything else.

Now Zee was going to die over it.

"Goodbye, Zee," Azevedo said, walking over to get a closer look. "I wish things had gone differently."

The pain amped up. Zee screamed even louder.

Then the world exploded into a ball of static and light.

Zee was on the ground in the actual, physical world. There was a buzzing noise, coming from a security drone hovering overhead.

It was the drone Zee had co-opted in the Prague office. One of its manipulators was still extended, with a tactical laser powering down. Zee looked around and saw that the neuro-link cable that plugged into the console was burned cleanly through.

"What the fuck," Zee whispered. Standing up brought an

echo of pain everywhere, but it quickly faded.

"Best I could do on short notice," the drone said in Darma's voice. "Didn't have a lot of options, but this got the job done." The manipulator waved. "Please tell me you've got a spare cable lying around somewhere."

"I don't."

"Then you're out," Darma said.

"I can log back in wirelessly."

"And you will die," Darma replied. "Jesus, Zee, do you have any idea how close you came to dying just now? The only reason you didn't was because of a physical cable cut. You go in wirelessly, you won't have that safety net."

"I gotta fix this," Zee said, staring straight at the drone's camera. "I fucked up."

"You sold us out, you mean," Darma said.

"I..."

"I saw," Darma continued. "Accelerated perception, remember? Even if it was only for a second, I saw what I needed to. You and Azevedo were pretty cozy in there, and he bought you with a price that was... understandable."

"Did you cut me out to help me?" Zee's throat tightened. "Or keep me away from the run?"

The only sound in the room for a few seconds were the rotors on the drone. "I don't know," Darma said finally.

"Are you going to tell Cloke?"

"How could I? You're going to slap that Goddamn censor on me if you haven't already. You've got all the bases covered in successfully fucking us over."

"I'm not fucking you over," Zee shouted, surprised at the depth and place the words came from.

"Cloke brought you into this scene, and what did you do? I can't even say. I showed you the ropes, and what did you do? I can't even say. Em is one of the nicest people you will ever, *ever* meet, and what happened? I can't even say. And when the guy who has brought us all this grief waves money under your nose, what do you do, Zee? Do you give him the finger and delete his ass? No. You take it. You *take his fucking money*.

"You know what's the worst part of all this for me? The waste. You've wasted Cloke's trust. She believes in you."

"Well maybe she *shouldn't*," Zee shouted, surprised at the ferocity of it. "Maybe some of us don't deserve that kind of trust, because all we can do is survive, and that means doing what we have to. Maybe some of us have shit that's too big to fix all nice and neat, tied up with a ribbon on top, and we have to do what we can when we can. We're not all magical girls that the whole world needs. Fuck her anyway, she's never said anything about trust. Not to me."

"Does she have to say it? Cloke? Do you know her at all yet? She believes in you," Darma said again. "She trusts you. You wanna know how I know? She actually *disapproves* of the things you do. If she didn't give a shit about you, she wouldn't care what you did. She sure as shit didn't with me at first. She let you in. You may not know it, but she let you in, and you're burning that all down because you *think* it might go bad later and want to make sure you're ready if it does? Well guess what? Doing this? Guarantees it goes badly."

Zee couldn't speak. Something inside squeezed hard, and even breathing was difficult, like it had to get around a lump of grief before clean air could be reached. Maybe Zee wasn't a bad guy, not like Azevedo, but it wasn't easy to use the label "good" either. Which shouldn't have mattered to Zee anyway.

Except now it did. And even though Zee couldn't see Darma's face in the lens of the drone, it hurt. It hurt to imagine what he must have looked like right now as he said these things.

"What about you?" Zee asked.

"What about me?"

"Are you…"

"Does it matter? I'm just another program to hack to you. I have to accept that, don't I? Why the hell would you care what I think of you?"

"I was just… I…" Zee stopped. There was no point.

"I don't have any more time for this," Darma said. "I got some shit to un-fubar. You just stay out of our way."

The drone swayed slightly as Darma's presence left it and it returned to control under Zee's console.

The displays above the console were still lit up. Things were still happening, some things still spiraling straight down the toilet.

This had been a huge fuck up. Zee ignored the tears and got to work, rerouting a wireless connection to get back into the console's workspace, analyzing the code Azevedo had used to break into the workspace. There was still a virus package in reserve that Zee could ride in to kick Bad Azevedo out: it wouldn't take long to prep.

The chatter on the tactical network kept up as Zee hacked together some workarounds.

The comms continued to act up. "–eady yet?" Marcus asked.

"He's plugged in," the female cyborg Marie said. "That gear is smooth like chocolate, all automated, practically rolled out the red carpet for him and handed him a daiquiri."

"You're good to go?"

"I'm stable on life support. Neurolink interface holding steady… and I can't launch."

"What, why not?"

"This thing is locked into some kind of diagnostic with the Prague site, won't revert control until that's done."

"Fuck," Zee said, and checked to see if he was right.

He was. Azevedo's virus was already spreading. It was going to take another counter-virus running in full, constant riot mode just to keep it at bay.

Fine. This was it. This was a sign.

Zee deployed the virus package that had been intended to open the way straight and safe to Bad Azevedo, letting Marcus' portion of the tactical network benefit. The effect was almost instant. Then it was a matter of just hacking together a not-very-safe solution while listening to the professionals at work.

"Wait, what? Negative on that, I'm locked into full control."

"What about the rest of you?" Marcus asked.

"I'm out of the way," the other male cyborg said.

"I'm nearly in position," the female said. "Good to go

anytime. Comms are clear now too, what did you do?"

"Nothing. Must be Darma. Release Gamera," Marcus said. "And rain it down hard on the witch."

On one of the displays, Zee finally saw what the other cyborg mercs had shipped into Dubai. The roof of a warehouse curved and expanded like a balloon being inflated, seams of light forming cracks that turned into full-blown shafts lighting up the darkened, stormy sky. The roof burst into fragments from the volley of a laser barrage. Something climbed out of the hole, a metal claw gripping onto the ragged edges, pulling itself out. The Jane's Military Recognition software on the console tagged a massive rail gun moving into firing position on the back of the unit. Marcus and friends had smuggled Mobile Armor into Dubai.

It was massive, the size of a small building, a heavy weapons platform. It was four legged, and it was hard not to see it as some kind of giant, mechanized turtle, thanks to the obscene amount of armor and weapons piled onto its back. The sensor package that made up its head and targeting systems had been painted over with eyes and shark teeth, and tiny letters spelled out "Kaiju Express" on the side.

"Light it up," Marcus said.

Another laser barrage burned through the sky, like the world's greatest arena concert light show, vaporizing everything in its path.

The audio pick-ups from the security cameras caught the Mobile Armor as it reared up, standing on two legs, and belted out a roar from its own speakers.

"Ease up on the testosterone," Marcus said. "We're here on a job."

"You never let me have any fun," the cyborg complained.

"You lost fun privileges when you lost your legs," the female cyborg said. "Now either redeem yourself and finish this job, or I'm taking your share of the pay."

"I'd authorize that, by the way," Marcus said.

The rail gun screeched into life and fired. Buildings in the firing solution blew apart, sending shrapnel everywhere in a growing echo of destruction. A rail gun was just as easy as playing horseshoes or firing a nuke; it didn't have to be on target, it just had to be close.

Something exploded in the distance with enough force that downtown Dubai shook. They could probably make a new pond or lake with the crater that would be the end result.

The lightning stopped abruptly.

"That's going to give her something to think about," the cyborg in the Mobile Armor said.

"Is she KIA?" Marcus asked.

"Holy *shit*. Negative," the female cyborg said. "I've got visual. Still breathing but knocked on her ass. All her friends still alive too. She had some kind of shield up, I think, but that rail gun just broke it. That should have leveled the street, and all we did was break her concentration. *Fuck*, I hate magic."

"We've got a window. She'll need time to work up another spell. Suppression," Marcus said. "The uncomfortable kind."

"Roger that," and the Mobile Armor retracted the rail gun while a new, wider barrel, almost like an old style 19th century cannon, slid into position.

"Spot me," the cyborg in the Mobile Armor said.

"Tagged," the female cyborg said. "Targeting laser is right on the money, you don't worry your pretty little head about anything, just pull that trigger."

The Mobile Armor fired off a single round. It flew in a slow, almost lazy arc through the air, following the path the targeting computers had laid out based on the female cyborg "painting" the target with a laser, and then descended on its destination, exploding in the air.

A mass of jelly expanded into the size of a small house and landed on the target area.

"Report," Marcus said.

"She's fondue," the female cyborg said. "Riot jelly is doing its job. She's trapped in the suspension, getting regularly zapped by low level electricity. She won't be speaking or concentrating enough to get any magic off any time soon. And that shit will be in her hair for weeks."

"That should make the boss happy. Set the rest of the area on fire to scare off her support and force an evac. They won't waste her if they know she's beat. Then it's back to work," Marcus replied. "There's a building what needs smacking down."

Zee looked at the work on the console. This was going to be messy and full of holes and exploits, but it only needed to hold together for a few minutes, maybe less, depending on how vindictive Azevedo was feeling. Everything was ready.

"It's messed up over here," Zee said on the comm channel. "But I'm gonna fix it. Now."

"Wait, Zee, where the hell have you—?"

"You just tell everyone else I'm sorry, all right?" Zee swallowed hard. "I really wanted to go to your barbecue and meet the family. Maybe in the next life."

"Zee, what the fu—?"

Zee broke the connection and punched entry into the simulation.

Azevedo wasn't there, which wasn't a huge surprise. There was no reason for him to hang around once his attempted online execution had been aborted. But it wouldn't take him long to come back, especially since the workspace had been left unattended, and he was experienced enough to know he'd need to solidify the beachhead he'd established.

Zee resumed the work of deleting Bad Azevedo. It was surprising how much of the attack was still at work even without supervision. Some of that probably had to do with Darma's intervention.

Zee felt Azevedo's presence before even seeing him. The console detected and attempted to blunt the full effects of Azevedo's lethal neural feedback attack. It helped that Zee had some opportunity to survey how it worked, and formulate some rough and ready defense, but it wouldn't work forever.

Azevedo finally put in an appearance a few seconds later, applying more pressure.

"Maybe I overestimated you," he said. "Even when you have the good fortune to escape, you don't do the smart thing and run away."

"Smart's not always the best thing," Zee said, watching the console's defense erode against Azevedo's redoubled efforts.

"I feel a defiant speech about faith and integrity coming on," Azevedo said, a look of clear disappointment on his face.

"Not much for speeches," Zee said. "I figured I'd just die and take you with me."

Zee kicked in the crudely hacked together link program and blocked off access to the workspace: nothing was coming into it, and nothing was going to leave it now—including Azevedo. Then Zee charged him and reached out, making the virtual contact that was required for the hack to properly work.

Zee dropped the console's feedback defenses and Azevedo's eyes widened as he realized, finally, what Zee was doing.

Zee was a conduit. The lethal neural feedback came in at full force, attacking Zee, but also passing straight through to Azevedo, filtered through the hack Zee had put together to convert into a virus that would delete Azevedo's emulation code.

Azevedo tried to disable the lethal neural feedback. Zee was ready for that and let the countermeasures kick in, blocking his commands.

He redoubled his efforts. So did Zee.

Zee pulled him in closer and looked him in the eye, managing to ignore the pain for a few seconds. "Looks like neither one of us wins today. I'm fine with that."

And then Azevedo screamed.

Chapter XXIII:
Debris

CLOKE DISCONNECTED FROM the simulation just in time to bounce against the ceiling while a combat cyborg crashed into the other side of the room. At her back, Ototo was ringing with a clear, sibilant, tone of alarm. Darma was screaming something in her ear.

There wasn't even time to say, "What the fuck," only react in a fast, clumsy way.

She reached out and did a basic student maneuver, converting the cyborg's artificial right arm into hydrogen gas.

The cyborg was completely surprised and failed to catch himself now that his limb was gone. He was spewing lubricant and hydraulics everywhere, but his emergency systems would block that off in a few seconds.

Cloke did it again, this time to his left leg.

She pulled away the neurolink cabling that had been pasted to her head, and then pulled out her sword and pointed it at him as she floated above him on the ceiling.

"You're down to two limbs. That's just enough to get you to an escape pod if there are still any left," she said. "I'm making you a good deal right now; I suggest you take it."

The cyborg's eyes shifted once, towards the rifle that he had brought in, still floating in the air. Cloke caught the expression and sent a bolt of lightning into it.

It exploded. A small piece of shrapnel scratched her face with a thin line of blood beside her lip, but she didn't even flinch. She tilted her head at the cyborg. "Your move."

The cyborg finally got the message and pushed against the wall with his remaining leg, passing her without making eye contact.

"You're welcome," Cloke said. "Do you have a name?"

He stuck his left hand out to stop himself from drifting. "Does it matter?" the cyborg asked, and Cloke was surprised at how young his voice sounded.

"It might," Cloke said. "I'm always on the lookout for a reliable hand. If you ever get tired of working for corporations, look me up. I just want to know what name I should look for on the application."

The cyborg grunted once, then pulled forward to resume his exit. "Bae," he said over his back.

"That Korean?"

"That's all you're getting out of me today, lady."

Cloke nodded. "Have a nice trip," she said. She watched as the cyborg made his way out of the room. It was a dicey chance he had of surviving this, but it was still a chance. "Tell me what I missed," she said to Darma.

"First, you should know I saved your ass by keeping you away from your new intern by hijacking the thrusters in your suit. It was like trying to steer a truck in a tango final. No, no, please, no thanks necessary, it was all in a day's work, no one needs to know how fucking brilliant that was. My reward is a job well done."

"I'll get that Amsterdam red light sim installed that you were always pining for," she said. She turned back to the terminal. "You ready for this?"

A hologram of Azevedo appeared. He closed his eyes and nodded once. "Thank you, Cloke," he said. "But I've been watching the progress of the others. It's still a little touch and go."

And that really didn't sound good. She hit the comm channel. "Marcus, sit rep."

"Breaking down the door, getting ready for a nice little visit."

"Darma, what's happening with Zee?"

"That's… complicated. But xie's back in the saddle, doing what xie has to."

"What does that mean?"

"Zee's dying. On purpose."

Cloke stopped moving, stopped concentrating on the zero gravity and the tornado outside and, for a second, forgot to breathe. "What?"

Darma brought up situation displays to show her what was happening. On one, Marcus and friends were bounding towards a hole that a giant mechanical turtle had opened up in the Dubai office. Things were exploding.

On the other, Zee was in a chair, completely reclined, hands dangling limply on the floor, while every system warning imaginable flashed on the displays and covered hir body in rapid, blinking emergency light.

"Bad Azevedo paid hir a fuck ton to walk away, so xie did. Then xie changed hir mind and he tried to kill hir. I stopped it by using a drone to cut the cabling and xie jumped back in wirelessly."

"Jumped back in why?"

"Xie said to fix hir mistake and get the job done."

"Is xie?"

"I think so. My read on the situation is that Azevedo is in the middle of fending off some serious deletion, but it's a losing proposition. He tried to get Zee with lethal neural feedback and now xie's turned that back on him and disabled his failsafe mechanisms to shut it off. They're both going down."

"No."

"C, xie sold you out. I was in there. I saw the money, xie'd already accepted it. Xie may have changed hir mind, but the initial instinct was to go for it. Zee can be bought."

"If that were really true, xie wouldn't be dying right now," Cloke said. "We're getting hir out of that."

"I don't think that's possible."

"Don't think or don't want? We're getting hir out of there."

Cloke went straight to the comm stone, hoping Zee hadn't ditched it. "You tell me what the fuck you think you're doing, and stop it. Right *now*."

"I thought they would have told you by now," Zee said, voice already sounding strained over the stone. "I don't need the lecture, mistakes were made, I'm doing something about it. I'm getting the job done."

"You're dying."

"That's what it takes to get the job done at this point. And that's my fault. I'm owning up to it. Some people call that being responsible."

"This is not the only way, we can—"

"It is the only way. I messed this up so bad that this is the only way to fix it now. Just let me do this, Cloke. Out of all the people I know right now, I'm the only one I don't respect," Zee said, voice breaking. "Maybe this will fix that."

"Zee, you've got to... Zee? Zee?"

There was nothing else on the comm stone. Possibly Zee had torn it off.

"Cloke, just let hir go."

"*No.*"

"Why are you—"

"I'm not losing hir," Cloke said. There was a sick, familiar feeling in her gut, and it made her both nauseous and furious at the same time. "I already fucked this up with yo— I'm *not* losing another one. Not again. This is not up for discussion."

Darma said nothing.

"I can't go through that again," Cloke said. "I... I just can't. So, you're going to tell me exactly what's happening, and we're going to find a way to stop it."

"You can't stop it," Darma replied. "Bad Azevedo just put himself on top priority for all of Majitsu's distributed computing to end this shit, so Zee is committed."

"What are you saying?"

"Any Majitsu computer with spare computational power is pouring it all into trying to keep him alive. The only way xie's going to pull this off is if Zee stays the course."

"So, if Azevedo pulls back…"

"No, not him. If he loses priority and the other computers pull back, xie might be able to do it without the kamikaze. *If* xie decides to take that option. But that's not going to happen. Every top-level executive at Majitsu is probably screaming at all their coders to keep their one cooperating emulation alive."

Cloke looked at the hologram of Azevedo standing in front of her, and started putting pieces together in her head. "So, you're telling me that all these honchos are propping up Bad Azevedo."

"Yeah," Darma said.

"And if they decide to withdraw their support, we have a chance."

"But that's all it is. A chance. Zee's still gotta take it."

Cloke walked up to the Azevedo hologram. "How much does the bad one know about what you know?"

"Very little," he admitted. "When I was still alive, I'd laid out the groundwork, but the development, the refinement, all the things I taught you… that came afterwards. The other hasn't been doing the same work that I have, because he was cooperating, channeled into different pursuits, just bolstering what's already been known."

"So, what you just taught me…"

"He doesn't know. No one else knows. Aside from what the other emulation in Dubai and I have shared together, no one else knows what you know."

That was enough for Cloke. She nodded, more to herself than anyone else. "Then it's time for a tease."

Darma chuckled. "Oh, I see where this is going. That's evil."

"It's business. Or fucking with the business mindset. Whatever, I think this is going to work. Azevedo, do you have any kind of outside communication access?"

"Very limited."

"I can help with that," Darma said.

"Then drop some hints," Cloke said. "You just need to give them two things. Just enough of a framework for the magic that they get a rough idea of what it is, where it could go. That'll get them salivating and high fiving all at the same time."

"What is the other thing?"

"That when backed into a corner, you've realized the value of life, virtual or otherwise."

Azevedo nodded. "So, you are going to—"

"I'm not doing anything. You're waving a ton of future profits under their nose that the other Azevedo hasn't shown them. They'll do whatever it takes to try to save that."

"How?"

"We're going to leave network access a little vulnerable," Cloke said. "They won't care where it came from, if it gives them an opportunity to try and dupe you and save the information you've put on the MOP-2 central database. They'll have to reroute a lot of distributed computing resources in a hurry if they want any chance to salvage this."

"And why would they do that?"

"Because," Cloke said, running unfamiliar keys a few times through her head to make sure they felt right. She lowered herself to the ground and touched the floor. "You always have to try and back up your data when the space station holding it is falling out of orbit."

"WHAT?" Darma asked.

"Just work with the man and make it happen," Cloke said, concentrating on the immediate task at hand.

She'd never tried this type of magic on this scale before. She was surprised, almost in awe of how it easy it was with the right understanding. There was a pounding sensation in the back of her head, a harbinger of either a very bad headache, or the near-total exhaustion she was going to experience at some point from using so much of this unknown, not precisely refined magic so quickly. This was new magic and on some level it was probably going to wreck her for a while.

But it was working. MOP-2 groaned as part of its structure went to zero mass.

"*Why are you so crazy?*" Darma yelled over the comm

channel. "How many times did you have to get dropped as a child to be this fucking suicidally crazy?"

"Shut up, please, and just do your thing. Get that information into Majitsu's hands. I'm working." She pushed out the energy, making sure that her sword was watching.

The entire MOP-2 station responded to her command. What had required several mass negation mages working in concert to keep the entire structure manageable, she'd just done by herself. She'd completely canceled the mass of everything in the station. For all intents and purposes, it was lighter than a feather.

She consulted her combat visor and it showed in three-dimensional space her position relative to Earth. She adjusted her position until she was pointing herself down, back towards the cradle of human life.

Cloke activated the Vernier maneuvering thrusters of her armor and the entire station moved smoothly downwards, its orbit completely destroyed as it aimed itself towards some desolate point in the Pacific between Wake Island and Micronesia.

Cloke could already feel the resistance from MOP-2, trying to regain its original mass. It was going to be a fight to keep the entire station stuck to a controlled arc of descent; probably requiring some give and take on the mass side to keep the trajectory consistent, then give it enough mass to make sure it didn't bounce right off the Earth's atmosphere.

"Tell me Majitsu is biting," Cloke said to Darma, never taking her eyes off the display on her combat visor that showed the descent of the station.

"Odds are good," Darma said, but she could tell from the tone of his voice that he was still pissed about her dropping all of them out of orbit. "Seeing a lot of network activity on the high end. I think the higher-ups are being informed right now that a lot of money is about to burn. I put out some of Azevedo's simulation models and a few incomplete equations on the station database. They'll run those numbers and see it's legit."

"And what about Zee?"

"No change on hir end, but we're not going to see anything until Majitsu management starts making their move. If they do."

"Then there are only a couple of things left to do," Cloke said. She assessed the feel of the magic around the station. They'd already passed the point of no return: gravity had noticed MOP-2 making its moves and had reached out to grab it. The descent would have to be precisely controlled. Or, at least, as controlled as anything could be when it came to magic.

The entire station rumbled as the first strains of structural shock reverberated through. The rumble continued, becoming a low, steady roar.

The station, complete with tornado raging in the heart of its space, fell towards Earth.

"I cannot fucking believe you just did this," Darma said. "What's next, bringing back Hitler?"

"No, something a little more pressing."

"Oh good, at least you're still worried about getting out of this alive."

"I'm going to need to make some calls," she said.

"I retract my previous statement."

MOP-2 continued to fall.

Cloke wondered how much time she would have before the heat of re-entry started to cook everything—including her.

Chapter XXIV:
Karma's a Bitch

ZEE WAS DYING and that was okay.

It was going to be a contest between consciousness and rationality, and which one was going to quit out first. Even now the defenses of the console were trying to keep Zee alive, which just went to show that ruthlessly following what Darma would have done under similar circumstances had been a pretty smart thing to do.

The workspace shuddered, systems struggled to hang on, fighting against whatever resistance Azevedo was putting up—which was sizable. He was getting the royal treatment from Majitsu, but it wasn't going to be enough. Zee wasn't playing by the conventional rules anymore, which all assumed the console jockey was trying to get out of the job alive. They had few precautions against someone who didn't give a shit anymore about only being able to breathe with life support.

Surprisingly, it was one of the few things over a short, largely brutal life that did feel one hundred percent okay, even with qualifiers like, "for a life that was artificial," or, "for someone with no experience." This had been a real, actual choice. No rail-roading, no snap judgement based on fear or survival.

For once, Zee had looked at everything that had come before, and everywhere things would go from this point, and the choice had been made on that basis alone.

It felt good, which was unexpected.

Azevedo was screaming, which was almost funny, because Zee had fully expected to be the one making all the noise. But somehow, having made the choice and knowing that the pain was just brain-killing, heart-stopping signals on a wire, it was easy for Zee to simply stand and endure. It was like a little ray of dignity that the world had decided to allow because Zee had, at long last, done a grown-up thing.

It was just too bad it had to happen right at the end.

The workspace, even as it slowly fell apart under the Majistu resistance, did due diligence and displayed everything that was important.

On one window, Marcus and friends got ready to deal their deathblow.

"The welcome mat is pretty much laid out," the female cyborg said. "I'm happy with what I did, you boys can enjoy yourselves."

"Still going to need confirmation on the hit," Marcus said.

"You worry about that after I'm done," the cyborg still plugged into the Mobile Armor said. The mechanized quadruped reared up and a trail of missile exhaust streamed from its back zeroing towards the gaping hole in the target building. The camera trembled with the shockwave from the impact.

"That's a confirmed kill," the cyborg said, and even with audio only, the smugness in his voice was apparent.

On the display, Marcus performed one final hurtle into the depths of the smoking building. It was radio silence for a few moments, then came a long sigh.

"Never send a giant robot turtle to do a man's job," he said over the comm channel. The sound of his carbine firing filled his audio channel. "You hit it, but didn't destroy the unit," Marcus said. "Had a hologram sitting there with a look on his face like, 'seriously?' Had to apologize for your sorry work and finish the job."

"A missile is not the answer to every problem," the female cyborg said.

"A good gun? That's debatable," Marcus said, hopping out of the building. "I just checked the sit rep; we got our job done first."

There was a half-hearted "Yay" from his crew of combat cyborgs. The one in the Mobile Armor made the weapons platform roar again.

"Okay, everyone we're done here, that's RTB," Marcus said.

Zee felt a pang of jealousy. Even when things had messed up for him with the addition of a combat mage hurling lightning, Marcus had actually managed to finish his job first, and with a bit of flair.

Azevedo, on the other hand, had no flair to him at all.

This close, it was easy to see the panic in his eyes as he struggled in futility against the virtual iron grip Zee had on him. The pain he was experiencing now must have been tremendous.

This wasn't the first time the death of someone else had been this close. It wasn't even the first time Zee had been responsible. But this was the first time it had been so direct. The intent so focused. It was hard not to see Azevedo as just a person in this moment, rather than a memory that just wanted to keep echoing in its own digital chamber. His eyes held real fear, and it was just like the fear Zee had seen in the others, all those years ago, the first time one of them had died in the lab and realized that nothing was going to stop it from happening. Zee was surprised to feel something like relief at the prospect of what was about to happen, and wondered if there should be shame in that. At least now there was no doubt. It took a certain kind of something to kill. Or maybe a lack. And whatever it was, it was in Zee.

"Please!" Azevedo shouted. "PLEASE!"

And that was the wrong word, the one that caused bile to rasp in up in Zee's mouth in recent years. It was the word that defined everything that was wrong with the world. Zee didn't bother to reply; just gripped him tighter and maintained a hard, steady stare. There was no point in words anymore, and the neuro-simulated pain was so intense now it was doubtful anything coherent could be spoken beyond a guttural howl.

Things were beginning to bleed into white around the edges of Zee's vision. It was probably going to all be over soon.

Then the pain dimmed.

Not all of it, and not right away, but what felt like fires and needles and explosions in Zee's heart that wouldn't stop became muted, almost tolerable.

Zee looked at Azevedo. He was still in the throes of his pain and deletion, completely oblivious to anything else.

On the displays monitoring the run, two things that shouldn't have been happening were happening. The first was that Azevedo's digital reinforcements were, to Zee's complete bafflement, backing off. The second was that Zee's own hack was getting buttressed from the outside. And not from any traceable source.

A comm channel on priority override broke through into the workspace and Cloke, in a voice that made no attempt to hide her irritation, said, "We have to have us a little talk about chain of command."

Zee bore down and fought for some control now that the pain was subsiding. "I'm just—"

"No, you don't get it. I give the orders. No one gave you permission to die. You don't get to be wiped by a poncy emulation unless I say you do."

Zee shouldn't have been surprised. Even when someone was dying, Cloke was a bitch.

"You're getting help," Cloke said. "You're not dying—not today anyway—so when the shot comes, you take it."

The comm channel shut down and Zee was left alone with the angry, panicked emulation that was still clawing to get away.

Committing to this death grip with Azevedo had been weirdly uplifting. It was like some part deep down inside actually had the confirmation it had always been hoping to find; that Zee could actually do something that wasn't entirely motivated by profit and survival. There had been relief in that.

But then there was Cloke's weird, contradictory message. She was mad. That wasn't such a big deal, it seemed like Cloke was always pissed about something. But there was a tone in her voice during that dressing down that was different. There was something familiar about the way she had been mad, and it took a few moments for Zee to remember that Cloke had been like this the day her sister had been locked off and tortured by Azevedo.

This was the kind of mad when Cloke was scared for someone else.

Then a big warning light went off on Zee's displays and something arrived. It was the killware that had been helping Marcus. It was back, inactive, and ready for more as something else took up its duties on the tactical network.

The lethal neural feedback backed off even more, and that was all that was needed, the room to breathe and move again.

Zee broke contact with Azevedo, and he threw up an impressive line of defenses. But it was improvised, unprepared, and ultimately not enough for what Zee had in store.

Zee looked at the money that was still floating as numbers in the workspace and pushed it back towards Azevedo, transferring it back out. "You can have that back. That was my second mistake."

"I can give you more" Azevedo said. "I'll give you the name, please, just stop and listen to me."

"And that was my first mistake," Zee said, cutting loose the killware and letting it do its thing without restraint.

Azevedo screamed and parts of him tried to implode into a digital black hole from which nothing could escape, while other parts of him expanded like a star being born, emitting heat and light and a scream that ran up and down the spectrum of fear and pain in a way Zee hadn't thought possible.

His death filled the room with light and warmth as the dying code struggled to find some kind of structure in a dying simulated space. It faded away with residual pieces of light floating through the air like snowflakes.

Azevedo was gone. In another minute or two, the same thing could be said about the space Zee was in. It was continuing to collapse.

Then a golden rectangle of light appeared, and something stepped through. It was the GIS artificial intelligence, Athena.

"There are actually a half dozen GIS processing centers experiencing some minor outage right now because of you," Athena said. She broke into a smile. "I hope you're grateful."

"How..."

"I got a call from your chief. She told me you were about to make the world a less interesting place by removing yourself from it." She looked back at Zee. "That simply won't do."

Zee checked the displays in the workspace. Athena, even though she was standing there with complete apparent casualness, was holding off the destruction of this space and everything that was inside it.

"Now, while I'm sure you want to take some time to admire my amazing work here, the clock is ticking. And I brought a friend."

Athena looked back towards the door she'd stepped through and someone else entered the space.

Miriya stood there, still clearly dressed for a club or some other kind of outing.

"C was right, this is more interesting than the after-party I was just at," she said. She looked uncertainly at the oscillations of the workspace as it struggled to destroy itself. "This doesn't look entirely safe. Am I okay to be here?"

Zee frowned and stared at Athena. "Why did you bring her here?"

"Because I asked her to," Miriya said. She took a step into the workspace. "Now, I was under the impression that you had something to finish up."

"It's done," Zee said, gesturing towards the falling bits and pieces of Azevedo that looked like snowflakes made of light. "What is that?"

"Bad Azevedo," Zee said.

"Well," Miriya said, a baffled look on her face. She was brushing bits of light off her arms and dress. "That was either pretty. Or gross."

"Pretty gross," Athena said.

Miriya shook her head at the AI. "And that horrible pun settles the argument of whether you're truly sentient for me." She sighed. "If you were just code, you would have had no problem resisting the impulse to go there."

"A pleasure seeing you all again," Athena said with a curtsey. She looked to Zee. "Don't make this a habit, please."

And then she was gone.

Zee's system alarms blared the imminent death knell of the workspace as Athena's protection was withdrawn.

"Now what?" Zee asked.

Miriya reached out. "Take my hand, Zee."

Zee reached out. Miriya's hand was warm and soft to the touch.

Miriya smiled and pulled, and Zee followed her through a tunnel of white light that swallowed everything up.

When sight, sound and feeling returned, so did Zee's lack of awe.

They were back in the shitty Jersey apartment.

"Not you too," Zee said, taking in the same decrepit couch, the windows that still had plain dumb glass installed and actually needed to be manually opened and closed.

"Roots," Miriya said. "Important. This is where my career started you know." She pointed to the couch. "Right on that."

Zee sat down on it and leaned back. It felt good to not have six different kinds of shit going down. Not dying was also an extremely underrated experience. "Why did you do that?"

"Because you needed help," Miriya said, and now, sometime in the space it had taken Zee to blink or look away, she was dressed in a simple t-shirt and sweatpants. "And you did me a good turn."

"So it was payback?"

Miriya sighed. "Why does everything have to be about debts and payments? You want this binary? Fine. I heard you were in trouble and it would have pissed me off more if you had died than it would have if you didn't. That was my selfish motive, to avoid being pissed." She sat down on the couch. "Sometimes people just do stuff because they want to. The kind of motives you think make up reasonable human behavior don't always apply. You were in trouble. I didn't like that."

"I fucked up," Zee said finally. "I sold out your sister."

"Did you?" Miriya leaned back. "Then why was that guy trying to kill you?"

"I changed my mind."

"So, you didn't sell out."

"I did. I just tried to undo it."

"You made a mistake," Miriya said. "When that happens, you can do two things. Live with it or fix it. Guess what you did."

"Yeah, but—"

"You tried to fix it," Miriya said with a firm, insistent voice. She reached out and held Zee's hand tightly. "And you are what you do when it counts." She patted Zee's hand. "That's the only thing that matters."

"I've fucked up more than once," Zee said.

Miriya shrugged. "You fixed the most important one. That means there's hope. We'll give you the benefit of the doubt on the other things."

Zee could feel tears threatening to form, but tried to push past them. "There's still a job to do."

Miriya swept her arm across the apartment. "Be my guest. Mi casa and all that."

"Eve, give me a basic config area," Zee said.

"Compliance," the VI said. And all the most important status indicators, meters, and displays from the Majitsu run popped up in a semi-circle around Zee.

Marcus was in the middle of his Return to Base, but it was still a mystery to Zee how they were going to get a giant robot turtle out of Dubai undetected.

On the news feed, there was a lot of priority reports about Majitsu Orbital Platform-2, which was no surprise since there was a tornado ripping through it and it had stopped rotation.

Zee's mouth dropped open when the reports mentioned it was now falling from orbit and headed for impact somewhere in the South Pacific.

Zee looked at Miriya. "What the fuck?"

Even Miriya looked pale. She shook her head. "I didn't know about that. She just told me you needed help. Is she on that thing?"

Zee nodded.

"Oh shit," Miriya said in a near whisper.

Zee looked over the display. Watching the Majitsu corporate activity and going back over the timeline of events. It made a queasy kind of sense. The distributed computing of Majitsu had been poured into the station that was now about to burn up with Cloke in it.

Zee peeled back the layers of simulation just enough to be able to put the comm stone back on in the real world.

"Cloke?"

There was no response.

"Cloke? Boss?"

Still nothing.

Zee ran through the communication channels on the tactical network.

"Cloke? Darma?"

"Hey, the kid's back," Marcus said.

"Marcus, you get anything from Cloke?"

"No, why? Something wrong?"

Zee switched off his channel without answering and boosted the other channels. This was not fucking funny. Cloke had saved Zee's life but at the cost of her own. That couldn't be right.

"Cloke, Darma, someone fucking speak to me *now*," Zee said.

"Hey," Cloke said. "I was wondering if that worked."

"I tried your comm stone, but there was nothing."

"Yeah, that's gone. Not sure where it went. Lost it once the station started swinging around when gravity caught up with us. Things are pretty messed up. Re-entry is gonna kick in any second now, and we'll lose conventional comms. Are you okay?"

"What?" Zee asked.

"Are you okay? You're not hurt?"

"Yes," Zee said. This time the tears did come. The guilt was a tangible ball of pain. Even after all this, Cloke still wanted to know. "I'm okay. I did the job. Bad Azevedo is done."

"That's good," Cloke said. She sighed. "You did what you promised. That's important. Thank you. You're fired."

There was a burst of digital feedback and the channel went dead.

"Cloke? Cloke?"

Zee looked at Miriya. Miriya's hand was covering her mouth.

On the news, the Majistu station continued to fall and burn.

Chapter XXV:
The Direct Route

CLOKE KEPT HER muscles relaxed as Majistu Orbital Platform-2 continued to spin and plummet back towards the Earth. The electromagnetic clamps on her combat boots were the only things keeping her stable as the structure dangerously pitched and yawed while it fell.

She stopped attending to the descent of the station to put things to a final end.

Azevedo was still in the room with her, watching her with his hands behind his back.

She opened up access to her visor and let him look while satellite communication was still working and updating her systems. The Majitsu Dubai building was collapsing on itself, and the Prague network looked like a digital asteroid had made a huge, smoking crater in the middle of its infrastructure.

"It's done," she said.

"Thank you, Cloke."

"You kept your word. You did other things I didn't appreciate, but you did keep your word. I do the same."

He gave a slight bow. "Then there's nothing else left."

She nodded and pulled out her sword. "It's time."

"I suppose it is," Azevedo said. He looked at Cloke, but didn't seem to be looking at her. "And what about you, Darma?"

"What?" Darma asked, clearly caught off guard by the sudden attention.

"When will it be your time?"

Darma said nothing, letting the question hang in the air.

Azevedo shrugged. "I didn't have a choice about my death, or what came after it. But you did. Is it what you wanted? Is it worth it?" He walked up to the terminal that housed his emulation and ran his hand over it. "Magic taught me one thing over the years. There are many things in this world we don't know or understand, but that doesn't mean they aren't working the way they are supposed to. Do you suppose death is one of those things?"

"That's an incredibly optimistic attitude you have," Darma said. "You act like we'll actually survive this experience and I'll have time to think about the question."

Azevedo smiled. "I believe Cloke is committed to that proposition, yes. After getting this far, I'm reluctant to doubt her credibility."

"I still need to weigh my options," Darma said. "I did sign on for this."

"It was a choice," Azevedo said. "And you are free to make more later. Just take the time to really consider what is the right choice."

"You've already made yours," Cloke said.

"I have, yes," he said. "And you will have your own choices to make now. About what you will do with what I have given you."

She gave a single nod. "It was never just about mass negation, was it?"

He shook his head. "That was the start, but no, the potential was always greater than that. And you can be the start of that."

"If I live long enough," Cloke said. "That particular condition always seems to be a part of the deals I make."

"I have faith in your resourcefulness, Cloke." He stood up straighter, bringing his head back, holding it high.

She held the wakizashi in front of her. "Just give the word."

Azevedo closed his eyes and nodded once. "It feels good. To finally know the end is here." He opened his eyes. "Do it."

Cloke switched her grip to hold the wakizashi in two hands. She walked unsteadily towards the console, letting her boots get a firm electromagnetic grip on the floor to ensure she was in striking distance. She raised the sword and looked at Azevedo.

He nodded again.

She swung down. The cut, as expected was clean, like the blade was slicing through air.

The hologram cut out.

Arcs of blown circuitry sparked around the terminal. Small bursts of flame flared in the air as the sparks reacted with the hydrogen she'd transmuted into the air earlier. She swung two more times, carving a chunk out of the terminal and it detached from the mass of the hardware, floating away.

For the final coup de grace, lightning arced out of the sword, enveloping the shattered fragments of the console. The air cracked once, sharply, as any remaining circuitry was fried.

Cloke sheathed her sword.

The station leaned. Then kept leaning. And then it was no longer a lean, it was a tumble. MOP-2 had gone into a spin.

"We're fucked," Darma said. "This is atmospheric entry, isn't it?"

She double-checked the seals on the combat armor, saw the puncture on her arm. She still had oxygen, she was going to be able to breathe, but the suit wasn't airtight.

It was time for more student work, the basic stuff that would fix this quick. She'd converted some of that cyborg's mass into pure hydrogen, so she already had that to work with. She shut her eyes, forcing the elementary alchemy principles to rise up from the murky shadows of her first-year classes and held the keys in her mind.

She just needed carbon and hydrogen, and plenty were available here. She transmuted it, mixing it together into C5H8, and watched as a small amount of isoprene formed on the floor. She grabbed it, slapped it on the break in her armor and applied some flame to its edges to melt the rubber across the break.

It wasn't going to stop a bullet or a blade, but her suit confirmed it would keep air in. She was airtight once more. She turned her attention back to the falling station.

MOP-2 groaned again, like some weathered, ancient beast that knew its time was nigh.

"Whatever you're doing, do it better," Darma said.

She'd already given up on trying to keep the entire structure at zero mass; too many parts of it were flying off to keep that task simple. She leaned down towards the ground, resuming the mass negation work, just doing what she could to keep the arc of re-entry going in the general direction she'd picked.

"I don't suppose there's a parachute on this thing?" she asked.

"There actually is," Darma said with no small amount of surprise.

"I was kidding."

"You may have been, but there really is at least one on this station. 20th century, nylon ram air parachute. According to the local guide it's in one of the restaurants you passed by. They've got it stretched out along the wall as part of the décor. 'Freefall' the place is called. Fusion cuisine."

"So, it's actually possible," Cloke mused.

"Assuming you get over a few humps," Darma said. "Like surviving the actual re-entry—"

"I'm working on that."

"—then somehow finding a way to get back to that restaurant in a space station that's spinning out of control. Then check to see if a 120-year-old chute still works the way it's supposed to, then stuff the chute back into its pack, then strap on and figure out how to bail."

"That doesn't sound as good as I was hoping."

There was silence. "Please don't tell me that was seriously your plan. Drop a station out of orbit and hope there was a parachute somewhere? Really?"

"No," Cloke said. "But I figured if it was the easier solution, I might try going for it."

"*Easier?* What you've got in mind is now easier than that?"

"Well, more variables under my direct control."

"So, there's a plan?"

"Fuck no, you think I actually wanted to drop us out of orbit and laid out an exit strategy for that?"

"So, what are you going to do?"

"Improvise," she said. "I've still got oxygen, so breathing's not a problem."

"Cooking is," Darma said.

"I told you, I'm working on that."

She engaged the grips on her gloves. Her left hand she kept firmly spread on the floor of the station, as it rapidly switched from being floor then ceiling then floor again as MOP-2 spun.

The other reached over her back and pulled out Ototo. She showed the little sword the keys, running them fast and clear through her head.

"Keep it small," she said to her blade. "Localized. Keep adjusting to compensate."

The sword glowed, and Cloke saw her suit's indicators notify her that the local temperature had just dropped by 10 degrees centigrade.

If Ototo was doing this correctly, Cloke was in a six-foot sphere of cool air, and the sword would maintain that temperature even as the air around them heated up from the descent through the atmosphere.

"Oxygen, check. Temperature, check," Cloke said.

"So, what's next?"

She brought up the interface for her visor and keyed up her music selection.

The synth sound flooded her ears, followed by the discordant, opening moans of Holly Johnson.

"Oh, sweet crying baby Jesus, is that what I think it is?" Darma asked.

"Time for Frankie to go to motherfucking Hollywood," Cloke shouted, as 'Relax' got into full swing.

"Your taste in music is so, so bad," Darma said.

Cloke tensed her muscles and focused on keeping the magic

under a tight leash. "Tell you what, the next time we have to deorbit without a re-entry vehicle and you're getting us out of it, you can pick the goddamn song."

She checked communications. Nothing was coming in; there was probably already interference building from re-entry. On her visor, the computer pulled telemetry from both the station and defense satellites tracking MOP-2, showing the arc of descent that was ideal, as well as clear indicators that the station, stubbornly, was not falling according to plan.

"Ride 'em cowboy, I guess," she said, and then pumped up the bass on the song. She concentrated, going over the keys slowly to make sure she got them right. Her environmental monitors showed that the temperature was starting to fluctuate; going up a few degrees then going back down. Ototo was already going to work.

Cloke focused her efforts directing the mass negation. She was no longer concerned with keeping the entire station weightless, and concentrated her efforts on keeping the areas "above" her at zero, while the "ground" that she was on retained its true mass.

Gravity went along with her adjustments and the tumble of the station stopped, as the heaviest portion weighed down the rest of the structure. She applied a few seconds of zero mass to the entire structure periodically to fire her thrusters and keep the station following the arc her computer had mapped out for her.

The entire station shuddered as atmospheric entry began in earnest.

"Darma, you still have access to the local network?"

"For now. Power's gonna go at any time, but you knew that."

"Show me the station's damage control system."

Darma put it on her visor. Parts of the station were already flying off, which was no surprise whatsoever; it was never designed to be aerodynamic and never designed to reenter the Earth's atmosphere, so if any of this survived in salvageable condition it was going to be a miracle. ·

Cloke tried not to think about that same principle applying to her. Ototo was acting like a champ; despite the fact that the station was hurtling through the atmosphere now with the tremendous roar of re-entry reverberating through the structure, the temperature was holding more or less steady. She had to admit, even with the new tricks Azevedo had just taught her, none of it would have been possible without this little sword keeping her from burning up.

Everything was shaking now.

She ignored the vibrations and concentrated on the task at hand. It was a crazy bit of on-again-off-again magic, adjusting wherever she could to the angle of descent. Atmospheric entry wasn't something many people did anymore once the LUMO was finished, so aside from escape pods, no one built anything anymore to withstand the 1500 degrees centigrade of heat any vehicle would have to sustain for the minutes that the process took.

Cloke's own notification went off with a beep that informed her outside communication was gone. Ionization blackout from the intense heat was causing the expected interference.

"Even if you got up this morning thinking you'd be the first woman in space to make a tornado, I bet you didn't see first space station re-entry coming up on the itinerary," Darma said.

"How much of this station is going to make it?" Cloke asked.

"No reliable way to tell," he replied. "Anything that falls out of the sky retains anywhere between ten to forty per cent of its original structure. Depends on the material and the atmospheric entry. Got a lot of carbyne and diamond analogs in this station's structure, hard to say how much of that will hold together."

"Whole lotta variables," Cloke said, gritting her teeth.

Absolute focus was critical.

She knew there was no way this was going to be a textbook atmospheric entry. MOP-2 wasn't aerodynamic, and it had no maneuverability to speak of except what she'd been able to initially provide with her thrusters. The only problem was now that gravity had them deep in the well, her thrusters weren't going to cut it even if the entire mass of the station were zero. All she could do was try to control the mass of the station to roughly keep the speed in check. The reactor blew somewhere in the core of the station and all the power went out. It didn't matter. Cloke could see light from outside this room: the light of the entire station as it burned up.

MOP-2 was shrieking now. It was a chorus of sounds from the station as it burned and twisted through the air, riding a path that Cloke was forcing on it through a series of mass-negation tweaks that someone at the College was going to get a thesis out of when the time was right. The station shuddered through a combination of stresses from re-entry and explosions that rocked various portions as anything remotely combustible burst into flames.

It felt like forever. She knew it would have only been a few minutes, but eventually Darma cut in.

"Okay, we've got wireless access back. Congratulations, you somehow survived the burn through re-entry." He patched back into satellite communications, hopping over to a news broadcast from which several news network drones were diligently following the station all the way down.

Cloke grunted.

"Now all you have to do is survive the actual impact into the Pacific Ocean."

Cloke checked her visor. Ototo had done brilliantly. She had no idea how cooked the rest of the station had been, but this tiny area wasn't. The temperature in this area was holding steady, and they were rapidly plunging through the stratosphere. After this it would be clouds, turbulence, and, once properly in the troposphere, only 10 km before impact.

"I sure hope you have a plan for this," Darma said.

"I have a theory," she replied. The pain in her head was throbbing now, but she couldn't resort to painkillers just yet. She needed to be sharp for what was coming next.

She gave her sword the signal to stop and it did. Then she

redirected the mass of the station, making the area she was in zero, while returning the mass to the area directly "above" her.

MOP-2's tumble changed, and she felt the shift in her stomach as she found herself upside down, still gripping the floor, which was the ceiling now, by the grips of her boots.

She wasn't sure how long it would be before she told the College about what happened next.

Matheus Azevedo had been right. Mass negation had only been the start. What he'd given Cloke would change many things. Including the ability of mass negation to only work on inanimate objects.

She made sure she had the keys right, and then pushed the energy forward.

The magic coursed through her, reducing her mass to zero. Then her armor.

Cloke held out Ototo and cut the floor she was standing on.

"WHAT THE FUCK—" Darma screamed.

The response was immediate, like being ejected. She simply "fell" upwards, the station continuing to plummet below her. She cut the grips on her boots and the floor she'd been magnetically clinging to spun away.

She fell back on more familiar keys, and got the wind going. It came up behind her, pushing her, and she tumbled in one direction for a few minutes before getting the application of it right. But she wasn't falling. She weighed nothing and the wind, when she finally figured out how best to use it, carried her along.

She was flying. She put up an altimeter on her visor, then looked at the map. The weather was clear, at least she had that going for her.

"Get an evac out to Wake Island," Cloke said. "I'm not going all the way home like this."

"Holy fuck," Darma said. "Holy fuck, holy fuck, you crazy fucking witch bitch, you even ditched the goddamn broom..."

"Focus, Darma," Cloke said. She'd had dreams like this. But not with a sea glittering with lights underneath and a dead friend whooping in fear and excitement at her ear.

Even she had to have a moment right now.

She removed the visor, and her mask, so she could look down at the world with her own eyes, and breathe in the thin, crisp air.

She remembered darker times, earlier times, sitting on a Jersey rooftop, hot and sticky in the summer night. All around was a starless sky because the lights of the city drowned it all out. It didn't matter: there were still lights in the sky too, the countless planes and gyros flitting up and down, forcing the birds out of the way—even though it was the birds that belonged there.

Cloke had watched those lights, those vehicles, and had idly wondered if she could just shoot flames out of her hands and soar into the sky like a rocket.

They'd laughed at her, of course. All the gang members there. Even they knew that only machines could fly.

"Birds aren't machines," young Cloke had said.

And they'd told her that they were supposed to be there, but people were not. People could never fly, only machines could. Even magic couldn't make a person fly, only a miracle could do that.

Now Cloke looked down, at the shimmering sea with its reflection of the sun, and the shadows of clouds creating dark patches on the water. The wind felt cool and inviting on her face.

Mass negation had just been the start. This was really about something more fundamental.

This was about gravity. And Cloke had to decide what she was going to do with all this. She was the world's first gravity mage, not a specialty she had ever thought she would take up. But here it was.

And here she was. Soaring.

Cloke laughed and looked down at the sea and the birds below her.

And she flew.

Chapter XXVI:
New Terms

ZEE WAITED A few days before going to the hospital to visit Cloke.

From what everyone else had said, Cloke didn't even need to be hospitalized for that long, but there were a battery of tests everyone from GIS to the College had wanted to conduct. There had been eyewitnesses on the scene, even if scrubbers had eventually tracked and killed the footage from drones sent to document the death of MOP-2.

Both GIS and the College had seen what she'd done. And the College wanted to wring every last bit of biological and theoretical data they could out of it. Cloke had flown. She had negated mass on living, organic matter. No one had done that before. They wanted to know how.

It suited Zee just fine.

Zee was in limbo now. The job was over. The run, with all of its many, many hitches had been completed, and everyone had held up their end of the deal. Just mere minutes after confirmation that bad Azevedo had been deleted, and that the Majitsu Prague office was just fine but in the middle of some kind of apocalyptic network failure, Eve had gotten online notification of payment for services rendered.

Zee had checked the bank account, and there it was. Money for a job, if not well done, at least done. It was also severance pay, since being fired had also come in right at the end. Which, admittedly, had been deserved.

Zee had stared a long time at the number. Then walked away from it.

The next few days had been a blur of activity. There was the news of course. It was difficult for three separate, major Majitsu installations to all get hit and not have people connecting the dots, even if they weren't sure what the dots formed. Dubai in particular was a spectacular, news-friendly topic since there had been confirmed reports of Mobile Armor deployment and, incredibly, it managed to evade detection once it hit the desert. The re-entry of the MOP-2 station was also fair game, since it had been nearly thirty years since anything that big had fallen out of orbit and this time there were no casualties on the ground.

Marcus disappeared to be with his family. He sent a message saying that they would catch up once he'd fulfilled his Dad Duties back in the UK.

Darma had been entirely radio silent.

So Zee went into a holding pattern, renting out a loft in a submerged apartment complex in Hawaii, watching the sun set from under the water, drinking alcohol and clearing out all the furniture in the living room to make space for a console. The rest of the time was spent getting caught up with news, counting money without spending it, tweaking and updating Eve and the workspace to get them both back in fighting shape, and then feeling absolutely caged and restless with no goal, nothing to hit, nothing to chase, and all the food and rent concerns not a problem.

It was maddening. For once the fight for survival was taken care of, and it was proving to be a lot less fun than Zee had been expecting.

But then maybe that's because things were still left unsettled. Unanswered.

And that's why after a few days of circling around the messaging system on the console, Zee finally got around to requesting a visit at Cloke's hospital, once again in New York, and was granted rights immediately.

Now, the time had come. Zee was standing right in front of the door and all that was left was to push it and walk in.

This was really hard to do.

Deep breath.

Just push the fucking door open, there isn't a torture chamber back there, just Cloke...

Except that Cloke wasn't just anything, and everyone knew it, which made Zee even more nervous.

Whatever. Fuck it. Time to commit.

Zee walked in.

Cloke was in a short, red silk robe. She had opened the window and was sitting half in, half out, one leg dangling over the drop down to the ground, the other carelessly propped on the frame itself, showing some extremely fit thigh. She had the sword still strapped to her waist, like some hilariously out of place geisha masseuse samurai.

She was smoking, and Zee wondered for a second how the alarms were not going off before finally realizing, after staring at the scored, blackened ceiling, that alarms and sensors had to have not been zapped by lightning in order to work properly.

Cloke turned her head to look back, the cigarette dangling in her mouth. She nodded and threw the pack at Zee.

Zee caught it.

Cloke held her index finger up and a tiny flame danced there. Zee took the light and then, wordlessly, sat down in a chair at the far side of the room.

"No ash tray, but I'm sure the floor can deal with it," Cloke said.

Zee took another drag but didn't reply.

Cloke looked totally okay. This was a woman that had dropped an entire space station out of orbit and had somehow survived unpowered, unshielded re-entry, and then thrown an entire magical research body up in arms with what she could now do that no one else could. And it didn't look like it had even messed her hair.

And she had done it all to save Zee's life.

Zee wanted to ask why.

"How are you?" Zee asked instead.

Cloke shrugged. "I slept for nearly forty-eight hours, after I touched down," Cloke said. "It's a magic thing. New spell, no tolerance for the drain. You have to build it up over time. Most kids want to sleep for a week after their first fireball. I feel fine now, but they want to keep taking blood and cell samples hoping to find something that isn't there."

"So why bother?"

"Diligence. Like when Glamour mages tuck a chin, or a healing thaumaturge treats a burn wound, there are changes at the cellular and genetic level. They don't want to take the chance on missing out on some change with something like what I did, just because it's not likely. You never know. So, they keep taking pieces out of me hoping something weird will come up on the microscope." Another shrug, another drag on the cigarette. "How've you been? Keeping busy?"

"Not really."

"You got paid, right?"

Zee nodded. "Really fast."

"Good. I don't like messing around with that. You do what you promise, you get what you're promised. That's the deal."

And whether Cloke had meant it or not, Zee felt like a sucker punch to the heart had just come in with the force of a freight train.

"You know what was the first word I learned that had any important meaning?" Zee asked.

Cloke shook her head.

"It was 'please.'"

Cloke stopped and appraised Zee for a few moments. "Now that I think about it, I think that's the first time I've ever heard you say the word."

"It's an ugly word for me," Zee said, taking a drag from the cigarette and sagging down in the chair. "But it was the word we used back then."

"With the man who made you."

Zee nodded. Another long drag. Silence for a few moments.

"I heard one of the others use it first. 'Please.' 'Please stop,' 'please don't hurt me,' 'please, no more.' Every time one of us used it, it made him smile. Sometimes it worked, sometimes it didn't. But we kept using it, hoping that this time would be one of the times it worked." Zee's head shook. "For the longest time, I thought that word meant, 'you win, I give up, you have all the power, I admit it.' That's the way we used it."

Zee watched as Cloke crossed her arms and stared, but she didn't interrupt.

"He moved us around a lot. Had little dens everywhere. When I got out, I was in Germany. Cologne. I didn't speak the language, I had no visor, no skills, nothing. I was just out on the street, in fucking pajamas. Trying to figure out what to do next and how the hell to get far, far away from wherever I was.

"I just ran. I ran in any direction. I couldn't even tell you where I was. Somewhere in downtown, big buildings. I thought that this was it, I was out, I was free. Everything was going to be okay from now on. I hit up a group of guys coming out of some dive. I asked for help. They made fun of my English. They told me they would only give me help if I asked the right way, if I said 'Bitte'."

"German for 'please'," Cloke said.

Zee nodded. "And so I said it. And they laughed, and they dragged me into an alley, and they started beating me, looking for a wallet, debit chip, anything. I was crying. I kept screaming 'bitte' and they just kept kicking me and tearing at my clothes. Even though I was using the word, they wouldn't stop. And then they left me there, and I couldn't even go to the cops. So I learned. I learned how to steal, I learned how to work, and I never, ever used that word again. I was never going to let that word put me in my place. I wasn't going to ask any more. Asking doesn't work. You see something you have to take it. You can't let anyone dangle it for too long, otherwise you're just a mouse being toyed with. When someone makes you use that word, they are shit and need to be smeared out." Zee shrugged and took a very long drag from the cigarette before finally making eye contact with Cloke again. "I'm not trying to justify what I did, or make you feel sorry for me. I'm just telling you because you probably want to know why. That may not be a good enough 'why' for you, but it's mine. You can take it or leave it."

Cloke nodded and stared, taking a long drag from her cigarette.

"Well?"

Cloke kept staring.

"Aren't you going to say anything?"

"Not really. I thought you might want to do more of the talking today. I think that's why it took you so long to come down here."

"I wasn't even sure I was supposed to be here."

"Why?"

Zee stared. "You fired me."

"I did," Cloke said. "But I saved you first."

And then, to Zee's complete surprise, the words came out as a raw scream. "*Why did you do that?*"

"Because I didn't want you to die," Cloke said. She turned to Zee, kept the eye-contact steady. "Because I already lost one jockey when it wasn't his time, and I wasn't going to let that happen to someone who was still just at the start of whatever life was supposed to give them. You're supposed to stay here. You're supposed to do something, it wasn't time for you to leave."

There were tears coming down. Zee knew it, but it didn't seem to matter.

"A long time ago," Cloke said. "There was this kid. She had a mouth on her. Attitude a mile wide and five miles tall. She was so up on herself that she nearly threw away the chance to make something out of her life. She was so pissed at life she was ready to burn it all down rather than take a risk on people that were just trying to help her. But one guy put up with her shit. And it was abominable amounts of shit. There were fires, there was mass property destruction, there was a lot of screaming and 'fuck yous.' And everyone told him that kid was a lost cause, better to let her burn in her own fire if she wanted to so bad. But he believed in her. He looked at that kid and he didn't just see trouble. He saw someone that didn't know what she could do, who she could be, but she needed to give herself a goddamn chance. So he didn't give up." Cloke took a drag from her cigarette and let out a long stream of smoke. She watched the smoke drift before finally looking at Zee. "And neither will I."

Zee tried to speak, but it came out as a choked cry at first. "You should. You should just give up right now. I'm shit."

"Why?"

"I... I stole. I stole from you. From your sister. From everyone."

Cloke smiled. "I know."

Zee blinked back the tears. "What?"

"I know you were stealing. I know about the Ad Bucks, the dips into accounts. We told Em to turn a blind eye to what you were doing, and she did. Too quickly for my taste, but she's never cared much about the money."

"What, but... how?"

"Darma told me."

"That's impossible, I—"

"You really should pay more attention to him," Cloke said, her smile turning into a grin. "He's quite good, you know. I think you owe him an apology, by the way. He thinks you've dismissed him as nothing but a bunch of code. Anyway, that censor of yours might have stopped him from saying anything, even trying to type out a text message and send it. But it didn't stop him from piecing together time codes from different video and audio content so that a bunch of different media strung together could say the thing he couldn't."

Zee's eyes widened. "Why didn't you stop me?"

"To see what you did," Cloke replied. "How you did it. How far you would go. You can learn a lot about a person when they think no one's looking."

Zee had been played. All this time being careful, and

everyone had just been watching, letting that rope for self-hanging just get longer and longer.

"You want to know what I saw?" Cloke asked. She finally left her perch on the window, and stood a few feet away.

Zee only stared at the floor, taking a drag from a cigarette, unsure how to respond.

"Somebody smart. And scared. And constantly thinking xie was backed into a corner and had to fight it out, even when there were no walls and it was a sunny day in the park. But I also saw someone with limits. Good ones. You may be greedy, but you kept it in check. Maybe because you wanted to be smart and not get caught with a big red system flag. Or maybe you just didn't want to take more than you needed to. And you didn't like what you were doing, even when you were doing it. I know you corrected one of your VIs when it tried to make a move on the college fund Marcus is running for his kid. And when your VI notified you that it had access to the very first savings account I ever opened for myself when I was seventeen, you told it to leave it alone."

Zee's hands trembled.

"And I saw that you don't want the big shot glamour or riches. You didn't go out and buy a house somewhere, even though you should—real estate's always a good investment. You didn't buy better clothes for yourself, or better gear. You didn't even do that with the stipends and per diems we gave you, and that's what they were for. And I know you don't want to hurt anyone, because you could have outted Emily and her problem to the public anonymously, you could have deleted Darma at any time and just bailed on us. And you could have taken that deal with Bad Azevedo—"

"—But I *did*. I did take that deal. And then I fucked up. I fucked up so bad... And you... you *knew*. You knew I was stealing from you, from your sister, and you..." Zee leaned forward, staring at the floor and broke down. There was nothing stopping the tears now, the choking cries. "You still did that... for *me*. I was so shit to you, and you went to the wall. For me. *Me*. WHY?"

Cloke finally left her perch on the window and leaned against it, looking taller somehow, more like she did when she was on the job, even though she was in a robe, with a cigarette in a hand, and a sword dangling out of place off her hip. "Azevedo was smart. He gave you something that actually mattered to you. I know what that's like. Someone gives you something that can make the biggest difference in the world to everything you think your life is. So you took it. But then you didn't. Because of Em?"

Zee nodded, unable to stare Cloke in the eye, the floor swimming through tears. "He said he was going to finish her."

"So you made a choice," Cloke said, walking a few steps closer. She dropped the cigarette as a tiny cap of ice formed on the tip, extinguishing it before it hit the ground. "You decided that the people in your life, your team, your friends... your *family*... mattered more." She put her hand out and let it rest on Zee's shoulder, and Zee felt the firm, gentle pressure there. "Anyone that can make that choice, and turn hir back on something that could change hir whole life, give hir the freedom xie thought xie wanted... Someone that can make the tough call like that for the people who matter... I don't think xie deserves to be turned into a twitching pile of meat plugged into life support. I think xie earned hir shot. And that's worth a lot to me." She bent down, filling Zee's view with her face. "So, I did whatever it took to make sure xie had that shot. Does that answer your question?"

Zee wept and hugged Cloke. Cloke allowed it for a few seconds, then tapped Zee's shoulder three times. "Okay, mush is over. I've got intimacy issues, pull yourself together for my sake."

After a time, Zee felt collected enough to speak. "But you fired me."

"I fire everyone," Cloke said. "Marcus got his walking papers once his robo-turtle was out of the country and Darma quit before I could even open my mouth about it. Which is the first time I think he's ever gotten the jump on me in the dismissal merry-go-round. Being dead must have sharpened his game." She pulled back and shrugged. "Whatever. Next job, I hire 'em again. That's the business. Everyone's hired until they're not. Then they're hired again. That's the way freelancers work, from job to job."

The sound that came out of Zee's throat was half laugh, half cry. "You bitch."

Cloke smiled and pulled back. She took out another cigarette, magically produced from a pocket Zee hadn't even noticed was there. "So, I'm going to be stuck here for a little while longer, even though I'm totally fucking fine, because some people think if they stuff enough hospital food in me, I'll spill everything just to get a decent meal." She made a face, put the cigarette in her mouth and lit it with her finger. "I'd probably be doing this whole place a favor just chucking a fireball into the kitchen. Anyway, they're going to keep giving me the old passive-aggressive, not-quite-interrogation, and I'm going to give them the finger, and they're going to shout, and I'm going to laugh, and at the end of it all I'll still get out, because something will go down and they'll need me to deal with it. Then afterwards, we'll all just be that little bit less cordial with each other at staff meetings because they still want what's in here." She tapped her head and walked back to the window. "But in the meantime, if you've got nothing better to do, I think you should make sure your gear is polished and your ware is ready. There might be something coming up. I might need a jockey for it, so I might be hiring." Cloke turned around and started at Zee. "Interested?"

"Maybe," Zee said, wiping at the tears. "So... you saved my life."

Cloke waved it off.

"Does that mean I owe you?"

She smiled. "Oh my God, does it ever mean you owe me," she said. "The only thing better than being paid is being owed a favor. Don't worry. I'm sure we can work something out."

And Zee felt like something already had. And everything was new.

IV
Coda
January 1, 2139

Another Dull Affair

NEW YEAR'S EVE was always a big deal in São Paulo.

Cloke had one of the best seats in the city, but she'd been here before; standing off in a corner somewhere while the rest of the kids, professors and VIPs counted down along with Emily, or Miriya as the kids knew her. Her sister was projecting on a stage as a full color, high resolution hologram, whipping the crowd—even the normally staid instructors—into a frenzy.

Cloke had not picked her own gown. Victor had sent people over to make sure she was properly presented for the occasion. It was black, frilly, and was transparent enough down the right side that that people could have friendly debates about whether she was wearing anything under it. Her hair had been done up in such a way that a passing bird might see it and decide it would make a perfect nest.

She smoked her cigarette and blew out a long stream of smoke.

The crowd was huge; scattered across the many galleries and obscenely large balconies built around the College complex. The complex was, of course, part of the show itself; throwing up lights and plasma—both technological and magical—into the air for people on the ground to "ooh" and "aah" over. The concentrated capital of magic for the modern 22nd century world had temporarily converted itself into the world's largest and most ornate aerial light show for the people of São Paulo. A lot of the administrative staff grumbled about having to pander to the common man, but fights broke out every single year over who would get to take part in the show and come up with new tricks and performances.

Cloke nursed her brandy.

Somewhere on one of the lower balconies, Marcus was throwing his daughter up into the air with every number shouted out. Darma was here as well, smuggled in with Zee, and he was quietly reinforcing and spreading out the initial network infiltration Zee had installed months ago. It would make the surveillance of the College network more invisible and more complete.

Zee was supposed to be helping, but had problems of hir own. Victor's people had worked a minor gender-neutral miracle on Zee's hair and clothes, and xie'd been almost immediately swamped by many admirers from both sexes and many age brackets that wanted to know who this mysterious young ingénue was. Zee looked out in desperation for either Marcus or Cloke to help, but was being patiently ignored by both and forced to deal with this popularity. It was something xie'd have to get used to if xie were going to be out in the world more.

Rector Ortega was here, along with a few of the other Wardens. Cloke and the Rector stared in silence at each other for a few moments before Ortega finally broke eye contact, going back to her drink and talking to the crowd. Her irritation was easy to read. Cloke wasn't sure which one pissed the Rector off more; that Cloke had gotten away with deleting Azevedo, that Cloke's crew had neutralized a combat mage without magical assistance, or that Cloke could now fly but still wasn't telling anyone how she did it.

Even Athena was here, standing beside Emily and performing cheap, quantum computational parlor tricks for the masses, while a huge, impossible-not-to-see GIS logo floated over her head, reminding everyone who and what she was. She kept winking at some of the men, and they kept getting smacked by their companions when they were caught winking back.

"HAPPY NEW YEAR!" Emily shouted. And the world, or at least this part of it in UTC -5 time zone, shouted along with her.

Down below, Marcus' little girl screamed in delight as Marcus threw her high into the air with one hand while embracing and kissing his wife with the other. Zee broke into a run from the crowd, as a fight broke out about who got to hug and kiss hir. Emily made a ridiculously dramatic show of shading her eyes with one hand to pretend to scan the horizon until she saw Cloke and blew a kiss. Cloke gave a quick salute back. Darma sent a quick update saying he was about eighty per cent complete on the job, no thanks to Zee abandoning him, accompanied by a quick, simple graphic of two martini glasses clinking together with the words "happy new year" going off in fireworks.

"Happy new year," said a familiar voice behind her.

She turned and raised her glass to complement a tuxedoed Victor, who had already raised his own. They both took a sip and then he gave her a warm hug and kiss on the cheek.

"Happy new year," she said back, and looked him in the eye to see that even though his gestures had been genuine, his face looked serious.

"And a happy new year to you too, Cloke," said another voice from the shadows.

Victor's frown deepened and he stepped aside. "Cloke, I'd like you to meet Andrew Komarov. Chief technology officer of Majitsu."

The man stepped out of the shadows. He was dressed in a tuxedo with a slightly more modern cut to it than the one Victor sported. He looked only a little bit younger than Victor. But colder. More immediately dangerous.

"He was quite insistent about meeting you," Victor said, looking unhappy with the situation.

Komarov's one eccentricity was the very obvious cybernetic right eye that he hadn't bothered to customize in any way.

It was devoid of any living color; shiny, inorganic, a reminder to everyone that he had a camera on his person, and it was trained right on you. And now it was staring straight at Cloke.

"Thank you for the introduction, Victor," Andrew Komarov said, not looking at him in the least. "That will be all."

Cloke crossed her arms. "I'm not sure you get to talk to him like that."

Komarov smiled with all the warmth and naturalness of a mechanical grinder. "My apologies, no offense meant. I just wanted to speak to you."

"We can do that."

"Privately." The smile, if possible, became even less human.

Victor stood by, ready to step in. Cloke gave him a single nod. "I think you need to save Zee," Cloke said. "Xie's probably hiding in the plants somewhere."

Victor sighed, but that was the extent of his protest. He looked at Andrew Komarov, gave him a nod, then left the balcony.

Komarov was insensitive to everything except Cloke, keeping his eyes fixed on her.

"You're actually much more attractive than I imagined," he said.

"You're not."

He laughed, and that was even colder and less welcoming than his gaze. "It's not part of my business to look good for the cameras."

"Not mine either," Cloke said. "I hope you weren't counting on that eye of yours to do the job. The firmware update you had to install before you came up here is going to keep me off your records." She finally smiled, took a long drag from her cigarette and blew the smoke past his face. "Now was there something I could do for you, Mr. Komarov? Or was this just holiday decorum?"

"To business then. I see." Komarov walked up until he was standing beside her. He looked over the balcony down to the crowds on the lower floors, and the lights of São Paulo far below. "I assume you know why I'm here?"

"I really can't imagine why," Cloke said. "After all, a man of your stature probably has better things to do than give holiday well wishes to little old me. A man of your stature wouldn't be in the legally questionable position of keeping an iron fist over three illegal emulations of a mage." She took a sip from her brandy. "And he'd certainly not be baffled as to why three offices were tragically put out of operation for no discernable reason. Especially if those reasons suddenly came up in a court of international law complete with an interesting set of digital records, videos, conversations and confessions. I'm sure you have better things to do than put up with all that. And frankly so do I."

Komarov's smile twitched ever so slightly.

Cloke smiled. She always enjoyed it when she hit a nerve. "So, I guess I'll have to just keep wondering why you're here now, won't I?"

Komarov was rigid. "Pettiness suits you."

Cloke shrugged and turned back to look down at the hugging and kissing as "Auld Lang Syne" started up in dozens of thick accents from hundreds of people.

"I will try not to be petty," Komarov said. "I came here to concede. That was an expensive project, quite a promising one. You have created a major setback for our firm."

"That project was kept a prisoner and had his rights ignored for decades," Cloke said. "And when it finally asked for help, and someone agreed to give it, setbacks started piling up the moment it was decided the way to deal with this was to threaten someone's family. With torture." Cloke tilted her head. "Quite a setback, I'd say."

"Indeed," Komarov replied. "And more importantly, you have created major setbacks for me and my career within the company. And I will not forget that."

Cloke turned and looked at him. "I was wondering what was more important. Your ego or your curiosity." She tapped her head. "I guess you don't care about what's here at all. That's useful to know."

"On the contrary, I'm very interested in what's in there." He leaned in, taking Cloke's hand in his and giving it a slow kiss. "And I will have it. And then you'll give me everything else I'm due."

"Let's start with this, then. I'm pretty sure you've earned it," Cloke said, and sent a small charge of lightning through her hand and into his cybernetic eye.

He backed away, shouting. No one heard. He clutched at the side of his face and stared back at her.

"Let's talk about your setback now, shall we?" Cloke said, stretching out her hand, fingers spread wide. "Someone very smart once told me that mass negation was just the start."

Komarov groaned and sank to his knees, then put his hands out in front to support himself. He groaned again and collapsed to the ground, the floor cracking underneath him.

"I guess you weigh at least three hundred pounds," Cloke said. "You must work out. You don't look 300 pounds, so good on you. This floor is probably rated to take about 1000 pounds of force. Your mass just increased by three times. Or is it five? I'm still getting the hang of this."

Komarov groaned again. Cloke walked over and dropped the cigarette she was holding, stubbing it out with her high heel beside his face. She pulled out another. "So, not only can I affect living organics, I can increase mass. But it's more than just mass, isn't it? I'm locally distorting gravity. That's two things setting you back. How many other things can I do now? You've got to wonder." Cloke lit the cigarette. "How many years did you have Azevedo under lock and key and he never gave you this? Me? He handed it over without even asking. Want to know why?"

Komarov tried to speak, but it came out a gurgle.

Cloke bent down and looked at him. "Because unlike you, I actually give a shit about something beyond my own fucking percentage." She took a drag from her cigarette and blew the smoke at him again. "If the positions were reversed, and that was me on that floor being crushed by my own lungs, this would probably be my execution date. But I'm not like you.

I know we're in the middle of a nice, harmless New Year's celebration and you'd make a big enough hole that people would notice. And I know you've got people in your life, and your staff that would be affected by whatever happened to you. I'm considerate that way. So, I'm going to make you the same offer you made me, but I think I've got a lot more weight on my side." She knelt closer until her mouth was close to his ear. "Don't pick a fight with me. Stay out of my way, and I'll stay out of yours."

She stood back up and snapped her fingers, restoring his mass to normal.

He rolled over onto his back, coughing, then gradually got to his feet.

"You're also going to be apologizing to Victor Chapman. I'll spare you the indignity of doing it in person, you can send off a message tomorrow. But I want to see you dictate the order to your assistant. Now."

Komarov did it. He stuttered and he glared, but he gave a quick order to a virtual assistant and then it was done.

Cloke smoothed out her dress and raised her glass. "Happy New Year, Mr. Komarov. I think we're done here."

Komarov collected himself, got his breathing back under control, then pointed at Cloke. "You set us on this path," he said, straightening himself. "Now we are both committed."

"You should get that eye looked at. Someone around here can probably help. Just make sure they're still sober," Cloke said. "I'm sure you remember the way out."

Cloke turned away and listened to Andrew Komarov walk out.

She sipped her brandy and watched Victor, Zee and Marcus with their arms around each other, singing down below.

It was going to be a very interesting year.

—End—

Acknowledgements

DEBUTS ARE FULL of long, rambling acknowledgments when they take a few years. If they take a few decades, the list grows even longer. This is one of those long lists.

The first thank you goes to Ms. Pinces and Ms. Palazzo and the English Teachers at ArchBishop O'Leary for encouraging me to consider the possibility that words could do more than just be weaponized for snark. Thanks also go to Candas Jane Dorsey, as a writer-in-residence at the Edmonton Public Library. She steered me in the right direction towards a group that would be critical to my development. The second thank you goes to that group, the still up and running Cult of Pain writers group, for putting up with a kid that wanted to write and believing he could do it.

More thanks go to Professor Greg Hollingshead, for sticking his neck out and believing I belonged in a Creative Writing Class and not rejecting me at the last minute since he'd called me up to do just that. Warm thanks also go to Kristjana Gunnars for taking me aside on the night of my last Senior Creative Writing Class and telling me she believed in me and expected to be hearing about me.

Thanks also go to Brian Henry and his writing workshop classes for keeping me engaged and active in my work. Following that, more thanks go to Eugene Goh, who was one of the first people ever to read this novel and Tim Ashdown for his speculations about what a future with magic might be like in Europe. Thanks as well to Catherine Thorpe and Sabrina Noble, who punched this thing up every Friday night for months while it was being written. A very big thank you to Jeff Seymour, who was a crucial "last mile" editor for providing the final, professional critical eye that got this book ready to hit the query trenches. And thanks also to Chuck Sambucino, who helped me bang out a query that was far more effective than anything I could have come up with on my own when the time came to start submitting to agents.

I'd also like to thank Jack Byrne, my first agent. He was curious enough to answer a random email query from a hopeful writer and find something worthwhile in it. Those books didn't get published, but they were proof to me that I had stories that some people thought were worth telling. Huge thanks to my literary agent, Jennie Goloboy, for not laughing my query straight out of the room and wanting to read the whole thing, then sending a "let's talk" email. She shepherded this whacked up "cybersorcery novel" into the right hands where it finally found a home. Thanks also to Katie Shea Bouttillier for audio rights representation, and the whole Donald Mass Literary Agency, for somehow letting me stand in the same agency air as the Heavy Hitters; I promise I'll take short, shallow breaths. The biggest of thanks go to Kate Coe, who was crazy enough to read this book and say, "Yeah, I'd edit and print that," and David Thomas Moore for the green light, and Donna Bond for her copy editing. Thank yous also to Rebellion Publishing for letting Kate cut the check to buy this book. Thanks also to Michael J. C. Rowley, Rehema Njambi, and Hanna Waigh and all the rest of the Rebellion staff for additional editorial and public relations support because I have no idea how to do this stuff, nor how it works. Thanks also to Jon Dunham, who gave the cool, shiny sheen of cyberslickness to the book.

Thank yous and goodbyes to my cats, Zero and Uno. Neither of you lived to see this book come to print, but both of you warmed my lap sometimes while I was writing it.

Finally, and of course, many, many thank yous to Charlene. You believe in me; you put up with me, you let me play video games when I should be working. You are important in ways it's impossible to convey, and every day I wake up and see you think, "This is a good dream."

About the Author

Wayne Santos has been an ad copywriter, a TV script-writer, a magazine contributor, an editor, and a free-lance writer for too many things on the Internet to count. He grew up in Alberta, lived in Singapore, and settled down in Ontario with his wife and an ongoing rotation of two household cats. He is a multi-disciplinary geek with a double major in science-fiction and fantasy, specializations in novels, comics, anime, TV and film, and a minor in video games. Under no circumstances should he be approached to discuss 80s pop culture unless you are fully aware of the toll this will expend on your remaining lifespan.